SWEET SURRENDER

Alexandra's lips were temptingly parted, expectant; she was waiting for the kiss that he almost dared not give, no matter how compelling his own desire. For he had seen in her eyes, in those great green shining pools, what he had not seen before and what he wanted so much to see and what frightened him to the very core of his soul.

Mikhail's mouth closed over hers gently. As his tongue teased past her lips and touched the edge of her teeth, he reached up into the pile of her hair and pulled out the pins. One by one the locks tumbled free, falling around her shoulders, in her face, over his head. She wore no perfume, yet the scent of her hair was more heady than gardenias, clean, sweet, lingering lightly in his nostrils when he pulled himself away from her.

Her eyes looked up into his, caught them, held them.

"No, Mischa, please. Don't," she begged.

Had he heard her correctly? Were her lips saying "no" at the same time her arms tightened around his neck and pulled him closer? Angry at the thought that she could toy with him now, Mikhail decided he no longer cared, but before he could grab her and teach her a lesson, she had pulled herself to him and kissed him hungrily.

With the first touch of her mouth on his came understanding. She had begged him not to *stop;* he had misread the meaning of her plea.

Careful not to break the seal of their kiss, Mikhail gathered her like a child into his arms and carried her toward the door of her bedchamber . . .

LEGACY OF HONOR

Linda Hilton

LEISURE BOOKS ∞ NEW YORK CITY

A LEISURE BOOK

Published by

Dorchester Publishing Co., Inc.
6 East 39th Street
New York, NY 10016

Printed in the United States of America

Chapter 1

NAPOLEON'S TREATY with Alexander, Tsar of Russia, had brought peace at last to Europe, and Russians to Paris. Among the Russian diplomats, most of them dull and insufferably clannish, was one who seemed to have no other duties than to dazzle society with his flamboyance and his irresistible charm. On a particularly fine October evening his arrival was eagerly awaited by Madame Rosalie de Beaumartin at her latest soiree. He was late.

When he was announced, Count Mikhail Pavlovitch Ogrinov entered the suddenly silent ballroom and greeted, with his usual gallantry, his hostess.

"My dear Madame de Beaumartin," he said in his perfectly accented French. His lips brushed her hand and sent a tingle up her arm. "You are as lovely as ever, Rosalie. I am sorry for my tardiness, but I am here at last, and very thirsty!"

She found him a glass of champagne while he let a footman relieve him of his light cloak. He did not at once step into the crowd but rather waited until he had surveyed the guests and room and set up, like a skilled actor, his entrance. Every eye was upon him. Mikhail let his gaze wander casually about the assembled men and women until he knew that he had their complete attention, and only then did he walk into their midst like a conqueror.

Many were well acquainted with him since his arrival in Paris nearly a year ago. Yet no one, no matter how many times they had seen him, could ignore his presence for those first few minutes. His effect on men was no less intense than on women, though the men seemed to recover more quickly and within a short time had resumed their discussions of Napoleon's latest conquests—romantic as well as military.

But no woman could escape the spell cast by blue eyes and his enigmatic smile. Even the young wives and fiancees, the cautious mistresses, felt the physical power that surrounded him. They listened for his voice; out of the corners of their eyes they watched for his tall figure. If he approached, they preened and giggled and let him know, each in her own way, they were available.

This was his third party in as many days. Not only the faces, but the gowns and jewelry were becoming familiar. Mikhail, who noticed such things, was bored and tired, and he had half a mind just to yawn and ceremoniously leave, which would mean the instant demise of Rosalie's career as a hostess. A middle-aged widow living beyond her means who needed his influence, she was shallow and greedy and not as worthy of his approval as others he had snubbed. He had been told that she was to provide him with a unique diversion. Curiosity was a strong force; he would stay if only to see the surprise.

The champagne was excellent and abundant; long before supper Mikhail felt a need for fresh air and a walk in the garden to clear his head. He had had his fill of dancing with the same women he had danced with the night before, the week before, and always they stared at him without speaking or babbled as though he were a country lout never before in Paris. He excused himself and made his way out the doors to the terrace and then the garden.

Rosalie was justly proud of her little garden, with its fountain modelled after one in Rome and the most beautiful roses in France. It was also cunningly planned to provide as many hidden benches and concealed nooks as possible for the lovers who took advantage of evenings like this. Mikhail discreetly avoided these trysting places until he had made his way to the torchlit fountain. Here he sat down on a carved marble bench and leaned back to enjoy

6

the peace and gentle music of splashing water.

His solitude lasted only seconds. At first he heard just footsteps on the gravel walkway, but then he became aware of a very feminine voice whispering abominable threats.

"Damn you, Yvette. When I find you and that idiot lieutenant, I swear I will kill you and castrate him. Of all the stupid officers in Paris, he is the stupidest. And I must have been a fool to listen to him, or to you for that matter."

By the tone of her voice and the words she chose, Mikhail guessed she was alone, and there was only a hedge between her and the very intrigued Russian. He heard her stomp her foot and turn around several times as though looking for someone, or something.

"Damn!" she swore again, a bit louder.

Another step toward the fountain and she would be in his sight. Should he let her know he had overheard, for it was only a matter of seconds before she took that single step and found him? Well, it would depend on the woman herself; if she was pretty, perhaps he would pretend to have been asleep and not have heard a thing.

The silence stretched out to a minute or more, until Mikhail began to wonder if she had left. The only thing to do, he decided, was to get up and see for himself. Supper would be served soon, and he had no partner as yet. If he wanted to maintain his reputation, he knew he dared not enter the dining room alone. As he brushed a bit of dust from his sleeve and smoothed the wrinkles from his gloves, he spied a perfect white rose, hardly more than a bud, that, if the face and figure belonging to that intriguing voice were pleasant enough, he might cut and give to her.

He stared at the rose too long, for when he looked up, the girl was there, quite as astonished as he. The flower was instantly forgotten; she was more exquisite than any rose in any garden in France.

"Excuse me, monsieur, but I'm afraid, well, I'm not sure — you see, I don't know quite . . ."

She was too startled by his sudden appearance to think

straight, for she hated to make a fool of herself by admitting to a strange man that she was lost. Her large dark eyes, though he could not see their color, were bright as she looked up at him, and their black lashes sparkled with traces of tears. Her vexation had apparently given way to despair. She was angry and embarrassed, but unlike every other woman to whom he had spoken tonight, this one, a total stranger, was not in the least intimidated by him. He could only surmise that she had not recognized him in the dark.

"It is easy to lose oneself in Madame de Beaumartin's garden, and if intentional, it is quite pleasant. But being lost and unable to find one's friends can be very disconcerting," he observed. "Sometimes, however, if one knows how, such distress may be turned to one's advantage."

She was not tall and needed to look up to meet his eyes, but in doing so she took the firelight full on her face. He could see now the green eyes spark behind those wet lashes.

"I'm sure I don't understand you at all," she said haughtily.

Could she really be that innocent? He doubted it. She was dressed too enticingly for innocence in a gown of ivory muslin that revealed rather more than it concealed. And she was not as young as he had at first thought; the figure so delightfully displayed by her decolletage was that of a woman, not a girl. He guessed her to be nineteen or twenty, all the more desirable for a bit of maturity.

"I only meant that you could have made very good use of your plight if you were so inclined. It has been done before."

"I'm sure it has. But I consider such theatrics as distasteful as they are dishonest. Since you have discerned my trouble, I shall simply ask you to show me the way back to the terrace."

"And for this favor what is to be my reward? I daresay I'm not certain I wish to be alone with you after you have threatened one poor soldier with such torture. Have I any guarantee that if I ask you to honor me by being my dinner companion you will not wish a similiar fate upon me?''

He watched her expression change from anger to embarrassment when she realized he had heard her tirade. He had gambled that she would accept his honesty, but it appeared he had lost, for her smile dissolved and she drew away from him. At any moment he expected her to slap him for his insolence or simply turn on her heel and march away, lost or not.

Then the smile returned. She took his proffered arm and let him lead her back through the hedged walkways toward the sound of the orchestra. Recovered from her earlier embarrassment, she strolled at his side and chattered, rather animatedly, about the predicament she had been in when he rescued her.

Mikhail tried to imagine the scene she described. An innocent girl, a very drunken young officer, a secluded garden path. What confused him was that here she was, soon after having been insulted and abused by one amorous young man, now walking as casually as could be with him, with Mikhail Pavlovitch Ogrinov, the most notoriously amorous of all the Russians in Paris, as though he were an old friend or a brother. The explanation, though incredible, was obvious; she had no idea at all who he was. Such a situation had definite advantages that must not be taken lightly.

Unfortunately, he had no time. Already they stood on the terrace; the doors to the ballroom were open to admit fresh evening air into the stuffy house where dancing and champagne had raised the temperature to an uncomfortable level. Other couples were returning from the garden as the supper hour approached, leaving little of the privacy Mikhail wished for. He could hardly prevent her going inside now that she was no longer lost and at his mercy. Yet when he paused on the steps, she stopped too and waited without protest.

''We can't go in just now,'' he explained.

''Why?''

''Because very soon Rosalie is going to announce supper.

I have asked you to join me and you have accepted, I think, but —''

''But I am your second invitation of the evening and you were really only being kind and now would I please return the kindness by getting lost — again.'' she finished for him.

She had shocked him thrice over, first by interrupting him and completing his sentence in such ridiculous fashion, second for being neither humiliated nor angry at the shabby treatment she obviously had expected, and third because she made no move to leave. Her hand still rested very lightly on his arm.

Impulsively, because she had left him speechless, he bent down and kissed her cheek, then chuckled.

''You have a very poor opinion of me already,'' he said. ''Why would I do a terrible thing like that to a lovely lady such as yourself? A knight does not abandon the damsel so quickly after saving her from the dragon. I merely meant that I would find it most unpleasant to spend the evening with you —'' He held up his hand when he saw she was about to interrupt again. ''— And not even know your name.''

Now it was her turn to laugh.

''Forgive me, monsieur, but is it not proper for the gentleman to introduce himself first?''

She was teasing him, he knew, and yet he still could not be sure that she really did not know who he was. Never once taking his eyes from hers, he did as she requested.

With a heavy Russian accent and a theatrical flourish he said, ''Count Mikhail Pavlovitch Ogrinov, at your service.''

''Alexandra Marie Valenceau, Monsieur le Comte,'' she whispered, the awe in her voice and the grace of her curtsy more in honor of his rank than his name, for when she rose to take his arm once more, the laughter had returned.

''Shall we go in?'' he asked.

Knowing only her name and that she was the most charming woman he had met in Paris, he escorted her into Rosalie de Beaumartin's elegant dining salon.

His hostess was thrown instantly into a panic at the sight of her guest of honor leading Alexandra Valenceau through the crowd of other guests. This wasn't her plan at all, and she must make adjustments quickly. In the old days, such a situation could not have existed. Tailors' daughters did not attend fashionable dinner parties. They stayed within the confines of their status, visiting the homes of the well-to-do only when their proper services were required. Now, with the whole world turned upside down, such unthinkable things were happening that a seamstress at a dinner party was not only common but almost acceptable. The few aristocratic families left after the horror of the Revolution intended to keep any taint of bourgeois blood from their daughters, so the hostess who did not want a crowd of unaccompanied young women into the circle. It was a necessary, but unpleasant, show of democracy.

But to have one of the little adventuresses flaunt her privilege; it was almost more than Rosalie could bear. What were her responsibilities in this kind of situation? Was it more important not to offend the sensibilities of her old friends, who were still recovering from the trauma of a generation of revolution and war, or to ensure the pleasure of her most important guest? His opinion might ruin her if she failed to please him; he was that powerful.

When Rosalie arrived in the dining room, she saw that there was nothing to be done. Everyone had already been seated; there was no way to move the girl to a more suitable place without calling far too much attention to the problem. All Rosalie could do was make the best of it and be sure that at the earliest possible moment she rescued the Russian from this impossible situation.

But as Rosalie took her own place at Mikhail's left, she learned to her dismay that he did not seem to want any rescuing. He was listening to the Valenceau girl's chatter.

"And so, my father threw the coat on the floor and told him, 'Monsieur, there is where I found it and there is where it shall remain!'"

That remark, the end of a story Alexandra had been

11

quietly relating, sent Mikhail into gales of laughter. Rosalie had been in his company often enough to recognize that this was not the usual snickering at a bawdy joke nor polite response to some silly tale. Whatever the story, he had found it very, very funny; his laughter was honest, his delight, real.

"Oh, my dear, dear Rosalie!" he exclaimed as he rose to greet her finally. "I must remember to send you a very special gift, for I am sure this is the most delightful evening I've spent in months."

He kissed Madame de Beaumartin lightly on the cheek, but it was impossible for her not to notice that even while he thanked her for providing a splendidly unique diversion, he could not wait to return to the attention of Mademoiselle Valenceau, the tailor's daughter.

Chapter 2

YVETTE VALENCEAU entered her father's shop and closed the door behind her. A little too much brandy left her less than perfectly steady; she tripped on the edge of a rug and nearly fell. Regaining her balance and suppressing a giggle, she kicked off the shoes that had pinched her feet all evening and she made her way in the dark to the stairs.

"Where is Xan?"

Justine's voice cut through the darkness as brightly as the candle she carried in her shaking hand. Yvette opened her eyes to see her older sister glaring at her.

"Did you hear me? Where is Alexandra?"

The anger was so intense it completely masked the fear in her voice, but Yvette, now sober, knew the fear was there.

"I — I don't know. She hasn't come home yet?"

"Obviously not, fool."

"Justine, you're making too much of this," the younger girl said. "Xan could hardly be in better hands."

"That's what I'm afraid of," Justine muttered, but she followed her sister down the stairs and into the little room behind the tailor shop, well out of their father and step-mother's hearing.

"I assure you she was having a marvelous time, especially after she got rid of the lieutenant and came back from the garden with the Russian."

"A Russian!" Justine crossed herself automatically. "Why couldn't she —"

"Oh, no, he's not just *a* Russian. He is *the* Russian, the talk of all Paris, the guest of honor at every important, or interesting, affair. He has been involved with nearly every available woman in France, unmarried or otherwise, and I can honestly tell you that he is in love with Xan."

That was more than Justine could believe, though she knew Alexandra was a very attractive young woman, a fact which had all too often distressed both Justine and her stepmother.

"Besides, you mother her too much," Yvette scolded with a yawn. "Xan's twenty years old, not twelve. If she doesn't know how to handle a man by now, it's because you and Maman Therese won't give her a chance to practice all you've taught her."

Reluctantly Justine admitted that her sister was right. They had all protected Alexandra too much; she was probably in more danger from their sheltering than from her infrequent forays into society. But it was hard to do otherwise; she seemed always to need protection.

It would have been difficult to imagine anyone less in need of protection than the girl being handed into the magnificent black carriage decorated with the Russian eagle. Everything about her bespoke calm and self-assurance and complete control, from the way she stepped into the vehicle to the way she allowed the gallant Count Ogrinov to take her hand in his for a moment as the carriage began to move through the silent streets of pre-dawn Paris.

Nothing quite like this had ever happened to Alexandra before, and she was well aware that the honor might be less than honorable. Though her position as a trademan's daughter kept her on the outer fringe of society, she knew enough of what went on in the elegant mansions and townhouses to know that gentlemen could often be more obnoxious than Bernard the silk merchant or Pierre Rochais who delivered lace from Brussels. And this Russian nobleman, whose French was so exquisite and whose manners towards her, throughout dinner and dessert and a few glasses of cognac—it was the cognac that made her a bit tipsy—had never once been anything other than perfectly polite.

She had, she thought, handled the situation rather well. Refusing his invitation to a very private salon would have labelled her as strictly bourgeois, something she wished at all costs to avoid. But that was not the only reason she accompanied him into Madame de Beaumartin's elegant drawing room and allowed him to lock the door.

She could not possibly have resisted his polite entreaties any more than she could have resisted his pleading eyes. Alexandra tried not to be mesmerised, to keep her mind clear, to remember who and what she was, and it was only with great effort that she succeeded in maintaining conscious control of her actions. Alexandra Valenceau the seamstress had seen both sides of too many well-bred young men, and most of them either bored or disgusted her, or both.

Count Mikhail Pavlovitch Ogrinov did neither.

He fascinated her.

The years spent in her step-father's shop had given her an appreciation for that rare quality of elegance in a man of fashion, a quality sadly lacking in most of the men she met. They were far more concerned with being current and being noticed, and the resulting dandyism was hardly less than the over-indulgent splendor of the Bourbon court.

Accustomed as she was to extraordinary clothes on ordinary physiques, Alexandra could not help but admire the wine-colored velvet coat the Russian wore over a black brocade waistcoat and strikingly white silk shirt. Not only were his clothes exquisitely subdued; his magnificent body did them justice. Tall, broad-shouldered, he was the kind of man who would be noticed for the way he wore his clothes, the way he moved in them, rather than for the garments themselves.

"You look amused, Mademoiselle Valenceau," he said when they were at last alone. "Did I say something funny?"

"No, I was just thinking," she replied, but her blush left him wondering.

He offered her a glass of brandy and carefully hid his surprise when she accepted. She continued to amaze him. Her composure and self-presence during the long supper showed quite clearly that she was not about to be intimidated by those who considered themselves her superiors. Her honesty in admitting exactly what she was left him convinced that she certainly did not see herself as anyone's inferior, even if her adopted father was a tailor.

There was a sudden twinkle in the Russian's eyes as he laughed and said, "Do you know what I wish right now? I wish I were a mouse in Rosalie's salon to listen to the gossips."

She shrugged and said, "What they have to say about me is of no importance whatsoever." She made it quite clear that her lack of concern was genuine. "Did you know that the only reason I am not one of them is that I had the 'great misfortune' to live in the household of a man who earns his living with his hands? I'm a simple seamstress, which is exactly what Madame de Vere's mother was before she married Albert Sauve, Viscomte de Lemagne, and she had to marry him at that. Nor is she the only one. Very few of those pompous fools realize what a farce their pride is."

"And I, am I one of those pompous fools?"

"That remains to be seen," she said, but with a smile.

He laughed, amused by her sauciness. There was something appealing about her freshness, a wide-eyed innocence that was all the more sensual for its sincerity. From her high-piled jet-black hair to the trim ankle she dared to expose as she sat down, she was as desirable a woman as any of the painted playthings drowning their sorrow at not being his companion. Let them gossip, he thought. It serves them right.

The ormolu clock on the mantel chimed very softly, but in the brief silence of a break in the conversation, the tones seemed inordinately loud, like the tolling of bells in a quiet church. Unable to believe that so much time had passed, Mikhail checked his own watch to find out that it was indeed two o'clock in the morning. Alexandra looked worried.

"Is something wrong?" he asked with concern, but before she could contrive a face-saving reply, he had guessed her predicament. "Forgive me for keeping you so late; I'm very sorry if I've caused you any inconvenience. Perhaps I can help by offering you the use of my carriage; I won't need it until tomorrow."

She was too surprised even to think of a way to express her thanks, but a greater surprise was yet to come.

"Better still, let me accompany you. I can then see you safely home and postpone the hour of our parting."

His sudden kiss, if a touching of his lips to her mouth for the barest whisper of a second could be called a kiss, caught her off guard. And his words—was he really reluctant for this evening to end? It seemed to be so, for no sooner had he handed her into the luxuriously appointed vehicle than he entered it himself and took the seat opposite her. Once the door closed, the small space within became charged with a power that could be felt, though not seen. Nothing could be seen in that complete and utter darkness, but the inability to see only served to sharpen the other senses.

Mikhail let himself relax, enveloped in the sweet fragrance of her lilac perfume. The scent had been with him all evening, light and fresh as the first blossoms of spring, reminding him of May and all the springtimes that had ever been, the newness and the innocence. The fragility of that innocence demanded protection, *his* protection, though he never once wondered why he felt this way. The last time a woman had shared his carriage and not spent the ride in his arms was before he had left Moscow, and the woman who sat where the intriguing Mademoiselle Valenceau now sat had been another fascinating Frenchwoman, his fiesty grandmother.

He reached to close the window curtain, for the air was

17

damp and cool.

"No, leave it open," Alexandra asked.

"Aren't you afraid of taking a chill?"

She paused, unsure which fear was the greater, but it took only a moment for the deeper fear to conquer. Her hand reached up to his, and he felt it tremble.

"I'm afraid of the dark."

His initial reaction was to laugh, to make a witty joke and banish the horror until, as the carriage entered an intersection and a stray moonbeam graced her face with silver, he saw that there was no jest in her eyes. The curtain remained open.

Had this been Moscow in October rather than Paris, Mikhail would have had fur lap robes to keep out the cold. He did what he could, however, and pleasant it was to change his seat and draw her close to him beneath his cloak. She welcomed the warmth as much as the pale luminescence of the autumn moon.

The opportunity to have the girl close to him had presented itself; the Russian had availed himself of it but very quickly began to think perhaps he should not have. It would have been impossible for him not to sense her complete trust of him, a trust he himself had built throughout the evening but which he was no longer certain he could honor. She was, without effort, the most desirable woman he had ever known. Had she been more bold, or more shy, the allure would have vanished, and Alexandra Valenceau just another pretty face and figure to be enjoyed or ignored. He could not ignore her. It was more than the scent of her lilac perfume or the curve of her thigh against his that taunted him, that produced the familiar urgency in his loins, an urgency he dared not ease, for this exquisite creature was not in the same class as the painted dolls he was accustomed to sport with. The contradiction itself was perhaps what he found so irresistable.

The steady clatter of the horses' hooves had gone on long enough, Alexandra knew, to have reached the Rue

Ste. Aurrienne, but occasional glimpses out the window told her that the carriage was taking a very long, round-about way to the tailor's shop. The handsome foreigner had not lied in wanting to delay their farewell.

Though she was grateful for his consideration in opening the curtain and sharing his cloak, she was not naive enough to think his motives entirely pure. He was too much a man. She felt it in his fingertips; nervously, involuntarily, they caressed her arm where her shawl had fallen away and exposed the silken skin. Yet even when the movement was unconscious, it was still the gently arousing touch of a man skilled in the art of seduction.

Why then, she asked herself, did she not move away from him? Why, knowing that his driver was taking a long detour, did she not demand to be taken directly home? No answer came to mind, and she remained content to ride with him because she knew such an experience would not come again. Tailors' daughters did not take romantic carriage rides through the moonlit streets of Paris with Russian noblemen. She must enjoy it while it lasted.

After a very long silence Mikhail said, "Mademoiselle Valenceau, we should be near your home now. I'm afraid my driver is not familiar with the streets of your lovely city and he loses his way often, though I have been glad for the delay tonight." He smiled at her, and when she smiled back he knew that she had guessed the truth long ago. "I am indeed sad to see this evening end."

But end it had. When the carriage came to a gentle halt in front of Armand Valenceau's shop, Mikhail opened the door and stepped out to help Alexandra. Before she could take his hand, he grasped her about the waist and lifted her down, set her gently on her feet and then looked at her for what she was sure would be the last time.

"Good night, monsieur. I shall always remember this," she said very softly.

This time his kiss did not surprise her, but she had not expected his embrace to be filled with such passionate fury. As his arms encircled her and his mouth covered hers, he knew that he would never forget her, the child-woman whose body he now crushed against his. His hunger for her became all-consuming, until he knew that nothing short of having her would satisfy him. He needed her as he had never needed any other woman before, needed to feel her body beneath him, her skin next to his, her flesh opening to receive him.

He let her go. As suddenly as it had begun, the passion ended.

"My apologies," he murmured sincerely. "I am very sorry."

He waited until she had gone into the building and locked the door behind her before he re-entered the carriage and told the driver to hurry.

The taste of her was still on his lips, a memory to linger with another, stronger. He leaned back, closed his eyes, and let the pain of denial slowly fade. As the pain receded, so his strength returned. He had called upon every ounce of control, and it had almost not been enough, for he had recognized, even in the heat of his own passion, that there was fire in her response.

Alexandra had seen the narrow band of light beneath the door but chose to ignore it. If Yvette and Justine wanted to stay up all night and speculate, fine; she wanted no part of it. All she wanted now was sleep.

She undressed and pulled her nightgown over her head quickly, almost as if afraid of watching eyes. As she took the pins out of her hair, brushed and braided it for the night, she listened for footsteps on the stairs. She heard only the indistinct whispers of her sisters' conversation and was glad they had decided to gossip rather than interrogate her. Perhaps by morning she would have a suitable tale fashioned for them, if she got some sleep first, sleep to restore her, to wipe out the memory of that kiss and the longing it had awakened in her. In those few moments while she lay there, on the edge of oblivion, the memory came back stronger and stronger, the image so clear that she felt his arms around her again, felt the beating of his heart next to hers. She fell asleep with his kiss still on her lips and an unknown delicious hunger burning between her thighs.

Chapter 3

WHEN JUSTINE and Yvette arrived in the little dining room for breakfast, they found Alexandra waiting for them. She glanced up from her newspaper and second cup of coffee to greet them and secretly to smile at their obvious discomfort. Three hours' sleep had left them barely on the walking side of exhaustion. Those same three hours had given Alexandra the most invigorating rest of her life; she awakened feeling more energetic than if she had slept the clock around.

"Good morning, my dears." Therese Valenceau kissed each of the girls before taking her place beside Alexandra, to whom she said, "I thought I heard a carriage outside last night. Did you not walk home with Yvette?"

"No, Maman. The lieutenant became ill early in the evening, so an acquintance of Yvette's Albert was kind enough to bring us in his carriage," Alexandra replied casually without taking her eyes from the newspaper.

"You were alone with a strange man in his carriage?"

"Oh, no, of course not. Albert escorted us," Yvette said quickly, then crammed a too-large pastry into her mouth, making it impossible for her to answer any more questions until her mind had thought out more lies.

"Albert even apologized for having kept them out a little too late," Justine added.

It was not a part of Justine's nature to take part in even the most innocent of Yvette's deceptions, yet this morning, without knowing any of the truth, she had fallen in with their story as if nothing was wrong. Even more surprising, when she took time to think about it, was that she felt no guilt at all.

Therese sighed with relief. She trusted Albert St. Croix, and not only because she had to. He, too, was a member of the *ancien regime* that the Revolution had tried so hard to exterminate. When the tailor's wife had been Therese-Claudine Aubertien, daughter to a marquis, Albert St. Croix was only an infant, but his father was more powerful than hers. And they had both died under the guillotine.

Armand Valenceau entered the dining room to find his breakfast, as always, waiting when he sat down on his chair. Therese, satisfied that nothing had happened to her adopted daughters, called the servant girl to pour his coffee.

Seated at the head of the table, he helped himself to his breakfast of eggs and sausage and thick slices of warm bread. Marie poured his coffee and then disappeared into the kitchen. Her presence was a direct result of the tailor's new prosperity, and he never failed to notice her and remember. He bowed his head as, with all her family gathered about her, Therese offered her prayer of thanks, not only for her life, which Armand had given back to her so many years ago, but for the bounty around her.

Justine and Yvette were as much her own children as if she had borne them herself; indeed they even resembled her, both of the tailor's offspring being fair-haired and bright-eyed like his second wife. It was one of the odd quirks of Fate that Alexandra had the dark coloring of her stepfather, but her eyes were her own, deep and sultry green. Therese could only wonder what the girl's mother had looked like, for Alexandra bore no resemblance to her father, Therese's beloved brother Charles.

"Whose carriage brought you home last night?" Armand asked, looking at Yvette. He did not mention that he knew how late it had been.

Alexandra answered quickly.

"A Russian diplomat Albert introduced us to last

23

night.''

"Must be a rich man. No goverment clerk can afford a coach and four just on his salary.''

"I suppose so. He's a count," Yvette replied, and almost ashamedly stuffed another bite of croissant into her mouth. Her eyes met Alexandra's, and the unspoken question was obvious. Did Armand know they had not come home together?

There was no time for further questions, however. A loud banging on the shop door interrupted Armand's interrogation, and Justine flew down the stairs to answer the very welcome summons.

Liveried messengers were not uncommon at the tailor's shop, but something told Justine that this one had nothing to do with business. He held a large envelope in one gloved hand, in the other the reins to his horse. The message must be terribly urgent: The horse was lathered and the messenger quite out of breath.

"For Mademoiselle Alexandra Valenceau," he gasped. "I'm to wait for a reply." The noise and the voices had brought everyone down the stairs, Alexandra first. Justine handed her the letter.

She broke the waxen seal hurriedly with trembling fingers. As her eyes scanned the first few words, she felt everyone staring at her, sensed their expectation and curiosity. There was no privacy here; she retreated to the back storeroom where Armand kept his desk.

It was dim, too dim to read, and by the time Alexandra found the tinder box and had struck a light to the candle stub, her heart was pounding and her unsteady hands were damp with nervousness. She lit a fresh candle from the stub and finally, with enough light to read without straining her eyes, she sat upon the high stool, opened the letter, and read it.

My dear Mademoiselle Valenceau,

There is to be a ball at the Russian ambassador's to-night. I would be greatly honored to be allowed to escort you. If you desire a chaperon, I shall see to it that Lt. St. Croix and your sister are invited as well.

Anticipating your acceptance, I shall send my carriage for you both at seven o'clock.

Mikhail Pavlovitch Ogrinov

His handwriting was so bold and clear that it was impossible not to be able to read it, even in poor light, but Alexandra read the letter several times before she was sure she had understood every word. She wondered, writing her reply on a sheet of paper found in the desk, how she could be so excited and so calm at the same time. There was no trembling in her hands as she dipped the quill in the ink and slowly scratched her answer on the paper. Declining this invitation was unthinkable.

He had opened a door to her, a door she had thought forever closed. The world of her dreams beckoned, but she knew that to enter it was to leave behind all she held dear and familiar. She also knew that this portal would not open again.

"Well, what did he say?" Yvette asked and rushed to her sister's side.

"Is it from the Russian count?" Justine queried, every bit as excited as before and completely forgetful of her lies and the consternation of a few minutes ago.

Alexandra was unprepared for their enthusiasm. "Yes, it's from the Russian. He has invited Yvette and me to a ball tonight at the ambassador's."

"He's invited both of you?" Therese exclaimed with a slight frown of disapproval.

"He was kind enough to invite Yvette and Albert so you wouldn't think me unchaperoned." The explanation was rather unkind, she knew, but Yvette was too entranced to notice. "I won't accept if you wish me not to."

Decisions had never been easy for Therese. Armand's attentive silence was his way of telling her that Alexandra was her charge, not his, her responsibility, and permission was only hers to give or deny. Even when she looked into his eyes, begging for some kind of guidance, he stubbornly refused.

"If I said no, Yvette would have you both out the window on your bedsheets. Of course you may go." With all three girls embracing her and yelling their jubilation, it was all she could do to tell them, "Settle down. There is a lot of work to do today before seven o'clock."

Within moments of sending the count's messenger on his way, Therese announced to Armand that she was going to the silk merchant's to buy fabric for the girls' gowns. He protested that there was cloth enough in his storeroom, but she merely snorted a reply and walked out the door.

Monsieur Tenard was a little man with bright eyes and an engaging smile that belied his greediness and almost unscrupulous business manner. Therese had never liked him, but she acknowledged that his goods were far superior to any others. She marched determinedly into his shop just minutes after he had unbolted the door to open for the day.

"Good morning, Madame Valenceau. What a rare pleasure to see you," he greeted.

"I want silk, your best," she said curtly, ignoring his chatter. For a moment she was that aristocrat she had been before the Revolution, before she had married the tailor Valenceau who had once been her father's serf. "Pale blue and white, for two ladies' evening gowns. And your best, I said, not that cheap, coarse stuff you tried to sell me last week."

Monsieur Tenard disappeared behind a row of shelves. When he returned, he laid several bolts on the counter for Madame Valenceau's inspection. She felt of each, sniffed in displeasure.

"I wouldn't scour pots with this," she snorted. "And I said pale blue, not violet."

She made a move as if to walk out of the shop to take her custom elsewhere. The wily merchant stopped her with his obsequious bow and begged her to remain a moment longer.

The bolts went back. He brought out a second armful and spread them in place of the discarded selections.

As usual, Therese had insulted the man into action, and he had produced his best. The blue was like an early morning sky, soft, light, airy in both texture and hue, as if

26

there could be no distinction between the two. It was Yvette's color, the perfect complement to her creamy complexion and sun-gold hair. Already Therese could picture her in a demure, simply styled gown with short sleeves trimmed with lace and a ribbon of blue velvet to accent the high waistline.

The merchant had not brought anything white, until after Therese decided on the blue and rejected all the others. She refused even to consider the pinks and yellows and palest greens. If he thought it odd that a tailor's wife was suddenly buying silk for evening gowns, he never gave a sign. He, too, was a survivor of another sort, and he had learned the wisdom of discretion. So he went back behind his shelves again and brought out one last bolt of fabric.

What he put before Therese was not so much silk as it was a fragile veil woven of moonbeams and ice. It was white, yes, not silver, and there were no metallic threads woven into it, yet still it shimmered like moonlight on new snow, glittery and dazzling. Against such a background, Alexandra's dark beauty would be impossible to ignore. And so, though the price Monsieur Tenard asked was outrageous, Therese paid it without protest and walked out of the shop with her bundle under her arm and a victorious smile on her lips.

Justine's fingers ached. She had finished putting the hem in Yvette's gown and now could only sit and try to make the pain go away. It hardly seemed possible that only a few hours ago the blue silk had been just so much cloth. They had worked, all of them, to get the two dresses finished. Even Armand, who was aghast at the cost of the garments, helped to pin and sew the seams while the women rushed around furiously, trying to get the two girls bathed and combed and perfumed and dressed in time for the arrival of the count's carriage at seven.

"I'll be done in a few minutes," Yvette said. "Three more buttons and it's done. Why don't you get some wine, Justine? You look as though you could use it, and I know I can."

She bent her head to bite the thread, and the movement brought a curse from Alexandra, who stood behind her pinning the blonde curls into place.

"Damn it, Yvette, don't move! I have enough trouble as it is."

"Damn it yourself, Xan. That is the third time you've stabbed me with a pin. How is it going to look if I have little streams of blood dripping down my neck all evening?"

"Sorry. I guess I'm just nervous." She quickly caught up the last lock of hair and, with it securely fastened, let herself flop onto a chair.

"You ought to be!" Yvette exclaimed. "This Russian count of yours—"

"He isn't mine."

"Well, whatever. Anyway, he's said to be the most eligible man in Paris. Now that I've seen him, I know why."

"You mean you've never seen him?" Justine was surprised. "I thought from the way you talked last night that you knew him."

"No, I had never seen him before last night. Albert does not yet move in the same circles as he, but my dear lieutenant is getting there. Tonight will help his career, too, I don't doubt."

"To hell with Albert! Tell us more about the Russian."

Yvette took the wine bottle and poured some for herself and her sisters, then simply shrugged.

"I only hear gossip. I believed all of it until last night." She glanced questioningly at Alexandra. "Unless you aren't telling us the truth, Xan, you're the first woman he hasn't seduced immediately. He rarely keeps a mistress more than a few weeks, and any woman who doesn't give in to him is instantly forgotten. Often he keeps his women for only a night or two, but that may be more than enough for them. I overheard Charlotte Bancon telling someone that she had spent one night with the count and didn't need her other lovers again for a month afterwards."

"What nonsense!" Alexandra protested. Her disinterested tone was betrayed by the blush that colored her cheeks. "He was very polite with me, never once tried to seduce me or in any way give me reason to think he wasn't a perfect gentleman. He didn't even kiss me but once." She felt the redness in her cheeks grow as the memory began to tingle within her.

Therese called Alexandra upstairs. Leaving her sisters to continue without her, Alexandra hurried to the parlor where Therese waited.

She ordered her niece to sit down and listen, in a voice the girl dared not disobey. There was something different about her this afternoon, something Alexandra had never seen before and did not understand, but whatever it was, it clearly meant Therese would stand for no interruptions.

"I never thought I would see this day," she said softly. In the quiet room, so comfortable and familiar, Alexandra could tell there were tears behind that softness and a lump in her aunt's throat that made this speech even more difficult. "Armand and I have argued most of the day about what I am to say to you. He, of course, is very cautious, as always, but he knows that you are no longer a child in need of warnings.

"You are a woman now, a very beautiful woman who perhaps has a chance to regain the place in this world that was stolen from me and from your father. Charles begged me as he lay dying in my arms to see that I never let you forget who you are. Armand and I love you very, very much and we would never think of doing anything that would cause you sorrow if it were in our power to prevent it. Therefore, we both give our blessing to you. We cannot deny you this opportunity."

"And if I do not want it?"

Tears slipped down Therese's cheeks, but she ignored them to answer, "Do as you think best for your own happiness. We are not forcing you into the world of the Russian duke simply because your own father bore a title. I only want you to remember that his world is as much yours as this shop is. You have a right to the kind of life a man like him can offer, but you also have the right to choose."

Embarrassed by her aunt's emotional declaration and by memories stirred at the mere thought of the handsome Russian, Alexandra put her arms around Therese and laughed gently.

"He is only a count, not a duke, and I am too much a tailor's daughter, by upbringing if not by birth, to hold his interest very long."

"No, Alexandra, you are an Aubertien, daughter of a murdered aristocrat, and you must never forget it."

Some of the pride in Therese's voice struck an eerie chord in Alexandra's soul. She knew she would never again need to be reminded of her identity.

Chapter 4

IF ALEXANDRA felt any nervousness, any fear at all, it disappeared in the glorious excitement that began the moment she and Yvette stepped into the carriage. By the time they and their escorts reached the home of the Russian ambassador, Alexandra had completely forgotten she was the bourgeois seamstress who had felt so out of place at Madame de Beaumartin's. She was instead, as Therese had reminded her, impoverished and illegitimate, but still the daughter of Charles Edmond d'Aubertien.

They arrived late; dancing had already started in the grand ballroom. The music drifted out to the street and as Alexander alighted from the carriage, she felt the melody fill her soul.

During a pause in the dancing, a butler liveried in black and gold announced the late arrivals, and Alexandra saw for the first time the reaction of the crowd to the name of Count Mikhail Pavlovitch Ogrinov.

There was absolute silence for a moment as all eyes turned to the tall Russian. He stood still as a statue, not smiling, but acknowledging their attention. When the silence stretched out longer than usual, he was quick to notice, with a barely perceptible shift of his gaze, that while the women still stared unabashedly at him, the men, who would normally have gone back to their drinks and conversation, were now staring at the diminutive, silver-clad girl at his side. Had Alexandra been aware just how much attention was centered on her at that moment, she might have lost her confidence, but the excitement of strolling onto the dance floor with Mikhail was enough to blind her to the fact that it was now she at whom the crowd had leveled surprised eyes. She was content to bask in his glory, unaware of her own.

He led her through first a gavotte and then a dizzying, exhilarating waltz that left her breathless and happy. She marveled that a man as tall and muscular as he could still be so graceful, so light on his feet.

Though the next dance was a stately minuet, Alexandra begged a respite until she had caught her breath. Mikhail did not argue, and after procuring two glasses of iced champagne, he suggested they join a group of his friends.

"No, please, couldn't we just walk out on the terrace?" Her reluctance to meet anyone was all too obvious, and he guessed why.

"If I for one moment thought that you were not good enough for this company, that you might embarrass me or yourself or them, do you think I would have invited you? Now, lift your head, smile, and let those green eyes sparkle. My friends won't care if you are a princess or a ragpicker or, Heaven forbid, a tailor's daughter."

His smile brought back her confidence, and she could no longer resist him.

They left the dance floor and were walking in the direction of a rather loud, noisy cluster of young men and women when a tall, clumsy man, his beard and curling moustaches labelling him a Russian, staggered by them and bumped Alexandra so hard she was thrown against Mikhail. Only her arm through his kept her from falling.

"Stupid drunken fool!" he muttered under his breath as he put his other arm around her and drew her protectively close. "Did he hurt you? Are you all right?" His concern was almost too sincere.

"Yes, of course. I'm fine."

Her answer, those few words, seemed to take forever to say. How long did they stand there, eyes locked to each other, seeing nothing, hearing nothing? A second? An hour? Neither could tell. Time had stopped the moment

Alexandra looked up to assure him she was not harmed.

He did not see the fire in her green eyes; he felt it, like a solitary ray of sunlight that pierces the velvet darkness of a forest, like the lightning that shatters a steaming summer night. That fire was the spark that ignited his desire again, and yet he was paralyzed, unable to move to take her into his arms and possess her. All he could do was stare into the well of her soul and try to fathom its depths.

Nothing existed for them, not the people around them, the music, or anything else.

"Oh, there you are, Mischa! I've been looking for you all evening!"

The voice burst upon them like a cannonball.

"I've only just arrived, Princess," he answered quickly, though not very politely. She did not seem to notice.

"And who might this pretty little snowbird be? My dear, that gown is the talk of all the ladies tonight. You must give me the name of your dressmaker so that I can be the first to copy it. Princess Vera Fyodorovna Ylbatskaya is not going to let these upstart Frenchwomen —"

The tall Russian woman immediately noticed the girl's blush and hastened to apologize.

"Not you, my dear. I've done it again, insulted without meaning to. I only meant these silly women who think that money and politics can make them better than they were born. They put on airs like the same aristocrats they were murdering a few years ago, but they are not aristocrats and never will be. You, on the other hand, anyone can see that such beauty and charm are the true marks of nobility. Besides, Mischa never bothers with common women. What did he say your name was?"

"He didn't," she replied with a little laugh. "I am Alexandra Marie Aubertien."

The sudden pride in her voice surprised Mikhail as much as the strange name she had used. He had no time, however, to muse over the situation.

"How patriotic of you, Mischa!" the princess said in Russian, with a laugh of her own. "Though I am sure it was not her name that attracted you. Each of us must serve our dear Alexander in his or her own way, however, and I see you have found yours." Then, in French again, "Please, my dear Count Ogrinov, you must call on me tomorrow, if you can. And, dear Alexandra, tell him who made that gown for you. I simply must have one like it."

A second later, she had disappeared into the crowd, leaving behind her only the impression of uninhibited, natural selfishness that one could not help but like.

"Are you going to tell her who made my dress?" Alexandra asked with a sly smile.

"Probably," he said off-handedly. "In fact, I'll probably tell her all about you and your family and your sordid little secret life."

He was not angry, just cold and bitterly, hurtfully casual, and she did not understand it. What had she done to offend him? She had introduced herself to the princess, but only after being directly asked her name. And Mikhail, who had been standing there listening to the two women the whole time, could just as easily have volunteered the information. Certainly the Russian woman had not seemed the least bit concerned about a minor breach of manners. Whatever it was, Alexandra knew her *faux pas* had cost her dearly. Humiliated, she turned to leave the ballroom before she lost control of her tears.

"Where do you think you're going?"

His voice was low and steady, but his hand gripped her wrist painfully, she could not mistake the unspoken warning: An outburst would not be tolerated.

"Home."

Tears of fright as well as embarrassment clouded her vision, but she kept them from falling.

"Alone? Don't be foolish. Besides, I intend to get some answers from you first."

His hand never let go of hers as he led her away from the crowd. She supposed he was taking her to some private chamber and was surprised when he opened the doors to the terrace, exactly the place she had wished earlier to go. Now she no longer wanted to be alone with him. He

34

handed her a glass of champagne and suggested in an angry whisper that she drink it and stop whining.

"I'm not whining; I'm crying," she retorted.

"Then stop crying."

This was no suggestion; it was an order that she managed somehow to obey.

To an uninformed observer, they might have been lovers enjoying a tryst in this shadowed corner of the terrace. Well away from the open doors and the light that came from within, Alexandra leaned against the smooth stone wall while Mikhail stood almost tenderly over her, his face in shadow so that she could not see even his eyes. His one hand rested on the wall above her shoulder; the other still held tightly to her wrist.

He kissed her ferociously, seeking her tongue and the sweetness of her mouth. Any struggle, she knew, was futile, for she was pinned against the wall as much by his strength as by her own weakness. Her head was swimming, her knees seemed to melt, her whole body felt on fire as though the very blood in her veins were boiling. He did not caress her. Save for his lips on hers and the gradually easing grip on her arm he was not even touching her.

There was no need for more. His fingers were barely curled around her slender wrist, just enough for him to feel her pulse racing. When finally he released her mouth, she was gasping for breath and limp as a wilted flower. Only the stone wall at her back kept her on her feet.

"Have you never been kissed, Mademoiselle Valenceau?" he whispered into her ear, his lips just grazing the soft skin of her neck. "Or should I call you Mademoiselle Aubertien?"

He stepped back to watch her reaction. What he saw was not what he had expected.

Even in the darkness he could see her eyes, wide and unblinking, staring at his with a look of utter horror. All the color had drained from her face, and she looked even more pale than he knew she must be, whiter even than the snowy silk of her gown. She tried to gasp, to make any sound at all, but was unable to force even the slightest whisper past lips that said no, no, no, no, over and over again—silently.

She was aware of nothing but the horrible reality of what she had done, and she saw only the glittering blue eyes filled with fire that was more than reflected torch-light.

"Oh, my God," she moaned, finding her voice at last. "I do not believe I have done something so foolish, so completely stupid." She was able now too to take her eyes from his and break their spell. She stepped away from the wall and into the shadowy light of a distant torch.

Some of the fire had left his eyes when he realized she was indeed upset, but there was still some anger in his voice when he said, "Stupid or not, I think you owe me an explanation."

He had seen too many women artfully faint when it served their purpose, but the continuing pallor of Alexandra's skin was the one sign of sincerity always lacking in those convenient collapses. He was concerned enough about her to force her to take a seat on a marble bench near the terrace railing but still in the half-light where she could remain unnoticed.

"If you think you're all right, I'll get you something to drink and then we'll find a place to talk where you can explain just exactly what is going on."

"I'll be fine. I'm really not the fainting sort."

Believing her only because a tinge of color had come back to her cheeks, he walked back to the ballroom, but not without several glances over his shoulder to be sure she had not fallen into a limp heap on the ground. He came back with a glass he pressed into her hand.

She expected wine or brandy; the fiery liquor took her breath away and forced tears out the corners of her eyes.

"It's vodka," he told her.

"It's awful!" she choked.

"Do you think you can walk without too much difficulty?"

"Of course! I've not been shot or hit over the head with a club." Though her voice sounded confident, she was not too certain she could traverse the ballroom without assistance.

She took his proffered hand and let him help her to her feet, then gratefully linked her arm through his. Her first steps were hesitant, and despite her own protestations she admitted she was more shaken than she had thought. The vodka that had so quickly cleared her brain a few minutes ago was having just the opposite effect now. She felt wobbly and dizzy and glad to have a strong arm to hold.

The ballroom was more crowded than earlier, making it more difficult to cross. The orchestra had begun another waltz; there was no choice but to wait until the music and whirling dancers had stopped. A servant passed with a silver tray laden with filled glasses, and rather than let all the liquor be wasted when some wild dancer knocked the tray down, Mikhail reached out and took two glasses.

This second vodka went down much more easily than the first, and Alexandra was just beginning to feel her strength return fully when the music and the dancing suddenly ceased. A strange hush fell that could mean only one thing.

The Emperor of France, Napoleon Bonaparte, had arrived.

Chapter 5

IF MIKHAIL had had any choice in the matter, he would have left Alexandra alone with the obnoxious little man, but he had no choice and glumly accepted the fate of a boring evening.

They entered the drawing room with Mikhail's questions still unanswered. Rather than risk any un-explainable confusion, he introduced her using the name she had given Princess Vera. It made little difference, for most of the guests in the gold and rose drawing room were more interested in the short gentleman with dark hair and piercing eyes. Alexandra hardly heard her own name in the excitement, but she did have the presence of mind to lower her eyes and drop a curtsy to the self-styled Emperor of France.

Napoleon Bonaparte, as she soon learned, was a conceited, insecure, arrogant little man whose hunger for power was matched only by his need for love. Surrounded by Russians whose watch chains hung at his eye level, the balding, rotund Emperor was delighted to monopolize the dainty Mademoiselle Aubertien and demanded that she sit beside him. She was the one woman he had met all evening who did not literally look down upon him. She was also the most beautiful woman at one of these damned diplomatic affairs in months, and it pleased him immensely to notice that her presence beside him on the brocade sofa aroused most intense anger in a particular young Russian, whose name the Emperor could not remember but whose face he recalled seeing at numerous parties around Paris, always in the company of the most lovely women.

His attention flattered her, and for a while this alone held her entranced. Before long, however, his exhortations on European unity and his emotional expressions of faith in the loyalty of the Russian people to his cause despite the cracks in his alliance with the Tsar began to bore her. It was all she could do to keep from yawning.

"The modern world cannot tolerate all these little states, petty kings and petty squabbles," he told her in all sincerity. "They must learn to accept change, regardless who leads them in their march toward the future. My dear brother Alexander, Tsar of Russia, understood this when we met and pledged our devotion to peace."

She wondered for whose benefit he made such a pompous statement. Surely not for hers. Was he trying to persuade himself that peace was possible, that the alliance could be saved? Not knowing quite how to react, she glanced across the room to Mikhail, seeking from him some kind of reassurance, a smile in his eyes, but she saw only boredom and disgust. At her? At the raving little man who now ruled half of Europe? She could not tell.

"It is the English who would destroy the dreams of all mankind," she heard the Emperor shouting. "The damned English and their navy! But they shall fall, the bloody fools; they shall fall. No nation that keeps importing her kings can long stand. Saxons, Normans, Stuarts, and now these German Georges. What strength can there be in a country that cannot even produce her own king?

The contradiction to his own status was lost on him, but not so to his companions. Alexandra barely suppressed a giggle. Why, she wondered, did Mikhail seem to be growing more and more angry? Napoleon Bonaparte was more silly than he was hateful.

"I'm tired of their damn conceit. A bunch of peddlers squawking because I've cut off their trade. Trade, that's all the English care about. Worried about their purses, more

39

concerned with profits than with progress. They are nothing but an entire nation of shopkeepers, greedy for gain. When did an Englishman ever think of anyone but himself?''

Now she felt that same anger rising within herself and she nearly choked on it. The little man was no longer just silly; he was vicious and mad, and she had to be rid of him before she went insane, too. Excusing herself with a headache and the need for fresh air, she hurried from the room.

''Bloody bastard,'' she swore half aloud when she was well away from the asylum-like atmosphere she had felt surrounding the Emperor.

''That's not a nice thing at all to say about a man so obviously taken with you.''

She recognized the voice, but the words, strange and unexpected, only slowly took on meaning.

''Shall we find somewhere private now?'' Mikhail asked, taking her arm gently this time. ''Do you speak English, or only curse in it?''

''When necessary, I can even think in it,'' she replied. She followed his lead reluctantly but did not dare to resist.

''Are you a spy?''

She laughed, ''No, though perhaps I ought to be. Is he mad—or am I?''

''We all are,'' he said, lapsing back into French as he opened a door at the end of a long corridor. ''I think we will be undisturbed here, for a while at least.''

The room was small, plainly furnished but comfortable, used possibly as a study. There was a large desk near the fireplace, and several bookshelves filled with massive leather-bound volumes occupied the far wall, but there were also two sofas and a number of mahogany chairs grouped around a table for conversation or cards. Mikhail gestured to one of the chairs and when Alexandra was seated, he offered her a brandy.

''In this city it is not safe to speak even Russian. Do you realize what could have happened if someone else had overheard your outburst?''

40

She seemed impervious to intimidation.

"You didn't seem overly cautious," she retorted. "And why should I worry about someone else? Why should I feel safe that it was you who heard?"

"That isn't the point. What the hell are you doing speaking English and calling the Emperor of France a madman and a bloody bastard? I thought the working classes adored him?"

He was more blunt than he had intended, but he had to get answers, and quickly. Their absence would be investigated without delay; Mikhail guessed they had less than ten minutes before their solicitous hostess followed them to this room.

"To begin with, what makes you think I'm from the working classes?" She tossed her head proudly, ignoring the furious stare he gave her.

"I want an answer. Are you Alexandra Valenceau, the tailor's daughter, or are you Mademoiselle Aubertien, someone—or something—else?"

Well aware that he was not about to let her escape without satisfying his curiosity, she told him the truth.

"I was born in England. My parents never married, but when my father, an emigre, returned to France, he brought me with him and put me into Armand Valenceau's keeping at his death. I don't know what made me give his name to the Princess; I can only think my senses completely left me."

"Your mother is English?"

She nodded.

"I was told that my father took me away from her to protect me. To this day I don't know if she is alive or dead or if she even knows or cares what happened to her daughter."

"And when your father returned to France he was executed?"

"No, he escaped that degradation. He was shot by a Jacobin bandit. My Aunt Therese then married Armand, and I was made a member of his family. Therese helped me with my English, either at my father's request or

41

because she thought we might have to flee again." She sighed wearily, and when he asked nothing further, she added, "I'd like to go home now."

He stood behind her chair and leaned over her shoulder to whisper, in English, "And I thought you were having such a wonderful evening!"

She tried to slap him, but he was far too quick, and she was in an awkward position.

"Your sarcasm is unnecessary, sir," she spat angrily.

He detected the hurt in her voice beneath the anger, and knew that he had been rather cruel even without meaning to be. He had never before felt a need to hurt and humiliate a woman, even one who no longer interested him. Why then with this one? Because she had sat beside a balding, middle-aged, overweight little Corsican and let the man put his hand on her knee? Of course not; the idea itself was ridiculous. Mikhail Pavolvitch Ogrinov was not the jealous type, and he knew it was impossible for him to be jealous of so pathetic a figure as Napoleon Bonaparte.

"Please," she begged politely after the silence got on her nerves. "If you have no further questions for me, I would like to go home."

"Not so fast. You see, my dear, it is not so easy for me as for you," he said in relaxed, unaccented English. "You can leave this house tonight and return to your life as the tailor's daughter with little effect on your future. I, on the other hand, must face these people tomorrow and the next day and the next. I have a service to perform for my government, and to do so I must maintain certain standards. You will leave when I leave, not before."

As calmly as he spoke, she understood the threat he had left unuttered, a threat not of any specific retribution, but only of some nameless, vague, and certain punishment if she argued. So be it. She was not foolish enough to oppose him or even to taunt him with insults already on her tongue. And it satisfied her to note the look of surprise when she refused to fight; she had disappointed him.

He was not, however, disappointed. He had merely

underestimated her, and now found himself once again amazed at her. Could the lost little waif of Rosalie's garden be this same carefully composed, proudly acquiescent woman? Then, remembering her vocal outrage, her colorful language when lost and angry, he knew that they were one and the same.

"Good, we have that settled, so let us make the best of it." He walked around the chair to face her. "The night is young, there are wine and music to enjoy, and I could not bear to see it all go to waste when I have you to share it with." He accompanied his flattery with a bow and said, "Shall we go back to the ballroom? I will make any excuses for you, a headache, whatever. There will be no gossip, no scandal, I assure you, for my own sake as much as yours."

She took his hand and, as she rose, looked up into his eyes once again and whispered, "You are a very strange man, monsieur."

"I? In what way?"

"You insult me, humiliate me, interrogate me as if I were a Spanish heretic, then you beg me to share the remainder of the evening with you. In my place, would you not think that slightly strange?"

"I assure you, Mademoiselle Aubertien, I beg for no woman's favors."

"No, you simply order her to remain with you. Really, I see little difference between the two except as degrees in politeness. You needn't worry," she said in an effort to calm his ruffled pride. "I doubt that I would be the one to run from such an opportunity. It comes so seldom to girls of my class that I would be foolish not to take advantage of it."

With a swirl of her skirts she turned away from him and strode to the door, only to be caught by his vise-like grip on her arm. Keeping her features steady despite the turmoil and rage and fear within, she whirled to face him with a stream of curses on the tip of her tongue.

"So, you are an opportunist?" he laughed. His smile disarmed her; his laughter put her off her guard. "To be honest with you, so am I."

43

So quickly that she had no chance to react, his arms encircled her and drew her to him until she was painfully aware of what her nearness did to him. In an instant he had changed from amiable to amorous with such unexpected ferocity that he did not try, as he had the night before, to control the urge that built up inside him like lava within a slumbering volcano. He could not fight it, nor did he want to.

Their animosity was forgotten; all that remained was the ocean of sensations that surrounded them, threatened to engulf them and drown them. The scent of her hair filled his nostrils as he buried his face in the mass of silken curls against her neck. His lips nibbled at the curve of her throat, sending joyous shivers up and down her spine and wringing little cries from her that only stopped when his mouth covered hers. The taste of his kiss, the sensuous caress of his tongue within her mouth, and she was powerless against the involuntary hunger that surged up from the depths of her soul. Her hand moved to the back of his neck and her fingers twined in the thick curls to pull him even closer, were it possible. Even through the fabric of their clothing she felt his need, his longing, the fiery wanting of his manhood pressed throbbing to her belly.

He didn't try to understand it, this strange longing that so blinded him to everything but the soft body his arms surrounded and his lips devoured. The need was physical and something more as well, something he knew he had never experienced before. Any woman, any of the dozens of willing females who were sighing over his absence from the dance floor right now, could ease the ache in his loins. He knew it would not be enough just to plunge himself into a body until the pulsating relief came. The need was deeper than that, deeper and more passionate, and it was a need not for any woman but just for one, the lilac-scented, silken-skinned creature now in his arms. Only she could quench his fire—with her own.

He nuzzled her ear, whispering to her words that meant nothing and yet everything. Little gasps of pleasure and longing escaped her lips, and he understood only too well what her wordless sighs told him.

His lips travelled seductively down her neck, caressed her bare shoulder, nibbled at the mound of creamy flesh that rose above her bodice.

"So beautiful, so perfect," he murmured as his hand cupped one lovely breast. Through the silk of her gown the nipple was hard with passion. He touched it with his thumb; she moaned and shuddered.

She was his now. With a single sweep of his hand he could have her dress in ribbons and her glorious body exposed for his delight. Already she writhed against him, seeking her own satisfaction and the release from the agony of desire. She was beyond resistance.

Mikhail heard the tapping on the door, heard it and tried not to ignore it. Discovery would mean little to him; it had happened often enough before and on several occasions he had been much further along in his seduction. For Alexandra it would be different. The thought of her embarrassment, of her justifiable fury, gave him the strength he needed to push her away, to quiet her passion and bring her attention to the repeated knocking. She blushed but in no other way displayed her feelings until Mikhail took her in his arms again.

"Shshshshshsh," he whispered in her ear. "What better excuse could we have for leaving Napoleon's very boring little party?"

Feeling betrayed and used, Alexandra failed to see the motive behind his actions. Her hand itched to slap his arrogant smile, but, as if he had read her intentions in her eyes, he gently pinioned her arms so that she could only let them hang at her sides—or embrace him. She chose the latter without realizing it and when Madame Roganskaya, the ambassador's wife, cautiously pushed the unlocked door open, she found exactly what she had expected.

She coughed.

"Dear Mikhail," she said when the lovers slowly released each other. "I do hate to bother you, but His

Majesty is about to leave and wishes to say good night to Mademoiselle Aubertien. If she is recovered from her headache, do you think she could come to bid our guest farewell?''

''Of course, of course. We certainly do not want to incur the imperial wrath,'' Mikhail said easily, completely unabashed.

Where Alexandra found the strength to control her shaking knees and put a conspiratorial smile on her lips she did not know. With her arm linked through his, she walked almost jauntily back to the ballroom, her non-chalance convincing the Russian woman that the meeting she had interrupted was nothing more than a common assignation. And why should she believe anything else? Mikhail Pavlovitch Ogrinov was too well known for his way with women, and this unknown little French bonbon certainly was attracted to him.

Had Madame Roganskaya looked closer, she might have seen the truth.

The passion that glittered in Alexandra's eyes was hatred, not love; the smile that curled her lips was more a sneer. Mikhail recognized it, and he knew that if the evening were to be saved from becoming an embarrassing fiasco, he must get both himself and Alexandra out of the house, away from the crowd and the pressure it put on her inexperienced head.

It was not to be. Napoleon, having lost his avid listener, was overjoyed at her return and demanded a dance, a waltz, with her before departing. The musicians changed their tune, the dance floor cleared as the other couples made room for the Emperor and the bright-eyed beauty in shimmering silk at his side.

Bonaparte was not a bad dancer; he merely lacked the emotional energy Alexandra had found so thrilling when Mikhail whirled her around the floor. The imperial hand on her hip felt no different than any other hand, except that perhaps it was less possessive as it lightly guided her through the steps in perfect time to the music. The slow, almost stately waltz was as much a boon to her nervousness as to Napoleon's age and occasional infirmities.

The room was swirling around her, the faces of the other guests becoming a blur of colors and sparkles, the polished floor uneven. Too many images scurried like frightened mice before Alexandra's eyes, scenes of the past day and night, memories and sensations that overwhelmed her. Was it possible that the girl who danced with the Emperor of France, the ruler of half of all Europe, had yesterday been unable to find her way out of a lovers' garden? No, it wasn't possible. It couldn't be. Something must have happened to her. Some unseen power must have transformed her, for she could hardly remember when she had not been just exactly as she was now.

It had to be a dream, a whirling, crazy illusion, a fantasy of light and music and laughter that her mind had created. Yet still she felt his hand at her waist, light and undemanding. Her feet followed his instinctively around and around and around until she lost all track of time and reality. She knew she was talking to him for she felt her mouth and throat forming words of answer to a question she could not remember being asked. Nothing made any sense at all, neither her conversation with Napoleon nor the music to which they danced. The feeling of floating was not altogether unpleasant, only slightly irritating, frustrating because she did not understand it. It was as though her mind had been placed in a strange body and, unfamiliar with the new environment, was totally incapable of controlling the muscles and nerves. She found herself giggling for no reason at all.

The music must have ended, for Napoleon had stopped dancing and now was leading her off the floor amid enthusiastic applause. He leaned over and whispered something in her ear, and though she understood not one single word, she was sure he had been at least a little improper. She wanted to slap his face and stomp away from him in extreme indignation, but could only manage another little giggle. When the Emperor kissed her lightly on the cheek, she somehow forced her uncooperative body to respond with a genuinely appreciative curtsy.

The nightmare came when she tried to rise again. Her legs had gone numb, her backbone turned to jelly, and even her arms hung limply at her sides. Panic flooded her brain, panic born not of fear at her inability to move but of the humiliation her paralysis brought her. Her ears rang with the gales of laughter that surrounded her on all sides, laughter that stung worse than the lash of a whip, for it raised welts on the tender flesh of the soul. Even when someone's hand touched hers and she felt a strong arm helping her to her feet, hysteria seemed her only escape. Some part of her befuddled brain, however, made the effort to keep her under control, but she had neither the will nor the strength consciously.

In the confusion of chattering and gossiping that followed Napoleon's departure, Mikhail found it a simple task to spirit a very willing Alexandra away from the crowded ballroom and outside to his waiting carriage. The night had turned damp and chill, with thick clouds overhead that obscured the moon and threatened rain, and it was the cold, fresh air that finally brought Alexandra back to her senses. Shivering and with a dull, annoying ache in her head, she felt as if she had awakened from a restless and most unsatisfying sleep. Worse, there was the mocking smile on the face of the man seated across from her that told her the very thing she did not want to know.

"Drunk?" she asked needlessly.

"Not quite. Just very delightfully tipsy."

"On what? A few glasses of champagne and brandy and that horrid stuff you forced on me?"

He nodded and said, "No doubt it was the vodka. Madame Roganskaya has already scolded me for deliberately giving it to you, and I do apologize."

Not yet able to recall what exactly had happened or what she had done, Alexandra felt no great remorse or shame. Curiosity about that blank space of time was her prime concern when she asked, "What in the name of heaven did I do?"

48

His laughter at first was the cruelest sound she had ever heard, until she realized he meant only to ease her worry.

"Absolutely nothing to be ashamed of, my dear, or at least not yet. Here, let me make you more comfortable." He found her cloak, which he had retrieved from a servant earlier, and gently placed it around her shoulders. "Better? I hadn't expected it to get quite so cold."

"Much better, thank you."

She was aware that the carriage had stopped, but a glance out the window told her they were still in the neighborhood of the ambassador's residence. Her momentary trepidation diminished somewhat at the knowledge that Mikhail was not abducting her.

"Do you still want me to take you home?"

It would have been so easy to say yes, to put an end to this evening of disillusionment and humiliation. Instinct, always surer than thought, told her to do just that but she hesitated for a tiny fraction of a second and she allowed the wisdom of instinct to be defeated by the logic of her heart.

"I promised not to leave until you wished me to, and I will keep my promise. For the rest of the evening I am at your command."

Words of submission spoken almost defiantly, leaving only one course of action open to him. Mikhail shouted a curt order in Russian to his driver and the carriage lurched into motion with a whistle and crack of the whip. As he had expected—indeed he had planned it so—Alexandra was flung into his arms by the sudden jolt and found herself fast in his embrace.

His intention was to tease her, to show her that he would brook no impertinence from her. Already an idea had formed in his mind, a plan to use this girl's very special talents, but such a scheme required her complete submission to his authority. And how better to ensure such obedience than to charm her into falling in love with him. Even if her story of an aristocratic father were true, though he doubted it, it would only serve to strengthen her desire to escape the bourgeois existence she must truly despise. Whether her tale were truth or fiction did not matter so much; she hated Napoleon with a passion as fierce as any he had seen before, as fierce as his own, and that could not be wasted.

Even her drunkenness formed part of his carefully calculated plan, though he had to admit to himself that he had been more than necessarily cruel. She had performed splendidly, better than he had dared to hope; the final waltz with the Corsican had proven a windfall. Her helpless embarrassment had driven her back to Mikhail, and now she was at his mercy.

Or was she? She lay in his arms passively and made no effort to defend herself against the savage attack of his lips on hers. He forced her mouth open, a wasted expenditure of strength, for she welcomed his kiss eagerly, hungrily, responding so quickly that she startled him. Still in control, but thrown a little off balance, Mikhail released her as abruptly as he had seized her.

"So, you *have* been kissed before!" She did not know if pleasure, surprise or anger tinged his voice, but something was there, something that alarmed her as much as his inexplicable retreat.

"Indeed, it was you, and certainly not so long ago that you've forgotten already," she retorted. It took an effort to keep from saying, I know I have not forgotten.

It was just as well, Mikhail thought with a shrug, that they had returned to the brightly lit entrance to the ambassador's house. Mikhail had no wish to start another argument with the little tart, though she deserved a lecture—and more—for her insolence. She had become too valuable to him to risk anything simply because she had a sharp tongue. Besides, she had a point. And he had not forgotten.

If the first half of the evening had been hell for Alexandra, the remaining hours she passed in paradise. Long before the late supper was served, she had become the belle of the ball.

Bonaparte's attention earlier had turned her head, but subsequent events sharpened her wits and without the influence of the potent vodka, she kept her mind clear and her emotions under control. She enjoyed the pretty speeches and passionate declarations of the Russian nobleman whose French rivalled hers for preciseness. She never danced with Mikhail again, but whenever the music left her breathless or a clumsy partner crushed her toes, he was there instantly to rescue her and give her a few moments' respite from the unrelenting stream of propositions that came her way.

Any number of these gentlemen—and they remained gentlemen in spite of their lascivious invitations, begged to join her for supper, to be seated next to her and perhaps continue their amorous pleadings over a sumptuous feast of Russian and French delicacies. To each and every one she replied the same. she lowered her eyes and said nothing, but the flutter of her long lashes seemed to promise everything. In the end she found herself seated with Mikhail on her left and on her right a very distinguished looking gentlemen she had not previously met.

She guessed him to be fifty years of age, perhaps an ex-officer now in the diplomatic corps. He had the rugged, clean-limbed physique of a man accustomed to action; the creases around his eyes could only have come from weeks and months and years in the field. The only real sign of age about him was his iron grey hair. She suspected it was a reflection of his personality.

"Good evening, my dear Baron," Mikhail said to him. "Alexandra, this is my uncle of sorts, Baron Andrei Nikolaievitch Tchernikov. Uncle, may I present Mademoiselle Alexandra Marie Aubertien."

When the only response was a grunt and a cough, Mikhail whispered rather loudly to Alexandra, "I am not his favorite nephew, and he sometimes ignores me."

"I am not ignoring *you*, Mikhail Pavlovitch; I do not care to make the acquaintance of whatever tart you have brought with you tonight and insulted my friends with," the baron replied without looking at either Mikhail or Alexandra.

Her face turned scarlet and tears of shame sprang to her eyes, but Mikhail's hand on hers and his stern glance kept

51

her in her seat and gave her the courage to hold back the tears. Then, with supreme indignation, Mikhail addressed his uncle again.

"You surprise me, Baron. Judge me on the basis of what I have or have not done in the past, but do not condemn an innocent young woman without a trial. Mademoiselle Aubertien is certainly not what you have called her, and you owe her an apology for this insult. You should be more open-minded," he scolded, "and perhaps you will find Alexandra to be the kind of lady even my father would approve of."

The baron raised an eyebrow and finally, with a look of intense confusion in his eyes, he turned to Alexandra. The confusion did not abate as he stared boldly at her, examining her as though she were a horse he contemplated buying.

"So this is a girl your father would approve of," he said slowly, quietly, more to himself than to Mikhail. "Then, of course, Mademoiselle Aubertien, I offer my deepest, most sincere apologies. I have, as my nephew so justly accuses me, jumped to an erroneous conclusion. I beg your forgiveness, and if it is possible for an old man to change his ways, I promise to be less prejudiced of Mikhail's friends in the future."

His smile could not have been more glowing nor his eyes more merry as throughout the long, elaborate meal he entertained her with tales of his native Russia. He neglected his wife shamefully to charm Alexandra with stories of dragons and witches, of brave Cossack warriors and Circassian damsels of unsurpassed loveliness. At times she was laughing so hard she could neither eat nor drink. Then he spun a tale of tragic love so moving, so sad, that it brought fresh tears.

After the last dessert plate had been removed from the long table, brandy and tobacco were brought out for the men while the ladies retired to either Madame Roganskaya's quiet drawing room for gossip or to the music room where the effervescent Princess Vera Ylbatskaya entertained at the harpsichord. Without

Mikhail, Alexandra felt lost and bewildered, until Baroness Tchernikova took her hand and led her to the music room.

"You must excuse Vera," the baroness said. "She was raised by her father and seven older brothers and they spoiled her beyond redemption. The result is what you see there, wild, unmannered, and full of the very devil."

"But a damned sight more fun than the twits in the drawing room!" Vera shouted back with a grin. She sat at the rosewood instrument but had not yet begun to play. "Sonia, my dear friend, has our little snowbird told you who made her gown?" she asked the baroness. "I *must* know."

"Don't tell her, Alexandra," Sonia Tchernikova warned, "or she will have a dozen copies made for herself and her friends."

The princess laughed heartily and made it quite clear that whether Alexandra divulged the desired information or not, Vera Ylbatskaya would remain a friend.

"Do you sing, Snowbird?" she asked.

"No, not very well."

"Then, if there is no one to sing, I shall not play. Come join me over here and we will talk."

Her invitation was more a command, but Alexandra willingly followed her to a small circle of chairs around a low table.

"Vodka?" Vera offered from a selection of decanters. "No? Well, if you intend to chase after our Mischa with any hope of success, you must learn to be as Russian as he." She poured a little of the clear liquor into a glass and handed it to Alexandra. "And stop that silly blushing! It isn't hard to see you two were made for each other."

"Stop it, Vera!" the baroness scolded. "The poor child is red as a beet from all your nonsense."

In spite of the baroness' light chuckle, Vera took on an aspect of seriousness, and she leaned forward to whisper earnestly, "It is not nonsense. Look around you once and you'll see I'm right. Maria Palichnikova has three marriageable daughters and she is watching our little

Snowbird with envy. Have you noticed your own niece this evening? She knows there is a new temptation for her philandering husband, and I don't think she's had a peaceful moment since Alexandra entered this house. I'm not the only one who wants that gown; every woman tonight has asked about it, and about her. More important, every woman who wants Mischa now knows he is lost, and every man who wants the Snowbird dares not even hint at his desire.''

''Still nonsense.''

Vera shrugged.

''Your Andrei hardly looked unhappy to share a bit of conversation with her over supper. Which reminds me. I must tell our hostess that her new cook is a jewel. The fish was done perfectly, and the *peches flambees*—mmmmmmm.'' Alexandra relaxed and let her companions gossip. They seemed to have forgotten her, but she did not complain. Left to herself she was free to let her gaze travel about the room and to eavesdrop on a few of the conversations nearest to her.

For the most part the ladies of the music room had only one thing on their minds, and when Alexandra discovered that she was it and that they had little to say about her that was flattering, she returned to Princess Vera's passionate denouncement of a certain diplomat who had left his wife in Moscow and brought his mistress to Paris. Such talk, when she didn't know either the man or his mistress, bored Alexandra, but at least it did not make her cheeks burn.

''You should have warned me, Mischa,'' Baron Andrei chided. ''That was a very unkind thing you made me do.''

They had left the noisy, smoky dining hall for the privacy of the library.

''There was no time, Uncle. I only met the girl last night, and it was only a few hours ago that I learned what unique talents she possesses.''

''Such as?''

''Besides the obvious, she speaks fluent English and

54

hates the Corsican as much as we. And she has one advantage we don't: He likes her."

"And that comment about your father, rest his soul. You mean she's English?"

"At least as much as I am. I don't know a great deal about her, but with an English mother and an emigre father, she's got scant loyalty to the self-proclaimed Emperor of France."

"Does she have any loyalty at all?"

Mikhail flashed a very knowing smile and said only, "She will."

Chapter 6

RAIN STREAMED down the windows of the tailor shop, dreary and sad as tears. Despite a fire in the grate, the damp was penetrating. Yvette rubbed her hands together before rethreading her needle.

"I wish this whole thing had never happened, Xan. I'm really sorry."

"That is the thousandth time you've apologized, and it really isn't necessary. I keep telling you there is nothing to be sorry for."

A week had passed since the ball, a week with no message from the Russian count. Alexandra had been disappointed at first, but within a day or two she seemed to have forgotten all about it. She had been warned of his reputation and blamed no one but herself for the heartbreak his rejection caused, but it had begun and ended quickly. The pain could not last long.

At least that was what she told herself.

He had not accompanied her home that night. In the garden he had kissed her once, very sweetly, before telling her he had been called to attend some urgent business and that he could not go with her. She said she understood, and then he had kissed her again. It was the memory of his kiss, of his hand touching her cheek, his arm holding her, that kept sleep from her no matter how exhausted she was. The blue eyes that had never left hers as he whispered his farewell still haunted her, invading her troubled sleep with dreams so real she awoke more than once with his name on her lips and an ache in her heart.

The past night had been no different. After a few hours of fitful sleep she had opened her eyes on a still dark bedroom with the dream more vivid than ever. Even in the cool room, her thin nightdress was plastered to her skin with sweat. She kicked off the quilts and lay shivering with cold and tension, waiting for the dawn and the start of another day so she could forget the cruel tricks her mind played.

It had all been so real, this dream. His hands, his lips, his blue eyes, even the passionate whispers he poured into her ear. She saw only his face, shadowed as it had been in the garden; the rest of his body was only a warmth that enveloped her, consumed her, devoured her. No man had ever aroused her the way the mere memory of Mikhail Pavlovitch did in her dreams.

How was such passion possible in a woman who had known few kisses and fewer caresses? she wondered. She was no naive child; she knew what the delicious warmth that began between her thighs and spread to become a tingling in her toes meant. Wanting him more now that he was gone, Alexandra got out of her bed and faced another day determined to forget.

"Perhaps he's just busy," Yvette continued. "More than likely he'll send you a long letter explaining everything and we'll feel so foolish."

"You might, but I won't because I really don't care." Alexandra folded a blue spencer she had just hemmed. "By the way, where is Justine? I thought she said she would be back by one o'clock."

"She did, but between you and me, I don't expect her back until later."

"Oh?"

"I don't know who it is, but Justine has a lover. I'm sure of it."

Alexandra chuckled, "You sound so surprised, so indignant. Is she not entitled to a lover? You have Albert,

57

and you keep trying to imagine some liaison between myself and Count Ogrinov. Why not Justine?''

''It isn't the affair that bothers me. She has to sneak around all the time. I get suspicious very easily, and it doesn't seem natural to me that he never calls on her. She always goes to him, and always during the day. It just isn't at all like her.''

''That is her business. She is old enough to make up her own mind, to know what she is doing. I only hope he isn't a philandering husband or some filthy degenerate who will abuse her and break her heart.''

Before Yvette had a chance to reply, the door crashed open and Justine, soaking wet and shivering, burst into the shop. Leaving a trail of mud and rainwater on the floor from door to hearth, she hurried to the warmth and rubbed her hands together over the fire. Yvette ran upstairs to get her sister dry clothes while Alexandra threw another shovel of coal onto the flames and stoked the fire until it licked hungrily at the fresh fuel.

''In my pocket, Xan, there's a letter for you,'' Justine said once her teeth had stopped chattering enough for her to speak coherently. ''A man came up to me and said, 'Give this to your sister.' When I asked him which one, he answered, 'The one who is not your sister,' and then he dashed out into the rain again. I couldn't even tell you what he looked like.''

Her hands, wrinkled with the wetness of her clothes, were little help getting the envelope from the pocket of her skirt, where the letter had remained relatively dry. Tucking it into her own pocket, Alexandra helped Justine out of her sodden clothes, and as it was late and there had been no customers since noon, she locked the door and pulled the curtain across the window.

''I'll keep Yvette busy if you want,'' Justine offered.

''Don't worry about it. With Therese and Armand gone until Friday, I gave Marie the day off, so there will be time enough for me to read this while I fix you some hot tea.''

Yvette arrived, breathless, with an armload of dry clothing. She had forgotten nothing; the pile she unceremoniously dumped on a chair included underdrawers and stockings as well as a warm flannel blouse and skirt.

"It's warmer up in the kitchen, so get dressed and we'll have some tea there," Yvette suggested. She was so intent on gathering up the wet clothing that she did not see the look of frustration cross Alexandra's face. "Marie left us some onion soup and there's a bit of yesterday's bread, too."

Even in the cozy kitchen Justine shivered, though certainly less than before. She sat as close to the fire as she dared and with a heavy quilt wrapped around her, she let Yvette wait on her.

"It will be a miracle if you don't catch your death of fever," the little blonde clucked like a mother hen. "Now, here, eat this and then you are going straight to bed."

"With a bit of brandy to warm you and help you sleep," Alexandra added. "I'll go down to the cellar and fetch a bottle."

Justine protested such pampering feebly; she knew only too well that the brandy was an excuse, nothing more, though the idea of a glass of the fiery liquor was welcome.

Alexandra strode into the kitchen only moments later, bottle in hand. As nonchalantly as ever, she removed the cork and poured the clear amber fluid into three glasses.

"I can just see us an hour from now, all drunk, lying on the floor for Marie to find us in the morning," Yvette laughed.

With each sip of the strong liquor, Justine felt warmer and sleepier, but kept seeking Alexandra's eyes over the rim of her glass.

Why are you back so soon? she wanted to ask. Did you read the letter? What did he say?

It never entered her mind that the sender could have been anyone but the Russian.

Alexandra fussed around the kitchen, ladled hot soup into large bowls and set bread on the table with a crock of butter and the remains of a cheese. As the savory steam filled the room, it awakened appetites that were not satisfied until all the soup and cheese was gone and only a crusty end of the bread was left. Full, warm, and a little light-headed, the three girls left their dirty dishes on the table after promising to help when the servant arrived in the morning, and then they wandered off to their beds.

For hours, it seemed, Justine lay awake, shaking off the effects of more brandy than she was accustomed to and trying to listen for Yvette's snores, a sure sign that she had fallen into a sound sleep. Only silence came from her bed, though Justine could tell by the perfectly even breathing from the far corner of the room that Alexandra, too, was waiting, unable to sleep.

"Yes, I intended to read it when I got the brandy, but I was afraid," Alexandra whispered. She had laid the letter, still unopened, on the work table in the back of the shop. A single candle glimmered between them, the yellow flame casting eerie shadows on the walls and brilliant highlights on honey-gold and raven-black hair.

"I even took it out of my pocket and held it a moment, but I just couldn't bring myself to open it and read it."

"Why?" Justine pulled the quilt tighter around her, for there was no fire to warm this room and the night was cold.

Slowly her thoughts coalesced and formed words of a reluctant answer.

"Because I was afraid it wouldn't be from him."

In a quavering voice, Alexandra poured out her feelings, the heartbreak she had not dared to acknowledge all this past week. All the dreams he had wakened, dreams of a life she had never believed could be real, had been dashed so quickly.

"I was silly, I know, to let myself be carried away by two evenings with a man so completely beyond my reach, but it happened. My imagination took over and wouldn't let me see the truth that I had to accept. I thought I was getting over it, until *this* arrived."

But dreams die hard in the soul of a girl with tales of

past glory and tragedy as her only legacy. She fingered the letter without picking it up.

"If I don't open it, if I just think it's from him, I can go on with my little fantasy, imagining all kinds of wonderful things he has written to me." she sighed. "I won't have to face the real world, the world of this shop and ordinary people in ordinary houses, leading ordinary lives. If I were sixteen again, I would have ripped it open the instant you gave it to me. At that age I had only the future. Now I have a past, a few memories that are very precious to me. I am so afraid of tarnishing those memories with the ugliness of the present, with the hurt of losing him, that I would risk all hope of the future to keep what I have."

Justine's clear blue grey eyes searched Alexandra's green ones, looking for tears. There were none, though her voice still trembled.

"Open it," the older girl said calmly. "Open it now, or you'll live the rest of your life wondering, never knowing the truth, never living."

The thoughts that flooded Alexandra's brain as she gingerly touched the drop of red wax that sealed the letter almost frightened her and yet almost made her laugh.

I am twenty years old, hardly a child any more. Most girls by this age are married, have children, and are looking around for a lover to break up the boredom of their lives. I've never even been in love! Even dear Justine had a broken heart or two when she was my age; now she has a lover she meets secretly, and when she comes back here she is both happy and sad in such a way that she glows. I am like a candle that has never been lit, just lies on a shelf gathering dust and dirt and someday will end up melted by the summer heat into a shapeless lump, to be thrown away without ever having brightened someone's life.

Her green eyes sparkled, but the tears did not spill onto her cheeks. A bit of romance had come into her life, a spark that might touch a flame to the candle, and she could no longer find the strength to deny her heart its moment of brightness. She broke the letter's seal almost violently.

The page was covered with careful, bold masculine script. In the unsteady light the letters seemed to dance as if they, too, heard the music that soared within her, ringing in her ears and pounding in her blood.

"It's from the count, isn't it?" Justine asked, though she knew the answer.

"Oh, yes, it certainly is!"

Alexandra had been too excited to eat any breakfast other than a cup of bitter coffee, but by the time Marie had lunch ready, she was famished and wolfed down everything set in front of her. Yvette had gone out with Albert, leaving Justine alone to share the afternoon with a very nervous Alexandra.

"You'll get sick if you eat like that," she warned. "How will I explain to him that you can't go riding because you've a bellyache from eating like a pig?"

Alexandra made a face and took another bite of bread.

"I shan't be sick. Only death could keep me from seeing him. Oh, Justine, I can't believe this is really happening to me." She burst into half-hysterical laughter that frightened the older girl. "All these years of listening to Therese and her stories of the life I ought to be living have made me an incurable dreamer, almost unable to accept the reality of life, of being a very ordinary person, the daughter of a prosperous but still ordinary tailor. When I was old enough to understand it all, I began to envy you and Yvette."

"I'd have thought you'd despise us."

"No, never! You were happy, you had no noble heritage to defend, no slaughtered family to avenge. I hated that responsibility, and even more, the burden of self-pity and guilt." She paused, then turned away. "I'm sorry. That was cruel and I didn't mean it to be. You're the last person in the world I'd want to hurt."

"Xan, you haven't hurt me! Look at me, please, and don't cry. You'll get your eyes swollen and red if you start

62

crying." More tenderly than a loving mother, she took Alexandra's hand in hers and gently raised her face until green eyes met grey. "Did you think we were not aware of—and constantly reminded of—the differences between us and you? Yvette and I were no less guilty of those thoughts, yet what a miracle it is that we still love each other the way we do. Did Therese ever let you neglect your part of the work in the shop? Did you ever want to? Were you ever less a member of the family—or more? No, of course not. You are feeling guilty for nothing you have done, only for what you are, and who of us can change that?"

There was such strength in those eyes, a strength born of love, faith, and an almost saintly sense of justice. For how many years, Alexandra wondered, have I been turning to Justine with my problems instead of to Therese? Therese was as lost as I, but Justine always gave me comfort and knew the answers.

"He will be here in just a little while, so you had better hurry. Have you decided what to wear?"

Alexandra's choice of a modest green twill dress with a long row of buttons down the front came as close as she had to a riding habit, and with the addition of a wide-brimmed, high-crowned hat borrowed from Yvette, she hoped the costume didn't look too unfashionable. Justine brushed her hair into a simple coiffure held in place with half a dozen adroitly placed pins and the green hat. After sliding her feet into a pair of brand new boots, Alexandra stood before the long mirror in the fitting room downstairs.

"It's the best we can do," Justine apologized. "With so little time . . ."

"Nonsense! It will do just fine. If he is more concerned with what I wear, let him buy me a velvet riding habit. He knows what I am, even if his friends don't."

The bell jingled as the front door was pushed open. Justine put out her hand to restrain an over-anxious sister, then went into the shop alone.

This had to be Alexandra's Russian. No Frenchman ever

had shoulders that broad or arms so muscled that the fabric of his sleeves strained almost to bursting. He was dressed in subdued greys more elegant than any flashy fop, and he knew without conceit that he easily impressed the girl who stared at him.

She could see how Alexandra had been captivated so instantly by this man. He was in every sense magnificent, more so than Justine had imagined from the simple description her sisters had given. Tall, strongly built, with an aura of raw power surrounding him, he still did not intimidate, and Justine felt no awe of him. He had no airs of an aristocrat, only the essence of nobility. And when Alexandra walked from the back room and into the shop, Justine saw his bright blue eyes shine with a new sparkle.

He had brought her a very gentle little grey mare and lifted her easily into the saddle once they had left the shop.

"You ride well for someone who says she's been on a horse only once before in her life," Mikhail teased as he held his big black beside her, but there was sincerity in his compliment. "If I ever doubted your claim to English blood, I cannot do so now; no Frenchwoman has your instinct with a horse."

She blushed but said nothing, only smiled at him, and he at her.

The afternoon, graced by sun, a gentle breeze, and the lingering warmth of autumn, passed pleasantly and without incident. Alexandra surprised herself at how quickly she caught on to the art of managing a horse, though the mare needed little enough managing, and she began to believe Mikhail's praise. They were not the only ones taking advantage of the lovely day; the Bois de Boulogne was crowded after two days of torrential rain had kept everyone house-bound, and autumn had not long to last. On horseback, in carriages, and even on foot, nearly everyone who could was outdoors enjoying what might be the last nice day before winter.

Alexandra lost track of the people Mikhail introduced her to. She recalled a few names and a few faces, but doubted she could match any of them. Was Madame Yolande Romantiere the elderly woman in the open phaeton with the dogs on her lap, or was that Mademoiselle Pantouille? She could not remember. But she did know that many of the people she met smiled and said, "Ah, the celebrated Snowbird!" and she blushed quite crimson then. She was not the anonymous seamstress she had been ten days ago. Perhaps that door had opened and now shut once again—behind her.

So much time was spent meeting and talking with all these people that hardly ten words passed between Mikhail and Alexandra, and then most of the conversation centered on her horsemanship. Not until early twilight and a growing chill in the air put an end to the afternoon did they have time for each other.

"There is a little restaurant not far from your home," Mikhail said. "Shall we stop there for coffee?"

"I think I'd like that very much," she answered as he helped her off the mare and into his waiting carriage at the edge of the Bois.

The vehicle moved off slowly, and, Alexandra was quick to note, took a direct route towards their destination. She leaned her head back against the black velvet upholstery and closed her eyes in the refreshing exhaustion brought on by a day spent in the open air.

"You enjoyed today?" Mikhail asked.

"I most certainly did, even if I pay dearly for it tomorrow." She laughed at this innocent implication of discomfort in places not mentioned in mixed company.

He laughed, too. "That will pass with practice. If we could delay the winter, you'd soon be as much at home on a horse as in the tailor's shop."

Then he asked, "Do you trust me, Alexandra?"

Flabbergasted, she stammered, "Really, monsieur, I—I don't know!"

"Good. That was a nearly honest answer, because of course you don't trust me. You can't. At least not completely. After all, I am a man with a ruthless reputation, a breaker of young ladies' hearts, a destroyer of happy marriages, a scoundrel and a rogue. Definitely not a man to be trusted, unless by a silly, foolish girl.''

Those last words were murmured slowly, softly, as he gathered her into his arms. His lips touched hers gently, persuasively, in a kiss that sent a wave of warmth over her. Nothing in the world seemed more natural than that she should kiss him back, parting her lips to his seeking tongue, revelling in the taste of him. The world beyond the carriage, the world of pain and pity and unattainable dreams, slipped away, dissolved into nothingness as she let herself succumb to her desires.

His kisses grew more passionate, more demanding, and his hands began a wondrous exploration of her body. The buttons of her dress opened quickly under his expert fingers; he had travelled that road before. With only the thin fabric of her chemise between his flesh and hers, he cupped her breast in his hand and felt the nipple tighten at his touch.

"Shall I ask Vasili to take a long detour?" To whisper the question he had freed her mouth, but his hand never stopped its caress.

"No, please, I must go home." The words seemed to come from someone else, not from the girl whose arms tightened around him and pulled him closer. "Will you take me home, or are you really not to be trusted?"

He could not help but laugh again, this time at himself. He had touched her, aroused her, but this time she remained in control.

"First some coffee and some talk, and then I shall take you home."

They rode the rest of the way without talking, save for Alexandra's giggles as she let Mikhail refasten the buttons on her dress. She wished for a mirror to examine the damage done to her coiffure but had to content herself with pushing a few loose curls back under her hat and blaming the rest on the breeze. Satisfied that she did not look too dishevelled, she sat back to think.

No man willingly begins that which he has no hopes of finishing, she told herself, yet this is not the first time he has started and then desisted so easily. If he has no intention of seducing me, what *does* he want?

She glanced at him from the corner of her eye. Legs stretched out before him, eyes closed, he might have been asleep, except for the steady drumming of his fingers on the back of his other hand. He was deep in thought, obviously, and Alexandra did not find it difficult to imagine what kind of thoughts brought that ghost of a smile to his lips. As the flush of her arousal waned and sensibility regained control over sensation, she knew she should feel some remorse, some guilt for the shameless way she had acted, but all she felt was happy. Not even the apprehension of their upcoming conversation over coffee dampened her spirits.

There were only two other patrons at the restaurant, a pair of elderly chess players who sat at the table nearest the window, when Mikhail led Alexandra to a quiet table in the far corner. An over-solicitous youth took their order and returned almost instantly with Mikhail's cognac and a steaming cup of strong black coffee for Alexandra. It took an extra coin in his palm to ensure their privacy.

Mikhail took her hand across the little table and found it trembling.

"Are you cold?"

"No, monsieur, just nervous."

Hesitant, she took a sip of coffee before saying anything, then whispered, "Mischa?"

"Perhaps if you would call me Mischa, you'll be less nervous. Only favor-seeking Frenchmen and women with favors to grant call me 'monsieur.' Try it."

"Perfect! and what do your friends call you? I think Alexandra is too long, especially for one as tiny as you."

"Xan, spelled with an 'X', spoken with a 'Z'," she replied. "Really, though, it is getting late, and I mustn't worry Justine."

"Of course, forgive me. I shall get right to the point, if you promise to hear me out completely. I don't want you running off before I've had a chance to finish."

"I promise—Mischa."

It did not help at all; she was more nervous than ever.

"I would like to make you a business proposition, Xan. In exchange for certain favors, I will make you the most fashionable hostess in Paris. A house of your own, servants, jewelry, clothes, everything you need or could possibly want. Effective tomorrow, if you wish."

She had not expected anything like this, but her surprise was overshadowed by curiosity. She had given him a few kisses, allowed him a few liberties, but surely he had not been so smitten by these tidbits to offer so much for future favors. No, it had to be something besides her body that he wanted; she ruefully admitted that he could have had *that* for a much lower price.

"A tempting offer," she heard herself say in a strange, detached voice that betrayed none of the anticipation of her soul. "But are you sure I have all the qualities you look for in a mistress?"

"No, not yet," he answered with a grin she could barely see in the growing dark, "but I do know you have everything I need to make you the perfect spy."

Chapter 7

ON A dreary January afternoon, despite the commotion of servants preparing for a dinner party, Alexandra retired to the quiet of her blue and silver sitting room to enjoy her weekly visit from Justine. For a few hours she could forget the unrelenting pressures of her new existence in the pleasant company of the one person with whom she felt truly comfortable. Too much of her life since accepting Mikhail's offer was sham. Indeed she often reminded herself that her name was the only thing she could claim as her own; nothing else said or believed about her bore any resemblance to the truth.

Still she could not say she did not like the luxury and elegance his generosity afforded. Less than a week after their conversation in Gofanier's, he installed her in this modest but exquisitely appointed townhouse furnished with what she soon came to know was his own quiet good taste. There followed on the very next day the first of several sessions with dressmakers, milliners, cobblers, and jewelers until her dressing room was filled with more gowns and shoes and hats than she could wear in a lifetime.

At first the sheer novelty of it all kept her enchanted, and she shared her joy and excitement each evening with Mikhail as they dined together, either in her own dining room or at some intimate restaurant where they could easily be taken for lovers. When the newness began to wear off and the business for which they had contracted the liaison occupied more of their conversation than the latest bauble or pair of slippers, Alexandra noticed that Mikhail spent less and less time with her.

She told herself that she should have expected nothing more. Had he not laughed when she asked if she qualified to be his mistress? She was a spy, or soon would be, and that was quite enough. Somehow she must help to bring about the demise of the madman who ruled France and much of the rest of Europe, but her hatred of Napoleon Bonaparte was not the only reason she had left her safe and secure home on the Rue Ste. Aurrienne. Nor had her curiosity, fueled by her aunt's stories, about the aristocratic heritage a revolution had stolen from her pushed her into this masquerade. She simply could not refuse the opportunity to spend some part of her life with the man who had come to mean everything to her.

Justine alone had guessed this part of the truth. On those occasions when Yvette or Therese accompanied her, the charade was played out for their benefit, but today she would come alone.

Her note had arrived while Alexandra was eating her breakfast and having her hair done by Giselle, the maid she had selected after interviewing a dozen or more. Not that she considered Giselle any more competent than the others; the girl was simply the youngest and least haughty of the women Mikhail had sent for Alexandra's approval. Over the months a kind of bond had developed between them. Not exactly friendship, for Giselle was too shy and Alexandra too unsure of herself, but a vague something that went beyond the duty of a servant to her mistress and vice versa.

"You may tell cook that only Mademoiselle Justine will be here this afternoon, and we may go out for a while, so he need not prepare anything for us."

"I'm sure he will appreciate that, what with the dinner and all," Giselle replied candidly as she twisted another curl to dangle behind Alexandra's ear. "Will you want the pearl earrings or the amethysts?"

The dress laid out was pale grey muslin, simply but provocatively cut, almost too revealing, Alexandra thought, for morning. The lace on the long sleeves and the ribbon that graced the high waistline were off-white, as were the satin slippers and kid gloves, the beaded reticule, and the low-crowned hat that completed her ensemble.

"The pearls, I suppose. Who am I receiving this morning? I do hope it isn't Madame Souvin again. She drives me nearly mad."

It was an unkind thing to say about the woman who had spent so much time over the past months making Alexandra what she was today, a poised, exquisitely gowned young woman whose coming soiree was the talk of Paris today. But Alexandra could not disguise her feelings toward the woman. She had begun to irritate Alexandra no more than a month ago, about the time Mikhail announced that he wished her to host a small dinner party, a very intimate dinner party, on the fifteenth of January. The implication was all too clear; he considered her ready for the important business of their bargain.

Alexandra was not certain what about Madame Souvin so upset her, but she could not settle her dislike.

When Giselle made no reply to her question, Alexandra protested with a stomp of her foot and a determined shake of her head that set the carefully designed curls to swinging. "Tell Henri he is not to let that woman in this house again."

"You will tell Henri no such thing."

Both women turned toward the voice, firm and allowing no argument, that came from the open doorway between the dressing room and Alexandra's bedroom. Giselle had only seen the man twice before, and his presence terrified her to the point that she let out a mouselike squeak and tried to hide behind her mistress.

Alexandra never took her eyes off him, even as she said, "And why not? It is my house and I do not wish her inside it." Then, to Giselle, in an entirely different tone of voice, "Stop it, child! He won't bite. Go get us some coffee."

The girl scurried, still like a mouse, from the room, but Alexandra was not altogether glad to see her go. She had spent very little time alone with Mikhail recently, and on those few occasions it was always in the drawing room, the library, or the dining room, never once in her private quarters in the two months since she had taken residence here.

"Madame Souvin is not calling today, that's why," he answered after a long anxious silence that filled the room once Giselle had gone. "In fact, she will not be here any more at all. Does that look in your eyes mean you are pleased?"

"A bit surprised, but yes, pleased also. Something about her . . . ."

He laughed at her mock shudder, and the tension was broken.

"So you were not fond of Madame Souvin. Was she unkind to you? Did she beat you when you did not know your lessons?"

"I always knew my lessons," she tossed back tartly. "Who could not learn how to stare sideways, to walk with just the right wiggle, to laugh just so, to smile just so? One would have thought she was grooming me for a brothel rather than a drawing room."

Why was he laughing so uproariously at her? Laughing so hard that tears began to dribble from the corners of his merry eyes. This was more insult than she could stand.

"What did I do?" she shrieked. She stormed around the room in wild circles, her pale blue negligee foaming about her ankles and opening in the front to reveal the sheer white nightdress and a glimpse of very small feet in blue satin mules. "Can't you even share your amusement with me? Surely I might find it funny, too, whatever it is."

She stopped her pacing long enough to stand before him, hands on her hips, and glowered at him with all the outrage she could muster, outrage that began to disappear the instant he reached up and took her hands in his. His laughter subsided, but there was still mirth in the sparkle of his blue eyes.

"Honestly, Mischa, you can sometimes be the most

rude, the most infuriating creature," she continued in a vain attempt to maintain her anger against the swell of other emotions brought on by the mere touch of his hand.

"My dear Alexandra, I most humbly apologize for my laughter, not only because I can see how it has upset you." He paused, took a deep breath to still the last chuckle. "I employed Marianne Souvin because I knew she, of all the women in Paris, was the best qualified to teach you what you needed to know. I had no way to guess how accomplished you might be, nor had I the time to find out on my own. Marianne cost me a small fortune and a lot of talk to persuade her, but she was the one person I could trust to turn you into the most irresistible woman in Paris." He paused again, then said, "As if you weren't already."

"And what is so funny about that?" she asked, trying to ignore his last remark. "What does that have to do with embarrassing me the way you just did?"

"Only if you promise not to go into another fit. Marianne Souvin runs the most exclusive pleasure house in Paris, and I told her you were destined to be Bonaparte's next mistress." His hands tightened their grip as he felt new fury rising in her.

"That is not the least bit amusing; it is disgusting," she hissed. She tried to turn her back to him, but he held her fast.

"No, it isn't, especially since Marianne idolizes the little fool and would do absolutely anything for him. What *is* so funny is that you, whom I believed so innocent, so naive, should know right away what she was. In you, my dear, the game of espionage has gained perhaps its greatest player."

He stood and at least released her hands as he bowed, only half mockingly. She had caught a new gleam in his eye, a brightness that was neither passion nor humor, and the tone of his voice was changed, too. He had underestimated her before; he respected her now.

Fighting the desire to break one of the cardinal rules of his profession, he persuaded Alexandra to sit down beside him and have a cup of coffee while he detailed the strategy for the evening's dinner party. He had spent months preparing these plans and now considered the time perfect to put them into action. But as he described them to her, he felt a vague uneasiness. For some reason he was reluctant to begin the deadly game, and he hoped it was not because of the newest player. Every time he saw her, he wanted her more, and he dared not let such desires interfere with his work.

Baron Tchernikov was waiting in the library when Mikhail returned shortly before noon to his own apartment. Eager to hear what news his uncle had brought, he headed straight there, issuing orders for luncheon as he strode down the long hallway. He had walked from Alexandra's in a sleety fog that had chilled him to the bone but had not cooled his internal fire one degree. Only sheer determination took the look of worry from his face.

The library was not particularly large, but on this cold and damp day, the coziness of a small room and a roaring fire made it more than comfortable. In the flickering light of the fire, Mikhail saw the baron seated in one of two leather armchairs that flanked the hearth. He was reading, or trying to read, for the fire provided but poor illumination. Several pages of the long letter lay in his lap. Not until he heard the click of the latch as Mikhail closed the door did he look up.

"A letter from the Tsar?" Mikhail asked.

"Worse yet. It's from my sister, and I know of no other woman who can write such long, boring missives as she." He gathered up the various sheets of paper and returned them to their envelope. Then, after a long swallow of vodka, he asked, "How fares the little Snowbird today?"

"Very well. I expect great things of her." Mikhail poured himself a long draught of the same liquor and took the other chair. "She's much quicker than I had guessed, and she has cooperated completely."

"If I were you, I'd be a bit suspicious."

"I was, at first. I laid a dozen traps for her, and even more for the people I thought might have provided her. That week last November that I spent in the worst holes of

74

Paris seeking information that would give me the slightest doubt told me that she is absolutely genuine.''

The baron harumphed and wished he had thought to light a candle or two. In the dimness it was hard to see Mischa's face, where Andrei was certain lay the clue to the strange tone in his voice. Tchernikov had long held a deep respect, even admiration, for his nephew; now he was concerned that something might go wrong with this fantastic plot of his.

"The girl knows what is expected of her?" he asked.

"Of course she does. Uncle, you are living proof of how good she is. Already you are in her power." Mikhail smiled, pleased with himself. "Tonight's target has already put one foot in the trap, and I am certain that by tomorrow morning we will know as much as he about the Corsican's plans.''

Tchernikov harumphed again. Knowing that any advice he gave would be unwelcome and unheeded, he gave it anyway.

"It is not a good idea in this business to count on anything, Mischa. And especially on a woman. You should know that by now." He reached for his glass but found it empty.

Mikhail shrugged. "Alexandra is like no other woman you've ever met. I think after tonight you will change your mind.''

"Are you sure that keeping her as your mistress hasn't put you, too, in her power, as you call it?"

Coolly, almost coldly, Mikhail answered, "She is not my mistress. This is a business arrangement, not sexual. I have too much respect for her to let myself become one of her victims. I have been in that position before; never again.''

That was precisely the answer the baron had expected. A spy could not afford to mix his business with his pleasure; Mikhail was experienced enough to know that and strong enough to follow his own wisdom. Then why was there that odd tension in his voice, the same tension Andrei had noticed before and worried about?

* * *

Justine's departure left the room cold and empty. Alexandra sat quietly on the blue brocade and silver gilt chair until Giselle appeared with a message that Count Ogrinov was waiting downstairs in the parlor, that he had been there for almost an hour.

"Tell him I'm tired. I'm going to take a nap and I don't want to be disturbed unless the house catches on fire."

With a mumbled "yes, mistress," the maid bowed her way out of the room. She half expected the count to be waiting in the hallway. To her surprise he was not only still in the parlor, but he seemed to accept the excuse without argument. He muttered something about Alexandra's being rested for the party, to which Giselle nodded polite agreement. It was all she could do to mask the terror she felt in his presence. More than anything she wanted to run from the room and hide from him, from those icy blue eyes that pierced her like long slender knives. She had heard stories of men who could bewitch girls with their eyes and no doubt this Count Ogrinov was one of them. With her gaze fastened on the floral pattern in the carpet, she stood as tall as her shaking knees would allow and tried to answer his questions as best she could.

He asked about Alexandra's visitors, who they were, when they came, how long they stayed. When she went out, where did she go and with whom? Had she ever been gone from the house overnight? Had other guests ever spent the night with her?

"What business is it of yours?"

Alexandra stood in the doorway, her face flushed with anger, her eyes alive with the green fire of rage. Yet her voice remained amazingly calm. Neither she nor Mikhail said another word until Giselle, frightened and relieved all at the same time, hurried out of sight.

"Everything about you is my business," he answered easily. "Have you something you are hiding from me?"

"Hardly. When do I have the time? You keep me too busy to have any visitors, and I only go out when you approve. You know my habits as well as I, perhaps better. There was no reason to scare the poor girl out of her wits."

"My apologies." He had stood at her arrival but now returned to his chair. He took a thin cigar from his pocket, then, noticing the look of distaste she gave him, he put it back. "I thought you were napping."

"I came down to find a book I started reading yesterday. Do I have your permission to read, or is that proscribed?"

"Certainly not. Do anything you like this afternoon, so long as you are ready to receive your guests on time tonight."

The silence that followed was unbearable. The ticking of a distant clock grew louder and louder; the crackling of the fire became a roar; the pounding of her own heart deafened her. What did he want of her? He sat there so arrogant, with a wicked half-smile on his lips and that frozen glitter in his eyes, eyes that never left hers.

Not waiting for the inevitable, she spun on her heel and retraced her steps to the bedroom. It would do no good, she knew, to let him see what he was capable of doing to her.

With the door securely locked, she set about undressing herself and sliding into the great canopied bed. Sleep was impossible; she knew her nerves and her emotions were too agitated now. But she could lie here and think, try to puzzle out some of the questions that haunted her every time she saw him.

The moments of passion they had shared were distant memories now. Why had he never kissed her since that November afternoon in his carriage? He rarely even touched her, except to dance with her now and then or take her hand as he had that morning. It almost made her laugh to know that all Paris considered her his mistress. If only the gossip-mongers knew the truth! It would indeed have been amusing had it not been for the fact that Mikhail himself fed those rumors.

And he was very careful to see that they were believed. He never looked at another woman, and his jealousy when a gentleman paid too much attention to Alexandra was most unpleasant. At first all this had flattered her and she had waited, not without some fear, for the night when at last he would make her what everyone believed her to be. That night never came. Week after week passed and finally she accepted the truth, but she did not understand it. Nor did she understand why tears came to her eyes when she pondered this strange situation.

It was all so confusing. How did he expect her to seduce this Colonel Trabert when she herself had never been seduced? Once, in a spell of desperation, she had tried to ask him, but he merely smiled, patted her hand in a comforting way, and told her that she only needed to trust him, he knew what he was doing. So the subject of her inexperience had never really been discussed and she dared not think he considered her anything but what she was. Never had she given him reason to believe otherwise, not since that moment of weakness after leaving the Bois de Boulogne. He had never given her a chance.

If you had any brains at all, you silly goose, you'd not be letting him get away from you right now, she scolded herself. He's the one who keeps saying how irresistible you are. What makes him think he's immune?

She reached for the bell pull, stretching languorously until only her fingertips touched the cord and her toes wriggled into the crisp coolness of the sheets. A smile curled the corners of her mouth. When Giselle came into the room, Alexandra yawned and snuggled yet deeper into the luxurious comfort of the bed.

"Has Count Ogrinov left yet?"

"Yes, mistress, he has. I was just seeing him out when you rang."

And the tears came again.

Chapter 8

THE HOUSE was quiet now that the guests had gone, and darkness began to envelope the silent, empty rooms as the servants snuffed out the candles and banked the fires. Alexandra watched them for a moment or two, until she finally made her way upstairs.

Exhausted mentally as well as physically, she was in no frame of mind to face the ordeal of the next few hours. Her head throbbed from the prolonged effort of concentrating on conversation that seemed so unimportant, so trivial compared to what was on her mind and in her heart. Hours and hours of forced laughter and mechanical smiles had left even her facial muscles painfully fatigued. Every inch of her ached, every muscle screamed in protest of her abuse. Her whole body cried out for rest, from her swollen feet in too-tight slippers to her pounding head.

And the evening was not over yet.

She had laid out very specific instructions to the servants, which they had followed perfectly. Her bed had been turned down and a sheer peach-colored silk night-dress laid out for her. Giselle had been told to go to bed early; Alexandra would ring for her when necessary. How pleasant it would be to pull the tassled cord and let the maid help her out of the green satin gown. How relaxing to lean back in a soft chair while experienced hands pulled the pins from her hair and brushed all the tangles and troubles away. How glorious to curl into a tiny, secure ball

79

beneath the warmth of a silken comforter, to sleep and sleep and sleep until all the weariness was gone.

How fiendishly satisfying to ignore the man who waited in the adjoining sitting room.

She had met Colonel Augustin Trabert a month ago and had taken an almost instant dislike to the man. The death of his wife some years ago had left him both wealthy and eligible, two qualities he had seen fit to maintain and even improve upon since then. Until his recent reassignment to Paris, he had served with the Army of Italy for a number of years, and if nothing else, the soldier's life had kept his body trim. He was, at forty-three, attractive, intelligent, wealthy, and he held a position of some authority in the procurement division of the army staff.

But Alexandra had protested immediately when Mikhail told her Trabert was the target, not on any particular grounds but because, as she told him over and over, the colonel gave her a chill feeling in the pit of her stomach. After an entire day spent contemplating the situation, she still could not put a finger on what she found so objectionable, except that his eyes seemed too small and queerly lashless, and he drank far too much. When Mischa pointed out that the colonel's predilection for fine brandy was one of the reasons he had been selected, Alexandra wrinkled her nose and forced a shudder to express her displeasure.

Now, with her hand on the latch to the door connecting the bedchamber with the sitting room, she wished she had a glass of cognac herself. Yet she found herself remarkably calm even without the extra fortification. She turned the handle, and firmly committed to the ideals she believed she was serving, she entered the room.

"Well, good evening," he said, rather unemotionally, she thought.

"I'm very sorry to have kept you waiting, Colonel. I had to see that the servants were in their quarters first." She had moved closer to where he stood, and seeing his glass empty, refilled it and poured a bit for herself. "I'm so glad you were able to wait."

"I would not have missed the opportunity for

80

anything," he gushed in her ear. He stood behind her and leaned over to nibble at her neck and almost bared shoulder. "I do not know where that Russian bear found you, but I am very glad he did."

His hand began stroking her other shoulder in a slow, circular rhythm. Around and around his fingers traced their pattern on her skin, sensuously, tenderly, insistently. As impossible as it was for her not to feel his caress, it was equally impossible to respond to it.

She had been warned. Mikhail had warned her long ago, and now the colonel himself warned her, not with words but with the nervous glitter in his eye and the snarling smile that curled his lips as he came to stand in front of her. She had no more than a second or two to prepare herself for what lay ahead, but in that brief space of precious time, all manner of visions sprang forth from her imagination.

Neither the warnings nor the visions of hell her mind had glimpsed could match the unmitigated horror of reality. Like a crazed animal, he attacked her with the brutality of blind lust, of angry, drunken rage, tearing at the satin gown with such force that her flesh was bruised before the fabric gave way. He clutched her naked arms with strong fingers that bit into her skin, and he brought his mouth down on hers in a savage, nauseating kiss.

It was not just the stench of his liquor-laden breath that caused her stomach to knot and roll. Fear, utter terror, gripped her vitals; her lungs could not draw breath and her heart froze into a lump of icy pain in her chest. Seduction was one thing, lust another, but this was beyond even the basest animal rutting. This man hurt her and was intent on inflicting more and more pain. He pressed her head back until she expected at any moment to hear the sound of her neck snapping, while his mouth moved viciously on hers, biting until the blood ran salty down her throat.

In the first few seconds she tried to think of a way to tame this ugly passion; then she struggled merely to survive. He held one arm so tightly that her fingers began to numb, and he had let go the other only to pin it between their bodies, rendering it useless in her defense. His free hand now reached behind her to shred her chemise and drop the torn ribbons of silk to the floor. The touch of his fingers on the unprotected skin of her back sent a fresh wave of revulsion through her. The exertion had spread a light film of perspiration over her entire body, and this seemed to increase the ferocity of Trabert's caresses as he slid his hand up and down her back, across her shoulder blades, around the smooth firmness of her buttocks, kneading the flesh until she felt she had been beaten.

Despite the futility of her resistance, she refused to give up. With her left hand finally freed, she pushed his head back, and her lungs sucked clean air through her nose and mouth in frantic gulps. Then excruciating pain exploded in her head as he swung his arm and struck her with the flat of his hand on her temple, and she felt unconsciousness drop a welcome blanket of blackness over her.

It was not to be; self-preservation was too strong an instinct to be easily defeated. Battling to maintain a tenuous grip on consciousness, Alexandra found a new strength in the anger that burned within her, anger at this madman who seemed bent upon her brutal murder, anger at the cold-hearted Russian whose schemes had put her into this struggle, and most of all anger at herself for being such a willing victim.

There was blood on her hands from the long row of scratches she had clawed on the side of his face. No other part of his body was vulnerable; he had not so much as loosened a button of his black tunic. Buoyed by even this small measure of success, Alexandra struck again with her nails, aiming for Trabert's eyes.

She fell short of her mark, but even as she felt her wrist grabbed by his iron hand, she had the satisfaction of feeling her nails dig once more into his cheek and come away with skin and blood wedged under them. More satisfying still was the hot, sticky, salty taste of his blood as she sank her teeth into the back of his hand and bit down hard.

The colonel tried to shake her off and let her go long enough to strike her again and again, but she had fastened onto him with a death grip and did not intend to let go. She had both hands free to ward off his blows, but the man was too big, too strong, for her to continue much longer. Why didn't he shout, or make some noise to rouse the servants? To scream, Alexandra would have to release him, something she could not do voluntarily. Though the blood was choking her and he had landed a dizzying blow to the top of her head and another to her shoulder that almost jolted her loose, she held on like a tiny bulldog, grinding her teeth together until her jaw trembled and she could hardly breathe.

The last of her strength was almost gone when Alexandra realized Trabert was weakening. Whether with exhaustion or drunkenness or both did not matter, for though he was still far superior to her in strength, she felt some frail vestige of hope spring back to life. Instinctive reaction gave way to calculated strategy, and she had time to think.

The opportunity for victory came just as she knew she had reached her limit. Her attacker stepped back to gain momentum for a full swinging blow when she opened her jaws and freed his mutilated hand. He had only a moment to inspect the damage before something burst like a powderkeg between his legs. The pain in his hand was forgotten as he doubled over with the agony of her well-placed kick. Then she spent what strength she had left in a two-fisted thud on the back of his bowed neck. He slumped to his knees, then toppled over and lay in a grotesque, bloodied heap on her pale blue carpet.

Minutes ticked by slowly. The colonel stirred and moaned, but Alexandra held a bronze candlestick in her hand ready to put him out of her misery again if necessary. With a long sigh of relief, for the candlestick was heavy and her arm felt almost too tired to lift it, she watched him sink into drunken oblivion, snoring loudly.

She found a rather large remnant of her ruined chemise and carefully, though none too gently, wrapped it around the torn and bleeding hand, not through any kindness but only to keep the bloodstains from marring the carpet and raising questions from the servants. More minutes passed and slowly some of the pain and exhaustion eased. The decanter Trabert had drained was not the only one in the room, and though the other was some fifteen feet away, Alexandra managed to walk to it and pulled the stopper out. A swallow from the crystal bottle brought back a measure of strength, and a warm glow of sleepy satisfaction crept from her stomach to her arms and legs. It was possible now to stand without swaying.

The quietly ticking clock clanged raucously, jarring her back to wakefulness. While Trabert snored on the floor, his open mouth drooling an obscene trickle of saliva onto his sleeve, she stepped over him and walked to the closed door. It was three o'clock in the morning.

Her first task was to make herself presentable. Leaving the colonel where he lay, she returned to her bedroom and locked the door behind her, then made her way to the dressing room that adjoined on the other side.

It was cold, especially to her exposed flesh, but the carefully banked fire leaped to flaming life when she raked the coals and tossed on a fresh log. There were, however, more important things to do. She pulled on a heavy robe of red velvet and, almost afraid of what she would see, sat down at the dressing table to inspect her face in the mirror.

Once she had cleaned the gore from her mouth and chin and looked at least human again, she was able to see that the damage was not as extensive as she had feared. None of his blows had hit her squarely on the face, thus saving her any obvious and unconcealable disfigurement. The bruises on her arms could be covered by long sleeves, and no one need see the dark blotches on her side and shoulder except Giselle, who would say nothing. Her hair, however, was a total loss. There was nothing to be done but comb out the elaborate curls and plait the long locks down her back to make a knot on the top of her head. She chose the latter as it required less time and effort. When she finally had the lop-sided chignon in place, the improvement was considerable.

She found and put on clean undergarments, then selected a simple dress of deep gold wool with touches of lace at the wrists and throat. Though it was both fashionable and attractive, she chose it more because it covered her almost completely and it was the warmest gown in her wardrobe. The long row of buttons down the back gave her some problem; she had to leave two undone for the moment.

Shoes were another matter, for most of hers were dainty slippers more suited to dancing than what she planned to be doing in the next few hours, but she found a pair of brown half-boots that would serve nicely and quickly pulled them on over the same stockings she had worn throughout the evening. Ignoring the flecks of blood on the fine white silk, she laced up the boots and pulled the cord to rouse Giselle.

Wearing only a cotton nightgown, the maid entered the dressing room and yawned. She was more asleep than awake and her befuddled senses failed to notice her mistress' changed attire.

"Are you going to bed now?" she asked, thinking she had been summoned to undress Alexandra and brush her hair prior to retiring.

"Not yet. I have some business to take care of first, and I need your help. Go get dressed, warmly, and meet me in the parlor. You'll be running an errand for me, but under no circumstances is anyone else to know about it."

"Yes, mistress." The chill had driven away some of the drowsiness and now excitement took care of the rest. "Shall I be going far?"

"Only to Count Ogrinov's."

A light shone in an upstairs window when Giselle, muffled in a heavy hooded cloak borrowed from Alexandra, mounted the ice-slick steps and approached the door. She held the note in her left hand; with her right

85

she crossed herself three times before lifting the massive brass knocker. It fell with a thud that echoed in the cold silence of the winter night.

She barely had time to mutter a hasty Ave Maria. The door was flung open by the count's servant Vasili, who stood frowning down upon the quaking Giselle. He terrified her, but loyalty to her mistress was stronger, and she demanded to see Count Ogrinov.

"My lady gave me orders to deliver this into his hand only and to await a reply," she stated flatly, though she was unsure he understood French.

Without a word, Vasili ushered her into the vestibule and left her there, alone and growing more and more frightened. She kept her eyes lowered, stared unseeing at the tiled floor, and did not move a muscle until the sound of footsteps drew her attention to the doorway.

She expected to see a man roused from sleep, bleary-eyed, dishevelled, grouchy. Mikhail was none of these.

"Give me her letter, Giselle," he ordered quietly. "Vasili, take her into the drawing room and find her something warm to drink. I'll take this into the library."

He left the timid girl in Vasili's capable hands and made his way down the corridor to the oaken doors of the library. They swung inward silently and just as silently closed behind him. He had expected Alexandra to come herself, either hysterical or triumphant, and he had waited up for her, fully dressed, alert with anticipation, only to have her out-guess him and send the maidservant.

The lamp lit on the desk shed better light, but Mikhail chose to sit in his favorite chair before the fire. He lit a candle from the glowing coals and held it in one hand while the other unfolded Alexandra's letter.

She wrote little, and what she wrote told him nothing except that he was to come immediately. Something had happened that he had not provided instructions for. He was to return with Giselle, she ordered, and bring no one other than possibly Vasili.

Well, he supposed he would have to go, if only to satisfy his curiosity. And he did owe it to her.

Within five minutes, the three of them—Mikhail, Vasili, and Giselle—were out in the damp, cold night. The maid was forced almost to run to keep pace with the two Russians, but she did not know that even Vasili was walking faster than normal in an effort to keep his master from quickly outdistancing him.

Alexandra met them at the door, opening it before Mikhail had a chance to knock.

"Giselle, you may go back to bed. Sleep as late as you like tomorrow. I shall be able to take care of myself," she said after a barely courteous greeting to Mikhail. She waited until the girl had disappeared down the long hallway and up the stairs before saying any more. "If you will instruct your man to wait here, I have something to show you in my room."

He gave her an odd look but no protest, and did as she asked, speaking very quietly in Russian to the enormous blond serf and then following Alexandra along the familiar way to her rooms.

"Did you get any information from Trabert?" he asked casually.

"I learned a great deal from the colonel, as a matter of fact," she replied with a bitter smile, but he was behind her on the stairs and could not see her face. "I do hope I didn't get you out of bed, but as you'll soon see, I had no choice but to send for you. Colonel Trabert has become incapacitated, and under circumstances that are best kept from the servants."

They had reached the second floor where, in much better light, Mikhail saw that the dark splotch on her neck he had thought was the shadow of a stray lock of hair was in fact the beginning of a nasty bruise. He could not resist the urge to touch it very tenderly with his finger; he was shocked when she jerked away as though burned.

What in the name of Heaven could have brought about this change in her? Just a few hours ago she had been bright and alive and warm. Now there was a strange fire in her eyes, a dark fire of fear. What had Trabert said that had so terrified her?

It was all clear the moment Alexandra unlocked the door to reveal the snoring, bloody obscenity that had once been the dashing colonel.

Mikhail bent over the unconscious officer. "You were right; the servants must know nothing of this." He glanced up at the sound of her moving about in the next room. "What are you doing?"

When she made no reply, he stepped over the slumbering body and approached the open door to her bedroom, where he saw her, in the dim light of one candle, standing very, very still. She turned her head slowly, taking a last survey of the room, from the graceful canopied bed to the hearth and its crackling fire, symbols of the luxury and comfort she had enjoyed these last few months.

"I said, what are you doing?"

He was a step or two behind her, yet she could already feel the powerful nearness of him.

"What does it look like? I'm leaving. I'm getting out of here while I still can." She did not look at him, could not, though it took every ounce of will power she possessed not to fall into his arms.

She lifted her head still higher and straightened her shoulders under the heavy cloak, but such a show of determination could not fool him.

"I'm very sorry, my dear, but we made a bargain, and you have not yet delivered your half. I'm afraid I can't let you leave."

Chapter 9

THE FIRST cup of coffee he poured for her was heavily laced with brandy; the second she drank black and bitter. As the clock chimed eight, Alexandra glanced up at it, unable to believe four hours had passed since she watched Vasili carry the limp form of Colonel Trabert into the hired coach. In those four hours she had said nothing to the man who sat beside her, not a single word. With more resignation than patience she had listened to him explain why she could not go back to the existence she had so eagerly left, and she admitted very reluctantly that he was right.

"Disappear now and you'll have all of Paris talking, asking questions until they find out the truth. Is that what you want?" Half of what he said was flagrantly untrue, but he said it anyway, knowing only that he could not let her walk away from him. "Will you be able to live with yourself when Bonaparte enslaves the rest of the world and you have done nothing to stop him?"

So she agreed at last to stay, or at least did not leave immediately and that gave him hope. But his words had not persuaded her. She heard nothing that he told her, only his voice, and it was his presence, his attention to her, that kept her with him. And she knew, too, that the door back to that other world was now not only closed, but locked and barred. She could not go back, only further forward down that dark corridor.

"I'm going to send someone for a doctor. You are to follow his orders explicitly, even if he tells you to stay in bed for a week. I've already cancelled your engagements for today and tomorrow." He lit a cigar with maddening casualness. "I hope you'll be able to attend the ball Friday night, but of course it depends on how you feel and what the doctor says."

"I don't want any doctor; I'm fine." The look he gave her, with one eyebrow cocked, prompted her to repeat herself a little more forcefully. "Really, I'm perfectly all right, or will be after some sleep."

"Then why do you wince every time you move that arm? If you won't let a doctor see you, at least let me look at that arm and the bruise on your neck. And then rest, for a day or two. You've been up all night and you've been through a lot these past few hours."

Her complacency exploded without warning.

"How can you know what I've been through? You haven't bothered even to ask me what that animal did to make me nearly chew his hand from his arm!" She stood up and crossed the room, carefully stepping around the spots of blood that remained on the carpet in spite of Mikhail's personal scrubbing. "I don't think you care at all about me, about what happens to me, so long as I get you what you want. It is one thing to whore for a cause, to trade my body for the lives and freedom of my country-men." Which countrymen? she thought briefly, wondering which country she was fighting for, France, England, or even Russia. "But I refuse to submit to what-ever it was that that beast wanted of me for any cause, no matter how noble. I'd rather die."

She was speechless then, because so much of it came back to her and she couldn't find the words to describe to him all the pain, the terror, the humiliation of last night though she wanted to scream it all at him. In those moments of angry silence, her hatred returned. The coffee was keeping her barely awake while the combined forces of exhaustion and strong brandy fought to close her eyes and her mind in blessed sleep, but more than anything else, the burning fury within her kept her from taking his advice for rest.

"Sit down, Xan."

The quiet calm in his voice fueled the fire of her rage. In a seething whisper she ordered him to leave.

"Get out! Get away from me, now, before I scream for every servant in this house. I don't ever want to see you again!"

He still spoke softly, "Alexandra, please, you are becoming irrational. I do not intend to leave until I am sure you will do nothing foolish. Now, come back over here and sit down."

Her mistake was in turning to look at him. The instant her eyes met his she knew she was lost, for in their depths sprang the bluewater coolness that quenched the flames and soothed the pain in her soul. Without another word, with only the steady, gentle gaze of those penetrating blue eyes, he brought her beside him.

"That's better, isn't it?" He handed her a glass of brandy from which she took a small sip. "While you finish that, I'm going to have your bath drawn. After you have soaked in some nice hot water for an hour or so, you are to get into your bed and sleep." His voice as well as his eyes, which continued to stare unblinking into hers, mesmerised her. She was powerless to disobey. I'll be here when you wake up, and we can talk then."

A few pinches of a sedative powder in the brandy assured him she would sleep untroubled for most of the day. By then, rest would have worked its usual miracle, and the process of rebuilding what the colonel had destroyed could begain.

He watched her stifle a yawn; a moment later, she succumbed to another. His stream of chatter became incoherent music, like a distant lullaby, fading and softening. Too late, much too late, she realized what he had done, but of course by then there was nothing she could do to prevent his picking her up and carrying her to the bed. She had neither the strength nor the desire to resist when he unbuttoned the gold dress; by the time he pulled her arms from the sleeves, she was asleep—and smiling.

*　*　*

There was no time for the sleep Mikhail needed as desperately as Alexandra had. More than anything else he wanted a bottle of brandy and eight hours in bed, but a hot bath and a pot of coffee would have to suffice. While he lounged in the steaming water and submitted to Vasili's razor, Mikhail tried to doze, tried to find some respite from the images that brought both mental and physical anguish.

Until he saw the bruises that disfigured the pale ivory skin of her arms and back, he had not fully grasped the extent of her suffering. Though most of the purplish blotches were little more than ugly discolorations, several were raised and swollen. She had concealed the damage done to her face quite well; only when he gently pulled the coverlet over her did he notice the puffiness and tiny cuts on her lower lip, and the long scratch Trabert's ring had cut just above her ear.

Feeling pity for the innocent victim of such cruelty was perfectly normal, and anger towards the perpetrator. But neither pity nor anger brought the warmth to his blood and the ache to his loins. He knew he should have put her to bed fully clothed or called her maid. He knew it then and he knew it even better now, when the memory of her wakened the desires he had fought so long and finally, he believed, had conquered.

That he had not conquered them was all too obvious in the way his body reacted. After sending Vasili for fresh coffee, Mikhail stepped out of the tepid water to stand naked and dripping wet until the chill that set him to shivering destroyed the evidence of his arousal. When the servant returned, he found the count half dressed, pulling a comb through the damp tangle of his curls.

"You took long enough," Mikhail growled.

Vasili merely shrugged and poured coffee into Mikhail's cup. The count was in one of his rare bad moods this morning, probably a continuation of the same one he had been in last night before Alexandra's maidservant had come. Vasili had learned to get sleep whenever the opportunity presented itself and so was in much better spirits than his master, having dozed quite comfortably in the kitchen while Mikhail and Alexandra talked. He was glad for the rest; he knew there would be no chance today.

Mikahil arrived at Tchernikov's not long after eleven o'clock, only to learn that the baron had overslept and was not receiving anyone for an hour. Frustrated and more than a little angry, Mikhail had no choice but to wait. He poured himself a glass of brandy, then threw the liquor down his throat without tasting it.

The long wait, the cups and cups of coffee, the sleepless night, the spoiling of his plans: all nagged and irritated him. He had hoped to have this unpleasant interview out of the way before noon; now it appeared the baron would not even see him until well after that hour. The thought of Vasili napping in the kitchen made Mikhail just that much more tired, if Andrei did not come down very soon, Mikhail's hopes for an hour or two of sleep in the afternoon would be dashed.

"Sorry to keep you waiting, Mischa. I hope you have good news for me."

Andrei's sudden greeting brought him rudely out of his reverie. He had heard neither the creak of the door nor the baron's booted footsteps on the parquet.

"Unfortunately, Uncle, I have only bad news."

"Then sit down and tell me about it." Andrei offered him a cigar and then lit it. "I suppose she refused at the last minute to go through with it."

Mikhail pulled the smoke deep into his lungs and exhaled slowly but felt no better. He reached for more brandy.

"No, as a matter of fact she didn't. But our pigeon turned out to be a vulture. She'd have bedded him willingly if he hadn't decided to beat her."

"Is she hurt?" There was too much concern in his voice to escape Mikhail's notice.

"She'll be fine. I saw to it that she'll sleep for a good ten or twelve hours and that is what she needs most right now. The bruises will heal; in no time she'll be herself again, ready for a new assignment.''

"Did she say that, or did you trick her?''

"No, not really. I simply told her that she hadn't lived up to her end of our bargain.''

"Then you are a worse scoundrel than I ever imagined. You may be able to persuade or cajole her into continuing this madness, but how long will it last? She is no fool; she's going to find out how you've used her, and when she does—''

"Now, hold on, Uncle!''

"No, you hold on, MIkhail Pavlovitch. And I am not your uncle.'' Tchernikov smiled inwardly, satisfied with himself at having, for a change, talked the headstrong young man into silence. "Alexandra is no servile peasant girl. Threats and beatings will never bring her into line. She's like that Spanish mare your cousin tried to break. And break her he did. Ended up with a cart horse old Granny Gurtcha could drive. That's what you'll have if you force the girl into submission.''

"I have no intention of forcing her into anything. Trabert frightened her half to death; I will do everything I can to see that she recovers. And when she does, I expect you to have another pigeon ready.'' He sipped his brandy slowly this time, swirled the liquid into the glass as though there were nothing more important at this moment than savoring his liquor.

"Find your own pigeon, Mikhail Pavlovitch. And I urged you to find another woman to play the whore as well.''

Mikhail held his glass still but continued to stare at the gold fluid. Knowing Tchernikov was waiting for him to speak, he chose his words with the utmost care.

"I did not think it would be necessary to remind you, my dear Baron, of your duties to the Tsar. We must not let personal feelings interfere with the mission we have undertaken.''

Words in his defense were on Tchernikov's lips when he caught the icy blue eyes. The agony was all too evident; Mikhail admonished himself as much as he did the baron.

94

But an instant later all signs of turmoil were gone, or cleverly masked, and Tchernikov wondered if he had indeed seen it.

"Of course, of course." He made a weak attempt at his usual harumph and tried to think quickly of something to say. The silence fairly crackled. "If Alexandra is recovered by Friday, I think I can have a nice assortment of pigeons, as you call them, for you to choose from. But I warn you, if anything happens to that girl, anything at all, I'll see you skinned alive."

And he meant it. Of that Mikhail had no doubt, and he frowned at the thought that Tchernikov was under her spell so completely that he made no effort to fight her.

"She is far too valuable to me to let any harm come to her."

The baron, though he did not like Mikhail's choice of words, accepted this and contented himself with that small consolation.

"I'm sure that Toliere will be in attendance; he's the first possibility that comes to mind. Or his brother-in-law Lamargue. If Chacliot didn't prefer pretty boys, I'd suggest him."

"What about Gravîmes or even Sarbeau?" All animosity was forgotten as they settled down to discuss the possible choices for Friday's winter ball at the Luxembourg Palace.

"Gravîmes you can't separate from his latest mistress, that insufferable Clothilde. We'd have more luck setting you after her; she probably knows as much as Gravîmes."

"She's too fat for my taste!" Mikhail laughed.

"And Sarbeau has been reassigned to Spain. It's not official yet, but he has been out of favor with Bonaparte for some time."

"Is there no one else, just Toliere and Lamargue?"

"St. Ypres, perhaps, or the old general, Ricardot."

'No, not Ricardot. He's lost two young wives because of his inability. He has no use for Alexandra." Mikhail paused, lost in thought for a moment. "Or has he? Who would be better than an old man, impotent, easily won by a pretty girl who is the talk of Paris? Will he be there?"

Something in Mikhail's eagerness confused Tchernikov, but he was too enthusiastic about the prospect of saving the girl from another disaster to question his nephew now.

"Bonaparte keeps him in an apartment in the Luxembourg. It should be no trouble to arrange getting her to him from the ball."

Ricardot was the perfect choice, but that was only one of the several reasons for Andrei's sudden smile. Now he could trust Mikhail to do everything possible to protect the girl, for though Mikhail might deny it vehemently, Andrei knew he had indeed let personal feelings interfere with his work.

Chapter 10

NOT EVEN the bright lights that glittered along the graceful facade of the Luxembourg Palace could dispel the cold knot of apprehension that formed in Alexandra's stomach. Mikhail helped her down from the carriage, holding her arm until she was steady on the icy pavement. A gust of angry, sleet-laden wind whipped her cloak around her. By the time she reached the door and stepped into the glaring brilliance of the foyer, she was numbed to the bone and shivering.

After allowing a footman to remove her cloak, Alexandra stood for a while both to let the warmth soak in and to still the quaking of her knees. She was aware of a dozen pairs of eyes staring at her from behind black silk masks, but she did not let it upset her carefully developed composure. When Mikhail offered her his arm, she took it and with studied indifference entered the great ballroom of Napoleon's palace.

The slightly bored pout she wore belied her dizzying excitement. She dared not gawk, much as she would have liked, at the ornate chandeliers, the exquisite paintings hung on the walls, the opulent furnishings and even more opulent costumes of the people gathered around her. The mask provided a certain concealment for the wonder in her wide eyes, but it was more the man beside her who kept her exuberance under control.

She did not need to see his face to know that his features betrayed no emotions, no thoughts. If he had any feelings at all about what was to happen this night, he kept them well hidden.

Despite the music and the glitter and the mystery of the Empress' masked ball, Alexandra discovered that she was not enjoying herself at all. Every fear that had built over the last two days remained with her, strengthened each time a strange man asked her to dance or brought her another glass of champagne. For long, long stretches of time, Mikhail was lost in the crowd and she could not see him. The longer he was out of her sight, the more nervous she became, the more she wished this night had never been.

Or at least that it would be over.

Quickly.

But it was not.

Mikhail had told her that the man she was dreading to meet, Jean-Gabriel Ricardot, had been a military genius and national hero before Bonaparte had begun soldiering, and that he adored, even worshipped, beautiful young women. How could a man with such a reputation fail to scare her half to death?

But for Mikhail's patient attention these last few days, she would not have had the courage to endure the strain. Something had happened since she awakened Wednesday evening to find him, asleep in a chair by her bed, waiting and watching over her. There had been a change, though it was nothing she could pinpoint; neither was she certain which of them had changed, Mikhail or herself. He seemed so tender toward her, so genuinely concerned when he asked about her injuries, that at first she been too surprised even to answer him. When the potent sleeping drug left her slightly dizzy and weak-kneed, the Russian swept her into his arms and carried her, still clad only in the sheer silk chemise, down to the dining room for a late supper. Not until she showed him the goose-bumps on her arm did he send a maid for warmer clothes, but when he wrapped the quilted robe around her, he apologized so profusely she could not help laughing at him.

For a moment he looked at her with a kind of hurt in his

eyes, then he, too, shared in the tension-relieving laughter.

He told her about the general on Thursday afternoon, briefly but not harshly. The words of protest never reached her lips. It was not just a matter of keeping a promise to him; it went beyond that simple breed of honor. Deep within her flowed a force that was both need and fulfillment, and it was this almost mystical force that gave her the strength to fight down her protest as well as her hunger for—

For what?

She had no more idea now, dancing beneath the glittering chandeliers of the Luxembourg than she had earlier in the silent privacy of her room. But the hunger remained nonetheless for being unidentified.

Exhausted by the constant dancing, Alexandra threaded her way through the crowd towards the ladies' retiring room. The salon was crowded with Italian peasant girls, Columbines, a deerskin-garbed American savage, even a curvaceous Harlequin, but Alexandra managed to find a vacant chair in a rather secluded corner and flopped onto it.

Less than half an hour later, a greatly refreshed Alexandra adjusted her mask and stepped out of the room, ready if not willing to return to the festivities.

"I thought you had decided to hide in there all night," a voice behind her said.

"And I was beginning to feel a bit deserted," she replied without bothering to turn around.

"I came to tell you that the general is waiting. And as for deserting you, that is exactly what I shall *not* do." Mikhail came up beside her and slipped his hand under her arm rather possessively. "Though I do not anticipate any trouble with Monsieur le General, I shall be no more than a quiet scream away."

Much as she welcomed his protection, Alexandra felt her cheeks redden when she realized he might also be close to listen to exactly what occurred in the room she was to share with Ricardot. And she worried that she might need the protection he so kindly offered.

"Are you expecting a repeat of Tuesday night?" she asked cautiously.

"No, but as I told you yesterday and again this morning, you are far too precious to me to let any harm come to you."

As he led her along the wide corridor, the heels of her Cossack boots clicking loudly on the marble floor, she said nothing. Her mind was struggling to find some significance in what he had just told her. Twice before he had told her, and quite solemnly, too, that he would protect her, using almost exactly the same words.

But his words *were* different. He had called her "precious" instead of "valuable," and the manner he used was altered, too. He was almost lighthearted, neither serious nor intense as he had been. She wondered what could have caused this sudden gaiety. The carnival mood of a masked ball? Too much champagne? Trying to match his long strides she nearly had to run, until he joked about her lack of stature in an almost cruelly jesting tone. This was not the same man she had come to know over the past months; he had grown brittle, shallow, nervously bright.

Such a deviation from his usual determined self-control quickly affected Alexandra. She felt all her resolve slipping away, and just as she had made up her mind to ask him for an explanation, he stopped.

"That door leads to Ricardot's apartments," he said, pointing to the last of several opening off this hallway. "It is time for your last instructions."

His hand tightened on her arm. In spite of every effort she made to resist, Alexandra felt her eyes drawn inexorably to his; she was powerless once she had looked into those blue depths, and yet she knew that he was offering her his strength.

"Be yourself, little Snowbird," he whispered. "If you are frightened, do not try to hide it; he will expect it. And should he try to hurt you in any way, I will be close by. Remember, he is one of *them*, the enemy, worthy only of our contempt." He paused to search her green eyes. "You are not afraid?"

"No, not now." And somehow it was the truth.

He took her hands in his and raised them to his lips. They were such little hands compared to his. They reminded him of the fragility of the girl, her weakness and vulnerability in the vicious game he had made her play.

He meant only to plant an encouraging kiss on her cheek as he let go her hands, but found her lips beneath his and could not resist the hunger that welled up inside him. So great was his need, so ferocious the desire to possess her, that he was incabable of either stopping himself or realizing that Alexandra did not want him to stop. Demanding what was freely given, he slipped his tongue between her parted lips to savor the delicate sweet taste of her.

No thought was possible while he held her soft and yielding in his arms. He could only want, not think, and what he wanted, he dared not have. He knew even as he crushed her to him and felt her response, that he must again force himself to push her away and deny his desires their fulfillment. Yet his arms would not let her go.

To hold her so soft against his hard maleness and then to push her away was more torture than he could bear without protest. As he loosened his embrace, unsatisfied desire became white-hot pain that brought an agonized moan from his lips.

"It hardly seems fair that I must now take you to the general," he laughed.

But there was bitterness and anger, no humor, in his laughter.

Alexandra could make no reply. Breathless and confused, she felt tears spring to her eyes and had no idea why. Mikhail saw the sparkling drops fall onto her cheeks and gently wiped them away with his thumb.

"Now, now, there's nothing to cry about. Put your mask on again, and I shall take you to Monsieur le General."

Mikhail's knock was answered by an elderly man in the uniform of the late Bourbon king's army.

"Monsieur le General has not retired, I hope?" Mikhail asked.

"I have not!"

The voice boomed from behind the servant, from the shadows of a poorly lit room.

"Come in, my dear Count Ogrinov. Have you brought me something to enliven my evening?"

The old soldier opened the door wide enough to admit the general's guests, and Mikhail stepped into the room with Alexandra clinging very tightly to his arm. She could see almost nothing, and when the door closed again, she felt as though she had dropped into a mine.

"Ah, yes, I see that you have. The Snowbird?"

"General Jean-Gabriel Ricardot, may I present Mademoiselle Alexandra Aubertien, known also as the Russian's Snowbird."

She dropped as respectful a curtsy as her Cossack costume allowed. Now, even in the deep gloom, the scene grew clearer. Ricardot's voice came, oddly enough, from a much lower plane than normal for a man standing to greet visitors. And the creak of slowly turning wheels further defined his position. As her eyes slowly accustomed themselves to the dark, Alexandra saw the general, robust and almost handsome despite his years, yet from the waist down a pitiful creature confined to the narrow prison of an invalid's chair.

"Emil, this room is a veritable dungeon! Light the candles, then bring us some brandy," the invalid ordered.

"Excuse me, but I cannot stay," Mikhail apologized. "There are other pressing matters I must attend to tonight."

Ricardot shrugged but did not insist on the Russian's company.

To Alexandra, Mikhail added, "I shall tell your driver you may be a bit late and just to wait for you, however long."

So he is going to wait for me, Alexandra thought. She had no driver, having come with Mikhail, and he could only mean he himself would wait.

Emil brought the brandy after lighting enough candles to break the darkness but not so many as to brighten the room overmuch.

"You may go now, Emil. I shall ring if either Alexandra or I requires anything more. Good night, Monsieur le Comte."

It happened so quickly that she did not even realize he was leaving. She was alone with the general almost instantly.

"Do you play chess, Snowbird?"

Mikhail had told her to be honest, to be herself. And she had no lie ready to tell him.

"Yes, I do, but very poorly."

"Then I shall endeavor to improve your game. You'll find the board and chessmen in that cabinet. Bring them over here to the table."

She did as instructed, and while the general unlocked the box that held the ivory and ebony pieces, she moved another chair into place on the opposite side of the little table.

"Now, my dear, remove that silly mask and that ridiculous costume."

She was about to protest almost hysterically until he snapped, "I can't hurt you, you fool. I've been impotent for the last six years, since one of my own infantry officers shot me in the back. But look at you I can do, and I shall. Get out of your clothes!"

Angry and frightened, Alexandra still felt a queer kind of pity for this strange half-man. He had the strength to desire, but not the power to find satisfaction.

"Slowly, my dear, Do not rip them off as if you were some lust-crazed slut." His eyes never left her, and she began to realize they were the only part of him that was truly alive, but they were so very much alive that they lent a false sense of vitality to the rest of him. "That's better. Some modesty is becoming. Too much is hypocrisy; too

103

little is ill-mannered. The skirt next, then the smock."

He continued to direct her disrobing until she stood naked except for the soft black leather Cossack boots. Though the room was quite warm, she shivered with nervousness.

"You'll get used to it," he told her casually. "Nakedness is the normal condition for every creature save the human one. Come over and let me have a closer look at you."

First he merely stared, letting his eyes examine her from top to booted toe. A warm flush spread all over her when she saw how long his gaze lingered on her breasts. Then he ordered her to turn slowly as he studied her profile. He made no comments about the fading but still purplish bruises on her back; he was more interested in the voluptuous curve of her buttocks.

"So far you please me rather well, though I usually prefer blondes."

Another blush, for she knew by the direction of his stare that he did not refer to the loose mass of curls on her head.

Finally he told her sit down, that it was time to play a game of chess.

It was hard to overcome the embarrassment of being unclothed and utterly impossible to concentrate on the chessboard. The General, however, corrected each move she made until the game ended in a stalemate, no victory for either side. Immediately, he began to position the pieces for another game.

"This time I shall let you play for yourself."

And she lost, quickly, foolishly.

"You have much to learn, but I shall teach you," he laughed, making her wonder if he meant only chess. "You must now walk about the room for me. I wish to see if a body so beautiful as yours can move beautifully, too."

Though the room was too small, he complained, for adequate exhibition of her talents, she felt like a horse led into a ring at a fair, put through her paces for the judgment of those who would buy her. She walked at the various speeds he ordered, slowly and seductively or authoritatively, according to his command. He liked the play of her muscles as she moved, the firm yet feminine strength of her legs, buttocks, and back.

Weary of crossing the room so many times, Alexandra was almost relieved when the General ordered her to be seated for another game of chess.

As difficult as the other games had been, this was a thousand times worse. That she was a poor player to begin with and was further handicapped by her self-consciousness seemed not enough disadvantage. In addition to correcting her chess moves and explaining the folly of her choice or the wisdom of his own, Ricardot kept a running commentary on feminine charms in general, hers in particular.

"The sacrifice of this pawn is unnecessary, for the bishop can as easily take the knight and not put himself in jeopardy. You have probably the most exquisite shoulders of any woman I have ever seen. Very delicately straight and square, strong in a determined rather than muscular way. You see how I ignore the temptation to capture your other pawn? I would be left open to attack by your other bishop. And the curve of hip, the tapering of thigh to knee, all nearly perfect. Men do not like fleshy thighs, blubbery bottoms or fat-rippled bellies. No, no, no. Leave the castle alone and move the Queen. You must remember that she is a warrior queen like the ancient Britons once followed against Rome, not a simpering plaything like our Empress. I admit I did not at first fully appreciate your dark coloring, but now I see it as a most welcome variation. My last two wives were blonde, pale-skinned, blue-eyed beauties with few brains and large appetites which I was unable to appease. I move the pawn again and threaten your knight, who has several roads open to him. My wives also had small breasts with pink nipples. Your breasts are full and ripe, with nipples like dusky rosebuds."

He reached across the table to touch her, but she drew back, instinctively avoiding his grasp.

"I am patient," he shrugged. "Next time you will let me touch you, perhaps. Anyway, it is late. I will leave the game just as it is, and we shall resume, say, Tuesday night?

You may come for supper at eight.''

Only a nod of his head towards the pile of her clothes gave her any indication that she had his permission to dress again. Putting her clothes back on seemed almost more degrading than taking them off, but at least the night was over. Nothing else mattered now but getting away, getting back to Mikhail and his sheltering embrace.

''Show this to the guard at the door when you come and he will notify Emil,'' Ricardot said and pushed a large, ugly pearl ring into her hand. ''I expect you to be on time.''

The air was tingling cold and clear, with the frost already beginning to sparkle on the railings and bare-limbed trees. The clouds had disappeared to leave the sky bright with a waxing moon and a million stars. The cold made her shiver and the crisp air hurt her lungs, but Alexandra was too glad to be outside, too happy to be away from the degradation and filth that lived in the shattered body of Jean-Gabriel Ricardot to complain about such slight discomfort.

Mikhail's carriage stood outside the gate, with the ever faithful Vasili waiting to help her inside. He stood by the door, not bothered in the least by what she took to be bitter cold, and opened it as she ran up. But he did not offer his hand to help her. Instead, a pair of strong arms reached out and lifted her bodily into the welcome shelter of the vehicle. The latch had hardly clicked when those same arms tenderly encircled her.

She began to sob the instant the carriage jolted into motion, and did not stop crying until Vasili opened the door and announced that they had arrived at her house. Henri, her steward, waited with the usual brandy and claret, both of which were politely declined.

''Mademoiselle Alexandra is to go straight to bed,'' Mikhail ordered. ''And I am going straight home.''

There was not a trace of a question in his voice. He stated his intention succinctly, and she had not the slightest reason to doubt that he planned anything other than what he said. Yet he stood there almost as if waiting.

"No, please stay, just a little while," she pleaded, wondering if that were what he waited for or if he had just been gathering his courage to face the cold outside.

"I'm sorry, Xan, but I simply can't."

She gave Henri a nod, and when he had gone, she looked full into the Russian's eyes and asked, "Why?"

"You know why," he answered sharply. The pain was returning, stronger than ever. He had to leave now. "Let's not stand here in the foyer arguing about it. Good night."

He spun on his heel and walked out the door, slamming it angrily behind him. Enjoying the brisk air, soft and almost spring-like compared to a Moscow January, he drank it deep into his lungs to cool the fires that threatened to consume him entirely. He must not give in to this temptation. The carriage and Vasili were only a dozen strides away and the flames were dying inside him when Alexandra called to him.

"Mischa, please! Don't leave me alone again."

He stopped but he did not turn, not even when he heard her footsteps pattering down the icy walkway.

"You promised, Mischa, if I were afraid you'd always be there."

Chapter 11

MIKHAIL HAD rekindled the fire, but the sitting room remained uncomfortably cold. Hungry for comfort as well as warmth, Alexandra snuggled into his arms as she watched the flames lick unconcernedly at the logs. Not a word was spoken, and there were no tears left to cry. They sat in silence.

With no idea what had happened in Ricardot's apartment except that Xan had not been driven to call for help, Mikhail tried to keep his imagination from running away with him. She had told him nothing yet, and he did not ask her. She had called to him, begged him not to leave her alone; that was enough to let him know she would eventually unburden her soul. Until then he could do no more than he already had: provide a shoulder to cry on and a strong arm to hold her close.

For the moment, that was enough. Even his own desires seemed to be somewhat satisfied just to have her near. He wanted her as he always did, but at least now there was no pain.

Alexandra dozed off into a light, troubled sleep until a loud pop from the hearth startled her back into wakefulness. She yawned.

"It's half past five. Don't you think it's time you went to bed and got some sleep?" Mikhail whispered.

"Not yet, not until it is light outside. I don't think I could sleep knowing it is still dark."

"What will you do tomorrow night?"

She paused, then calmly said, "I shall cross that bridge when I come to it. One day—or one night—at a time."

Such brave words failed to convince him, especially when she burrowed closer still in his arms. Instinctively he tightened his protective embrace and kissed the top of her head.

"Let me get you something to eat, or a glass of brandy. Either a full stomach or a light head ought to make you sleep better."

"You sound just like Justine. I used to have nightmares that woke me up in the middle of the night and sent me running to her. Never to Therese, always Justine. I used to sit on her lap while she rocked me back to sleep."

"I'm sorry I have no rocking chair, but I can try if you want me to. Come sit on my lap and I'll rock you to sleep, though I confess I have no experience whatsoever."

She laughed with him for a moment, then became serious again.

"You want me to tell you what happened tonight, don't you."

He held his breath. He wanted to know, but he wanted something else even more.

"Only if you want to talk about it."

"But you *do* want to know."

"Of course, I do. But I can hardly tie you on the rack and torture the information out of you, can I? I am no Torquemada."

With his thumb he traced the line of her jaw and felt her lean into his touch. She spoke quietly, very, very slowly, choosing each painful word with care to express precisely and unequivocally what she had suffered. It hurt, physically, to tell him how humiliated she had been, stripped not only of her clothing but of her pride as well. Though Ricardot had not touched her, she felt dirtied by his presence, as though his eyes had caressed her as crudely as he had wanted to with his hands. The worst pain came from his assured nonchalance, as though he thought her accustomed to this cheap behavior, as though she was a whore. Not until she had finished the tale did she realize some of the pain came from Mikhail's steel grip on her arm, not just from the memory of those hours at the Luxembourg.

"I'm sorry, Xan, believe me," he apologized. "Did I hurt you?"

He kissed the reddened flesh of her wrist while she assured him that the damage was neither great nor permanent. As his concern became more intense and his apologies more profuse, she began to laugh, then to giggle.

"Please, Mischa, you are tickling my arm!" she cried when he let his lips nibble up the inside of her elbow. "Oh, stop it!"

"As you wish, my dear. Is this better?"

She knew, by the strange light in his eyes and the half-smile playing on his lips, that she was about to be kissed, and even if she had had the strength to fight him, she would not have done so.

The desire to kiss her had been growing steadily, had not in truth died in the marble corridor of Napoleon's palace. He had buried it, but it was still very much alive. Now, before he touched his lips to hers and abandoned all attempts to control himself, Mikhail searched her upturned face, studied the emerald depths of her wide eyes. Her lips were temptingly parted, expectant; she was waiting for the kiss that he almost dared not give, no matter how compelling his own desire. For he had seen in her eyes, in those great green shining pools, what he had not seen before and what he wanted so much to see and what frightened him to the very core of his soul.

There was no explosion when their lips finally touched, no clamorous ringing of bells, no shower of brilliant sparks. The fiery passion of their earlier kisses did not leap into flame. They were both filled with a warm, liquid glow. And that was exciting enough.

His mouth closed over hers gently. As his tongue teased past her lips and touched the edge of her teeth, he reached up into the pile of her hair and pulled out the pins. One by one the locks tumbled free, falling around her shoulders, in her face, over his head. She wore no perfume, yet the scent of her hair was more heady than gardenias, clean, sweet, lingering lightly in his nostrils when he pulled himself away from her.

Her eyes looked up into his, caught them, held them. "No, Mischa, please. Don't," she begged.

Had he heard her correctly? Were her lips saying "no" at the same time her arms tightened around his neck and pulled him closer? What kind of teasing was this that she practiced upon him? Angry at the thought that she could toy with him now, Mikhail decided he no longer cared, but before he could grab her and teach her a lesson she needed badly to learn, she had pulled herself to him and kissed him hungrily.

With the first touch of her mouth on his came understanding. She had begged him not to *stop*; he had misread the meaning of her plea.

Careful not to break the seal of their kiss, Mikhail gathered her like a child into his arms and carried her toward the closed door that led to her bedchamber. He expected no resistance from her when he turned the handle and pushed the door open. She gave him none. He kicked the door closed.

The room was lit softly with a pair of candelabra on the mantel and warmed by a brightly glowing fire. The bed had not been turned down. Mikhail set Alexandra on her feet, keeping his arm around her shoulders to steady her.

"There is a bottle in the desk if you want it. I don't."

"Well, as a matter of fact, I do. Now, you go over to the bed, pull down the covers, and climb in." He spoke so slowly, and stared at her so mesmerizingly, that she was completely oblivious to his hands. Long strong fingers brushed her hair back from her face and caressed her temples. "Can you do that?"

"Yes," she murmured dreamily.

"I really think you ought to have a bit of this," he pressed. "It will help you relax, let you sleep better. And I promise I've put nothing in it."

He found the liquor and a single glass, filled it with

hands that trembled ever so slightly, enough to make him wonder why.

Despite her protests, she took the glass from him and swallowed a sip or two. It burned her throat, but the warming glow it quickly spread through her was soft and delicious.

It all seemed so natural that at first she thought she was either dreaming or drunk. Mikhail unbuttoned her blue dressing gown, one button after another until the garment fell open. He pushed it off her shoulders, and she let it fall to the floor in a satin puddle around her feet. She stood like a shy Venus in just her white nightdress.

More tiny buttons, enough to try the patience of any saint, yet somehow Mikhail kept his hands steady and refrained from tearing the thin fabric in a single stroke. He could feel the warmth of her skin through it, though the dim light and shadow hid the charms that would have been clearly visible otherwise. It didn't matter; he didn't need to see to know she was beautiful.

He was nearly done when Alexandra handed him what was left of the brandy. He threw it down his throat and set the glass down, then returned to the last fastenings.

"Am I expected to stand here shivering while you stare at me?" she joked as she shrugged out of the nightgown.

She giggled when he swept her off her feet and carried her to the bed. Tossed there unceremoniously, she rolled up in the counterpane only to find herself imprisoned when Mikhail sat down beside her and prevented her wriggling out of the quilt.

"I do believe you are drunk," he observed while pulling off his boots. "Is it the brandy, I wonder, lack of sleep, or perhaps something else?" He cocked an eyebrow at her and received a sly, lash-lowered glance in reply. "I'd prefer not to take advantage of you if you plan to cry 'Foul!' in the morning and accuse me of abusing you when you were least able to defend yourself."

"It's morning already," she said, "and I'm not drunk. I know exactly what I'm doing."

But do *I*? he thought.

112

His coat was gone, his shirt opened to reveal the powerful muscles of his chest rippling beneath a mat of curling dark hair. He dropped the shirt to the floor and stood to unbutton his trousers. When he heard her laughter, he stopped.

"Do you always laugh when a man undresses?" he growled. "Or do you find my body amusing?"

With laughter still in her eyes, she looked up at him. And the laughter died.

The fun, the teasing little game that had eased her fears was suddenly gone, replaced by an eerie apprehension. This was a man beside her bed, a magnificently sculpted man who was obviously intent upon possessing her. He was a stranger, not the same gallant Russian count, but a powerful, vital animal. Alexandra felt her eyes drawn, against her will, down the length of his body.

"You are blushing, my dear," he commented. "The sight of *you* does not embarrass *me*."

She felt the rush of warmth to her face increase with the knowledge that he was visually devouring her. He, however, had no doubt seen many women in similar state; she had never looked upon a man without at least a pair of breeches, and certainly never one so heroically proportioned. There was nothing soft about Mikhail at all. From his broad shoulders, his chest tapered to flat belly and trim hips without an ounce of fat. Each muscle and tendon of his long legs showed cleanly as he moved, like a supple hunting cat. Without the moderating effect of silk shirt, coat, and trousers, he seemed taller, stronger, almost barbaric.

Then he was beside her on the bed, drawing her to him in an embrace that, though gentle and undemanding, was still passionate and determined.

Her skin was like silk to his touch, cool and smooth beneath his caressing fingers and teasing lips. He showered kisses on her eyes, her cheeks, her nose, ears, neck, throat. Like butterflies on daisies, his fingertips fluttered circles around her breasts until the nipples tightened into hard, dark rose points. With a low moan she pulled herself up to

113

him, demanding his kiss; she was not refused.

He had expected more resistance than he encountered when he touched, as lightly as possible, the inside of her knee and began to stroke the satin of her inner thigh. Higher and higher, closer and closer to his goal he tantalized, making her writhe against him when he finally reached the warm triangle of dark silk between her legs.

A soft animal sound of pleasure escaped her throat, half cry, half groan, as she struggled against her own increasing desire. This suddenly seemed so very wrong; no matter how delicious it felt to have his hands soothing as well as arousing her, it was wrong. She had to stop him before it was too late, before he found the wellspring of her need and made it impossible to stem the current carrying them towards disaster.

"Stop, Mischa," she moaned. "Oh, God, please, Mikhail. Please stop!"

He pried her fingers loose from the curls at the base of his skull where she had entwined them and, after placing a kiss on the warm palm, pushed her hand slowly down his chest and belly until she encountered the pulsing shaft of his virility.

"Do you really believe I could stop *now*?" A groan of pleasure mixed with pain exquisitely delightful followed his question as she wrapped her slender fingers around him. "Do not deny us this moment of joy."

She tried to fight him, but she was beyond stopping herself. He was too strong, forcing her legs apart to touch, probe, explore, and excite the secret innermost places until she nearly screamed. She begged him again, implored him to stop even as her body arched against his.

"Don't cry, little one," he crooned as he kissed the salty rivulets of tears trickling from the corners of her eyes. "I shan't hurt you, not as ready as you are to be loved."

Her warm, undulating body belonged to him, and he was about to possess it, from the sweetness of her mouth beneath his kiss to the hard points of her breasts against his chest to the glorious silky warmth between her legs. His kiss smothered any cry she might have made as he entered

114

her, slowly, easily, never forcing himself until he felt her ready. But still she fought him, twisting her body in a vain effort to escape his unrelenting attack.

He had never known a woman so awakened to desire. Why then did she tense with fear when he slid just within her? Had her lovely body been less perfect, less desirable, he might have found the strength to stop and withdraw, but abandoning what he had only begun to enjoy lay beyond his capacity for control. He had wanted her for too long. Ignoring her pleas, her tears, and her now feeble struggles, he persisted.

Then the pleasure became flawed. No coherent word passed her lips, no scream of pain or terror, just a gasping sigh. He understood, too late, the glistening tears in the great green eyes. It was not possible, he tried to make himself believe. It could not be true, and yet he could no longer deny the truth that made itself plainly evident.

So physically ready for a man that the desire dripped from her like honey from a comb, she resisted him with the simple power of her virginity.

He tried to summon from the innermost depths the strength to stop this seduction that had become a rape. The self-control he had taken almost for granted during all the days and evenings he had spent with her seemed to have disappeared, melted by the heat of his passion. With an exasperated sigh, he knew the triumph of the body over the mind. He felt her maidenhead break; it made no difference now whether he withdrew or not. The irrevocable damage had been done.

Alexandra must have known, too, for she ceased her struggling as the pain tore through her. Resigned to her fate, she relaxed, or collapsed, and the brief moment subsided, only to be replaced by a newer, stronger agony. As it grew, it blocked out all her thoughts, erased her shame and guilt, filled her with a crazed longing of a kind she had never known. All that mattered was the man in her arms, inside her body, whose powerful thrusts drove deeper and deeper within her, deeper yet not deep enough.

She was crying, sobbing, almost screaming. Every nerve in her body stretched taut as a violin string. It was unbearable, this torment of body and soul that made her do things she would have thought inconceivable only hours ago. Hours? It seemed years.

He could hold back no longer. Already he had gone beyond what he had thought himself capable of, but now he had indeed reached the limit. As much as he wanted to prolong this love-making and bring her pleasure, his own needs demanded release. One final plunge, and the warm, sweet explosion ripped through him. Before the last wave had spent itself, he felt her tighten around him.

The line between torture and ecstasy blurred as a great bubble of rapture burst within her. Exhausted, breathless, sapped of all strength and will, she surrendered completely to the strange sensations swirling around and through her. The nameless hunger had been sated.

She was warm, tired, and contented, and thoroughly unable to sleep. As her heart ceased its frantic pounding and returned to a normal pace, she tried to assess her situation.

It was hopeless.

"Ah, precious little bird," Mikhail whispered against her cheek. "You should have told me all the truth."

He had not left her, seemed to have no intention of doing so. Indeed, the kisses he rained upon her could only serve to arouse her again.

"I tried. I thought you knew."

"I should have. But perhaps I have had too little experience with delectable innocents." He nibbled at her ear. "Would you care to teach me more?"

She expected a repeat of the first violent intensity; his gentleness surprised her as he led her step by joyous step to another roaring crescendo. She quivered with exhausted delight from head to toe, while above her Mikhail smiled contentedly.

Later, he lay beside her, one arm under and around her shoulders, the other crooked behind his head. Staring at the ceiling, he was not unaware that she had fallen asleep,

116

or at least dozed, and she desperately needed that rest. In spite of the fact that the morning was well advanced and he had a great deal of work to do, Mikhail made no move to leave her bed. The fire was dying, but he needed no glowing hearth when he held her warm, naked body next to his. She had brought him the most exquisite, most complete sexual satisfaction he had ever experienced, even though she was innocent and unpracticed, but that was not what made her a woman he could want again and again.

"Mischa?"

She whispered his name sleepily; her lips nuzzled his ear in a drowsy kiss.

"Mischa, I'm hungry." She bit his earlobe. "Can you reach the bell?"

"And bring your maid in here with us like this?"

She pulled the sheet up to her chin.

"I think we'd best get some clothes on," he suggested. His hand, however, had reached under the sheet to caress her breast.

"Are you sure you wouldn't rather stay the way we are?"

Her own fingers went exploring when he pinched her nipple in answer; she found him and closed her cool hand around his hardness to draw a long sigh from him. He took her quickly, with little foreplay, then deliberately prolonged the act until he had brought her to the summit of joy once more. Not until she lay sated beneath him did he seek his own satisfaction. Even before the last of her spasms had passed, he caught his breath and let his passion spend itself in throbbing release.

Chapter 12

THE GOWN was cream-colored satin, with mameluke sleeves slashed to reveal the lining of robin's-egg blue silk. A petticoat of the same color hung six or seven inches below the skirt; matching ribbons bedecked her hair and held a nosegay of silk flowers at her waist. Alexandra's costume was the height of fashion, but she took no pride in her reflection. Indeed, she could hardly bring herself to look in the mirror. It made not the slightest difference to her if she wore a satin gown or beggar's rags.

"I do believe your choice was best," Mikhail commented as he surveyed her appearance. "The opals certainly are lovelier by themselves, but the Mexican stones give you something of a wild, untamed look. No one at the Opera will be able to resist you."

She shot him a warning glance.

"When I am in the company of a creeping serpent like Ricardot, I do not care to be noticed at all. I am only going tonight because he can hardly expect me to undress and play chess with him in public." She adjusted the fur-trimmed cloak about her shoulders and pulled the hood down over her hair. "And this rain! Will it ever stop?"

She glanced at the darkened window streaming with a March downpour, another like the past three days and nights. When last she had turned that way, she saw heavy droplets beginning to form on the glass; now the water ran in a ripply sheet from one pane to the next. Had the night been clear and spring-like, she might have been less depressed. The rain plunged her into an abyss of despondency.

Only a few hours before, she had felt quite the opposite. Justine had come for her usual visit, but it was a different Justine. The hint of romance that hovered about her had grown these last months to a bright, illuminating radiance. Staring out into the darkness, waiting for the arrival of the despised general, Alexandra tried to concentrate on the happiness of the afternoon.

It was not easy to envision steady, practical Justine in love with an opera singer, but such was the case and by now even Armand and Therese had given their approval to the young man's attentions. He had been a proper enough suitor and finally, on the preceding Sunday, he had asked Justine's father for permission to wed her in June.

"But what kind of life will you have with a singer of songs?" Alexandra asked.

"No worse than I have now." Her eyes twinkled as she spoke of him. "You must meet him, tonight maybe, if you can arrange it. He is really quite shy and not at all what you must expect."

Arranging a meeting with an opera singer was no difficult task, and though she expected to find this Guy Chaldimond frightfully boring or unbearably conceited, at least a visit with him would delay the time when she must return with the general to his apartment and the customary entertainment there.

"How much longer?" she wondered half aloud.

"Not much. It is nearly eight o'clock now; he should be here any minute."

"I wasn't talking about that. I was wondering how much longer this would have to go on. I don't know how much more I can take."

This was not the first time she had warned him. His shrugged shoulders were his only reply; he did not meet her questioning eyes. How could he look at her, feeling the way he did about her and about the extraordinary circumstances of their relationship? More than he could ever tell her, it hurt him each time he thought of her alone with her half-human lover. There were evenings when, after leaving Alexandra in Ricardot's company for several hours, Mikhail had wandered the streets of Paris in frenzied rage, spending the energy of his anger in long strides down narrow alleys and up broad avenues. He felt nothing of the damp, cold winter weather, only the fire of his emotions.

He had at first thought he would have no trouble controlling his feelings, keeping them separate from the work he and Alexandra had to do. It had taken the incident with Trabert to show him how much she had crept into his thoughts and he had quite firmly believed that putting her with the invalid Ricardot would eliminate the pangs of jealousy. He had failed. He hated the idea that Ricardot could touch her, even look upon her, and found that all too often he had to remind himself how much worse matters could have been.

"Mischa, he tells me nothing. I have told you everything he says to me, every question he either asks or answers. If I wrote down every single word he spoke, I could not tell you more than I have. Is there not someone else, someone who could give me information of some use, some value?" She began pacing the floor angrily. "I could endure it so much easier if only I felt it were worthwhile. But this kind of torture for no reason at all is becoming more than I can stand."

"Only a little while longer," he said softly, wanting to tell her how he shared her pain. The truth was there, just waiting to be said, but he could not do it, not yet. "I know you don't understand, but believe me when I tell you that what you are doing has had its results. I am getting the information I need, and it is reaching the proper ears."

She understood, a little, but seeing the carriage pull to a stop at her door destroyed the momentary lift to her spirits. Black depression settled over her again. Not even Mikhail's light kiss on her cheek helped. Dodging the raindrops, she scampered to the waiting carriage and allowed herself to be whisked away into the darkness.

"You should have told her, Mischa," Baron Tchernikov

scolded. His hair was wet with the rain, and a few drops of water glistened in his beard. "Or do you plan just to be here one day and gone the next?"

"Calm down, Uncle. I plan to tell her just as soon as I know exactly when I must leave. It may be next week, it may not be for a month or more."

Tchernikov lit his pipe and settled himself into the chair beside the fire. This damned rain had chilled him through and through as no Russian weather could. In a way he hoped Mikhail was right; a war at least would get him out of this silly diplomatic post and back where he belonged. But there were still no outward signs of war, only rumors. Mikhail, keeping his secrets to himself, would tell Andrei only that his informants had assured him there would be war before the end of summer.

The baron had learned one thing, if nothing else. Ogrinov was not a man to be underestimated, nor second-guessed. Perhaps it was his mixed blood that made him more Russian than any pedigreed boyar. At any rate, Tchernikov admitted months ago that he knew no one quite as devious, cunning, sly, and well-informed as his sister-in-law's nephew. Mikhail was far too complex for a man of Tchernikov's experience ever to understand.

"I remember, Uncle, that you once doubted the girl's loyalty. Do you still?"

"It depends. I remember, too, that you promised me her loyalty, but you did not say where it would lie. I have a feeling hers is a woman's loyalty, not a man's."

"And just what is that supposed to mean?"

Mikhail asked the question, but he did not listen to the answer; he had known it far too long to need to be told.

"She is in love with you, Mischa. You wanted that and now you've got it and you don't know what to do with it. You've traded her adoration for information and I do not doubt for one moment that she is going to demand payment in return. You've used her, Mikhail, just as I knew you would."

Pain choked off the younger man's reply, and rather than admit how deeply those words had cut, Mikhail merely shrugged his shoulders and tossed another swallow of brandy down his throat.

"And then to put her in the hands of a monster like Ricardot. I am a soldier and have lived my life like any other soldier, yet the things I have heard said about her and that half-human eunuch are not repeatable."

"Nor are they true," Mikhail at last managed to say. "I promised you I would not let her be hurt, and Ricardot can do her no harm. And I have not traded on her affection for me, either. I have bargained Ricardot's affection for her."

The words stunned Tchernikov. He sat back down on the chair he had just prepared to leave and stared open-mouthed at Mikhail.

"Ricardot, by the way, is too damned smart to fall for any trap I might lay for him; he tells her absolutely nothing, which she has realized. But her attention to him has made every other officer in Napoleon's army eager to share her favors. And they come to me to bargain. So she is safe, and I get what I want. It is as simple as that."

"Is it? Are you sure she is so safe? No, don't try to tell me that you don't care."

"Alexandra is capable of taking care of herself. When I leave, she will simply go back to being what she was before. No one knows where she came from; they will forget her soon enough."

"But will you?"

Mikhail laughed so artifically that he knew the baron was not fooled.

"I have forgotten many women, Uncle. One more will make no difference."

"There is one I know you have not forgotten and never will."

He watched as Mikhail's eyes darkened with hatred.

"Tamara betrayed me, used me, nearly destroyed me. No woman will ever do that to me again. Never."

Andrei puffed thoughtfully and stared through the smoke at Mikhail's carefully masked features. Time was running out, and not only for this evening's conversation.

Andrei knew he must speak now before it was too late and tragedy could not be averted.

"You gave Tamara the power to hurt you when you fell in love with her, Mischa, and you have put that same power into Alexandra's hands. Don't force her to use it. Take care of her, or you'll find out just how capable of taking care of herself she is."

"I will do what I can," Mikhail assured him in a slightly chastened tone that led the baron to believe him. "And now, dear Uncle Andrei, if we do not hurry, we shall be late for the opera."

The performance had already begun by the time they arrived. There was no opportunity for polite conversation, or conversation of any kind, for the baroness had not seen this particular opera before and was thoroughly engrossed with it. Mikhail did not complain, for he could keep an eye on the occupants of the box directly across the theatre.

This was the first time he had seen them together. In the darkness of the Opera, Mikhail had only slight difficulty discerning the two figures seated side by side. They sat not very close to one another, causing Alexandra to lean in the general's direction whenever he spoke. Mikhail watched the shadowy silver movement as she listened to some whispered comment, then straightened again to stay as far away from her escort as possible. Even from his distant vantage point, the Russian could almost feel the shiver that crept along her spine when a gloved hand settled on her knee. The intermission could not be more than fifteen minutes away; her torment would at least be interrupted for a short while, and perhaps during the change of scenery Mikhail could speak to her, give her a word or two of encouragement to get her, and himself, through this evening.

Bored with the opera, which he had seen twice before, he let his mind wander from the poorly sung duet to plans and schemes for what little time might be left to him before departure from the French capital became imperative. Already he had felt the pressure. It had started only a few weeks ago, almost imperceptible at first, but building gradually nonetheless. Certain doors had suddenly closed; others opened where he did not wish them to. He had seen the signs of danger and did not ignore them. To do so, he knew only too well, was an even greater danger.

Reluctantly, for he was still half trapped by his thoughts, Mikhail rose and joined his companions for the intermission.

"You look as though you do not feel well, Mischa," Baroness Tchernikova whispered to him.

"Actually I do have a bit of a headache. I believe I'll forego the champagne and take some air instead, if the rain has stopped." The Baroness' concern provided a rare opportunity.

He excused himself and made his way through the crowd towards the exit. Once certain that he could no longer be seen by those who had heard him announce his intentions, he turned in the opposite direction.

He did not return to the box until well into the next act, his absence and impolite entrance severely denounced by the baroness' scowl. Not even the obvious improvement in his appearance, which she noted and ascribed to a walk in the cool of a rain-washed evening, could keep her from disapproving his rudeness.

A page brought the note to General Ricardot's box not long before the beginning of the final scene. Alexandra took it and slipped out to read it quickly. If Mademoiselle Aubertien would so honor him, the note read, the humble singer Guy Chaldimond offered to share a late supper with her in his room beneath the theatre. Such a rendezvous was rather irregular, but not altogether unheard of. She had now only to explain it to Ricardot.

"I've taken it in my mind to become his patroness," she explained with a lie that came easily to her lips. "The young man strikes me as exceedingly talented, but untutored."

Ricardot looked up at her from his chair.

"Then go, silly thing, though if you think his pretty face and voice will satisfy you the way your Russian does, you will be sadly mistaken."

Ricardot, who had been quick to spot the changes in her after that first January night, never let her forget that he knew, and like any man denied the fulfillment of his natural desires, he imagined that lust alone motivated her every action. She found it convenient not to persuade him otherwise.

He had agreed to wait for her at a nearby restaurant frequented by opera patrons, but at midnight, if she did not rejoin him, he would leave her to find her own way home. No sooner had the curtain fallen than she dashed from the box and hurried toward the darkened hallways and labyrinthine passages that were the performers' world behind the stage.

The maiden who had just died so tragically and beautifully brushed by Alexandra. The voice that had sung so sweetly of her undying love now cursed the orchestra, the audience, the weather, the theatre with all the gusto of a drunken sailor. Gaping in astonishment, Alexandra found herself suddenly jostled by the entire cast, all anxious to be out of costumes and make-up. Wigs and false beards were pulled off before her eyes; fat men became miraculously thin as padded clothing was discarded. A shepherd boy with a mop of bright curls, dressed in a simple leather tunic and hose, turned into a lovely young girl with braids tucked under her boyish wig.

"It is fascinating, isn't it."

She whirled at the quiet voice behind her and came face to face with the hero-prince's faithful knight.

"Strange. Almost frightening. To see people's faces and bodies change, right before one's eyes."

Guy led her to a small, dim room, then quite unnecessarily introduced himself. He apologized for having nothing more to offer her than some cold beef, cheese, bread and wine.

"I came to talk with you, not to be served champagne and duckling," she laughed, feeling at once perfectly easy with him.

The beef was cool and tender, the cheese sharp and delicious. Guy sliced the crusty bread in thick slices and poured the glowing burgundy into glasses that belonged on a queen's table, not on the rough bare plank that served in the singer's subterranean chamber. He noticed Alexandra's attention.

"My father pilfered them during the revolution. They once belonged to Marie Antoinette, and it was his desire to return them to her someday. Alas!" He turned his hands up in resignation. "He was an avowed monarchist."

" 'Was' ?" she echoed. "Did he—"

Guy laughed.

"Oh, no! Actually, the old goat is very much alive. It's just that I see him so seldom these days. He and Mama and my sisters still travel with the circus."

He began to tell her about his childhood with the travelling circus. Year after year his tale stretched on, one of love and laughter as well as hardship, poverty, and thwarted ambition, until Alexandra realized she knew more about Guy Chaldimond than she did about Mikhail Pavlovitch Ogrinov.

"I heard the old general tell you he would wait only until midnight," Guy finally said. The meal was done, the wine nearly gone, and his story brought up nearly to the present. "Let me walk you to your 'rendezvous'," he joked, "and perhaps we can meet again, next time with Justine and without Monsieur le General."

He offered her his arm; when she failed to take it, he saw her eyes had fastened upon some object in the corner of the room. Thinking she had seen a spider, he went to step on it but found only a white linen handkerchief with an embroidered initial on the edge. The recognition in her eyes could not have been more instantaneous.

"Well, now, I've been looking for this all day!" he exclaimed innocently. "I'd hate to have you think it stolen. I have a very nice collection, all more or less honestly

126

obtained. Gentlemen are always dropping handkerchiefs and ladies have been known to lose earrings at the Opera. Lucky the sweeper or opportunistic singer who finds such valuables.''

She might have believed him but for the smear of rouge on the square of fine linen, a smear Mischa had put there when he wiped away a tear earlier in the evening. Mikhail had known nothing of Justine's engagement to Guy nor indeed to Alexandra's plans to see the singer after the performance. His presence in that little room raised a score of questions that puzzled her so completely that she heard not one word Guy said to her while he walked beside her to the door of the restaurant called the Barque d'Or, the Golden Ship. Only when he stopped, just outside the circle of light illuminating the entrance, and placed his hands on her shoulders did she listen to him. What he said to her created more mysteries, more fears, and it certainly answered no questions.

''Do not try to see in me anything but a singer of songs. It might prove dangerous to you, to me, to someone else. But remember, little Snowbird, that I am your friend. There may come a time when I can help you, and you must not hesitate to trust me, no matter how betrayed you may feel. On my love for your sister, I swear that I will do my best to protect you. If ever you are in need, I shall be there.''

He kissed her forehead lightly, with brotherly affection, then bowed and moved off into the darkness of the streets, leaving Alexandra more puzzled, and more frightened, then ever.

Chapter 13

THE WARMTH of early summer faded with the sunlight, causing Justine to clutch her shawl more tightly around her shoulders as she hurried home from an overly long visit with Alexandra. Not too distant thunder rumbled a warning that rain was on its way, a dismal enough prospect for one already half chilled. As she turned the corner to enter the familiar environs of the Rue Ste. Aurrienne, the first little droplets spattered on the cobbles. A few more steps, past Madame Columiere's millinery shop and the gay flower boxes outside the window where Elizarre Marligneaux sewed the most sought after gloves in Paris, and there was the warm glow beneath the sign that said, simply, Armand Valenceau.

Justine reached the doorway at a half run, but not before the rain had become a steady patter. It glittered in her lamplight-gilded hair like a chaplet of random diamonds, scattered unconsciously as she tossed the wetness out and stepped inside the shop.

Francois, the apprentice, had a mouthful of pins and was unable to do more than wave a greeting and signal that her father was in the back room. Armand looked up at the sound of her footsteps.

"At last! I thought perhaps you two had embarked on a double elopement!"

When Justine stood mutely puzzled, Armand quickly tried to mask his concern.

"Yvette isn't with you?"

"No, I haven't seen her since I left."

He laughed and reached for the shears.

"Then she has lied to me again, telling me she planned to meet you and Alexandra. Perhaps it is just she and Albert who have eloped!"

His chuckle and seeming interest in the task of cutting the lush fabric did not in the least hide his anxiety. The tiny momentary pause after she had confessed to not seeing Yvette that afternoon and then his laughter brought an ominous chill to her heart. With more practice at deception than her father, Justine disguised her own fears to set his at ease.

"And if they have, then it will save you the expense of her wedding and mine shall be all the grander for it!" She danced over to him and planted a kiss on his cheek. "She'll be home soon, never fear. With only a week until the wedding, she'll wait. Is Maman Therese at home?"

"Yes, of course. She has spent the whole day with Marie making plans for this wedding, and I've been fortunate enough to stay out of their way through most of it."

Now his laughter was genuine, and father and daughter shared a smile. But even as she whirled gaily out of the room and waltzed up the stairs, Justine knew that something had happened, and her fear intensified. Something had happened that was not tragic in itself, but it would have tragic consequences for them all.

Marie was setting out supper and a loud clap of thunder brought a shriek from the usually imperturbable servant just as Justine reached the top of the stairs.

"It's going to be a wild night, this one," Therese exclaimed when the rumbling had passed. "I'm certainly glad you brought Yvette home before this storm broke."

"But I didn't. I just told Papa that Yvette didn't come with me."

"She left not a minute after you, running like the Devil himself were on her heels, and she told Francois to tell me and your father she was going to catch up with you. She had something, probably wedding plans, to talk over with you and Xan, I supposed."

"Is that what Francois told you?"

"No, I heard her myself. I was talking with a customer and apparently Yvette didn't see me standing there."

Feeling only a little guilty for all the white lies of a similar nature she herself had told, Justine said, "I do believe our sneaky little Yvette has merely taken advantage of a golden opportunity. She hasn't had much time with Albert lately. All this war business has kept him rather busy."

Her nonchalance kept everyone from spending too much effort worrying about the prodigal. She helped her father and the apprentice close the shop before the evening meal and even assured Armand of Yvette's safety enough to persuade him to lock the doors. Yvette's knock could be heard if she came home to find herself locked out.

And she did. They had just sat down to supper, with a place set for the absent daughter. Therese offered grace for the meal and had begun to serve the food when frantic pounding on the door thundered above the storm.

"Ought to leave her out in the rain," Armand grumbled as he pushed his chair back.

Her continued beating moved him to hurry not in the slightest. His anxiety had given way to vexation. Justine followed him as Armand lifted the latch and pulled the door open. Her hair dripping a stream into her face so that at first it was impossible to see that she was crying, Yvette burst into the room and ran past her father to Justine.

"I knew this was wrong from the start!" she sobbed hysterically. "No, no, I don't have time to change clothes; it isn't important now. We've got to do something right away, before it's too late."

Nothing about her manner, let alone her bedraggled appearance, bore the least resemblance to the pretty, giddy Yvette Armand had watched race out of the shop so few hours ago. There was in her hysteria a kind of determination, even strength, that heretofore had been buried beneath her carefree bubbliness. Justine had always been the strong one, serious, not at all like her younger, sister, but now it was obvious the same fortitude ran in their blood.

By now the commotion had brought everyone downstairs, and the last thing Justine needed was an audience.

"Marie, bring me some brandy, and take Francois back upstairs. And stay there! Maman, get some dry clothes for Yvette, and a cloak for me, then you and Papa finish your supper and go to church for late mass. The less you know about what happens tonight the better."

Long-forgotten terror clutched at Therese Valenceau's heart. She fought it back, kept it from taking control, and then she did as Justine told her, for she knew that what the girl said was true. Tonight's events were best left unknown.

"Everything will be all right," Justine promised with a voice suddenly gentle, and as she kissed her stepmother she realized how much she loved her, as if there had never been another. "By the time the storm is over, we will all be safe and sound and home again."

Bright blue eyes beneath golden lashes sparkled with unshed tears as they met Justine's steady grey eyes, and nothing more needed to be said.

Finally alone, and remembering another rainy afternoon when it had been Justine who brought the fateful message, the sisters sat in silence for a moment in the near darkness of the shop.

"We have until midnight, at the very latest," Yvette began. "We have to get Xan out of Paris, out of France. Now."

In those few words lay confirmation of Justine's longheld suspicions.

"We'll work together, and it won't be so hard. Just you and I and Xan together again, and we can do it." She laughed, a brittle cackle that sent shivers down Justine's spine. "He's using us again, that scheming bastard son of a Russian whore. If it weren't for the fact that he's treated here even worse than he has us, I don't think I'd lift a finger to help him."

"Who? Count Ogrinov?"

131

"Who else? Through Albert he has used me, and through your precious minstrel he has used you. We are all tools in his little game, like pieces on a chess board." She started crying again, but a long swallow of brandy brought her back to clear-eyed sobriety.

"I heard this morning when I brought Papa's newspaper home that some regiments were to be sent out of France this week. That's why I lied to Francois this afternoon. I had to see Albert. I knew they wouldn't let me, with the wedding so close. I met him at La Miromelle, as always, and he told me he is to leave this Thursday morning for Poland or Austria or somewhere. So we got married."

Justine gasped but could find no words to express her surprise. It did not matter; Yvette gave her no time to speak.

"We went back to La Miromelle to celebrate with Brisceaux and Renouille. They started buying champagne and drinking it like water, and I wanted Albert to leave, but he wouldn't. He wasn't drinking with the others either, so I didn't know what was going on at all. I told him he could either come with me or stay with his friends, but I was leaving. He took hold of my arm and pulled me back to my chair and made me stay. Then I realized he was listening to some other men, officers they looked like, at the table behind us."

"Did you hear what they were saying?"

"Only part of it. At first I was too mad at Albert. But they were talking about a woman they all seemed to have, well, enjoyed at one time or another. They said they would take care of her at the Opera tonight, when she was alone with the old general who had no use for her. As soon as they said that, we were both sure they meant Xan, so Albert sent me running back here."

"You ran all the way from La Miromelle?"

"What else could I do? I had to warn you."

"Warn me? What about Alexandra?" Justine bellowed. Then, softening, "No, you were right. It's much too far to run to her house, and we need help."

Now it was clear, maddeningly clear. Albert had used Yvette, and Justine forced herself to accept the reality of her relationship with Guy. It was all so convenient, so carefully arranged. And so perfect was the scheme that they had been trapped into continuing the game in order to save Alexandra, the most sadly abused and innocent of them all. Their own revenge could only be at her expense, and the master spy had known they would never sacrifice her.

Alexandra stepped across the threshold and entered the darkened room. As usual, only a single candle glimmered on the mantel. Emil, silent and somehow menacing, took her evening wrap and disappeared into the shadows to leave her alone and apprehensive.

This was the last time. Mikhail had promised her, and she had made him repeat the promise a thousand times during the course of the day. There would be a game or two of chess, depending on how skillfully she played or how quickly she lost, and then the opera, just as if this were any other Tuesday. And so she would make it seem to the general. It was not, however, the same as all the other Tuesdays.

He kept her waiting for several minutes, wheeling himself into the room as the clock struck the quarter hour. Alexandra, her senses heightened, noticed changes in the man. He had become, in the five days since their last meeting, much older looking, frail, as though the strength had been drained from him. Yet he spoke with the same eagerness, and his voice had not lost its power.

"I've purchased a new set of chessmen," he announced. "This will be the first game I've played with them."

He held open the door and ushered Alexandra into the room where the game waited, the pieces on their appropriate squares of ebony and rosewood.

Nothing in the room had changed, nothing that could be seen, but the heat radiating from the fireplace was intense, the room stifling. Alexandra noted that the general had a heavy woolen rug draped over his lap, something he had never done despite the usually cool temperature he maintained in his apartments. And in the better light his deteriorated condition was seen to be much more pronounced.

A bare four months ago Ricardot had seemed in perfect health. How could he, in the space of so few days, have aged so many years? The hand that held the black marble chess king was bony-fingered and covered with transparent skin like fine but fragile silk.

"A remarkable likeness of our Emperor, don't you agree?" he asked. "And Marie Louise does indeed make a fine Queen. I commissioned this set myself, chose Murat and Ney as the black nights. The pawns were easy; it was not difficult to find eight expendables in the empire of our illustrious Bonaparte."

But she was not in the least interested. Her mind was working rapidly, analyzing what she could not diagnose. Silently labored breathing. A blue tinge around his mouth. Once she thought he winced with pain. She had to take note of every symptom, just as she had mentally recorded every idle bit of conversation over the months of their association.

"I had very little trouble finding a craftsman willing to undertake the commission. At least half a dozen wanted it. I chose a young Italian, a Michelangelo of miniatures. Mario Pardolini. Do you know him?" She shook her head but he seemed to pay no attention and chattered on. "Beautiful work, such splendid detail. They are worth every sou I paid for them. Shall we play? Do sit down, my dear. You know I can't stand staring up at you."

Doing as she was told, she took her seat opposite him, but there was no hope of concentrating on the game. She moved the pieces mechanically, without thought, captured a pawn, then a bishop, sacrificed one of her own "expendables" and took another of his.

"That's it, my girl!" Ricardot chortled. "Finally you are learning!"

His eyes glittered with excitement. They seemed to draw the energy from the rest of his body, for even as she watched, the flame grew brighter and she knew he was dying.

His breath became a series of slow gasps as more and more frequently he raised a trembling hand to his chest and closed his eyes against the growing pain. Determination kept a wicked smile on his lips, but not even the fiercest desire could forestall the inevitable.

"Some brandy?" Alexandra suggested with a calm she could not believe.

"Yes, please."

The decanter held only enough for two glasses. Alexandra walked to the bell cord to ring for Emil.

"No, let him be. One glass will be enough." It had touched his voice now, but his order was still firm enough that she dared not disobey.

And then the enemy caught him. The pain was no longer to be denied; he stiffened under its attack and clutched at the strangling fingers gripping his heart.

"Damn!" he swore through clenched teeth. "You must not be frightened, Snowbird. Sit down and listen to me. Listen carefully, for I will not be able to repeat this."

Whether the agony actually subsided or he simply found another reserve of strength to keep it at bay was impossible to tell. Alexandra, feeling no fear at all, believed him and gave him every bit of her attention.

"If I fail to hold off the pain the next time, and it may come at any moment, for I cannot maintain the force I have called upon, you must mix this powder into the brandy and pour it down my throat. It will keep me alive just barely long enough for you to get me to the Opera. No matter what anyone says, we must be seen together tonight. Do not let Emil keep me from attending, not even if I should die beforehand." He touched her arm for a brief moment, then sank wearily back into his cushions. "Pay no attention to Emil. Don't let him give you orders, and if he becomes insistent, shoot him. He is one of Napoleon's spies, *given* to me by the Emperor out of the kindness of his heart, but I know the truth." He laughed painfully. "I have my own spies!"

"I can't shoot him," Alexandra protested, frightened now more of Emil than by the man dying in front of her. "I can't shoot someone right here in the palace. Besides, I have no gun."

From under the lap rug, Ricardot pulled a silver pistol, primed and loaded.

"Do not hesitate if it becomes necessary to save your life. This wing of the palace is nearly deserted; there are no guards here any more, no one at all." He pushed the weapon into her hand with a strength that for a second made her forget what was happening to him. Then a gasp of pain brought it back.

"No, not yet!" he exclaimed when she began to open the slender vial of white powder he had given her. "This is but a warning tremor of the earthquake yet to come."

"Is there nothing I can do?"

"Nothing at all." He was still smiling, even laughing despite his agony. "You have hated and despised me all these months; is there now some tenderness in that sweet voice?" he mocked.

There was not, and he knew it. Alexandra was frightened of her own realization that she cared nothing whatsoever about the ordeal this man was suffering before her very eyes.

For God's sake, the man is going to be dead soon, perhaps in minutes, and I feel no pity, no sorrow at all. What has become of me? she asked herself. Can I calmly, even impatiently, await the final attack that will take him out of my life and feel nothing?

Less than ten minutes later it came, but not without warning. As the pain grew, like a hungry flame in dry tinder, the old man had time for one last instruction.

"Wait, not yet. A moment longer, please," he whispered between gasps, and she wondered if he spoke to her or simply begged for more time. "Before you give me the powder, for you will have no time once it has taken effect, go to the chessboard. Look carefully at the pieces, the black and white. See how they lie, and do not forget."

He could speak no more, could only gesture feebly with his shaking hand that she must now give him the potion. She poured the fine white powder into the remaining brandy and watched, waiting for some magical smoke to rise above the cloudy mixture. He reached for it desperately, but once the liquid flowed down his throat he could not even hold the glass. It slipped from his grasp and clattered to the floor. The drug worked almost immediately, sending him first into a series of horrifying convulsions that twisted his face, already a pale mask of death, into a grotesque nightmarish image. Then, almost as suddenly, the seizure passed and the medicine left him relaxed, euphoric, seemingly free of pain.

His voice was weak, so low that she had to put her ear to his lips to hear him.

"You must tell Emil that I have developed laryngitis. Call him now, and get us to the theatre immediately. We have two hours at the very most." His eyes remained open and alert, but the fire had gone out of them.

Alexandra retrieved her reticule from the table beside the chessboard and while stowing the pistol in it, took a last look at the hated game.

Her Napoleon-King, surrounded by his knights, was closing in on the white king of Ricardot's side of the board. It seemed to her, even without close study, that he had been right. She was on the verge of winning her first game. Then, while she stared at the pieces without his steady gaze boring through her to disrupt her concentration as he did during a game, she noticed what she had not seen earlier. With a quiet gasp of surprise, she picked up the two kings, the black and the white, and stared at the two very different figures.

The black king, her Napoleon, was a corpulent, balding little man, exactly the image of Bonaparte. The white was different in every way. He was taller, bearded, dressed in a tunic Alexandra recognized as the military uniform of the Cossacks. He was Alexandra, Tsar of all the Russians. His queen was a regal looking woman, but quite obviously not the Tsar's wife, as the black queen was Napoleon's consort. There was majesty in her tiny face, a look of power, but she was dressed in the simple clothes of a peasant woman, and she had a small child standing at her feet. Holy Mother Russia. Of course. Alexandra had heard Mikhail call his homeland by that affectionate term, and now she held her, carved in pure white marble, in the palm of her hand.

The Russian knights she did not recognize, but she had no difficulty imprinting their faces on her brain. They, of course, were the most important, but she did her best to memorize the pawns, the bishops, even the castles. Their positions were harder to remember. There was no time, no time whatsoever. She had no paper and pen to draw a diagram, and no time, as the loudly striking clock reminded her.

She turned back to the fragile figure in the chair, saw him staring quite placidly at her. His eyes moved towards the bell pull.

"You want me to call Emil now?"

He nodded, and with one last glance at the chessboard, Alexandra pulled the tassled cord.

The opera was a particularly boring one, although the absence of the lead tenor seemed to be an improvement. Mikhail mentioned to the baroness that the understudy had a far more powerful voice and that the part was suited to a younger man than the aging star.

"Yes, I agree, but he is so nervous. Perhaps it is his first chance at such a large role."

Or perhaps it is something else, Mikhail said to himself. Guy is too skilled a performer to display nervousness on stage unless he has a reason for doing so.

A movement on the other side of the theatre caught his eye; he glanced from the stage and saw the sparkle of Alexandra's jewelry as she settled into her seat beside Ricardot's wheeled chair. Her late arrival had caused him no little concern. Now he relaxed and returned his attention, what there was of it, to the performance.

Near the end of the first act, as the heroine and her

maid sang a duet mourning the duplicity of their lovers, it was Guy's role to appear in disguise and comfort them. In doing so, he produced two handkerchiefs which he flourished almost comically before handing them to the sobbing sopranos.

Mikhail saw the first gallant gesture and, even from a distance, recognized the square of plain white linen he had lost to Guy's clever fingers months ago. The signal had been employed several times before, but never had the actor made such a show of it. Rising and excusing himself from the box, Mikhail almost missed the other signal.

He had not expected it, though he knew the opera well and remembered that the masquerading nobleman gave an ordinary linen handkerchief to the countess-heroine and one of silk to her maid, in one of those silly, over-used plots of mistaken identities and exchanged positions. It came as a shock to him when the actor waved about a most familiar bit of lace-trimmed silk almost immediately after the first signal. It could mean only one thing: Alexandra was in danger. Mikhail left his companions and strode purposefully toward the rabbit warren of the dressing rooms.

"Mischa, dear, where are you going in such a hurry?"

Princess Vera Ylbatskaya possessively grasped his arm and matched his long stride with ease.

"Why do you not bring your little Snowbird more often, Mischa? She is such a delightful creature, so different from most of these French twits!" she whispered in Russian. "They bore me so! It is no wonder your grand-mother left this country!"

"Verushka, please, you must excuse me," he said as he extricated his arm. "It is not that I do not wish your company, but sometimes a man—" He surprised himself by managing a blush.

Unabashed, the Princess gave him a quick kiss on the cheek and laughed, "So even the magnificent Count Ogrinov must bow to the demands of nature! When you come back, then we will talk again of this matter. I do not like being bored, Mischa."

Vera spun on her heel and was gone on her way in an

instant. She was not fooled by his indelicate lie, but it did not matter. He could not waste either time or effort in worrying about what she might or might not think he was up to. As long as she did not know the truth, he did not care what she thought.

The first act was over by the time Mikhail reached Guy's tiny chamber. They had only a few minutes to talk, and most of what Guy had to say was muffled by the costumes he took off and put on.

"The time has come, my friend, much more suddenly than we expected." He deftly removed shirt and waistcoat at once and had his peasant's shoes and stockings off without using his hands. "The circle is closing very swiftly; by midnight you and Alexandra must be out of Paris."

"But I can't take her with me, not now. Give me another week to finish—"

"There has been a queer chance of circumstances. Justine was just here and told me that St. Croix has been ordered to leave for Poland in thirty-six hours, so he and Yvette were married this afternoon."

"Damn the fool! He deserves Poland!"

Chaldimond was stripped to his underdrawers when a timid knock sounded on the door. Knowing it was too soon for the warning signal preceding the second act, he shot Mikhail a puzzled glance.

"Who is it?"

Without bothering to answer, Justine threw the door open and shoved her sister into the tiny room ahead of her. Yvette sank silently into the chair Mikhail offered her and sat staring mutely into space.

"Albert has been arrested."

It took several seconds for this shocking bit of information to have its effect, but the reaction was not at all what Justine had expected.

Guy said nothing, nor did he even pause in his frenzied rush to don satin breeches, ruffled shirt, silk stockings, coat, wig, and all the other parpahernalia of a dandy for his role in the second act. But his mind was racing.

Mikhail spoke first, to the stunned Yvette.

"Nothing will happen to Albert, I promise you." His voice, soft and tender as a mother crooning to her babe, penetrated the curtain of oblivion she had woven around herself. She turned her face and let his eyes gaze hypnotically into hers. "By morning he will be free to spend at least one day with his bride before going to Poland or Prussia or whatever. I'll see to it personally."

Tears brightened her eyes, a sign that at least she was no longer benumbed by shock.

"I believe you, I think," she said.

Justine knelt beside her sister and took hold of her hand.

"Yvette, you have Count Ogrinov's promise that Albert will be free, and you have to believe him. But he needs your help. You must tell him everything you know so we can help Albert and Alexandra."

"I know, I know." She spoke to Justine, as though the others did not exist, and repeated what she had said earlier. Then, at the end, a few more details came back to her. "There were three of them at the table, one much younger than the other two and with a large mole on his chin. The others I didn't see well enough to recognize again because they had their backs to us. They said something about being glad that they hadn't been the only ones to fall for the trick, that someone else—I don't recall the name or maybe I didn't hear it well enough—had sold a great deal more than they had and with just as little success. I didn't know Xan was involved, at least I wasn't positive, until the man with the mole said, 'The Russian's little bird must have a well-feathered nest by now.'"

"You left then, when you knew who they were talking about?" Mikhail asked, showing no sign of any emotion but keeping his voice and manner soft and calm.

"No, they kept talking, but they were laughing, too, and we couldn't hear just what they said until one of the older men, I think he was a general or something higher than the rest of them, said that there would be more singing at the Opera tonight than just what the players did on the stage." She jumped at the knock on the door, then

141

calmed when a surly voice from the corridor muttered there was but one minute left until the second act. "I knew Xan always comes to the Opera on Tuesday, so dear Albert did not have to tell me twice what to do. I ran home to Justine."

"And then I came here," Justine continued. "When I got back, Yvette was hysterical. Lt. Brisceaux, one of Albert's friends, had come and told her that her husband had been arrested, and I could think of nothing else to do but come here, for a second time, and hope that Count Ogrinov could help."

Guy adjusted his neckcloth without the aid of a mirror and mentally calculated the seconds he had left before his presence would be required on the stage. They were few, so he chose his words carefully and efficiently.

"The best thing Yvette can do now is to go home," he said with gentle firmness. "And you, Justine, must get Alexandra to this room, before the next intermission. I want no one to see her, no one at all. Do you understand?"

She nodded. With an exaggerated flourish, he bowed his way out of the room.

The two women turned their gaze from the closed door to their remaining companion. His blue eyes steady and cold as ice, Mikhail Pavlovitch Ogrinov looked first at Yvette and then at Justine, before smiling with confidence he hardly felt.

Chapter 14

NOT UNTIL she had assured herself that Yvette was emotionally under control did Justine allow her younger sister to leave the theatre. She would have preferred to leave with her, but it wasn't possible, not now.

"When Papa and Therese come home, be sure they do not stay up talking," Justine whispered as they embraced in somber farewell. "You get yourself to bed, too."

"What about you? You won't be too late, will you?"

"Not a moment longer than necessary." She gave Yvette a reassuring kiss on her tear-streaked face. "Be brave. Albert will be knocking on the door before you know it."

Not letting her mind or nerves relax for a single second, Justine turned to Mikhail immediately after closing the door. Had she waited a moment, given in to the despair, the fear, the frustration, or any of the other wild emotions careering through her mind, she could never have continued. The strength did not falter; indeed, it grew, just as the hate she was beginning to feel toward the elegant, unconcerned foreign count who had said barely a word through the entire ordeal. But he had been patient, did not rush Yvette while she told her story or hurry her out of the room and into the lonely night. Nor had he displayed any anger. Still Justine dared waste no more time. She had no idea how much longer that patience would last.

"I've no paper or pen," she said bluntly. When he

looked at her rather quizzically, she added, "For the message to Alexandra."

"Just tell her Guy requests Mademoiselle's presence before the intermission. When you have delivered the message, come back and I will give you further instructions."

How could the man be so cold, so unfeeling? How many more lives had he ruined before theirs, and how many more would he ruin before his game was done? Glumly fighting back tears of rage, Justine made her way through the empty corridors to Alexandra's box. The music, gay and happy, added to the feeling of desolation and a weight of despondency fell on her shoulders.

"I do believe I shall depart early," Princess Vera announced in a rather loud whisper when Mikhail returned to the box shortly before the curtain rose on the second act. "This substitution is the worst I've seen, and you know how I hate understudies anyway." She yawned rudely.

He made no reply, just smiled in the dark and wished he could see her face at the end of this scene. Her reaction to Chaldimond's second act performance would almost be worth risking his neck for. His neck, but not Alexandra's.

Mikhail had a soldier's distaste for inaction, and the boredom of sitting and waiting for something to happen was a strain on his normally calm nerves. He paid scant attention to Guy's performance, though he was well aware the rest of the audience was now absolutely entranced.

The voice that had hinted so promisingly in the first act now bloomed into its full glory, power, and richness. The nervousness had disappeared; sure and confident, the understudy dominated the stage in a way his predecessor had never done. In manner as well as voice, he was magnificent. Mikhail smiled inwardly and wondered if he would have time to congratulate Chaldimond on a spectacular performance. Then turning his mind to other matters and his eyes toward a different part of the theatre, the Russian yawned in immeasurable boredom.

A quick flash of light from the opposite side of the auditorium caught his attention. He saw the curtain in the box open, and a small figure slipped out.

Justine had followed his instructions perfectly. She was certain no one had seen her in the corridors, and there was no one near now to hear what she had to say.

"Before the intermission, you must be in Guy's chamber," she whispered. Terror more than caution kept her voice almost inaudible. "You have to be out of sight when the second act is over."

"Why? What's happened?" Alexandra demanded to know. She had caught Justine's fear as easily as she might have caught cold.

"Later, not now. I don't have time now, but later I will tell you everything," was all the answer Justine could muster. "Don't be late!" she reminded softly as she edged away and retreated toward the dark cavern backstage.

Not until Justine's frightened figure disappeared did Alexandra fully understand what was happening. Petrified, she stood for a long, long moment in the corridor. The urge to follow her sister was strong, yet she knew she dared not, for there was a man within the shadowy box who still breathed, whose tenacious grasp on life threatened her as would a deadly weapon. She could not leave him, nor could she seem to find the courage to rejoin him. It was not superstitious fear of death or the dying that held her back; it was the dread that he might still be alive.

Ricardot had not spoken since they left the Luxembourg. At times he appeared to sleep, but most of the time he was alert and well aware of what went on around him. With gestures he indicated to her that the opera bored him or that the musicians played badly, but since the beginning of this act he had not made even feeble movement. Only his glittering eyes and steady but shallow breathing told her that he had not yet relinquished his spirit.

Die, damn you! she cursed silently. Die and rot in the deepest pit of hell!

The words were half formed on her lips when the sound of footsteps and approaching voices startled her into motion and she ducked with frightened eagerness into the box.

"Alexandra, my little bird."

The general's voice set her heart to pounding.

"The drug is wearing off," he told her in an almost normal voice. "Five minutes at best is all I have." He winced and tried to bring the cold hands to his heart but they did not respond and lay still in his lap. "Go now, while there is still time. Your head is too lovely to end in a basket beneath the guillotine. Yes, I know what you are," he said with a grim smile barely visible in the shadows. "I have known almost from the beginning and I have allowed it because you are so beautiful." The eyes grew misty for a moment, then cleared. "I was a fool, tricked by a man whom I hated because he could enjoy what I could not. And more than a fool, because I have done it with open eyes. I could still bring him down, but I will save him because of you."

He stopped suddenly, as though there were words yet to be spoken. Fascinated as well as horrified, Alexandra waited expectantly. Another song began on the stage, a gay chattering of feminine voices that was no more than a hum in the background of her consciousness. With morbid curiosity, she watched the impersonal fingers of Death reach out and pinch the last flickering flame of Ricardot's life.

"I hate the Russian, but I loved you, and it is for you that I do this. If they find you here, they will kill you. Perhaps he knows this already and that is why he wants you gone. Trabert and the others, they know. I told them," he whispered as his eyes slowly and gently closed. "Don't forget to tell him about my new chessmen."

The head sank to the chest with the last exhalation of breath. Not able to believe that at last her tormentor was dead, Alexandra stayed beside him, her knees and legs painfully cramped from so long in that unaccustomed position. She felt no grief, not even sympathy, and certainly no sadness. That he had loved her mattered not at all, for his love had manifested itself in too cruel a fashion, and she could not recognize it as love. When the orchestra struck up a march that was the final chorus before the intermission, she straightened her legs and with a light heart made her way to the dressing room. She made no gesture of farewell to the corpse, muttered no prayer for its soul.

"Where's Justine?" Alexandra wanted to know.

Only Mikhail occupied the little chamber.

"You'll see her later."

He opened a large trunk in front of him filled with costumes that he methodically threw out on the floor.

"Whatever is going on?"

"You and I are leaving Paris tonight."

She thought she should have been surprised at such a forthright statement but she wasn't.

"Justine doesn't know that, though I'm sure she suspects it. She knows that it has become necessary at least. By the way, Albert St. Croix was arrested today on charges of espionage."

That did shock her. Afraid that her suddenly weak knees would not support her, she sank onto the chair.

"He'll be free by morning; two of his accusers have already been dealt with and the third will be shortly." He looked at her for the first time since her entrance. "Is Ricardot alone?"

"Yes, but—"

"Good. It will be difficult—this theatre is too bright for my liking—but we will eliminate the prime witness against Albert and then let the last accuser see who listens to his tale. This will give Albert at least one night with his bride before he leaves for war."

One shock after another. Mikhail prepared her for none of it, gave her no words of comfort or consideration as he struck her blow after blow, until shock gave way to anger. Furious at such cold-hearted treatment, she seethed and vowed vengeance.

"Ah, here we go. This should do nicely."

"You expect me to wear *that*? I've seen cheap whores wear better."

"That's not the point. This should fit you fairly well, and I would hate to have you stumble over your clothes. I don't want anyone to see you in what you've got on now; you could be identified. Now, put this on quickly; we haven't much time."

It took no more than a minute for her anger to build to an explosive peak. He threw the garment at her, and when she was about to unleash a torrent of abuse and protest at him, he warned her, with his characteristic calm, that now was not the time.

"Do as you are told. More lives than your own are at stake." Sure that he had achieved the desired result, he added, "Take off your jewelry and put it in this satchel. You can tie it around your waist under the dress. I wish there were something we could do about your hair, but I neglected to bring shears."

Her hands flew automatically to her head, to the carefully curled and beribboned mass she wore like a crown. Again the anger rose, then fell as she knew what she had to do. There would be time later for hatred.

The lavender dress, she discovered, was sadly worn, poorly mended, and smelled like a musty cellar. The very idea gave her a shudder as she pulled it over her head and pushed her arms into the long sleeves. She buttoned it and looked down to find it still trailing three or four inches on the floor. It made her wish Mikhail had thought of the shears.

"I'll have to tear it off," he said. "Loosen your hair and get those damned flowers out of it. See if you can't knot it or braid it or something while I shorten your hem."

Pulling the dress over her head had mangled the elaborate coiffure beyond repair and also made removal of the tiny ribbons and silk daisies more difficult. One pin after another fell to the floor as she sought them in the tangle of curls and jerked them out. Then the locks tumbled free, until the whole gloriously unkempt mass cascaded down her back.

"I'm a fool," Mikhail muttered as he knelt on the floor to rip the worn fabric. "More fool than poor Albert."

"In what way?"

The material tore with a screeching sound under his powerful hands. There was anger in his action, and she decided not to press him with questions.

He rose from his undignified position and stood to look at her.

He twined his hand in her hair tenderly, then brought her face up to meet his. The instant his lips touched her, she felt that strange fire kindle in her soul. All the anger, all the hatred she had felt evaporated; only desire remained like a liquid flame coursing through her veins. What effort it took him to let her go, to break the molten bond of their kiss, she could not gauge, though she knew it would have been beyond her own powers to do the same. Still swaying slightly from the effect of so swiftly aroused and so suddenly thwarted passion, she gazed up at Mikhail, who calmly pulled on his white gloves without ever once taking his frightening eyes from hers. Through the months of their relationship, she had never forgotten the hypnotic power they had.

"I was a fool to believe that when I had finished with you I could send you back where you came from," he sighed. "You were perfect, but that very perfection will no doubt lead us all to disaster."

This was the consequence of her actions, and the realization shamed her. For herself she no longer cared what happened; she had known from the very beginning what risks were involved, risks far greater than any posed by Colonel Trabert or the others like him. After all, she told herself, I got only what I asked for, a life like what I would have led had there been no Revolution, and I got it, right down to the final terror.

But she saw now, too, the expanding horror, the danger that spread to touch others, innocents like Justine and poor silly Yvette. The thought was sobering.

"I'll do whatever you ask of me, Mischa, anything at all," she said in a voice so low she could not be sure he heard her. "I always have, haven't I?"

"Yes, you have, and you will continue to do so, because if you don't, you will leave me no choice but to see that no one else avails himself of your, shall we say, talents. Now, to the matter of shoes. Your slippers won't last a mile."

There were several pair of sturdy boots in the trunk, but none came close to fitting her tiny feet, and in the end she had to settle for the little kid slippers after all. She knew the first rough cobble would cut her feet to bleeding ribbons, but there was nothing else to do now. She must make the best of it.

He tossed her a ragged shawl, filthy with dust. Choking at the smell, she wrapped it around her shoulders and was preparing to follow him out the door when Guy burst into the room, slammed and bolted the door.

"I saw them. They're on their way to see Ricardot now, exactly as you suspected. Trabert is with them, too, and it can only be a matter of minutes before the general tells him she's here," he gasped. "You'll have to leave now and hope it isn't too late already."

Alexandra said quietly, "Ricardot is dead."

The astonishment on both men's faces might have brought a smile, but not tonight.

"He died fifteen minutes before I left him. I waited to be sure."

After taking a deep breath to collect his thoughts, Mikhail said, "Then he has given us a little extra time."

"Damned little," Guy swore. "But better than none. Let's not waste it."

"Of course. The sooner we are out of here the better. I had planned to be days ahead of them, not minutes, but this will have to do. Come on, Xan."

"I'm ready." She turned to look at Guy and said, "Thank you."

And then she could no longer speak at all.

"You have the directions?" Guy asked anxiously.

Mikhail tapped his skull and smiled. "I sent Vasili ahead to Lyons; he'll meet us in a week or two."

"Then farewell, my friend, and good luck." He embraced the Russian with genuine affection. "And you, little Snowbird, go with God."

He kissed her very softly, and then Mikhail was hurrying her to the door. She had time only to glance over her shoulder and say, "Justine?" The actor's smile and murmured "yes" were all the reassurance he could give her.

The corridor was crowded with men and women in gawdy costumes. Mikhail pushed them aside roughly as he headed for the stage door with Alexandra running to keep up with him. By the time they stepped into the pitch black alley, she had been jostled breathless and her feet already hurt from being trod upon so often. Stepping into a cold puddle did nothing to help.

"Good. The rain has stopped, and we will have no moon for hours yet. Perfect for an escape."

He had paused only long enough for his eyes to adjust to the darkness, a few minutes at most, but still it gave Alexandra the chance to catch her breath. She had no idea where she was, nor did she care, and when Mikhail moved off into the night she instinctively reached for his hand. His fingers curled around hers with a gentle, comforting squeeze, and she followed where he led.

Much to her relief, he kept his pace slow. Through narrow, unlit alleys and down the winding streets of Paris, he walked with silent determination. Her own knowledge of the city was limited; she could not have told where they were at any given moment nor what direction they had taken. They saw no one save a few harlots and a drunken soldier or two, not even a patrolling watchman.

It was impossible to avoid puddles she couldn't see. Her shoes sloshed noisily and the skirt, despite its shortened length, was wet nearly to her knees. The extra weight made walking more and more difficult, more tiring, yet she kept pace with Mihail without a word of complaint. He was only a shadow, a phantom moving just ahead of her in

151

the blackness, her guide into the unknown hell of the future.

The houses crowded together like beggars in a cold wind and were hardly less ragged. All manner of filth lay in the streets. Seeing how it fouled the rainwater, Alexandra almost gagged to know what she had been walking in all this time. She tried not to imagine what a stinking sewer these narrow lanes must become in the steaming heat of a Parisian summer.

They wandered, or so it seemed, in darkness longer than usual without seeing a single lighted window. Though she made no attempt to guess how long ago they had left the Opera, Alexandra knew it was late, near midnight or even later. She looked up towards the narrow ribbon of sky showing between the shabby buildings and discovered uncountable stars glimmering above her, clean and pure against their velvet curtain.

Her stargazing slowed her down; she felt Mikhail tug her arm roughly. They turned another corner in darkness so absolute she thought he must be part cat, and there, at the end of a short alleyway, bright lights and an open doorway beckoned. Alexandra moved toward it like a moth to a flame.

She had reached the edge of the lamplit circle outside the door before she bothered to look at what awaited beyond that welcome portal. Wrenching her hand free of Mikhail's relaxed grip, she backed away into the safety of the blind night.

A cloud of steam rose from the fresh blood on the floor to surround the half-naked man with gentle tendrils of horror. Massive muscles in his arms, shoulders, and chest rippled beneath sweat-shined skin at each ferocious stroke of the knife in his hand. Over the grisly swish and thud of the blade as it hacked through the flesh and sinew drifted the tune the man whistled as he gaily went about his labor.

"Come on, come on," Mikhail muttered impatiently as he grabbed her arm again and began to drag her towards the door. "Have you never seen a lamb butchered before?"

The stench was worse than the sight, but Alexandra forced down the rising nausea and followed him hesitantly.

The butcher saw the two figures step from the shadows into the circle of yellow lamplight. From the corner of his eye he watched them approach, never missing a stroke with his knife though his heart skipped a beat or two. The sweat of exertion mingled with the sweat of anxiety in steady rivulets down his face and neck. Not until the stealthy apparitions came near enough for him to recognize at least one face, with great relief, did he realize he had been holding his breath.

Claude Duquesne slammed the razor-sharp cleaver into the wooden plank table with such force the instrument quivered with a strange twang.

"Welcome, welcome," he whispered with a beckoning motion of his huge hands. When Alexandra exhibited reluctance to step on the gore-covered floor, the butcher smiled and said, "Walk on this side, and hold your skirt up. Manette will have something for you to eat in the kitchen."

Walking where Duquesne indicated, Alexandra found a relatively clean pathway that led to a door giving entrance to the living quarters, though it really made little difference to her dress. Surely lamb's blood was no worse than what the lavender poplin had already been dragged through. And she wondered how, after all that happened, she could possibly eat anything.

Mikhail's knock brought almost instant response, and Alexandra suddenly stood face to face with one of the most intriguing creatures she had ever seen. But Manette Duquesne wasted no time on formalities as she took Alexandra's arm and brought her into the warmth of a spotlessly clean kitchen.

"Claude will be in when he is finished, not a moment before. Sit down, both of you, please. I'll bring you some soup and some bread, and you can eat while I get Justine."

She bustled about the large comfortable room with such

energy that when she had placed bowls of thick onion soup topped with cheese and a platter of fresh, oven-warm bread on the table and then scampered off into another room of the house, Alexandra was the one left breathless.

"It isn't polite to stare," Mikhail admonished.

"I can't help it. She's absolutely beautiful!"

"She is also very happy, so don't ask me the question that is hovering in your mind right now." He spoke in English, as he often did when he wished his conversation kept private. "Sometime I will tell you about her, but not now."

He turned his attention to the steaming, delicious meal. Alexandra, her appetite revived by the savory aroma, swallowed each spoonful hungrily, and by concentrating on the food was able to keep from following her hostess' movements around the kitchen.

Tall and slender, Manette seemed to flit about like a butterfly from stove to cupboard and table and back again. She was obviously at home in her surroundings, yet somehow she did not belong here. The hands that ladled more soup into Mikhail's bowl were too fine-boned, too long-fingered, too aristocratic even though hard work had left them red and roughened. She stepped lightly, gaily, with no trace of a peasant's shuffle.

"Henri has the cart ready; he can take you as far as Etampes." She spoke with the same energy as she moved. "He's to pick up a load of swine from a farmer there, so he should not arouse any suspicion."

More than anything else, it was Manette's face that so fascinated Alexandra. As Madame Duquesne and Count Ogrinov continued to discuss plans that had apparently been made in advance, Alexandra stole occasional glances over her mug of bitter black coffee at this woman who chatted so familiarly, and yet did not flirt, with her handsome guest.

There was no guessing her age, for her beauty had a touch of maturity as well as youthful freshness. Her hair, braided and coiled on the top of her head, shone like afternoon sun on ripe wheat, a clear, pale, shining gold. Her eyes, perhaps the only steady feature about her, were deep, lustrous brown with thick feathery lashes. I have seen all the fabled beauties of the Empire, Alexandra thought, all the decorated ladies and harlots of Napoleon's court, but not one of them can match this. I ought to be jealous.

But envy was impossible, for Manette was as generous and cheerful and kind as she was lovely.

"You wait here for Claude," she told Mikhail. "I absolutely must get this poor child out of these wretched clothes."

Taking Alexandra by the hand, Manette led the way upstairs to a large room where, to both girls' surprise, Justine sat on a bed pulling on her stockings.

"Oh, Xan, I thought you'd never get here!"

As if years rather than hours had passed since their last meeting, they embraced with joyful tears.

"Why didn't you tell me she was here?" Justine asked, but without anger.

Manette laughed. "She has only just arrived."

From a pile of clothing lying on the bed, she drew a rust-red dress and clean dry stockings and undergarments Alexandra recognized as having come from her old wardrobe. Manette tossed the articles at her.

"Get rid of that filthy chemise and that horrible dress and throw them over here where I can burn them. Don't be shy now; just do it."

Too tired for modesty, Alexandra obeyed and stripped off every stitch of her soaked and stained clothing. Somewhere in the back of her mind she laughed at the idea of constantly changing her clothes all night, which was waht she felt she had done, but at least she found the new dress dry and warm and affectionately familiar. She pulled on warm cotton stockings and slipped her feet into comfortable shoes.

"Not even a grocer's daughter eloping with a farm boy would be caught dead with hair like that," Manette scolded, holding up the damp tresses.

"Don't cut it, please," Alexandra begged.

"Why would I cut it? No, I just want it brushed and

braided, so that you look like something civilized, not a ragged whore.''

The reflection staring back at a yawning Alexandra from the darkened window of the butcher shop was that of a very sleepy and more or less unremarkable young woman. Gone was the intricate coiffure and elegant gown and artful expression of General Ricardot's mistress. The shabbily dressed and wild haired harlot who had traipsed the squalid streets had given way to a modest, shy looking creature who let herself be lifted up into the butcher's cart. Finding the softness of the straw and the warmth of a coarse woolen blanket irresistible, she made a cozy nest for herself and quickly fell to sleep.

"Thank you, Manette," Mikhail said with a grateful smile. "You'll be well rewarded, whether you wish to be or not."

"You know it is not the reason I do this. Now get into the cart and be on your way or Henri will be late to the market." She smiled her own farewell before picking up her skirts and returning to the house.

He had one foot up on the wheel of the vehicle when he heard his name.

"Monsieur, I would have a word with you privately," Justine called from the shadows.

"I thought you had left."

"I said my goodbyes to my sister, but I wasn't ready to leave without saying goodbye to you as well."

Mikhail glanced at the boy holding the reins and nodded to him to go on ahead. The horse wakened and leaned into the shafts with a squeak of harness and groan of axle.

"What I have to say to you won't take long; you'll not have far to run to catch them," she said, nervous at being alone with this man for the first time. Even in the ordinary linen shirt and loose breeches of a tradesman he had the power to enchant. She knew now why Alexandra had been so willing a victim. "Albert St. Croix and my sister are enjoying a brief honeymoon, and for that you have my gratitude. And I am at least hopeful that, having got Xan out of one dangerous situation, you can get her out of another until she is safe, somewhere. You have treated all of us abominably, and her worst of all. She deserves better.''

"Alexandra did nothing unwillingly," he said gently in his defense, surprising Justine with his lack of arrogance. "But blame me if you will; it matters very little in the end. I will do everything I can to see that she comes to no harm."

"See that you do. Here is the letter Guy gave me for you. If it were your life alone at stake, I would have destroyed it, but you have cleverly made Xan your hostage and left me with no choice but to help you."

He said nothing for a while, and in the silence they both heard the distant slow hoofbeats and squeaking wheels of the butcher's cart. Mikhail could waste no more time.

"I said before that she came willingly. If she had not, I might perhaps have been forced to take her against her will, for her own sake as well as mine." In the dark it was hard for them to see each other's face, but Justine saw the spark of flame in his eyes and knew for herself the power of the soul that lived within those depths. His voice remained soft and calm as he told her, "Had I left her, she could have given information about me and my friends to the wrong people, resulting in much suffering and possibly my death, which I wish to postpone as long as possible. That alone would have been sufficient cause, as you put it, to make her my hostage. But let yourself imagine for a moment the fate of a very attractive young woman accused of using her body to bring about the demise of Bonaparte's empire. Had I strangled Alexandra in the alley behind the Opera and left her lying like some common slut in the gutter, she'd have been better off than in the hands of Napoleon's interrogators.

"So go on home to your family and assure them that Alexandra is as safe as she can possibly be. Save some compassion for your other sister; a soldier's wife will not have a happy summer this year."

He kissed her cheek very softly, and squeezed the hands she held out to him in a mute and hopeless gesture, then he turned and strode off into the inky darkness that would soon be the dawn of another day. Exhausted and frightened, Justine stood in the unfamiliar street until the sound of his footsteps faded into silence. Now came the task of breaking the news to her father and Therese, of supporting them and easing their fears as much as she could. In another day, Albert's departure would add yet more sorrow to the burden she already bore on her shoulders.

With a sigh of sadness and resignation, Justine lifted her hand to wipe her cheek as she began the lonely walk home.

She had been angry with the Russian, but anger did not make her weep. These were not her own tears that she brushed away, and the knowledge that she was not alone with her grief made it somehow easier to bear.

Chapter 15

ALEXANDRA WAKENED suddenly, startled out of her sleep by the mournful howl of a distant wolf. Satisfied that there was no immediate danger, she settled back down on her grassy bed and pulled the almost unnecessary blanket over her. As she rolled over to find a more comfortable position, she saw a tall, shadowy form silhouetted by moonlight against a star-filled sky.

She had been disappointed by Mikhail's determination to keep riding despite the pleasant looking inn they had passed in the village by the river, but here on the empty plain, beneath a summer canopy of sky and moon and stars, she felt at peace. There was security in the openness, in the endless expanse of countryside that stretched on and on into the darkness. The wolf howled again, a sound almost comforting in the loneliness.

It was good to be alone. The months spent always in the company of strangers had given Alexandra a longing for privacy she could not explain. At first, while they travelled with the circus, suspicion and fear kept her aloof from the others.

Mikhail had not encouraged her to change her cold, unfriendly attitude. They wandered through Europe as strangers to all they met.

As tired as she was after the long day of riding, Alexandra could not fall asleep again. It was not the wolf that kept her eyes open nor the naked brilliance of the moon hanging overhead. Memories of months and miles that separated this night from the night she had run from the Opera in Paris crowded into her brain. The travelling players who had sheltered them through the mountains of Savoy; the merchant from Milano who made them part of his enormous family on the road to Venice; the blacksmith from Trieste: Their faces passed before her mind's eye like a portrait gallery, these people who had believed the lies that came so easily to Mikhail's tongue. It was hard now, in the purity of the summer night, to imagine him as any of the things he had claimed to be: an actor, a thief, a disinherited nobleman.

"Aren't you going to get some sleep?" she finally asked him.

"No, not tonight."

He did not look at her, just called the words back over his shoulder. Such indifference gave her a feeling of not being wanted, a feeling she had not experienced often during the last months.

"You'll be exhausted tomorrow."

"Don't worry about me. Go back to sleep; we have a long way to go tomorrow."

"Mischa, I can't sleep."

He turned sharply, brought out of his thoughts by her nearness. He had not heard her approach, and the sound of her voice so close behind him made him jump.

Scolding words were on his tongue, but the sight of her took them away. With the moonlight full upon her face, her features seemed cut from translucent marble, her eyes like emeralds set in the stone to capture the soft light and reflect it like green fire.

"I'm sorry I didn't stop at the inn," he apologized. "I promise I won't make you sleep on the ground again."

"It's not the hardness of my bed that's keeping me awake. It's you. You frighten me, standing there alone as if you were waiting for something to attack us. Come lie down and sleep. You said yourself that tomorrow is going to be a long day."

"I can't sleep, not tonight."

"Then at least sit down and talk to me."

To her surprise, he did join her, sitting beside her on the grass. For several long minutes they enjoyed infinite silence, unbroken even by a wolf call or the snoring from the horses hobbled a few yards away.

"You are troubled," Alexandra said quietly.

He could not hide it. "Yes, I am troubled," he admitted.

"Maybe if you tell me about it you'll feel better and be able to get some sleep."

"It's too late. The sun will be up in two hours."

She sighed, frustrated in her attempt to draw him out of this eerie shell.

"Look, I said I was sorry I didn't stop at the inn. What more do you want?"

"I wasn't complaining, Mischa. Why are you so angry with me tonight?"

"I'm not angry, just tired."

"Then please, tell me what's bothering you. It worries me to see you so upset and not know why."

He plucked a long blade of grass just barely damp with dew and held it up until the moonlight struck it silver.

"Do you know where we are?" he asked.

"I've been lost since we left Venice," she answered, shaking her head. "I know we are travelling east, towards Russia, but that's all."

Very slowly, in a voice filled with mystery and reverence, he said, "My dear Alexandra, we are no longer travelling *toward* Russia. The river we crossed today—yesterday—was the Dneister, and now we have begun our journey *through* Russia."

"Oh, thank God, we're safe!" She kissed him wildly with joy. "We've done it, Mischa. We've made it!"

"Settle down, settle down. We are not safe yet."

"But I thought once we were in Russia—?"

"Russia is not safe." He paused, looked at her open, questioning face. She was eager to listen, perhaps even to share some of his burden. "Today is the sixth of August. We have over four hundred miles to go to Kiev, then another three hundred to Moscow. In Kiev I can learn something of what is happening between Bonaparte and the Tsar, and of course Vasili is to wait for me there. Unless Napoleon has already added another jewel to his imperial crown. All these months could have been long enough for another French conquest.''

"So we go on, not knowing what awaits us.''

"Precisely.''

He had not meant to diminish her joy and now found that he missed the sparkle in her eyes, the laughter in her voice.

"But at least we are in Russia," he said encouragingly. "That in itself is an accomplishment. We have eluded the Corsican this far and tomorrow, in celebration, I promise you a bed.''

Her smile returned, and the gentle curve of her mouth was more than he could resist.

To be taken in his arms, to feel herself deliciously imprisoned in his embrace, seemed the most natural thing in the world. His kiss was soft, demanding no more than she willingly gave. A warm and glorious thrill spread through her as she felt his tongue tease past her parted lips. Her heart thudded against her ribs as though it would burst.

"I had forgotten how beautiful you are," Mikhail murmured while his fingers traced the lines and shadows of her body.

She shivered, not with fear or chill, but with the sweet agony of longing. She could not control the low animal sound of pleasure that escaped her. His hand was on her breast, caressing the firm flesh that shimmered like satin in the moonlight. How primitive, how earthy she looked, a goddess from some pagan age sprawled naked on the summer grass.

Soft nipples hardened at his touch, and he smothered her moan with his mouth. The taste of her was sweet, fresh as the breeze that stirred the grass around them, light as the flutter of her lashes against his cheek. He wanted her desperately, as he always did, and he let desire rule his troubled mind. Forgotten were all his suspicions and worries as he gave in to pleasure. Forgotten, too, was the memory of another woman who had once delighted him as Alexandra now did. It was as if that woman—and her betrayal—had never existed.

His hands moved slowly, tenderly, finding the soft curves of hip and thigh familiar and yet more beautiful than he remembered. There was no shyness in her response; she twisted against him, pulled his hard-muscled body to hers until they met flesh to flesh, warmth to warmth, desire to desire. When at last he took her, easily, quickly, his sigh matched hers.

Mikhail felt no need to hurry. Hers was a body to be enjoyed, not merely used. It was enough to lie still, to savor each sensation possessing her brought him. Only with strange reluctance did he begin to move within her. She arched her body to meet his, and at each coming together the sensations grew stronger, the hunger more fierce, until time no longer existed for them, neither past nor future nor even present, in this dream world of glorious, self-fulfilling ecstasy.

Dawn had dimmed the moon but the sun had not yet risen above the horizon when they lay in the dewy grass, no longer consumed with need. They were satisfied but not sated. Alexandra's hands trailed lightly up and down his body as she curled herself against him and made him want her again.

"You are insatiable," he accused.

"I suppose I am," she sighed, twisting the hair on his chest around her finger.

"And brazen enough to admit it!" He laughed and drew her closer. "Ladies do not own to having such desires. Only men are allowed that kind of need," he teased.

"I know." She lay atop him, the steady pulse of his heart against her own.

She could not tell him, could not find the words to make him understand her need for him, a need that went far beyond the act of passion they had just shared. Touching him, being close to him, feeling secure in his nearness; all those were as much a part of her need as the physical coupling of their bodies.

"The sun will be up shortly," he commented. "We had best get an early start if we expect to arrive in Kiev on time. Come on, you lazy wench!"

He slapped her backside just hard enough to make her jump off him but was caught unprepared when she, with lightning reflexes, returned the gesture with a resounding whack. Growling like a wounded beast, he lunged at her. His fingers grasped a slender ankle as she scrambled out of his reach. She knew she had no chance to escape, for even had she been able to outrun him, there was nowhere to go. Laughter crinkled her eyes as she turned to face him.

"You are not so lazy after all!" he said with a grin.

She tossed her head with its tangled mane of hair and replied, "Then let it be a lesson to you. Never underestimate me again."

He could do nothing in the face of such arrogance save throw his hands up in submission.

"Indeed I shall not. Now let us be on our way, if you haven't already ruined me for a long day in the saddle."

Though she could not gauge how many miles they covered each day, Alexandra knew it was never enough. Each sunrise found them already mounted, whether they had spent the night in a farmer's cottage, at an inn, or on the open plain, nor did they rest until Mikhail feared for the safety of the horses if driven too hard.

It was the weather that turned against them. By noon the heat had become unbearable. Sweat dripped from the horses even when they walked, and Alexandra felt her own perspiration trickling down her back and between her breasts. Her thin cotton blouse stuck to her skin; braiding her hair and coiling it above her ears the way she had seen the peasant girls did little to alleviate the discomfort of the sun beating down on her head and shoulders.

They had been forced to stop for several hours each day because of the heat. Continuing under those conditions would have killed the horses, and it was only on their account that Mikhail halted.

On the fourth day, the weather relented, a bit. Taking advantage of a cool morning under cloudy skies, Mikhail spurred the great red stallion into an easy gallop that ate up the miles a dozen yards at a stride. The long-legged mare had no trouble matching his pace and it looked as if they might make up some of the time and distance they had lost to the heat. On and on they rode, slowing to a trot for a while, then to a restful walk, only to jump once again to the gallop when the horses had caught their breath.

The clouds afforded shelter from the blistering sun, but the day steamed. The dust kicked up in clouds by the pounding hooves clung to Alexandra's face like plaster. She tried to wipe it away and only smeared the mud into ugly streaks. It hurt her throat so badly that to cough intensified the pain rather than relieved it, and particles got in her eyes to scratch and burn and itch without mercy. Once she tried to call to Mikhail to beg him to stop. Whether he did not hear or simply chose to ignore her she could not tell. At any rate, he did not slow his stallion at all, thus forcing her to go on or risk being left behind.

A stream, nearly dried up from the drought, crossed their path. While the horses drank, Alexandra knelt on the bank and plunged her face into the cool trickle of water. Using her hands as a cup, she, too, quenched her thirst and then splashed the refreshing liquid on her clothing and hair. She was about to pull off her boots and bathe her feet when Mikhail, water dripping from his face, ordered her back into the saddle. Before she had a chance to form an argument, she heard the thunder that heralded the storm.

Lightning split the roiling clouds in jagged flashes, but the thunder was muffled by the cadence of hooves on dusty road. A town took shape on the horizon, a place possibly possessing an inn where they could shelter.

Had the horses been fresh they might have outrun the storm. Instead it hit them a mile outside the village. Great drops of rain borne on the rising wind splattered in the dust and almost sizzled on the horses' flanks. Alexandra, never afraid of nature's tempests, turned her face upward to accept the cooling downpour, and even the normally skittish animals seemed to ignore the frightening aspects in favor of relishing the relief of rain on their steaming bodies.

Dripping wet from head to knee and covered in mud from there down, Mikhail and Alexandra wandered into the nameless inn. Alexandra stood shyly in a corner, embarrassed as much by her appearance as by what she suspected Mikhail was telling the innkeeper. As the proprietor led them to their room, he leered conspiratorially, confirming her suspicions that Mikhail had told a particularly bawdy lie.

The sight of a bed with clean sheets and fat pillows drove all scolding from her. Though hardly luxurious, the room was spotless and bright and quite pleasant. She glanced down at her muddy boots and the puddles they were making on the floor.

"You can clean it up later, if you wish," Mikhail said, "or leave it for the servant. And just in case you were thinking how nice it would be to soak in a tub of hot water, I've ordered one. You first, then me. Or, if you prefer, we can bathe together."

She felt her face turn red and was extremely relieved to see that the tub hauled in by two lackeys was hardly large enough for one person and would never accommodate two.

"We have come almost halfway to Kiev in only four days, not nearly so bad as I had feared," Mikhail informed her while he shaved his week's growth of beard. "We need to arrive there no later than the fifteenth, so we can't waste any time."

"Can we at least rest this one night? Mischa, I am thoroughly exhausted." She lay in hot, soapy water up to her chin, though her knees were doubled up and poked through the surface. "By the way, what lie did you give to the innkeeper?"

"What difference does it make?"

"A lot. I may be called upon to play the part of whatever it is you've told him I am."

He laughed and angled the mirror so he could see her face. Her reaction would be interesting.

"You are the only daughter of a very wealthy farmer, the apple of his eye." He saw a smile of pride in such a pleasant fiction light her face. She was still an aristocrat at heart. "Naturally, he wanted you to marry well, so he arranged a union with his very best friend, a fat, bald, ugly and lecherous old goat named Igor Petrovitch."

"Then what am I doing with you, and who have you told him you are?"

"I am one of Igor's serfs."

Her face was crimson now, and she tried to sink deeper into the water.

"I can guess the rest. I chose love, or whatever, over money and we are running away together."

"You are too clever for me. That is exactly the case. Secrecy is essential, as both your father and your betrothed are looking for us. Luckily, the innkeeper and his wife are incurably romantic." He wiped his face clean on a towel and turned around. "Are you done?"

She was, though it was with great reluctance that she left the warm water to stand naked in front of him.

The common room was quietly crowded after supper, but Mikhail found a place to sit near the wall. With a bottle of vodka and a glass, he leaned back to drink and to listen to the conversation around him. For the most part it was talk of the weather and the crops and local gossip no different from anywhere. If only one of these farmers had a son in the army who had written of the latest developments! Such luck was more than Mikhail had a right to expect, but wishing was free.

He drank cautiously, as always, though boredom was more the enemy than the vodka. Exhaustion, too, had taken its toll; he was sleepy after the first glass. Listening to the sound of the storm raging more furiously than ever, he knew there would be no travelling the next day. To curse the weather was a waste of time and energy, two things he had little enough of to waste.

Especially energy. Christ! but he was tired. Too many nights with too few hours of sleep coupled with endless riding had sapped his strength. Were it not that he had had no news of Napoleon's movements for more than a month, he knew he was a fool for leaving the comfort of the bed, and the woman, upstairs.

A sudden commotion roused him from his gloomy thoughts and he had to rub his tired eyes to focus them. Another traveller had entered the tavern, a rain-soaked giant of a man who stood by the door and shook like a half-drowned dog. In the poor light, made dimmer by the thick smoke from strong Turkish tobacco the peasants preferred, Mikhail saw only the man's enormous bulk, but when the stranger quietly called for the inn-keeper, his voice identified him instantly.

"Vasili!"

The two men pushed chairs and tables aside in their rush to each other's arms. Mikhail paid no attention to Vasili's wet clothes or the strong smell of horse that surrounded him.

"I didn't expect to see you until Kiev," Mikhail exclaimed, holding his friend at arm's length and blinking back tears.

"It's only because so many things went wrong that I'm ahead of schedule."

They made their way back to Mikhail's corner and called the innkeeper to bring Vasili a hot meal and another glass.

"Mischa, before you ask me any questions, tell me about Alexandra. Is she somewhere safe? I have worried so about her."

"She's upstairs asleep. I had to bring her with me."

"She was in that much danger?"

Mikhail sipped his vodka and searched for an answer that would not betray his feelings.

"No, but I was. I didn't dare leave her behind for

Trabert and his spies to make use of. She knew too much.''

Vasili scowled and gulped his own vodka as if it were warm milk.

''I know what you are thinking, Mikhail Pavlovitch, and I do not like it. The Snowbird is not like Tamara; she would die rather than hurt you no matter what you did to her. You insult Alexandra by comparing her to that whore.'' He saw his supper being carried to the table and held his tongue, but only until the porter had left. Then, in a quieter but equally firm voice, he said, ''Forget Tamara. Let yourself love this woman the way you know you want to. The way she loves you.''

Chapter 16

ALEXANDRA WAKENED with a start when Mikhail returned to the room. The incessant thunder and shrieking wind had kept her from sleeping soundly in the unfamiliar bed, made less comfortable by Mikhail's absence, so that when she saw him, she smiled gratefully.

As always, there was a single candle burning, and by its light she saw that though showing clearly the effects of exhaustion and perhaps a bit too much vodka, Mikhail looked somehow relieved. So many worries over the past weeks had etched lines on his face that now seemed to have disappeared.

"I thought you would be snoring by now." He pulled out his watch and set it on the washstand before unbuttoning his shirt. "Damn near two o'clock."

"I couldn't sleep. I missed you. And anyway, I don't snore."

"No, you don't. At least I have never heard you. But Vasili does, and he has just taken the room next to us, so don't be surprised if you can't sleep even with me to keep you company."

She watched him strip off the rest of his clothing and then made a place on the bed for him. Here the light from the little flame barely reached, but he needed only her warmth to guide him to her.

"Why didn't you tell me Vasili was going to meet us here?" Alexander asked as he slid his arm under her shoulders and pulled her next to him.

"I didn't know he was going to. He was supposed to have waited in Kiev. He said all the news could wait until morning, when we've all had a good night's sleep. We can't go anywhere in this rain anyway."

He kissed her softly, comfortingly. Vasili was right. Alexandra loved him and he loved her. He must shut Tamara and all the evil she had done out of his mind. If Alexandra had wanted to betray him, she had had ample time and opportunity in Paris. She would never have left France and embarked on this journey with him unless remaining in Paris was more dangerous yet. She had to love him; she simply had to.

"All the world could be falling down around us," he whispered between kisses. "Napoleon could at this very moment be marching on Moscow and I really don't care." Another kiss, longer, sweeter. "I feel like a lost pawn in a losing game of chess: useless, defeated, just a bystander to the battle."

She began trembling almost convulsively and struggled free of his embrace. Confused, he let go of her.

"The chess game! Oh, Mischa, I forgot all about it!"

"What in the name of Heaven are you shrieking about now?"

She insisted that he relight the candles, that she could not talk in the dark, and though he grumbled about the lateness of the hour and their mutual need for sleep, he did as she asked. He came back to the bed to find her sitting cross-legged, only her lap covered by the sheet.

"The night we left Paris, the night Ricardot died, we had been playing chess, as usual, and for a change it seemed that I was going to win."

"Excuse me, my dear, but I cannot concentrate on something as mundane as a chess game when I am confronted with *these*." He brushed the back of his hand across her bare nipples, grinned to see them tighten.

Not to be distracted, Alexandra pulled the cover over her breasts and tucked it under her arms.

"Behave yourself," she scolded. "This may be the first time I've ever had something to tell you about Ricardot

171

that has any meaning at all.

"As I said, I was winning, but we never completed the game. Before we left for the Opera, he made me memorize the board, the positions of all the pieces. I tried, but I couldn't remember all of them."

"What is so important about it then if you can't remember anything?"

"Because, O Impatient One, the pieces were more important than where they sat. I was the black, he the white, but the two sets didn't match. My king was a fat little Italian; his was the Tsar of all the Russians!"

He made no reply at first, let her words register as he let a long, slow sigh escape him, and then he took both her hands in his and kissed them.

"You were right. I should never underestimate you. In the morning I'll see if we can come up with some chessmen and we'll find out just how much of that game you can remember." He pushed her gently back and rolled her on her side before pulling the blankets over her and tucking them around her. "You have just earned a night of uninterrupted sleep." Then he kissed her good night. "Well, almost uninterrupted."

Ten hours later, Mikhail joined Vasili in the common room for breakfast. They were the only patrons, yet they kept their voices low out of habit.

"The French will take Smolensk, have no fear," the servant insisted. "I do not think the Scot and Prince Bagration will abandon it the way they did Vitebsk, but it will be taken nonetheless."

"It is what lies ahead of Smolensk that worries me."

"Moscow."

Vasili had put their worst fear into a single word.

"If Moscow falls," Mikhail said, "then it is all over."

"Moscow will not fall. Kutuzov is in command of all the armies now, and he will not let Moscow fall into the hands of a madman."

Toying with food he had little appetite for, Mikhail thought out loud. "We have a choice then. A hard ride to

Smolensk in hopes of reaching Barclay and the prince in time to join the fight, or on to Moscow as we planned. I want to choose the former, but if we are too late, then we, too, are lost. Today is the eleventh of August. When do you estimate Bonaparte will reach Smolensk?''

"When I left, he was still in Vitebsk waiting for supplies; but Smolensk is no more than three or four days' march from there.

"So the battle could be over already. Is that what you are saying?''

Vasili only nodded.

"Damn!'' Mikhail's voice thundered through the empty room. He took a long, deep breath, held it a moment to cement his thoughts together, and finally exhaled slowly. "Moscow, as we planned from the beginning.''

"How soon do we leave?'' Alexandra asked as she walked to their table and took a chair.

"Tomorrow morning if the rain lets up by then. In the meantime, may I suggest a game of chess to while away the hours?''

He clapped his hands and shouted in Russian, bringing the proprietor at a run. A few moments later he returned with a battered wooden box and a worn chessboard. A queer kind of eagerness came over Alexandra as she began to place the crudely carved wooden figures she had found inside the box onto their proper squares.

"You see, Ricardot had a new set of chessmen that represented France and Russia,'' she explained. "Napoleon was the black king, Murat and Ney his knights. I knew the Tsar, of course, but not the white knights. One of them was a fat man with a patch over one eye.''

"Kutuzov,'' both men said in one breath.

"I don't remember the other very well; he just looked like a general on a horse.'' She held the two queens in her hand. "Ricardot made the white queen Mother Russia, just as he used Marie Louise as the black queen to symbolize Napoleon's false claim to royalty.''

More and more of that night came back to her, bits and pieces at a time. Satisfied that she had recreated that last game, she sat back in her chair and waited for Mikhail's comments.

She expected a cry of delight as he discovered some secret military strategy only a soldier could understand. Instead, he shuffled a few of the pieces around, then put his elbows on the table and leaned his chin on his hands to contemplate the game.

Something was wrong. He had moved only two or three pieces, but one was the black king, and she remembered his position exactly.

"It wasn't like that at all. He had all the pawns stretched out like that, but he never moved his king, queen, or the other knight. And he had been telling me all along that I shouldn't be so afraid to move my king."

She put the piece back where she knew it belonged.

Mikhail's shout scared her half to death.

"Oh, my precious little Snowbird!" He kissed her cheek with a loud and very embarrassing smack. "On your own, with no help from me, you have done it. I sincerely apologize for ever having doubted your abilities."

He rose and bowed to her with smiling but genuine respect. Her embarrassment grew until her face burned, for she had no idea at all what she had done.

"I don't understand any of this."

"Of course not. But Ricardot did. He understood it better than we gave him credit for. It is all just a matter of time. If we can get to Moscow with this secret before Napoleon does, he is beaten, once and for all. He has entered Russia a conqueror, but he will not leave it without paying a dear price for his conquest."

Chapter 17

"DAMN!" HE set the mare's hoof down and swore again, long and loudly in Russian.

"Another stone?"

"Yes, and this time she's cut the hoof badly."

He stomped his foot in frustration and stared in the direction of the lowering sun. Though he hated to admit it, he knew there was no chance of reaching the city tonight. Even if the mare had not gone lame—for the third time—the ten miles that separated them from the city's eastern gate was more than they could possibly traverse in the little time left before dark.

With a shrug of his shoulders, he resigned himself to yet another night under the stars, another night, but perhaps his last, outside Moscow. He could not see it from here, but he could feel it. Its warmth, its beauty, its splendor; he closed his eyes, blotted out the glare of the setting sun, and it was there in all its shining glory, golden in his mind's eye. Over the sounds of Alexandra unsaddling the mare and making preparations for their meal, Mikhail heard imagined traffic in Saint Helena Street, bells of Saint Basil's cathedral, jingling harness and the sleighbells that would fill the city when winter arrived.

"If I hadn't sent Vasili on ahead, we could have made it," he complained. "Ah, well, with a good night's rest, the stallion can carry us both."

They had only enough food left for a spare meal. A few chunks of hard bread, some cold chicken from the night before, and a bit of wine took the edge off appetites already dulled by disappointment.

Alexandra ate slowly, without a word. Nor did she even hear much of what Mikhail said to her, though she knew he was talking about Moscow. His memories meant little to her, especially when he lapsed into Russian. She had learned more of the language over the past few weeks, though still not enough to understand his every word. It had helped to pass the long, monotonous hours of riding every day, and Alexandra firmly believed the knowledge of even a few words might be useful someday, despite Mikhail's assurances that everyone in Muscovite society spoke French.

"Xan, are you awake?"

"Yes, of course."

"You've been so quiet. I wondered if perhaps you had dozed off."

"No, I was just thinking."

He lay back on the grass and gently pulled her next to him, cradling her head on his shoulder.

"Dare I ask you to share your thoughts with me?" he whispered.

When she replied, "Nothing important," she knew he did not believe her.

The thoughts that had plagued her for so many, many months were not ones she could discuss with him even had she found the words for them.

What is to become of me? she wondered. I have no idea where I am, where I am going, how I am going to live. This man who has been my lover is about to be reunited with his family, a noble family who cannot be expected to welcome with open arms the tatterdemalion French baggage he has brought home from his adventures. Will he set me up as his mistress just as he did in Paris? What will I do if he doesn't? What happens if he walks into his home and leaves me in the street?

Tears gathered in her eyes; a choking knot constricted her throat. She fought back the depression that threatened to plunge her into screaming, sobbing hysteria and forced herself to concentrate only on the present, a present which would last at least a few more hours.

Twilight died, and the darkness covered them with its chill blanket. The day had been hot, but the September night held a touch of winter. Snuggling close to him for warmth, Alexandra wondered if this was the last time she would lie in his arms, feel his strong yet gentle hands caress her, know the sweetness of his kiss.

Not know or caring what drove his passion, she answered with her own. Before the teasing pressure of his tongue became insistent, her lips parted and the taste of him engulfed her. Something deep within her burst to spread a singing fire through her veins. Response became demand.

He had seen her unclad body many times before, in sunlight, in moonlight, in candlelight, and never failed to be amazed at the perfection. Standing above her while he removed the last of his own clothing, he marvelled at this strange new vision of her revealed by the pale, eerie glow of the stars glimmering overhead in the moonless sky.

His eyes roamed from the shadow of hair tumbled about her head and shoulders to the slender line of her throat where he could imagine the pulse beating wildly. Tempting dark-nippled breasts rose and fell as she breathed. Tiny waist, flat stomach, deliciously curved hips and thighs all fell under his scrutiny. His gaze rested a moment on the dark triangle between her legs, then retracted its path until his eyes met hers.

"Sweet Heaven, but you are beautiful!" he breathed as he lay beside her. "If I weren't able to put my hand right here and touch you, I doubt I could believe you are real."

His eyes never left hers as he reached and placed his hand on one warm, full breast. She shivered, perhaps from the cool evening air, perhaps from excitement, and wrapped her arms around his neck. Her fingers found the thick curls at the base of his skull, twined in them and held them.

"I am real, Mischa, very, very real." she whispered as she pulled him closer.

Beneath his fingers her flesh was like velvet, soft, warm, tantalizingly mysterious. With his eyes still rivetted on hers, he slid his hand down the length of her, gently parted her legs, brought a little animal cry from her when he touched the secret place.

She needed no further arousing. Her legs wrapped like silken serpents around his, she drew him to her until she possessed him even as she was possessed by him. Every ounce of her energy was directed at pleasure, his as well as hers, and when ecstasy came, it took them both at the same instant.

Long minutes later, Mikhail rolled from his back to his side and propped himself up on one elbow to look at her. Her slow, even breathing and the steady pulsebeat at the base of her throat suggested that she had fallen asleep. The emerald eyes, however, glittered with starlight, and tears sparkled at their corners.

He kissed away one salty droplet and asked, "Is my love-making so inadequate it makes you cry?"

"Oh, Mischa, you know it isn't," she said, raising her hand to trace the line of his jaw and chin. "I'm afraid, that's all."

"Of what? Even if we should meet head on with Napoleon's legions tomorrow, we are in Russia now. The Tsar's army will protect us. All of Russia will protect us. How can you be afraid?"

"This is something different. I won't want tomorrow to come, not ever."

"Why should you be afraid of tomorrow? It will merely be the end of our journey, not the end of the world. I thought you wanted to reach Moscow, sleep in a clean bed, wear fashionable clothes again." He smiled, then commented, "Though I find you more fashionable just as you are."

His levity seemed to help, and for a moment the tears stopped and a smile turned up her lips just enough to invite his kiss.

"It will be daylight in a few hours," he said, reluctantly releasing her mouth. "Sleep and sweet dreams will banish all your worries. Come on, close your eyes and rest. In the morning you'll have forgotten ever being afraid.''

Looking at him, seeing the confidence and remnants of pleasure that lit his face, she could not help but feel her own courage return.

"You're right. Whatever happens tomorrow, my worrying will not change it. What's done is done and what is to be will be.''

She leaned back against him, molding her body to fit his. He wrapped one arm around her after pulling the heavy cloak over them. With her buttocks held against his thighs and her breast cupped in his hand, he could not quiet the urges that sprang to life. His sudden entry from this unfamiliar position startled a yelp from her and a moment of resistance until she became accustomed to it. Then, comfortable, content, and still holding the hard warmth of him within her, she closed her eyes and slept.

The night was silent and dark, the horizon barely tinged with the glow of dawn when she wakened. She felt so tired, so completely exhausted, that it seemed impossible morning could have arrived so quickly. Surely only a few hours had passed since she had fallen asleep in Mikhail's arms, but the evidence of the sunrise told her the night was indeed gone.

The setting quarter moon glistened on the dew, much heavier now on the cool late summer nights. Mischa had said that frost would soon coat the stubble in the fields and the branches of the trees would be bare before long. She was glad they had completed their trek before the onset of the Russian winter; his tales of its ferocity had made her wish more than anything to spend the cold months safe and warm in Moscow.

Gently, so as not to disturb his rest, she moved Mikhail's arm and extricated herself from his embrace. His passion had faded with sleep, or perhaps he had sated himself while Alexandra dozed, but at any rate he had withdrawn from her, leaving her to feel curiously empty and abandoned.

Her clothes, as she had suspected, were far from comfortable, but with the sunrise they would soon be dry and warm. Had there been any morsel for breakfast, she would have lit a fire both for heat and cooking. She contented herself with finding her own voluminous cape and a sip of what remained in the wineskin.

As the pale, pre-dawn light grew, so did Alexandra's impatience. Mikhail was always awake before she was, and she was not used to waiting for him.

"Mischa, please," she begged when even not-so-gentle nudges failed to rouse him. "It will be light enough in a few minutes to ride." He might be angry at her for disturbing him but angrier still, she knew, if she allowed him to oversleep. With both hands on his shoulder, she shook him.

"Damn it, Xan, what is it?" he asked, instantly alert.

"The sun is almost up. Look." She pointed behind him.

"In the *west*? Don't be silly. There's the moon just coming up over your shoulder; it can't be much past midnight. Come on back to sleep."

He held out his arms to her but she backed away. The moon she had thought to be setting was indeed rising over the distant line of trees. Yet in the opposite direction the glow continued to brighten.

Mikhail saw it first reflected in her eyes, staring wide and uncomprehending, then he turned and saw it for himself.

He grabbed at his clothing, and in the same motion got unsteadily to his feet. A cold mask was drawn over his face, betraying no emotion at all. Terrified, Alexandra took several steps away from him as she grew aware of the barely restrained fury behind his deliberate calm. Once the rage nearly burst its bonds; he struggled with the inside-out sleeve of his shirt and came close to rending the garment in two before finally thrusting his arm into it.

She followed him to the horses, still sleeping peacefully on their tethers.

"Where are you going?"

He mounted the protesting stallion without a saddle.

"Just stay here. Don't move from this spot until I get back," he ordered. Alexandra watched as he kicked the horse into a hard gallop and rode off towards the luminescence that was not the sunrise.

He smelled the smoke before he could see the flames, though he needed neither to confirm the worst of his fears. Moscow, the sanctuary he had almost reached, was an inferno. Sobs of frustration and pain stuck in his throat, and his eyes burned with the sting of smoke and unshed tears. Unable to do anything, he stood beside the horse he had nearly killed in trying to reach the city and he watched the sky change from gold to copper to fiery orange.

"Mischa, is that you?"

Mikhail heard the voice, heard, too, the pounding hoofbeats approach, and he ignored them both.

"Mischa, it's me, Vasili!" the rider called again. "Are you all right?"

He jerked his lathered mount to a halt just a few feet from Mikhail and jumped to the ground.

"Where is the girl?"

"Back there," Mikhail muttered, gesturing with a nod of his head the direction from which he had come. "I left the bitch at the side of the road, three, maybe four miles back. Her horse is lame."

He spoke coldly, the words coming from his mouth with no more feeling than the squeaks and groans of a machine.

"I'll go get her," the servant offered.

"No," Mikhail countermanded, anger in the way he snapped the word. "Let the lying whore wait for some French animal to get her."

Having no idea what had caused this ugly change in his master, Vasili stood in shocked silence for a moment. Three days ago, when he had gone ahead to make arrangements for their arrival at the house in Saint Helena Street, Vasili was certain that a betrothal would be forthcoming. Reputations and past scandals had never stood in the way of Ogrinov lovers before, not since the old Count had

181

married his children's dancing teacher and Mikhail's mother eloped with the English physician.

"I said I'll go get her."

He was in the saddle before Mikhail could stop him, but as he turned the horse around toward the east, he noticed that Mikhail had not moved. Vasili made a snapping noise and the animal jumped into an easy, loping canter.

The moon was high enough now to give some light. Eyes strained to note every detail of the countryside, Vasili searched to his right and left for some sign of the girl or the lame horse. Concentrating on finding her kept him from thinking about what had happened, trying to imagine what turn of events had changed Mikhail's attitude so drastically. Whatever it was, it was of recent origin.

He saw the pathetic figures clearly. The girl walked beside the poor beast, her hand on its shoulder as she coaxed each step out of it. Even with her face in shadow, Vasili knew it was Alexandra.

He said nothing, merely dismounted and walked the last ten yards to her.

"Sweet, Jesus, it's you, Vasili!" she cried. "Have you seen Mischa? He left me hours ago, and he said he'd be back right away. I'm worried sick and I can't drag this poor animal much further and I'm afraid she's going to . . ." She stopped, remembering that the servant spoke only Russian. Slowly, frantically, she wracked her brain for the few words she had learned.

"Mikhail Pavlovitch is all right; he's just a few miles down the road," he answered in perfect French. At the look of amazement in her eyes, he shrugged and admitted, "It has been convenient in the past for me not to speak your language. Now the reverse is true."

"Yes, of course. I see. Well." She tried to collect her thoughts, but it was not easy. "You say Mikhail is all right? I was afraid the horse might have thrown him or something."

"Quite the opposite. He has thrown the horse. He'll do no more riding tonight, and it is just as well. Moscow is burning."

"Oh, God!"

She wiped salty tears from her face with the sleeve of her blouse and with calm deliberation said, "I want you to take me to him. I have to see him."

"There is nothing you can do, nothing he can do."

"Take me to him, Vasili," she demanded. "We'll leave the mare; she can't go far anyway."

The big gelding hardly noticed the added weight of a second rider, but Vasili kept him to a steady walk. It gave him a chance to answer some of Alexandra's questions.

"I got into the city early last night, and it was deserted. Everyone was gone. I let myself into the house on Saint Helena Street and found it empty. The furniture, the paintings, the chandeliers, even the draperies and the piano: They took everything with them, and everywhere it was the same."

"The whole city?"

"Yes. They all left, everyone who could. Most took only what they could carry; there were few carts and wagons available and they went to whoever paid the highest price."

"So Napoleon's army entered a deserted city."

"Not just his army. The mad emperor of the French sits in the Kremlin now, watching the destruction he has wrought."

They rode in bitter silence then, slowly closing the distance between themselves and the funeral pyre of Moscow.

The stallion stubbornly refused to move. Mikhail cursed, kicked, and cajoled in vain, then gave up. Head hanging, breath wheezing, the animal was more dead than alive and knew it. The Russian swore again before turning his back on the beast and striding towards the flames. Two miles, no more certainly, and he could walk that in less time than he had already spent screaming at his horse.

The smoke grew thicker and tiny sparks filled the sky. Now and then he saw great chunks of flaming material shot as if from a cannon and then fall back into the inferno. Oblivious to any danger, he entered the outskirts of the city and walked as a man in a dream, a nightmare, down streets filled only with the sounds of the fire.

It was a roar, like the noise of battle. Explosion after explosion shook the very ground he walked on. No friendly crackle of a log on the hearth; it deafened him.

Above the fiery thunder, a scream and the clatter of stampeding hooves turned him around, and he faced a shadowy phantasm charging down the street straight at him.

Her arms felt pulled from their sockets, but at last she slowed the rampaging gelding to a manageable trot. He snorted in terror and pranced nervously even after she stopped him, a yard or two from the statuelike figure ahead.

"Mischa, wait!" she screamed again when he started to walk away from her. "Oh, God, make him wait!"

It was a long drop to the ground; she landed with a jolt. Taking care not to drop the reins, she ran after him, pleading with him to stop, to listen to her.

"Vasili said you were angry with me, that it would be better to wait until the anger wore off, but I couldn't wait. I have to know what I did to make you hate me so."

He whirled to confront her so suddenly that she jumped backwards.

"Look around you, bitch. This is your handiwork."

She gaped at him, unable to believe his words or the venom in them.

"I don't know how you did it, nor does it matter at this point." He took another step towards her. "You scheming, lying little slut! May you and your bastard Corsican emperor roast in this hell!"

Too terrified to move or make any attempt to protect herself, she took the flat of his hand across her face without uttering a sound. The blow knocked her off balance, but she kept her feet. When her vision cleared, she sought his eyes. They were like ice, a cold, malevolent blue that held no tenderness, no compassion, only deep, unrelenting hatred. She saw no reason for the tears that smeared the soot on his cheeks.

He struck her again, and this time she fell to her knees.

"You *whore!*" He grabbed her arm, hauled her to her feet. Why wouldn't she say anything, deny his charges? Her silence cut into his heart like a dagger, worse than the pain he already felt at seeing his hopes destroyed. "And to think my dear Uncle Andrei felt sorry for you, accused me of mistreating you, when all the while it was the other way around. You used me, just as Tamara did. Did you plan to turn me over to to Bonaparte once he was settled on the Russian throne so you could collect a nice reward for the capture of a notorious spy? Yes, you're just like Tamara. Andrei was a fool to think you were different, and so was I. But no more."

He was insane. He had to be. The shock of his disaster when he had been so confident of victory must have unhinged his mind, and in his agony he lashed out at the only available object, blaming her for his grief. How often had he teased her in the past that she had slowed him down, that he could have made the trip from Paris to Moscow in weeks instead of months but for the encumbrance of a woman? No doubt he now regretted those jests and blamed this tragedy on the delay her presence had caused. She could not deny that.

He would never believe the truth from her lips. Napoleon was not totally responsible for the fire: the Muscovites themselves had sacrificed their city rather than surrender it. Vasili had heard the orders and saw the citizens with their torches set the houses and shops ablaze before the French, led by their Emperor, entered the city.

Mikhail's tirade brought on a fit of coughing aggravated by the thick smoke, and in the brief space of time afforded while he caught his breath, Alexandra tried one last time to reason with him, to bring him back to reality.

"Please, Mischa, don't do this. Let me go, let me disappear from your life and your mind if that is what you want, but do not put more guilt on your soul."

185

His maniacal laughter destroyed her last shred of hope as he tore the clothes from her with his free hand. She had expected him to kill her, but this somehow frightened her more. She knew the power he had, the brute strength of that magnificent body. He meant to hurt her, and she held no illusions about his ability to do just that.

It seemed impossible that only a few hours ago this same man had loved her so gently, so beautifully.

He shoved her to the cobbles and was instantly on top of her, spreading her legs apart and ramming his swollen phallus into her with such force she felt torn in two. Like a madman he pounded her with savage thrusts of hate. Writhing in pain and horror, she tried to get away from him. She beat him with her fists and raked his back with her nails, even tried to sink her teeth into his shoulder. He was no drunken Frenchman. She had beaten Augustin Trabert, but she was no match for this crazed monster.

Through a haze of pain, she felt the spasmodic explosion within her. He grunted and rolled away, reached for his clothes.

"That's how a whore is treated," he sobbed as he stood looking down at her, tears rolling from his icy eyes. "You deserved it."

Chapter 18

ALEXANDRA HAD made a remarkable recovery under abominable circumstances. After a week of almost total bed rest and plenty of plain but wholesome food, she was every bit as healthy as she had been the day she left Paris.

"I want to go with you."

There was determination in those words, and Vasili knew she would be more stubborn than ever.

"If I don't find him today, you can come tomorrow," he promised.

"You said that yesterday. I'm going mad locked up here every day, not knowing what is happening, just waiting."

"I apologize there are no newspapers or I would bring one home to you!" he laughed. "I give you my solemn pledge, Snowbird, tomorrow for certain."

Not quite believing him, but with no other choice, she had to be content. He had, after all, saved her life, though she wondered at times if she were really glad he had.

She had reached a point somewhere between despair and hope, a kind of limbo where death was not actively sought but neither was life fanatically treasured. After burning for four days and leaving nearly all of Moscow a charred ruin, the fire she had begged to consume her finally died and with it her own death wish. Now she merely walked through the days, her only desire to see Mikhail, to ask him what she had done, to give and ask for forgiveness.

It did no good to think beyond that. The emotions she had discovered since that horrible night were useless, vain fantasies, the dreams of the girl she had been too long ago to remember. Love had no place in this mean, rat-like existence of scurrying and scavenging among the ashes. All around her ugliness and poverty and filth held sway, from the vermin that scampered across the floor at night to the spiders that infested the rafters, and survival took all one's energy.

Then why did she feel tears burn her eyes whenever she thought of him? She touched the almost healed cut on her lower lip and found solace in the pain it still brought, for that was a reminder of him. Even his brutality was a thing to be cherished now that he was gone; when the wound was healed and the pain only a memory, she would have nothing.

She sat down on the bench that was the only chair and wished she had some thread and a needle. Useless embroidery, which she had always hated, would have been better than sitting alone with her thoughts. The loneliness, intensified by silence, closed in on her, crushing her, squeezing a whimper out of her that turned to a blood-curdling scream.

The door not six feet from her suddenly exploded, and four bodies in French uniforms lay sprawled across the floor at her feet.

The uppermost body straightened, first rising from its belly to its hands and knees, then standing, though unsteadily. His bloodshot eyes took a long minute to adjust to the dim room after the morning sunlight outside.

"Empty, like all the rest, Jean," he drawled to his companions. "Get up and let's go back. At least there's liquor at the tavern, if no food." He stumbled back out the door without seeing Alexandra.

The others lay still, as if dead, long enough for her to tiptoe to the back room. If luck is with me, she told herself as she made the sign of the cross and folded her hands, they will all follow him.

She sent up a prayer that they would, then added

another in case they did not. A shadow darkened the doorway, and before she could commend her soul to God and ask Him to forgive Mikhail, she felt rough, hard hands drag her from her hiding place.

The grey gelding picked his way daintily down street after street filled with rubble from the skeletons of homes, shops, offices, and the mansions of the rich. In the blackened remains of a church an elderly priest dug among the smoking embers to search for whatever might be salvaged. Vasili stopped to offer his help, then rode away with the old man's thanks and blessing a moment later. There was nothing to be found.

The French were harder and harder to avoid. Knots of three or four of them seemed to stand on every street corner, and Vasili noted with anger that they all carried some sort of plunder. The way they swaggered, bloated with pride and drink, sickened him.

Worse still was the desolation. Where there were no French soldiers, there was no one. The undamaged sections of the city swarmed with looters; officers, soldiers, French officials, camp followers. In the areas of greatest destruction, nothing remained to steal. Not even the drunkest thief ventured into that charred void.

It was eerily silent. The gelding's hooves clattered on the street, but few walls stood high enough to echo the sound. A gust of breeze stirred the ashes and whistled around the corners of stone foundations and brick facades. Like an obelisk, the limbless trunk of a great tree marked the site where generations of Ogrinovs had lived. The house on Saint Helena Street was gone.

He came every day, at about the same time, hoping that Mikhail might by some chance come there, too. Vasili tied his mount to the heat-twisted iron railing that had once enclosed the door yard and stood, still not believing, at the edge of the pile of ash and cinder.

"It's like a grave, isn't it."

The voice came from a distance, clear and recognizable at once. With tears of joy streaking his face, Vasili ran to

189

his master and the two men fell into each other's arms.

"I've been all over this God-forsaken city looking for you these last three days. What corner of hell did you disappear into?" Mikhail asked.

"Only three days you've been searching for me? I've been trying to find you for seven! Even before the fires were out." Distressed by Mikhail's appearance, Vasili decided that this was not the best place to stand and talk. "Come. I think I can find you a change of clothes and something warmer than that cloak. And you look like a man who wouldn't know how to refuse a hot meal."

"Not now, Vasili, though it does sound delicious. I lost something the night the fire started, and I've got to find it first."

Vasili coughed nervously. "Alexandra's been with me."

"With you? Then she's all right? Where is she?"

"I wouldn't have left her alone if she weren't all right. Hurry up, we can be there in less than an hour."

"Sweet Christ, Vasili, you left her alone? Do you know what's going on in Moscow? What could happen to her if the French find her?"

"*You* couldn't find her," the servant retorted. "Take my horse and I'll follow you. She's in the midwife's house on Noblinska Street, just past Saint Elisabeth's church. Can you find it?"

"Yes, I know where it is. And I won't need your horse; I've stolen one from the conquering army, so we'll go together."

Vasili wondered which French general was seething over the loss of the pale gold stallion Mikhail had appropriated. They galloped recklessly through back streets often choked with debris, drove the animals over heaps of rubble and refuse when there was no way around. No Frenchman so much as turned his head when they raced by. Other matters more important than a pair of Russian madmen concerned the invaders.

The single spire of Saint Elisabeth's poked into the cool September sky. Untouched by the blaze, the church stood witness to the pillage of conquest. The wooden doors hung open to reveal the ransacked interior; even the pews were gone, and the holy icons lay scattered on the floor, stripped of their gold and silver frames. Mikhail closed his eyes, unable to bear the sight of the sacrilege. When next he opened them, he wished he had not.

Noblinska Street was little more than an alley, with but six or seven houses and shops on either side. It looked just as it always had when Mischa and his father paid visits to Madame Eva, the midwife, to see if any of her patients needed additional medical attention. The only difference today was that a fat corporal lay sprawled in the center of the street, a pool of bright blood spreading beneath him.

The gold stallion snorted at the smell, but Mikhail was off his back and holding the reins tightly. He knelt by the body and turned it over.

The blood was still sticky around the gaping slash in his neck, and the flesh was not yet cold.

"A broken bottle," Mikhail said in a weak voice as he pointed to the shiny slivers stuck in the wound.

When he stood up, he saw Vasili walking hesitantly toward the house where Madame Eva had lived. The splintered door gaped open.

"Stay back," the servant ordered. "I'll go in first."

But Mikhail had already looked past the door and seen the unmoving form lying on the floor. He pushed Vasili aside and ran into the room.

There was blood everywhere, filling the room with a stench that curdled his stomach.

"Is that you, Jean?" The question came from the corpse.

"Yes, it is I," Mikhail answered, lying as easily as always.

"The girl, did you get her? Is she good? You always liked them with spirit."

Mikhail's hands trembled with the urge to wrap themselves around the Frenchman's throat, but his voice remained soft and calm as he replied, "She's the best."

"Then tell that oaf Henri to hurry; I want her next."

"Of course."

"She swung the bottle at the corporal. Did she hit the fat fool or did he duck out of her way?"

"She got him. He bled to death in the street."

So there had been at least four of them. Impossible odds, yet Alexandra had somehow avenged herself on two of the bastards.

"Good for her!" His laughter ended in a choking cough. "By the way, Jean, did you find out her name? I ought to know at least that much before I—"

"Alexandra." He interrupted, not wanting to hear the dying soldier's desires put into words.

"Named her after her chicken-hearted king! How appropriate!"

He lay quiet for a while, his sightless eyes staring across the floor to the wall where glass fragments glittered in the sunlight, pieces of the bottle that had carved up his belly and cut the corporal's throat. He was close enough to death to feel no pain, and he grew weaker steadily, each chuckle or cough sending blood oozing through the gashes.

With it now apparent that two of the attackers were still alive, Mikhail could not hope that Alexandra had escaped. It was more likely that they had left their comrades for dead and taken her somewhere else away from the scene and the bodies.

"Isn't Henri done yet?"

Blood trickled from his mouth and nose, but his voice was still clear, his words devastatingly coherent.

"We took Moscow as easily as raping a whore. When am I going to get my chance to fuck the Russian bitch?"

The next sound in the room was the cracking of his windpipe as Mikhail's fingers crushed it like an eggshell.

"What are you going to do now?" Vasili asked.

"Try to find out who this bastard was." He searched one pocket after another until he found the sheaf of identifyng papers. " 'Bernard Choulier, born in Limoges, May 1793.' And he died in Moscow, September 1812."

He straightened up and turned his back on the young corpse.

"For whose soul are you praying, Vasili, mine or Bernard's?" he asked sarcastically.

"Neither. His soul is in the hands of either God or Satan, and I cannot change that. Yours is in your own hands, and I cannot change that either. I pray for Alexandra." He crossed himself and returned to his prayer after adding, "It's all I can do after leaving her unprotected against those savages."

He felt a hand on his shoulder, then Mikhail knelt beside him.

"There is too much guilt on my soul to expect God to hear my supplication. I suggest you ask Him to have mercy on the two who are still alive, for I shall have none."

"And Alexandra?"

"There is no guilt on her soul. Even I know that."

They spent the night in what had been a tavern. Vasili spread scavenged blankets on the floor close to the fireplace.

"When did you last eat?" he asked. "Yesterday? The day before?"

"I don't know. Yesterday, I think."

"Then tonight you'll eat."

He built a fire, welcome now that the nights were frosty cold, and set about preparing a savory mutton stew which they ate silently and washed down with a bottle of fine old brandy from the cellar.

"It's been a week, Mischa. Time enough to find her."

He expected an outburst, but none came. The blue eyes stared at the dancing flames yet saw nothing. He had pulled a veil over them, shutting out sight and the window to his soul.

"Your mother must be frantic now. Your letter told her you'd be home by the seventeenth and here it is the first of October. You know how she is. Let's go to the farm where you can rest and—"

"I can't rest, not there, not here, not anywhere until I find her."

"And if you find her dead?"

193

"She's not dead. She warned me long ago not to under-estimate her, and I know that somehow she will find a way to stay alive," Mikhail said, forcing himself to believe his own words.

Then a silence fell that neither man could bear. Vasili broke it.

"Whatever burden of guilt you carry, keeping it on your own shoulders will never lighten it."

"Are you turning into a priest?" He laughed harshly. "No, thank you. I'll confess my sins to God and no other. He alone can forgive them. No mortal, priest or otherwise, can pardon the crimes I've committed against her."

He buried his face in his hands as if weeping, but when he looked up again his eyes were dry. Now was not the time to give in to weakness, to tears and self-pity. He could not afford, even for a moment, to lose control.

"I knew after the first day that she was innocent of all I had accused. I blamed her for tricking me into changing my plans. If I had gone to Smolensk, I reasoned so wrongly, Napoleon would not be touching Moscow. I don't know what I thought I could have done to prevent it, but I blamed her for it. And then I deliberately hurt her in the worst way a man can possibly—"

A hand on his arm silenced him instantly. The crackle of the fire became annoyingly loud, yet above it they heard voices, boisterous, inebriated voices singing an obscene French ballad. They stopped when everyone suddenly forgot the words and broke into hysterical giggling.

"You stupid bastard, you've spilled my wine!"

They stood just outside the tavern door. Mikhail laid his sabre across his lap and picked up the loaded pistols that were never out of his reach. Without taking his eyes from the bolted door, he knew Vasili had done the same.

"Here, you clumsy oaf, have some of this Russian poison. It'll make a man out of you."

More laughter, then another voice, groggy with drink, gurgled, "Poor Georges will need it, too, if he expects to bed Jean Guignon's green-eyed whore tonight."

The words stabbed like white-hot daggers. Sweat

trickled between Mikhail's shoulder blades and dampened his palms. Revulsion filled him. He wanted to kill them now, all of them, and silence their obscenities forever. It nauseated him to listen, yet he had to hear more.

"They say she is cold as ice. Jean keeps her tied up like a horse in that barn, and all she has to keep her warm is that long black hair of hers."

"You've seen her?" Georges asked.

"Haven't you?"

He must have shaken his head, for the other went on, laughing.

"You gave up the pearl necklace for something you haven't seen? Christ, you are a bigger fool than I thought!" He continued to laugh, then swore violently. "Damn you, Georges! You made me laugh so hard I pissed my pants!"

High-pitched cackles came from the others as they left their incontinent fellow to urinate in the street while they went on. He ran to catch them, the footfalls loud and then fading, dying into silence.

The silence became a void, crying to be filled.

"You can tell my mother I'll come home once I've found Jean Guignon's green-eyed whore."

Chapter 19

JEAN GUIGNON tipped the bottle up to his mouth and swallowed two gulps of brandy.

"Want some?" He offered a drink to the creature cowering in the far corner of the horse stall. "Come here and I'll let you have a sip. It makes a nice warm feeling right here."

He patted the bulge of stomach hanging over the top of his trousers, but Alexandra kept her face turned to the wall and refused his generosity.

"I can't let you have the bottle, of course," he went on, "because sometimes you get careless with them."

He laughed raucously, drunkenly, at the same memories that brought nightmares even to Alexandra's waking moments. Listening to him, she saw it all over again, the broken bottle in her hand, the leering corporal, the spray of blood when she slashed at him. A knot of nausea rose in her throat, yet she felt no regret. She would do it again if necessary—if possible.

Jean grew tired of baiting her and settled back to the remains of his brandy and joint of venison. Food was too scarce for him to have come by such a delicacy easily; he could only have procured it by some foul means. Alexandra burrowed further into the pile of straw to escape the delicious smell of the meat and to find some measure of warmth. The thin blanket Jean had given her did little to protect her from the chill of the unheated stable.

In the three weeks of her imprisonment, she had learned

that she could not climb, dig, or break her way out. The stall had no windows, and the half-walls were too high for her to reach the top. Even if she could, the bars that ran to the ceiling beams prevented movement between the stalls or out to the corridor. The only exit was by way of the door, and Jean kept that effectively blocked with a bolt almost too heavy for him to lift. It came off only when he came in.

Or when he let someone else in.

"Not a bad night after all," he said as he tossed the empty bottle into the next stall, where it shattered with a tinkling crash amongst the others littering the floor. "That bumbling farm boy brought me a nice fur coat to keep me warm this winter, and even if he hadn't, it was worth it just to watch him." More ugly laughter. "Like a stallion he was, and he didn't even know where to put it!"

She wished there were a way to close her ears as well as her eyes. Surrendering her body to one man after another was humiliation enough, but to have to listen to Jean's perverted descriptions was the ultimate degradation. On and on he went, until the silent screams filled her head to the bursting point.

The only blessing in her private hell was that Jean himself rarely touched her. He preferred to watch others do what he was almost entirely incapable of.

There were times, however, when he forgot that drink rendered him impotent, and he tried to perform as a man. Only once had he succeeded, and Alexandra had vowed it would never happen again.

He threw down the well-gnawed leg bone and belched with enormous satisfaction.

"And now for some dessert!" he announced, and belched again.

So inebriated he could not stand, Jean crept towards her on his hands and knees, stripping off the filth-encrusted uniform as he crawled. She had hoped that drunk as he was he would fall unconscious and leave her alone, or at least leave the stall to vomit in the corridor and lock her inside, safe from his advances for the night. The sour, unwashed stink of him told her that he came closer and closer, and that luck was not with her again this night.

He pawed at her with a huge, callused hand, mauling her breasts cruelly. Despite the pain he brought, she tried to listen to the voice within her that told her submission was the only path to survival. He pinched the tender nipples until she cried out against his perversion. From some hidden reserve she drew strength to protest his abuse and shoved him away.

It took him by surprise. He was too heavy to push very far or to keep away very long, and in an instant he was back at her, snarling and spitting obscenities. She kicked at him, and though she missed his groin, she still landed a bruising blow to his thigh. His howl of pain brought only a brief satisfaction before he clamped her ankle in the vise of his grip and dragged her closer to him.

"I'll teach you, you stubborn slut." He spat in her face. "All I wanted from you was a farewell kiss, but now I'll get more than a kiss before I turn you over to Colonel Trabert."

His growled words barely registered in her frantic brain. Rage and fear and pain clouded her thoughts as she fought him, silently, with whatever strength remained. She held no illusions about the inevitable, but one small corner of her mind refused to let go without a struggle.

The brandy had made him dizzy and sleepy. He tried to hold her still while he fumbled with the last of his clothing. Off balance, on one knee and one hand while leaning across her chest, he was vulnerable. Alexandra gathered herself tightly and drove her knee into his belly.

He groaned but did not move except to throw his full weight on her. Enraged, he flung his leg over her to pin her beneath him. She seized the split second opportunity and doubled her knee once more.

Guignon closed his eyes and bellowed with the agony. Like a hairy, bloated foetus, he lay curled up in the straw, cupping his injured parts in his hand. Freed at last from his suffocating weight, Alexandra retreated in a daze to her corner, the only place she could go without stepping over the writhing obscenity before her.

She yelped. She had sat on something hard, the bowl Jean had served her supper in. It had been forgotten until now, a plain heavy piece of crockery he filled once or twice a day. While she watched him get slowly to his feet and start towards her again, she held the bowl like a weapon, one with which she could and would kill, if only given the chance.

Murder took complete control of her. It dissolved her fear, steadied her shaking hand, gave strength to her weary limbs. As Jean advanced another step, she stood defiantly to face him.

"There won't be much left for Trabert when I get through with you," he hissed.

She almost gave in to despair at the mention of the colonel's name. It took only Jean's sudden and sickening embrace to bring her back to the awful reality and arouse her instincts once again.

He pushed her against the rough boards of the wall and was forcing her legs apart with his knee when she hit him. She crashed the bowl into the back of his head and felt him slump like a sack of flour against her. Again she hit him, and again, until he slithered to the floor, dragging her with him. Another blow, another, another, another.

He had not moved for several minutes. Too afraid and too sickened even to touch him, Alexandra left Jean lying on his face even though it was harder to see if he still breathed. She could not remember how many times she had hit him, a dozen, a hundred, until the bowl shattered to leave shards embedded in the pulpy mass of his brain. Had she killed him? Had she committed another murder, consigned another soul to its destiny? No man could live with his skull so battered as Jean's was, she felt certain.

With her toe she nudged him gingerly, prepared to jump out of his reach should he grab for her. There was no response. When she kicked harder and again he failed to react, she let herself believe, with a whispered prayer of thanks, that Jean Guignon was dead.

She had nothing to cover herself with except the blanket, and neither shoes nor boots for her feet. Though light in weight, the blanket was large enough to drape around her like a Roman toga, and with Jean's belt to hold it securely around her, Alexandra felt almost warm for the first time in days. Somehow she would have to find clothes and covering for her feet, but for now she was glad just to be able to walk into the corridor of the stable and leave his foul presence behind her.

Silence greeted her, silence so deep that the sound of her naked feet on the earthen floor seemed loud. Ignoring the desire to run for the door that led to the street, she turned instead to the back of the stable where she knew Guignon stored his plunder.

She found the cache in a small storeroom and set her lantern on a crate of silver. She had no interest in the stolen valuables. Clothing was an immediate need, and second came easily transportable wealth to buy her way back to France. A small satchel of jewelry would do nicely, and she knew Jean had collected several pieces in payment for her services. She had, in a sense, earned the right to anything she took, and there was just exactly what she needed somewhere in this enormous horde, if only she could find it.

He had hidden it all. Angry and disappointed, she sat down glumly on an overturned crate and tried to think where else to look. She had found a warm shirt, a pair of woolen breeches, and boots that came close enough to a decent fit, but without the gems she had counted on, her hopes of leaving Russia died. She was left with the choice of staying in this alien, hostile world, unwanted and alone, or of trying to follow the retreating army back to France. Neither alternative held any particular appeal.

After a moment's reflection, she knew that staying in Moscow was out of the question. If Mikhail were still alive and wanted to find her, she was sure he would have. Much as it hurt, she forced herself to face the reality of either his death or his desertion.

That left only the long, slow march back with the army. Unlike the soldiers who followed orders without any thought to the reasons behind them or the consequences of them, Alexandra understood only too well the forbidding prospect of the army's retreat. General Ricardot had seen it, too, and she remembered the strategy displayed in that final chess game. Ricardot knew that Napoleon would invade Russia, but he also knew that victory would be the Corsican's downfall. Drawn further and further into the country, his illusion of triumph became a nightmare of tragedy. Russia had not surrendered; she had merely surrounded her conqueror and made him her prisoner. Now he must flee, across thousands of hostile miles with the enemy at his back. And winter, already nearly upon them, would be their worst enemy.

The creaking stable door jarred Alexandra out of her thoughts, and she recalled with fresh horror what Jean Guignon had said to her just moments before she killed him.

Augustin Trabert had come for her.

Her first act was to extinguish the lantern and, stunned by the sudden blackness, she lost all power to think. Then instinctively she began to react as survival became her prime drive. She hung the darkened lamp on the proper hook beside the door and listened.

"Guignon! Where in hell are you?" His voice echoed in the empty silence. "Christ, man, but it's dark in here."

He stumbled over something, for she heard a scuffle and then a string of curses.

"If you've run off with that slut, I'll see you guillotined," he promised. "I paid for her, and I don't mean to be cheated, not again. She owes me, and I am here to collect."

Panic could do her no good, but it came unbidden nonetheless. She felt trapped in the little room, strangled by the dark and the fear. Escape seemed impossible with Trabert between her and the door. She had only tasted of freedom and now was to lose it so quickly again.

Or was she? She had the advantage of knowing the stable better than he, and she knew exactly where he was, while he had no idea of her location.

"Damn you, Guignon, I know you're here. You couldn't leave with your loot until I brought you a cart."

She opened the door a crack and squeezed through silently while he spoke. He could not know his words covered the sound of her escape and she smiled at her cleverness.

He found one of the doors to a stall and opened it, the resulting squeak telling her that he was near to the one in which Jean's body lay. With the razor edge of his sword, Trabert slashed a long sliver from the edge of the wooden door, and Alexandra knew what he intended to do with it. She could see now a bit of moonlight shining through the open door. Before the colonel managed to strike a light to his hastily contrived torch, she had to make a run for that portal. Steadily, stealthily, she moved towards it, poised to run the moment he saw her. Twenty steps lay between her and the door. Then only eighteen.

A spark from the flint caught in a little pile of straw.

Sixteen steps, fifteen, a dozen.

She heard him fanning the spark to a flame.

The wood crackled, flared, burst into bright light.

"Holy Christ, the bitch has smashed his worthless skull!"

Ignoring the cold, she ran as fast as she could into the free night air.

Chapter 20

ONE DAY followed another with little change. Existing in a haze of exhaustion and numbing cold, Alexandra plodded along with the army and the unfortunate civilian followers. From dawn until sundown she struggled to put one foot ahead of the other and keep going until night brought rest. Survival was only for those willing to fight for it or to buy it, as she was forced to do with the only currency she possessed.

A few days out of Moscow, they encountered the Russian army and a half-hearted battle ensued that did nothing to change the direction of the march. The French continued their slow retreat. On the next morning, Alexandra saw the wagons of the wounded. At first she envied them, lying on their backs and being transported leisurely back to Paris while she, who had once danced with their Emperor, tramped in the company of common whores and looters. Then she drew near to one of the carts and almost vomited at the sight.

Bloody bandages covered the stumps of severed arms and legs. Smaller wounds were left open, to heal or supperate as nature would have it. She saw faces half shattered, minus a nose or an eye. And the stench! She pulled a corner of her blanket over her nose and turned her face away from the horror of the men she had been so jealous of.

Perhaps it was guilt over that moment of jealousy that made her seek out a doctor that night to offer her help.

The moans of the dying guided her to the hospital area, a vague defined space of ground occupied by the carts of wounded, huddled groups of the walking injured, and pitiful piles of corpses awaiting some kind of burial. In the circle of light surrounding a large fire, she saw a man and woman rise from the side of a bandaged form and walk away shaking their heads.

"Monsieur, excuse me," Alexandra said timidly. "Are you a doctor?"

He shoved her out of his way without a word.

"Please, I only want to ask—"

"Get out of here, you filthy harlot!" he snapped. "I've no time to do favors for the likes of you."

"You don't understand. I'm not asking for help; I'm giving it. Is there something I can do for them?"

He looked down at the scrawny, dirty, dishevelled figure wrapped like a mummy in its blanket.

"There's not much any of us can do to help these wretches," he said, "but come along."

The woman who had been with him when the soldier died had stopped to examine another and now hastened to rejoin the doctor. He paused, waiting for her, and Alexandra watched as she pulled a heavy hooded cloak tightly against the rushing wind and strode purposefully, energetically despite her disheartening work.

"He'll be able to walk by morning, unfortunately," she announced. "It never ceases to amaze me why one man dies of superficial wounds and another lives despite mortal ones. Who have you got here? Or should I more properly ask what?"

She stepped up beside the doctor, her face clear in the firelight as she came out of his shadow. Before either woman could say another word, Alexandra collapsed in hysterical sobs at Manette Duquesne's feet.

Alexandra soon learned to follow Manette's advice and slept whenever a minute was available. After a few days without a lengthy rest, she discovered that it was possible to doze even while walking, and the two or three hours' sleep at night became more than enough to see her through the exhausting day.

Just as there was no time for sleep, there was no time to talk. Too many men needed their attention. How much easier it would have been, Alexandra thought in an ungenerous moment, to let them starve to death, but Manette never allowed herself or anyone around her to consider the fact that most of these men would die anyway, no matter what was done for them. Her exuberance, her overwhelming reverence for life, surrounded her and all she did. Alexandra felt it touch her, and like a seed in fertile ground it grew.

Autumn was gradually drifting into winter. One morning they arose before dawn to find the world white with snow. The air was filled with fluffy white flakes falling gently out of the dark sky. How beautiful it was, so pure and untouched by the ugliness of defeat and disillusionment. And how deadly it would become.

There was nothing to cover the wounded men with as they lay in their wagons, so Alexandra kept their faces brushed free of the icy dusting with the edge of her blanket. Many of the men smiled at her kindness, even those who could not see her, and she blinked back tears at every murmured thanks. They did not care what she was or had been, only that she showed them some kindness.

As the snow continued to fall and the men continued to die, Alexandra lost sight of Manette, though she saw Dr. Vaniche frequently. When he spoke to her, the respect in his eyes was worth more than any words. She knew that the small measure of comfort she gave to the wounded and dying was more than he had ever expected from any army whore. Her life had meaning again for the first time in weeks.

Much later that day, she took a steaming mug of broth Manette pressed into her hands. A cold wind whipped at them, swirling the snow until it stung their faces and bare hands. Aleandra sipped the hot liquid even though it burned her tongue, for in a few minutes it would be cold and useless.

Thousands of marching feet had packed the snow on the road to a hard coating of ice that made walking treacherous. Throughout the day occasional gunshots signalled the loss of another horse to the slippery hills, its broken leg rendering it useless except as food for the starving multitude. As she swallowed the last of her soup, Alexandra wondered what kind of meat had flavored her meal. She refused to think about it; there was too much work to be done to waste time mourning a piece of horse-flesh.

Night travel was impossible, but there was little comfort to be found after a halt had been called. What kindling they carried was wet and scarce, and no firewood could be found under the growing shroud of snow. The night would be long and bitter.

Dr. Vaniche managed to erect a small shelter from some tent canvas and a broken cart that had not yet been scavenged for kindling and offered this fragile protection from the elements to Alexandra and Manette. When they protested his generosity, he ordered them into it for a good night's sleep.

"You are too valuable to me to work you to death the way the army does its horses," he snapped. "There is nothing we can do for the poor bastards in this weather anyway, without light or even a fire to warm them. They will die whether we sleep or watch over them, so we might as well sleep. I don't want to see either of you out of here before morning."

The wind howled around the flimsy canvas walls, and snow tapped with deceptive daintiness. Inside, there was scarcely room for the two women to lie down, and no space at all for a fire had they been able to kindle one, but at least the doctor had provided an extra blanket. They spread their other on the ground and lay together under the new one to share their body heat. In the shadowy dark Alexandra reached out to squeeze Manette's hand before they closed their eyes for the first real sleep they had had in days.

They had slept for a few hours, Manette guessed, for the moon was bright behind the clouds and cast an eerie blue-white glow over everything. The snow had not stopped, but the wind had died. She let down the canvas edge and found the warm place she had left beside Alexandra.

"How stupid it all was," she sighed. "Stupid and wasteful. Tomorrow will be a cold, white hell."

They could not see each other in the darkness; huddled together under the blanket, only their voices and the warm nearness of their bodies existed.

"I never got the chance to thank you for saving my life in Paris and now you've saved me again. I can never thank you enough," Alexandra murmured.

Manette's rushing brook laugh was gentle.

"My dear, child, you have no need to thank me. I do not choose who is to live and who is to die any more than the doctors who tend these soldiers. I simply happened to be there at the time you needed me."

"You did not just happen to be there the night Mikhail and I ran away from Paris."

"No, that is true. But one does what one must." She paused, then asked, "Whatever are you doing going back there? When last I saw you, you were most eager to *leave* France."

Alexandra made every effort to keep her story brief, but Manette demanded details, no matter how horrifying or sordid. Throughout the long tale, she expressed no anger or disgust, or even pity, only curiosity. When it was done and there was no more to tell, Alexandra sat silent, waiting as if for her penance after confession. It was not punishment she received.

"You are much stronger than I, Alexandra. I could not have killed them, no matter how well they deserved it. All around me I see men suffering, wishing for death to end their agony, and I cannot take their lives. When they die, I thank God for bringing them peace, and I curse myself for not being able to lift my own hand to do what must be done. I have seen men die who should have lived, and I have seen men live who have no right to walk on this earth, men who deserve death and an eternity in hell, but I can change neither.''

The gentle voice was so filled with ugly hatred that it frightened Alexandra. Another spirit had possessed Manette's soul for those short moments, for surely no one as kind and life-loving as she could feel such hideous emotions. But when she spoke again, after a long, tense silence, the lightness and grace had returned.

''Then you have not seen Mikhail since the night Moscow burned.''

''No. He left me there beside the road and I never saw him again. Vasili and I both looked for him, but he had disappeared.''

That was the only lie she told, for the truth would not come to her lips. Through all the torment and degradation she had endured, the memory of his savage farewell burned with far more hurt than anything else. It was the one wound she could not bear to reopen.

''I do not think he could have been taken by the French,'' Manette mused, talking to herself almost as if thinking out loud. ''And I know they cannot kill him. They tried once before and failed. The first time I saw him, I thought he was dead, but he survived.''

''When was this?''

''He told you, did he not, that he had been wounded at Friedland?''

''Yes, but he never . . .''

The crackle of gunfire interrupted her. The steady fall of snow muffled the shots and made it impossible to gauge their distance, but it was clear they came in bursts, as if a small group of horsemen fired together, then rode on to attack from another position. After the third such volley, the entire French camp was alive with men shouting orders.

Manette jumped to her feet and ran outside with Alexandra right on her heels.

''What's happening, Lieutenant?'' She had to shout to be heard. ''Have the Russians attacked again?''

''Just another of their Cossack raiding parties, nothing

more," Lascaux replied, steadying his horse. "They've killed a sentry and a few civilians, but now they've disappeared again, and I doubt they'll be back."

He wheeled the stallion around and cantered off to check on the rest of those in his command, leaving to Dr. Vaniche the task of calming the women's fears. The surgeon appeared a moment later, an apparition materializing from the storm. Snow covered him, and a coating of ice had formed on his beard.

"Go on back to sleep," he growled. "There is nothing we can do now." He tossed a large bundle at Alexandra. "Guard these with your life."

Before she had a chance to figure out what he had given her or to thank him for it, the doctor was gone, disappearing once again into the mist of the snow.

Wrapped inside a long, heavy coat were two pair of warm gloves. Alexandra shrugged off the worn and inconvenient blanket that had served her as a shawl for the past weeks and slipped her arms into the coat sleeves.

"He stole that from the body of the sentry the Russians killed," Manette said. "But where a sentry found those gloves I will never know."

"Let us not question a gift from Providence," Alexandra remarked as she pushed her frozen fingers into the warmth. "I don't care where he got them. Come on, let's go back and get some sleep, or we'll never make it through tomorrow."

They had just settled down in their shelter when Lascaux called to them.

"Is something wrong, Lieutenant?" Manette asked, poking her head outside.

"Nothing that a hot meal, a roaring fire, and three weeks' rest wouldn't cure. We'll be marching as soon as it is light, and sunrise is only three hours away."

"Then perhaps you ought to get some sleep yourself," Manette suggested.

"I shall certainly try."

When he had gone, Alexandra muttered a quiet curse under her breath.

"What was that for?" Manette asked.

"I had hoped for news of Albert St. Croix. I asked Lascaux about him several days ago, but he didn't know him or even of him. He said he would do his best to find out if Albert is alive."

In the last few minutes before falling asleep, Alexandra wondered if Lascaux had told her the truth, and the thought that he might have lied to her gnawed at her brain. Was Albert dead? Or worse, was he among the pitiful wretches who had no hope of life yet had not received the blessing of death? Lascaux no doubt believed that St. Croix had been her lover, and if he knew the truth to be unpleasant, perhaps he had lied only to save her further pain.

She understood then why her little kindnesses to the dying meant so much. She gave hope, not to those who would die, for they knew their fate and accepted it, but to those who would live and who therefore needed it most. Helping a blinded corporal lift a cup of coffee to his lips displayed a tenderness in the face of so much brutality and gave them the desire to continue life.

She had barely dropped off to sleep when distant shouting broke the stillness. There had been no gunshots, just the sound of men's angry voices.

"Probably someone drunk and protesting his orders," Manette mumbled. "Lascaux will quiet them down."

But the shouting continued, and Alexandra could not sleep. Whatever caused this disturbance was more than a soldier complaining about his orders. As she was about to get up and investigate the commotion, she heard the single gunshot that confirmed her suspicions.

"It's another raid," she whispered urgently to Manette. "And by the sound, they've struck very close this time."

In a moment they had both stepped into the frosty darkness, awake and nervous. Lascaux and another officer galloped past, and more out of curiosity than anything else, the two women turned in the same direction to follow them.

The sergeant had built a fire, a large one, and in the

bright light they could see him clearly, a man of perhaps thirty-five years, his head wrapped in a blood-stained bandage. The tattered uniform no longer fit him; it hung in rags on his emaciated frame, for it had been made to fit a man fifty pounds heavier, the man he had been when he left Paris six months ago. But it was his face that caught their attention, the face of a cornered, defeated animal making one last stand against destruction. He spoke with an inhuman snarl.

"Get away from me, all of you! No one is going to make me walk out there and chase those murdering bastards in the dark and the snow." He fired his pistol into the air to enforce his threat to kill anyone who came near him. "That goes for you, too, Lascaux. I've had my fill of this war, and I've had my fill of running like a scared rat. I'll stand and fight them, but I won't go after something I can't see in a country I don't know."

Alexandra inched her way through the crowd that had gathered to watch this gruesome diversion until she stood near the officer who had ridden past her with Lascaux earlier. The lieutenant was nearby, trying to reason with the sergeant. If he could persuade the man to give up his weapons and do no one any harm, they could all go back to sleep and get some rest before the next day's march began. Worried that he would fail to disarm the man and instead become his target, Alexandra wanted to be as close as possible to Lascaux in the event he was wounded.

The sergeant fired into the air again and continued his tirade, ignoring the lieutenant's pleas and promises of pardon. He cursed Napoleon who had sent him here, cursed Russia and all its horrors, cursed the officers who insisted on the folly of retreat.

"Damn you all to eternal hell! May you burn forever as payment for making us freeze to death in this wasteland!" he screamed.

Then an explosion ripped through Alexandra's brain. She watched as the sergeant gasped, and crumpled like an abandoned marionette, shot by the officer who sat so calmly on his horse beside her.

"He became boring," the colonel explained, more to himself than anyone else. "I have more important things to do tonight than listen to a fool's rantings."

She looked up to see what monster could do so horrible a deed and for so vile a reason, and found herself staring into the face of Augustin Trabert.

Recognition flared in his eyes a second later. He lunged at her, but his horse, already startled by the pistol shot, danced nervously and she dodged his grasp. Panic drove her through the crowd and away from the circle of light around the fire. She ran blindly, not caring or seeing where she ran so long as it was away from Trabert. His terrified mount danced and refused to calm down, and she knew she had to get far away before he finally controlled the animal and pursued her. Only the darkness afforded her safety, for she knew she could not outrun his horse.

Every step was agony. Knee-deep at best, the snow had drifted until it oftentimes reached her waist, making escape impossible. She heard hooves pounding behind her and turned defiantly to face the inevitable.

The horse stumbled and fell, pitching its rider to the ground a few feet away.

"I couldn't warn you before," Lascaux whispered as he dusted the snow from his uniform.

"Are you all right?"

"Oh, yes, I'm fine. Can't get hurt falling in this stuff." The stallion, too, had got to its feet, no more injured than the young lieutenant. He patted its red neck. "I don't have time to explain it all, but Trabert found out just hours ago that you were here. I didn't know he had been looking for you since we left Moscow. If I had known—but I didn't, and there is no time now. There is a Russian camp three miles or so from here, straight ahead, and from what St. Croix tells me, you should find shelter with them."

"Then Albert is alive!"

"Alive and well. He's the one who told me about Trabert. Now go, before the colonel finds you. Once over this hill, you'll see their fires." He mounted the red

212

stallion and turned back to his own camp. "Adieu, Snowbird!"

Before she had time to give him a message for Manette, he had charged off in another direction to draw the colonel away from her.

Chapter 21

MIKHAIL PACED furiously, his heavy-heeled boots threatening to splinter the polished wood with each step. In the doorway stood Vasili, his arms folded across his chest, immoveable.

"She has no right!" Mikhail thundered.

The servant merely shrugged and refused to comment. He had been standing, silent and determined, for nearly an hour while his master strode back and forth or sat sullenly in a chair by the fire. This was an unusually long fit of temper; Mischa generally vented his anger for a few minutes and then either got over the problem or quietly brooded. An hour of almost continuous fury was completely unlike him.

Yet Vasili admitted it was better to see a display of anger than nothing, for Mikhail had done plenty of that these last few weeks. He insisted he had come to the country house to recover from the ordeal in Moscow in the peace and quiet of winter's isolation. He did not like his plans overturned.

"I am not in the mood for one of my mother's entertainments."

"Then you had better get into the mood, because you are going if I have to make Vasili drag you down the stairs," his grandmother called from the other side of the door. "Let me in, Mischa. I want to talk to you."

Anna Petrovna stepped regally into the room and held the door open until Vasili took her hint and left her alone with her grandson. At seventy years of age, she was still a beautiful woman, though Mikhail did not in the least resemble her. She was tiny and fair and seemed always to be dancing, as indeed she had been half a century ago when she was Annette Louise Naronne, dancing and music teacher to the children of Count Ivan Andreivitch Ogrinov.

"Sit down, Grandmere. If I have no choice but to listen to your lecture, let us have it over and done with quickly."

She took the proffered chair and waited patiently, her hands folded demurely in her lap, while he brought another chair from his desk and sat in front of her. She stared into his eyes, tried to fathom the cold blue depths. A smile spread across her face.

"You can't intimidate *me*!" Mikhail snorted. "You've kept my uncles and cousins wrapped around your finger for years with that all-knowing expression, but I for one have outgrown it."

"I know, Mischa. That's why I smiled." She looked around the spartanly furnished room, noted with pleasure that the years in Paris had not softened his tastes and that he still seemed to belong to this strong, simple room with its chairs and desk and bed of unembellished oak. He was more like his father than she had realized. "Have you nothing to drink in this lair of yours? I could use a drop or two of vodka."

While he found the bottle and glasses, she said, "Your mother is worried to death about you. She has it in her mind that you need to get your mind off all your troubles, whatever they are, and she is merely trying to do that with a party, a houseful of guests all talking about their own trivial troubles."

"I have told her a dozen times, in no uncertain terms, that I wish to be alone, to rest and not be bothered by anyone. It's enough to be constantly nursed like an invalid by an uncle, two aunts, and a flock of bird-brained mother-hen cousins. Must I also put up with forty or fifty of her friends?"

"Mischa, she doesn't know what else to do. Frankly,

215

neither do I.''

"Good. Then do nothing, and I shall be quite satisfied.''

"We have done nothing for over two weeks, and there's been no change. You refuse to eat with the family, you mope around in this dismal room or ride around the countryside by yourself. There are times, Mikhail Pavlovitch, when I wonder if we will not find you someday in the stable, hanging from a rafter or with your brains blown out.''

There was concern in her voice and also in his when he asked, "Do you think I am so despondent I would take my own life?''

"We don't know what to think any more. Right now your mother is in the parlor with your Uncle Dmitri, crying her eyes out because she thinks she is the cause of all this. When you rode out of here this morning I spent an hour calming her down. She thought you were running away again.''

He lifted his gaze to the ceiling and his hands in mock supplication.

"I spent the last four months running from Napoleon only to find him ahead of me. I am tired of running, tired of just about everything. I want to be left alone. I do not feel up to playing the role of hero to a crowd of her friends.''

"I should think by now Napoleon would have ceased to be a problem. He's left Moscow, and he'll have a hard time getting anyone to follow him here again after the time he's having getting them all out of Russia.''

"Good! Since he escaped roasting in the hell he created when he burned Moscow, perhaps he'll freeze to death in Mother Russia's wintry embrace.''

Such fierce vindictiveness did not suit him, but it was not the first time Anna had seen him like this. He had been severely wounded in the Russian defeat at Friedland and had not come back with such hate festering inside him, so it was not the war that caused his curses. A different kind of wound caused the pain he was fighting,

216

and only once before had she seen him suffer this way. She would never forget it.

"Did you leave her in Paris?"

"No, she came with me to—"

He realized too late how easily she had trapped him into that confession.

"I know, Mikhail, what it is to live when another has died. When you feel you wish to talk about it, I will listen." She rose to leave, told him not to get up. "Finish your vodka and let Vasili get you ready for your mother's party. Do it not for her, but for yourself. If you don't go, everyone will pester you to death, wanting to know what is wrong and what they can do to help. Put in a fifteen minute appearance and they will think you well on the road to recovery and no longer in need of their unwanted attention."

The drawing room was half-full when, two hours later, Mikhail entered and greeted his mother with a perfunctory kiss.

As though he were a total stranger, she introduced him to her guests. He politely ignored the fact that he had known most of them all of his life. Everyone asked after his health and exclaimed over what they had been told was his miraculous escape from the French. Rather than set them to rights with a long and tedious explanation, he left them believing the tale, most likely concocted by his mother or uncles or all three of them together. If they were happier thinking him a hero, so be it.

One of the few people he had an active desire to avoid was his cousin, Ivan Dmitrievitch. Of course, it happened that Ivan had an equally active desire for just the opposite. Mikhail saw Ivan glance his way with a conspiratorial smile and knew that nothing had changed between them. He resolved that no such meeting would take place. Persistence, however, was one of Ivan's few strong points.

There was only one other guest Mikhail made an effort not to speak with. Unlike Ivan, Baron Andrei Tchernikov seemed almost as determined that they not encounter each other. He spent a good part of the evening with Anna Petrovna engaged in apparently very serious conversation. And that was very unlike Anna Petrovna.

Mikhail drifted through the crowded rooms for nearly an hour, certainly long enough to satisfy everyone's curiosity, when the butler announced supper was laid in the dining room. It seemed an excellent time to depart, but as Mikhail made his way back to the drawing room to bid his mother good night, the light touch of a woman's hand on his arm stopped him.

He fought back a flood of unwanted images and turned to find Ivan's wife Rosanna standing behind him.

"Good evening, cousin," she whispered.

She was a pretty woman, tall and rather pale, with a low husky voice that fit well her seductive blue eyes.

"Good evening, Rosanna."

"You are much recovered from your ordeal."

"Yes, quite."

She had walked around him to stand directly in the path of his retreat.

"It must have been terrible," she exclaimed in that sensuous voice. "Ivan and I had already left Moscow, but he returned the moment he heard about the order to evacuate. He stayed right until the last minute."

"I'm sure he was very heroic." It was impossible to keep the sarcasm at bay. "I'm sorry, Rosanna, but I'm afraid tonight's excitement has left me rather more tired than usual."

He hoped the excuse would suffice, but she did not release the arm she had twined hers through.

"Surely you won't leave without supper. Please, Mischa, join us for a bite to eat before you leave. I know Ivan wants to talk to you."

He had hesitated too long and been caught. Forcing a smile, he let himself be led back into the dining room, where Ivan waited.

"You know my sister-in-law Irina, don't you, Mischa?" Ivan greeted.

"Yes, Madame Drubetskaya and I have met."

He took Irina's hand in his and kissed it politely.

"How good it is to see you again, Mischa. It has been a very long time."

Irina Leevna, widow of the late Colonel Anton Ilarionovitch Drubetsky, was a much more beautiful woman than her older sister Rosanna, but Mikhail found little to attract him. Her pale golden hair was piled high to display her long and slender neck; her simple blue dress, which matched the summer sky color of her eyes, revealed far more than it concealed of her bosom. By any standards she was a desirable woman. Why then did he feel almost repelled by the hint of seduction in her smile?

He knew he was trapped, doomed to spend the rest of a tedious evening in the company of a beautiful young widow with hunger in her eyes.

The same snow Mikhail had earlier fervently prayed for as an obstacle to Napoleon's retreat he now silently cursed. It had been falling since early afternoon, but sometime during the party it had blown up to blizzard proportions. Most of the guests left in plenty of time to be home safely before travel became hazardous, but Ivan and Rosanna, as both near neighbors and family, stayed much later. It was well past one o'clock in the morning when they finally decided to leave. By then, of course, the snow prevented their departure and they were obliged to spend the night, as was Irina, who had come with them. Behind the facade of a weary but genial host, Mikhail seethed. After seeing them all to their beds with wishes for pleasant dreams, he found a full bottle of vodka and took it to his room.

Vasili had accurately predicted his master's needs. The bed was turned down, the fire roared on the hearth, and a full bottle of vodka sat on the table beside the bed. Mikhail smiled and set his own beside it. He stripped off his clothing and slid naked between the sheets. With a wish that his family could show the same consideration for his privacy that his servant did, he poured himself a glass of vodka and drank it down quickly.

He knew what Irina wanted. Like Rosalie de Beaumartin

and a thousand others before her, Irina was a widow with too little income to support her as she wished to be supported. She saw in Mikhail more than just a handsome lover; she had other things on her mind than simple seduction.

As he reached for a second glass of vodka, he heard a knock on the door.

"Hello? Are you awake?" a kitten-like voice called softly from the other side. "I need some help."

She held a taper in her hand, and the light flickered when he pulled the door open. Irina yelped at the sight of him with just a dressing gown thrown around him; she had apparently expected someone else.

"I'm so sorry to disturb you, Mikhail. I thought this was Rosanna's room."

"What was it you need help with?"

He did not care to acknowledge her lie by confronting her with it.

"The window in my room is stuck open."

He looked at her quizzically but followed her down the dark hallway, tying the sash on his robe as he walked.

"The maid opened it to clear out the smoke." He detected sincerity in that statement. "I told her I'd close it before I went to sleep, as I wished to sit up and read for a while first. Now I can't get it closed."

He began to trust her a little more when he stepped into the icy, drafty room. The chimney was drawing poorly and had no doubt spewed smoke into the room before the fire had kindled. On the comforter lay the open book, an English novel translated into French. And the window was indeed stuck. Mikhail put all his weight on it before it slid with a crash to the sill. He remained wary, however.

"You'll catch pneumonia standing around like that. Get into bed while I find more wood for that fire," he ordered.

He brought an armload of wood from his own room and on the way thought how convenient it was to have her put up here, isolated from the rest of the family in a wing of the house seldom used. And everyone knew the chimney in that room had never worked properly. The more he thought about it, the stranger the situation became. Why had the maid left no supply of fuel for the fitful blaze, especially since there was no bell to summon a servant? Mikhail smelled a rat but had no idea which of his scheming relatives the rodent was.

Irina had picked up her book and lay propped against the pillows when he returned. He felt like a damned lackey dumping the logs into the box beside the hearth and then poking at the embers. Adding another log or two, he was satisfied the fire would last until morning, then got to his feet and walked to the door.

"Mikhail?" A softly purred plea.

He kept walking. He had been toyed with enough for one night.

"Mikhail, please?"

At the begging note in the feline voice he turned. Irina pulled back the quilts, inviting him to join her. In the light of the candle he could see the long line of her leg pale ivory against the snowy linen.

He did not want her, did not even feel a need for her. Never in his life had he approached a woman with less desire than he felt for this cold seductress. He dropped his dressing gown to the floor and lay beside her, waiting.

"Do you really find me that unattractive?" she asked.

"On, the contrary, madame. You are an extremely beautiful woman."

She laughed in the same cat-like voice.

"What I meant was are you not attracted to me?"

"I repeat what I told you earlier. I am very, very tired. If I did not leap into your bed the minute I entered your room, that is why."

Whether she believed him or not did not matter. He *was* tired, too tired to fight or argue any more. Her cool, almost cold hand rested lightly on his thigh under the blankets. She began to purr again.

"So, you are attracted to me after all!"

He said nothing, for her fingers had crept to his groin and found the answer to her question.

He could not deny that she aroused him, physically at least. But where was the joy, the passionate celebration? Their union was as cold as the snow falling past the window. Even her body, as it covered his and took him inside her, was cool, lacking warmth or fire of any kind. He lay still beneath her and let her bring his desires to fulfillment as she wished, for he did not care at all. He had never known a woman like her, one who could arouse and satisfy a man without any feeling at all. Even a whore of the lowest sort showed something.

She moved away from him the moment it was over, but as she did, he grabbed her wrist, feeling for the pulse. It beat steadily, calmly, as though she had done no more than say good night to him.

"What are you doing?" she asked when he left the bed and slipped his arms into the sleeves of his robe. He did not bother to tie it this time. "Perhaps tomorrow night, when you are not so tired, we can—"

"By tomorrow night, madame, I expect to be far more tired than I am now and to have put as much distance between myself and this house—and you—as possible."

She tried to catch him before he was out the door, but he was gone too quickly.

Vasili answered the bell instantly, expecting to find Mikhail shouting for more vodka or needing assistance into bed. He was quite surprised to see his master not only sober but dressed and preparing to travel.

"It is three o'clock in the morning. Where do you think you are going in this storm?"

"I am well aware of the time and the weather, and despite both, I intend to be out of this house within the hour."

"Then I shall see to the horses immediately."

"Only one, Vasili. I'm going alone this time."

The serf look at him and said evenly, "Then I will follow. Do you think I don't know where you're going and why?"

Rather than waste more time arguing, Mikhail accepted

222

Vasili's companionship, and as the servant left to saddle their mounts, he added, "I'll want to see my grandmother before we leave. Tell her maid I'll wait in the study."

He shoved his feet into tall, fur-lined boots and pulled the tops over his thighs. Cursing the vanity that had made him shave his beard for the party, he turned up the collar of his coat. With gloves and lambskin hat in hand, he took the taper from the mantel and left the room to darkness.

The study was cold, but there was no reason to light a fire for so short a time. It would not even warm the room before he said what he had come to say. When Anna Petrovna arrived just a few minutes later, he wrapped a turkish blanket around her and asked her to sit beside him.

"So you are leaving us after all," she said with a mysterious hint of a smile. "I am not surprised."

"I have to, Grandmere. I can't stand it here any longer."

"You almost fooled me, Mischa. You have been away so long I became used to your cousins and forgot how different from them you are. You are like your father, and I sometimes think there is even more of him than half in your blood. He never mourned for the dead, only for the living, and that is what you are doing now."

She waited a moment to see if she had aroused any anger. When he made no reply or seemed to ignore what she had said, she went on.

"I should have known she was not dead. Have you any hope of finding her?"

"None," he admitted. "But it doesn't matter. I just have to get out of here and try."

"Of course it matters. Hope matters most when it is the only thing you have."

He knew there were unshed tears in her voice, and she was not a woman who wept often or easily. She understood what he could not put into words.

"In the morning you'll have to tell my mother something. Tell her whatever you think she'll believe. No one would ever believe the truth."

"Oh no?" Anna countered with a wink. "You go and find your precious Snowbird and leave your mother to me."

"Tchernikov told you," he snapped at the mention of the affectionate soubriquet.

She shrugged under the blanket.

"Andrei told me what he knew, though it was little enough. Now, forget him, and forget us, and most of all forget that icy slut Irina. If I hadn't known you well enough to guess your reaction to that bitch I would never have allowed your mother to go through with such a ridiculous scheme. And if you had fallen for her, I'd have disinherited you. That's all she's after, you know."

"I know. Don't worry, I'm not going to let her trap me."

So he had been right; his own mother had put Irina up to seducing him.

"Thank heavens you got your brains from your father and not from my daughter! Well, I hear Vasili outside with the horses." She kissed his cheek as he rose to depart. "When you find her—no, Mischa, there must be no *if*—let her forgive you whatever sins you have committed against her. She is the only one who can exorcise the demon of guilt that possesses your soul."

She walked with him to the door, held it open as he stepped out into the frigid night. He turned to salute her, then blew her a lover's kiss in farewell. Oblivious to the wind that whipped her nightgown against her legs and swirled the snow into the vestibule, Anna Petrovna watched horses and riders disppear like shadows into the icy murk of the storm.

Chapter 22

IT TOOK nearly what little remained of the night for Alexandra to climb the low rise, and by the time she reached the summit, her legs trembled with exhaustion and cold. The wind cut through her clothing, even the heavy coat stolen from the dead sentry. But in the distance she could see, just as Lascaux had told her, the glimmering fires of the Russian camp.

As the sky paled with the sunrise, the flickering lights grew less and less distinct, harder to see against the background of whitening snow. Without their light to guide her, Alexandra was forced to steer a straight path by glancing back at the trail she had left behind her. Every time she turned, she expected to see Trabert riding her down. The horizon remained empty and grey in the twilight, and the silence was broken only by the call of a wolf.

The animal howled incessantly, like the wind above her. She did not fear him. The cold, the hunger, the living death she had already endured were far more terrifying than any animal.

Again and again, plowing her way frantically through the snow, she fell. The land sloped downward again, until she found herself at the bottom of a shallow valley. Another hill lay ahead of her, and just beyond its crest waited the warm fires of the Russian army. Too tired to go any further without a rest, Alexandra dug a space through the snow and sat down to contemplate the distance that remained.

The hill seemed like a mountain, cold and forbidding. To climb it would require all her strength, all her determination. She closed her eyes against the dizzying glare of the sun for a moment to collect her thoughts and concentrate on the task ahead of her. A minute's rest was all she needed before starting that last climb to salvation.

When she opened her eyes again, clouds had gathered in the western sky to turn the sun pale silver behind them. She had slept, warmed by its rays in the sheltered hollow, most of the day.

"It's a wonder you woke up at all," she told herself aloud.

The words echoed in the stillness eerily. Nothing moved at all, except the sun in its inexorable descent. At least a mile of uphill agony lay ahead of her, and in the rapidly failing light it would be impossible to keep from getting lost.

"Please, dear God, remind Lascaux to tell Manette where I am. She will worry so," she prayed as she took the first step from her resting place.

It seemed to help a little to talk aloud, to divert some of her thoughts away from the pain in her toes and fingers. Her arms had grown cramped, bent to fit her hands into the opposite sleeves; she let them hang even though it meant exposing her fingers to the cold. She remembered the gloves the doctor had given her, but somewhere she had lost them, perhaps while running, or later, while she slept. She missed them desperately now. When the stiffness in her arms eased a little, she fumbled with the pockets of the coat and slipped her hands into them, though she knew the gloves would have been warmer.

She encountered a lump in one of the pockets, a lump bigger than her fist and so hard that she took it to be a rock. What she found upon pulling it out was a small cheese, frozen solid, but clean and fresh looking. How the unfortunate sentry had come by such a treasure she could not guess, only thanked Providence that he had not eaten it. Other pockets yielded more to her searching fingers: three slices of bread and a dozen wedges of dried apple emerged from one, which she knew were the remains of yesterday's rations, and several strips of dried meat, too hard to chew under the best circumstances, lay in the bottom of another. The bread she was able to break into bite-sized chunks that thawed slowly in her mouth. The cheese and apple slices she had to transfer to an inner pocket where the slight heat of her body could warm them soft enough to chew. She left the meat where she found it and wondered how she could ever make use of it.

Her appetite was hardly satisfied, but at least she had something to quiet the most urgent rumblings in her belly. She promised herself she would eat the cheese when she reached the halfway point on the hill.

Just short of that mark, she stumbled and sprawled face down in the snow. Scrambling to her feet, she angrily clawed her way through the enormous wall of snow, but by the time she reached the end of it and emerged into the relatively clear space on the other side, she was sweating with the exertion. And the sun was almost gone.

It hovered like a candle in the fog just above the horizon. Already clouds darkened more than half the sky, and Alexandra dreaded the snow they carried. Time was her greatest enemy, however. She had to reach the top of the hill and be able to see the Russian fires before night fell completely or she would lose her way.

She ate the cheese as she counted her steps. After each ten steps, she took a bite, chewed it slowly while she progressed another ten. Gauging by the distance she had covered since fighting clear of the shoulder-high drift, she estimated the summit as still an hour away at best. She would reach it shortly after dark.

As the sun dropped, so did the temperature. And the wind had come up again. Tears of panic and frustration dropped from her cheeks to fall and freeze on the collar of her coat. Her feet were too numb to feel anything at all, but her hands, even tucked once more into the protection of her sleeves, screamed with pain.

"Holy Mother of God, let me die!" she begged with a quiet sob as she fell into another drift. "I can't stand it any more. It hurts; oh God! how it hurts!"

She got up and fell again, driven by some deeper force than she had known she possessed. She crawled through the snow on her knees, tunneling like a mole, blindly guided only by the fact that she continued uphill. Utterly exhausted and shaking with the cold, she broke free at last. Kneeling in the snow, she could see that but thirty or forty feet further awaited the crest, her goal, but the effort was beyond her. In the fading glow of the sun, she saw the first flakes of new snow flutter daintily down from the sky.

Death was easy to accept now. Life and its torture became too great a burden to bear any longer. Unable to control the tears, Alexandra collapsed in the snow and spent the last morsel of her strength crying and listening to the fragile wail of the wolf. High and long he cried, as if calling to his mate or merely voicing some canine misery. When he heard the answering call, joy crept in and the lament became a song.

She could see nothing, not the hand she held in front of her face or the ground at her feet. Through pitch black night and blinding snow, she crawled like an animal, her mind forcing her body onward despite all protest. She had seen her goal and would not surrender so close to it.

She searched in her pocket for something to eat; there was only the unchewable meat. She had eaten the last slice of apple long ago, years ago it seemed. For a moment, hunger took control of her, driving her mad with the pain and frustration. Not even the thought of food waiting for her on the other side of the hill could calm the madness.

When had she last eaten a decent meal? She could no longer remember. Frantic visions of roast lamb and duckling and new potatoes and steaming cauldrons of stew danced before her tear-blurred eyes. Only a blast of snow-laden wind, hitting her full in the face, cleared her mind and brought back reality.

She had reached the top of the hill.

On the other side of the ridge, the ground had been

swept almost clear by the unrelenting wind. The way down, directly into the Russian camp, was covered with no more than an inch or two of crisp snow. It was a blessing this open road, though she saw no welcoming fires. The blizzard had become so thick she could see nothing, but she knew she would see the blaze once she came closer. Cautiously, for the hard packed layer was icy, she started downhill.

She walked and then ran until she could go no further, until each breath of air that she dragged into her lungs froze her on the inside as she was frozen on the outside. Peering through the storm she searched for a light, for the glow of a fire, but all was darkness around her. Darkness and the unbroken loneliness of a tomb.

Not even the wolf called to lift her wretched spirits.

She sat unmindful of the cold on the hard ground while the snow fell and covered her with its shroud. A misty luminescence pierced the night as the moon rose behind the thick veil of clouds, and by its spectral light she saw that she had not misjudged her course. The remains of campfires dotted the open plain, black circles of ash slowly being obliterated by the snow. Last night they had been her glowing beacons, and she had come to them unerringly, only to find the final disappointment waiting for her.

The Russians had deserted their camp hours ago.

Chapter 23

THE SOLDIER had died in his sleep, possibly of starvation, more likely of exposure to the harsh weather. Vasili left the corpse where it lay and remounted the grey gelding to ride towards the next group of ragged refugees. Frozen corpses of men and the carcasses of half-devoured horses marked the trail as clearly as signposts. Even the thick blanket of snow could not erase the traces of battle or the debris of retreat. Their horses were fresh and well-fed and considered the knee-deep snow only a minor nuisance.

He had not liked Mikhail's idea from the beginning, but it was impossible to argue. These last few days had brought a savage transformation, made him more stubborn, more possessed than ever with this insane and hopeless search. When the nightly Cossack raids on the French bored him, Mikhail decided to ride ahead, to join the army waiting to annihilate the retreating forces as they approached Smolensk. There, too, he would be in contact with the main body of the French and perhaps have a better chance to hear news of Alexandra. Vasili warned him of the danger, but to no avail.

"You know what will happen if they catch you."

"I do." He was so calm, so brazenly confident.

"Then I will come with you."

"No, not this time. I'll not drag you to hell with me. Besides, if I do not find her, we can work towards each other and search the entire column in half the time."

It made sense, but Vasili did not like it. Mikhail was not

himself any more. His recklessness wanted steadying. His mad raid on the French camp the night before had nearly been his last, though the few sentries had been too cold and hungry to fire their weapons with accuracy. His daring had earned praises from his Cossack companions, and a tongue lashing from his servant.

"I swear, you're as shrewish as my grandmother at times!" he retorted, half drunk on vodka. "Besides, where's the danger? They don't waste men protecting the dead and dying. I saw nothing but wagon after wagon filled with wounded, and I'd lay odds no more than one in ten lives to see France again."

In the morning, when they broke camp and Mikhail was preparing to leave, he seemed more himself. Sobriety had something to do with it, surely, but he looked weary, as though he had spent a sleepless night wrestling the devil within. The blue eyes were clear and serene, though they stared westward and did not look at Vasili.

"When it is over—if it ever is—we will meet in Saint Helena Street, agreed?"

The servant nodded. It had always been the same, but now, as he rode across the snow towards the straggling end of Napoleon's army, he could not help but wonder if anything would ever be the same again.

Heading west at a leisurely canter, he met several groups of stragglers, and always asked for news of Alexandra or even of Jean Guignon, but he learned nothing. Finally, well past midday, he came upon the main body of the French army's wounded. A shivering sentry, his eyes bloodshot from the blinding snow glare, merely glanced at the Russian as he entered their midst.

The squalor in which the alive yet dying existed brought the taste of vomit to his mouth. Filth covered everything, men, animals, weapons, wounds. The crisp clean air reeked with the stink of death and worse. A man in clothes so dirty and tattered they were no longer recognizable as a uniform paused just in front of Vasili's horse to relieve himself. Steam rose from the quickly cooling urine in a malodorous cloud. Mikhail had seen the worst of war and described it, but only now did Vasili believe it.

Despite the fact that he was obviously Russian, no one attempted to halt or harm Vasili as he made his way through the slow-moving throng. The only sounds were the shuffling march of the weary, frozen feet and the moans of the suffering. The remnants of Napoleon's *Grande Armée* were a pitiful sight indeed.

There were too many to question individually, and time did not wait for him. Already the sun had dropped lower in the sky, lengthening the shadows and blinding all who marched toward it. Searching for an officer, Vasili finally spotted a lieutenant riding guard on a supply wagon and turned the gelding in that direction.

He saw a struggle out the corner of his eye and would have ignored it had he not seen one of the combatants was a woman.

She fought with her fists, the only weapons she had, but the man was too strong and only time stood between him and victory. He pushed her out of the way and hoisted himself onto the wagon. There, he grabbed the unconscious body of a young captain and flung it to the ground.

"Stop it!" the woman screamed. "Someone help me, before he kills them all!"

The blood-red stallion jumped at the mere touch of the lieutenant's spurs, but Vasili's grey already raced toward the women and reached her first. The Russian leapt from his mount to the wagon and subdued the marauder with a single blow to the chin. When he turned, instead of the gratitude he expected, he found a pistol aimed at his head. From a distance of five or six feet, the lieutenant could not possibly miss.

"Lascaux, you can't shoot him. He saved my life," the woman said, her hand on the lieutenant's arm.

"He's a Russian, isn't he? For that alone he deserves to die."

"No man deserves death for what he cannot change. He has harmed none of us and he . . ." Her voice trailed off into silence.

"What's wrong, Manette? Are you all right?" Lascaux asked.

"I'm fine," she managed to whisper. "Is it really you, Vasili?"

"It is I, Madame Duquesne. Indeed, it is I."

"And where is Mikhail?"

"I don't know," he said honestly.

Lascaux had heard enough; he turned to Manette with his pistol still cocked.

"Who is this man? And who is Mikhail? If they are spies and you give them aid, you'll force me to shoot you as a traitor, Manette, and I don't want to do that."

"We're looking for Alexandra," Vasili continued, ignoring the lieutenant's interruption.

Manette turned away from him and sought the tender comfort of Lascaux' embrace.

"Alexandra disappeared last night," the French officer told the Russian, speaking as if to a friend. "Trabert found her, and I helped her to escape. Or I thought I did."

"Where did she go?"

"North, towards the campfires I saw last night when we chased after the bastards who attacked us. I thought it was a Russian camp, that she would be safe there. We didn't find out until this morning, when one of our sentries shot their scout, that she never made it."

Sorrow contorted his face, but he did not turn away from Vasili's accusing eyes.

"I went back to look for her, spent all day trying to find where I had left her last night, but I couldn't see anything in the sun, and I had to get back to my men."

"Tell me what you can of the place where you last saw her."

Manette stared at him incredulously.

"You can't go looking for her now, Vasili. It will be dark soon; you won't be able to see her even if you do find her."

"Let me worry about that."

Lascaux thought for a moment. "I can only estimate

that we've come ten miles since last night, at most, and the countryside is so barren there isn't a single landmark in this God-forsaken wilderness. There is only one thing I can think of as a guide of any kind. Alexandra ran when Trabert killed a sergeant of mine. If you can find the sergeant's body, you should be fairly close to where she set out. Trabert shot the man right between the eyes.''

Vasili mounted the gelding and turned him back in the direction from which they had come. He had little hope of outrunning the storm he had seen gathering above the sunset or of finding a particular corpse out of the hundreds littering the way in the rapidly deepening twilight, but if Alexandra were out there and alive, he had not a moment to waste.

Finding the dead sergeant proved far easier than expected, but beyond that point, it was hell. Vasili pushed the grey through one drift after another, some of them coming as high as the animal's chest. It was no wonder Alexandra had never reached the Russian encampment. The snow was far too deep, and the lieutenant's estimate fell two miles or more short of the actual distance.

The setting sun illuminated the snow-covered hills for only a few moments, just long enough for Vasili to make out the long scar on the pristine whiteness. More of the flakes were falling now, and the western sky was veiled behind the storm. The moon he had counted on to light his way would be hidden. Whether he found Alexandra now or not, his own survival rested on reaching the open plain where he and Mikhail and their rowdy Cossack companions had camped a single day ago. This was no ordinary blizzard blowing up, but a rare killer storm.

The gelding followed Alexandra's winding course through the worst of the drifts, and as his hooves cracked through the icy coating on the lower layers of snow, Vasili understood the secret to her success. The ice had supported her weight while the horses and men had broken through it and been unable to go on. The jagged edges of the broken crust and the two feet of snow beneath kept him back.

He felt pain in the horse and knew without seeing the blood stained the snow. Not even bitter cold could numb the lacerations on the gelding's forelegs, but he plunged forward, climbing the hill one painful step at a time.

Nothing could have prepared them for the shock waiting at the crest. The same wind that swept the snow away as cleanly as a broom knifed through man and beast alike. Even with plenty of dry kindling, no fire was possible now. It drove the snow like a thousand needles into Vasili's hands when he took off his gloves to check the horse's injuries. The cuts might leave scars, but otherwise the animal was unhurt.

Why then did he tremble and snort as Vasili urged him forward again? He heard no wolf call or any other sound above the howling of the wind. The animal tossed his head up and down, whinnied a plaintive note, then refused to move.

At first Vasili thought it was just another corpse, frozen by the storm. He stepped down from the saddle and walked cautiously to the snow-covered lump a yard or two in front of them. When he pushed it, it whimpered, and he knew the voice.

Pale orange in the winter blaze, the full moon scowled above the mountain peaks like an angry old man. Vasili let the gelding pick his own way through the snow as he plodded up one hill and down another, always drawing nearer to the forbidding mass of the mountains. Silent and still, but at least alive, Alexandra sat bundled in a heavy quilt in front of Vasili on the saddle.

She had been barely conscious when he carried her from the wind-swept plain to the sheltered side of the hill. There they had huddled for two days around a small fire that warmed them and provided enough heat to brew tea and fix a tasteless but filling broth made from the tough strips of dried beef in Alexandra's pockets boiled in melted snow. At first her hands were so numb she could not hold the bowl to drink, but when he held it to her lips she drank greedily. With wordless smiles she expressed her gratitude.

The storm subsided late on the second day, and after a long night's sleep they set out at dawn. She said nothing when he explained that Moscow was too far back to go and that only two days' travel would bring them to a Cossack village. Without a word of protest or complaint she allowed him to lift her onto the horse and then he mounted behind her. A weak November sun rose slowly, though they did not see it, for they rode westward, toward the sullen face of the setting moon and the mountains.

Alexandra's silence continued through the day. Several attempts at conversation failed. She answered Vasili's questions with a nod or a shake of her head, or she ignored him and retreated into her shell. Finding solace in the knowledge that she was alive and slowly regaining her strength, he ceased his questions. Instead, to lessen the monotony of their icy, lonely trek, he painted fabulous pictures of the village, the mountains, the rivers that in spring would rush jubilantly from the high snows to the lush meadows. When he thought she had fallen asleep and no longer listened to him, he was pleasantly surprised to have her turn her head and signal that she wished to hear more.

He found a shepherd's hut, abandoned until the grass returned, and though the dwelling was empty, it gave them shelter from the howling wind. Encased in an impregnable coating of ice and snow, the stack of firewood piled outside the door taunted them. After telling Alexandra to wait inside, out of the elements, Vasili tramped off to find fuel for their fire.

The trees near the hut were too large to fell with his small axe, but the lower branches snapped off easily when he swung the razor-sharp blade. In just a few minutes he had a substantial heap of limbs and smaller branches that, though awkward to carry, would kindle quicker than a large log and still make a fine blaze.

When he returned to the hut, dragging the bundle of wood through the snow, Alexandra stood exactly where he had left her. She had unsaddled the horse and left him to paw the snow in search of feed, and she had put the saddle and other gear beside the door, but she had not gone inside.

"Why are you standing here in the cold?" Vasili asked, almost angry at her. "Have you completely lost your wits? Your lips are already turning blue."

He lifted the latch and kicked the door open for her, but she would not enter.

"It's dark, Vasili," she whispered, barely audible above the wind. "It's so dark."

He had forgotten her fear. Taking her hand in his he led her into the stone building and waited until her eyes became accustomed to the dark. Some light came through the south-facing door, enough to cast their shadows on the earthen floor. Alexandra squeezed his hand tightly as she looked around and let go only when he told her he had to bring in the wood.

Using the last of his dry kindling, Vasili started a fire on the open hearth in the center of the small shelter. Twigs crackled and smoked, then flared and burned brightly until a bed of coals glowed red in the dark. Careful not to force the fire, he continued to add progressively larger pieces until at last the entire room was lit with the flickering tongues of flame. By then Alexandra had unpacked the cooking utensils and sad little bundle of supplies. All that remained was a bit of tea, half a small loaf of dark bread, and a single strip of dried beef.

Vasili looked at it and immediately got to his feet.

Fix some tea while I'm gone and keep the fire hot. I'll be back before the sun goes down."

There was no window from which to watch the sunset, but when Vasili came back through the door with the carcess of a roebuck slung over his shoulder, Alexandra saw that the sky was still grey, not black. He had kept his promise.

He dropped the carcass to the floor and began to skin

and butcher it. Alexandra handed him a cup of weak tea and then, much to his surprise, knelt beside him to help.

"I wasn't always pampered," she told him. "You've waited on me enough; it's time I started to help."

The meat sizzled and smoked and filled the air with a delicious aroma while it cooked, laid on flat stones set in the center of the coals. Impatient and famished, Alexandra poked at the venison with the end of Vasili's knife, turning each slab over until it was cooked on both sides.

"I was just thinking how much better this would taste with some potatoes roasted in their jackets and a bottle or two of fine burgundy," she mused, "but as beggars can't be choosers, I shall be satisfied with what we have." Then, the lighteness disappearing from her voice, she asked, "What's wrong, Vasili? Why are you staring at me so strangely?"

He blinked, then realized he had been gazing at her rather fixedly for some time, and he apologized at once.

"I have missed the sound of your voice, Snowbird."

There was such tenderness and concern in his words that she looked away from him, embarrassed by the emotion he did not try to hide.

"Let us eat first and afterward we can talk, if you feel like it," he suggested.

The weeks of near starvation had shrunken her stomach, and after only two small pieces of venison, Alexandra announced she could not eat another bit. Vasili, on the other hand, devoured a good portion of the buck, smiling almost sheepishly at his appetite. When he had finished, he placed the remaining joints near enough the fire that they would be cooked thoroughly during the night and provide meat for the next day's journey.

"I'm surprised there is any left," Alexandra commented.

"Not much, I'm afraid, but it should be plenty until we get to the village."

"What about the tea? Is there enough for me to have a bit more?"

"A bit is about all you'll get. I can make more, but then that will be the very last of it."

"Save it for tomorrow. I'll have what's left and that will have to do."

She held her cup while he poured, then made a face at the bitterness. Sugar was as unobtainable a luxury as wine.

He was waiting, she knew. It was in his eyes, in his expectant smile. He wanted to ease the burden of her nightmare, yet she held back the words.

"You are afraid of me," he said as the reality dawned. "Why?"

"I don't know," she lied, but she could not keep the truth from him for long.

"I think I can guess, and it is a very foolish fear."

"Is it?" she asked with sudden anger. "After what I've been through, I wonder that the sight of any man doesn't throw me into hysteria."

"You are too strong for that, Alexandra. When I found you, sitting there in the snow and the wind, you had come as close to giving up as I've ever seen anyone. But you didn't lie down to die; you sat there as if you were just waiting for someone, waiting for me to find you."

He threw more wood on the fire. Sparks flew up towards the ceiling and an ember popped loudly. Alexandra stared at the flames without a change in her expression.

"Manette told me the same thing, but I don't feel strong at all. I was waiting for someone out there, but it wasn't you. It was Death, in whatever form. I had no strength left to fight. I'm sorry that I snapped at you, Vasili. You know you're the last person I'd want to hurt."

"Then do not weep, Snowbird, for your tears hurt me. There is no need to cry, certainly not for me."

His hand trembled as it cupped her chin and tilted her face upwards.

"No tears, Alexandra," he commanded sternly. "I am too much a man to want your pity, especially when it is unnecessary. You think, because you feel the pain of love, that everyone who loves in the same way must hurt the same way. It is not true."

239

"I was right. You *do* love me."

He laughed lightly and kissed the top of her head.

"Must you be afraid of me for it? Look upon me as a friend, someone who will protect you and care for you at any cost. It is hard, I know, for you to understand this now, after what has happened in these last few months, but the time will come."

How much he wanted to take her in his arms, to hold her close and draw all the pent-up sadness from her. He let his hand fall, but she did not turn away as expected. He had only to put his arm around her and she would collapse in his embrace, yet he did not do it. More than her emotional gratitude, his own vulnerability prevented it. In her innocence she did not know, as he did, that what she offered him freely cost far too dear in the coin of the soul.

He could not afford that price.

The trail narrowed as they passed the rolling hills and entered the first mountain pass. Despite the noon sun bright in the southern sky, all around them was shadowed and cold. In the stillness, the steady hoofbeats echoed softly. When Alexandra turned to ask Vasili how much further they had to go, his name reverberated with haunting clarity, and she said no more.

She had slept well, in spite of the aches and pains brought on by constant riding, and now gazed all around her at the grandeur of the mountains. Massive walls of white, with grey outcroppings of rock here and there, they surrounded her with a sense of primeval power, and yet they did not frighten her. She felt enclosed within their fortress, safe and secure.

The road the gelding followed so confidently that he must be familiar with it wound through a dense woodland as it descended into a valley. The fragrance of pine needles and dry leaves mingled with a faint smokiness that grew steadily stronger. Hidden by the evergreen woods, the village could not be far.

A cluster of small, neat cottages, it spread out at the end of the road some distance below them. Though several hours of daylight remained, all was in shadow, for in this valley the sun set very early behind the peaks encircling it. The single broad street, if it could be called such, wandered between the double row of houses, smoke curling a welcome from their chimneys. Behind the houses, less orderly, were cowsheds and barns. It was a scene of peace and tranquility, so different from the tableau of war and death that it brought tears to her eyes.

"This is it?" she asked.

"Yes, this is it. By the time we get down there supper will be started and perhaps I can persuade Katrushka to heat some water for a bath. Would you like that?"

"I certainly would. But who is Katrushka?"

He took a deep breath and let it out with a chuckle.

"First she married my mother's brother, and then when my mother died, Uncle Nikolai took me in, making Katrushka my aunt. But then he died, and she married Dmitri Sergeivitch Tcheradzin. I'm not sure if she is still my aunt, so it is easier just to call her Katrushka, as everyone else does."

He stopped in front of one of the houses, larger than most of the others, and announced that they had arrived. She sat silently while Vasili mounted the stairs to the porch and knocked loudly.

The tall figure silhouetted against the yellow light within stopped her heart for a full beat. Her hopeful smile faded quickly, however, when Vasili and the young man came toward her. With disappointment obvious on her face, she slid off the gelding and into Vasili's waiting arms.

"Who is *he*?" she whispered as he set her on her feet.

"Grigori Dmitrievitch, Katrushka's son and my cousin, of a sort."

What followed was a confused and incomprehensible mixture of introductions, questions, and answers in wildly jumbled French and Russian. Alexandra had the advantage of understanding part of Vasili's explanations; the young Cossack spoke not a world of French.

He led them to the parlor, a small room sparsely

furnished with a few chairs, a desk, and tables for the oil lamps that provided smoky light. Two rugs woven in reds, blues, and bright golds covered the floor, adding color as well as warmth to this austere room.

Feeling uncomfortable in Grigori's presence, Alexandra chose to sit as close to the fireplace as possible, and as far from Vasili and the Cossack. She heard Grigori explain that his mother had gone to visit someone identified as Ipanov's widow and would return shortly. In the meantime, there was vodka, which Grigori poured into two glasses for himself and Vasili. It was as if she were not there at all.

He said something as he served the liquor that brought an angry frown to Vasili's face. His reply, whispered low and rapidly to prevent her understanding, astonished Grigori. He turned to her, stared with no trace of shyness at her, then shrugged as he resumed his conversation.

Finding the strain of translation extremely tiring, Alexandra leaned back in her chair and relaxed every muscle in her body for the first time in days. On the wall directly facing her hung a delicately painted icon of the Blessed Virgin. The prayers of a rosary came to her lips, the invisible beads slipping through her fingers. Each word had meaning it had never had for her before, and the silent litany blotted out the unintelligible sounds of masculine voices in a foreign tongue.

Heralded by her own footfalls on the steps, Katrushka entered the room with all the bluster of a winter storm. She scolded Grigori with a shake of her finger while at the same time kissing Vasili on both cheeks.

She was a strong, sturdy woman of perhaps fifty years, dressed in plain peasant garb of black skirt and white smock. Her reddish hair was for the most part confined behind a headscarf of bright blue, but several stray locks had come loose and she kept pushing them back.

When she had listened carefully to Vasili's mumbled introductions, Ekaterina Tcheradzina walked over to the girl and said, "Yes, she is like a bird, a scrawny little chicken!" Gruff words, but with laughter behind them.

Her dark eyes twinkled as she said, "Come, Alexandra, let us see if we can make a bit of stew from that skinny carcass of yours."

With one large, rough hand she grabbed a lamp and with the other took hold of Alexandra's arm to drag her almost forcibly into a adjoining room. The only furnishings were a narrow bed, a small wardrobe and washstand, and an empty wooden tub, but they made it so crowded that Katrushka almost had to stand in the tub to allow Alexandra room to get in and close the door. Katrushka shouted at her son and at another person she called Tasha to bring water, but Alexandra had eyes only for the bed with its gaily embroidered quilt and fluffy pillow.

Protests got her nothing but a stern shake from Katrushka's long finger. First a bath, she ordered, then a good supper, and finally sleep. After Tasha, the servant girl, had dumped the last kettle of boiling water, she stood by while Alexandra removed the blouse and breeches she had worn since killing Jean Guignon. Katrushka's command that the filthy garments be burned, and not in the house, was readily followed.

The water was barely warm, and it cooled quickly, but Katrushka's insistent scrubbing left no chill. As if she did not trust the girl's ability to bathe herself, Katrushka did the job thoroughly. From earlobes to toetips, Alexandra's skin was rosy pink as a result. She stepped out of the tepid water to be wrapped in a warm, rough towel and gently patted herself dry.

She still wished she could climb into the inviting bed and sleep for at least a month, but politeness kept her from protesting when Katrushka led her, dressed in clothes borrowed from Tasha, back to the parlor.

Strange faces greeted her. The man standing beside Grigori could be no one other than Dmitri Sergeivitch Tcheradzin. The resemblance between father and son was remarkable, down to the same puzzled frown that wrinkled their brows. Dmitri's hair, though dulled with grey, curled exactly like his son's, and no doubt had once glistened with the same bright gold color.

Alexandra's chair by the fire had been taken by a young woman whose instant dislike of the intruder showed plainly in the defiant set of her jaw. Half frightened by such blatant hostility, Alexandra sought the protection of Vasili's smile and walked to his side.

He introduced her first to Dmitri, in slow, precise Russian that she had no trouble following. Telling no lies, but neither revealing all the truth, Vasili explained only that she was a refugee from the French. Not a word about her reason for being in Russia nor her past, nor her relationship with Mikhail. She listened carefully for mention of him, but there was none, as though he had never existed, had never been a part of her life.

Was it the presence of young Grigori that made her think of Mikhail? His eyes, beneath his scowl, never left her, and she was constantly aware of his assessing gaze. She did not like the sensation it created, a nervousness that bordered on fear. It seemed to imprison her mind, so that when she was introduced to his sister, she barely heard the girl's name.

Between the parlor and the enormous kitchen at the back of the house was the dining room. On the long trestle table that dominated, Tasha was laying out plate after plate of food: slices of beef in its own juices, chickens roasted on a spit until their skin was a crackly golden brown, mounds of potatoes, baked apples, sharp cheese, and fresh dark rye bread. Such a feast put the crudely cooked venison of the night before to shame, yet Alexandra, as she took her place between Vasili and Katrushka, almost wished she were still in that little stone hut. Madame Tcheradzina was kind, and there had been some warmth in Dmitri's stern eyes, but Grigori and his sister Valentina made her feel much less than welcome in their home.

244

Chapter 24

VASILI SAVED her the embarrassment of falling asleep at the table. As soon as the conversation around them absorbed everyone's attention, he took her by the hand and led her back to the parlor.

"It is time we talk, Snowbird," he said firmly.

"Can't it wait until morning? I'm so tired."

He hesitated, wondering if what he was about to tell her was the right thing. Had he overestimated her resilience? Was she strong enough to take yet one more blow? He alone could judge that, for no one else had seen her as he had, at the height and at the bottom of despair's deepest pit. There was no alternative.

"No, it can't wait. I'll be gone long before you are awake."

She stared at him with unbelieving eyes.

"Vasili, you can't go away and leave me now. Let me come with you, please."

He remembered another time when she had begged the same favor, but this time, he told himself, was different.

"I can't take you with me, even if I wanted to. You need to stay here and rest and let Katrushka take care of you."

"I don't need to rest. You said yourself I was strong and could survive anything. Please, let me go with you, or at least stay here with me."

"I have to go, and we both know why."

She clung to his arm for a moment as though it might

245

change his mind, but beyond the window the night had grown dark and the thought that somewhere in the frozen void Mikhail waited restored her composure. He needed Vasili much more than she did. She let go his arm.

"God be with you, Vasili," she said, swallowing a lump in her throat.

"Alexandra, I promise you—"

Tears gathered, clouded her eyes, but her voice by sheer force of will remained steady and calm. "That promise is not yours to give. Let it happen as it will, and ask no more."

One by one the glittering droplets slid down her cheeks to fall silently to the floor. Her words gained rather than lost dignity in the face of her tears.

"I will tell him," he assured her. "Now, dry your eyes and get to bed."

He wrapped her tightly in his arms, then carried her to the small room and the bed Katrushka had piled high with extra quilts.

"Don't forget," she reminded him, growing sleepy as the featherbed embraced her with its warmth. "And when you come back for me, bring a horse that doesn't break my back."

There was something else very important she wanted to tell him, but she had already fallen asleep.

He smiled knowing that in the morning she would forget all the pain after a good night's sleep in a warm, cozy bed. He kissed her forehead as though she were a favorite child, but she never felt it. Nor did she hear him bid goodbye to his hosts just moments later. He had indeed meant what he said; he was gone long before she would awaken.

Impenetrable darkness surrounded her. She reached out of her dream for Manette's hand and found nothing. Just as she opened her mouth to call for Lascaux, she remembered that this was not the French camp.

The fire had nearly died. She spent several chilly minutes poking at the embers before the fresh log began

246

to smolder and burn. Her teeth were chattering but she was dying more of thrist than cold. There might be some water in the washstand pitcher. She groped her way in the dark to it, finding to her delight that it was full, and the water refreshed her with its icy sweetness.

Sudden dizziness assailed her, made her lean against the washstand to keep from falling. And the pain in her back grew unbearable. It spread around her hips, clutched at her belly until breathing was impossible. When it had passed, she wiped perspiration from her forehead.

Lying tense beneath the quilts, she waited. Too much food on an empty stomach combined with too much excitement, she decided, was the cause of this discomfort. That and apprehension about her future alone in a house whose members did not all welcome her with open arms.

The second attack paralyzed her just when she had thought it was all over. She could not breathe, could not move, could not make a sound. Sweat dripped into her eyes and burned, the pain unnoticed in the agony that tore at her vitals.

Then it was gone again, but she knew it would return. With a blanket wrapped around her, she padded into the parlor and then toward the kitchen where Tasha slept on a mat by the fire. Tasha could wake Katrushka, who perhaps knew of a way to stop these horrible pains that seemed to be squeezing the very life out of her.

Halfway through the pitch black terror of the dining room, she sank to the floor, unable to go on as yet a third spasm caught her. She fought it, loudly with screams and silently with prayers, but it did not let her go. A light pierced the darkness and she could hear voices around her, but all sensation came to her filtered through the pain. It was everywhere and constant.

She drifted, sometimes aware of the figures clustered around her, but more often lost in a shadowland between reality and oblivion. The pain, too, came and went, but when it came, it was more than she could stand and it pushed her back into unconsciousness.

Someone wiped her face with a cool, damp cloth, just as

she remembered doing to the dying soldiers to ease the fever that would kill them.

She tried to stand to run away from this nightmare, but found strong hands forcing her back against the pillows. Another pain seized her, more excruciating than any other, wringing scream after scream from her until, just before the darkness closed in on her, she knew it was over. It made no difference now that she had forgotten to give Vasili that urgent message for Mikhail. That message had no meaning now. The sudden rush of blood between her thighs told her that everything she had lived for was gone.

Katrushka covered the frail body with the quilt.

"She'll sleep quietly now," she told Tasha. "You'd best get some sleep yourself."

"Let me stay with her, please?"

"All right, but call me if there is any change."

"I promise," Tasha vowed solemnly as she took her place in the chair beside Alexandra's bed.

Tasha never took her eyes off her patient. When Alexandra dreamed and kicked the blankets off, the girl nearly overturned her chair in a rush to replace them. Such a great responsibility was to be treated with the proper respect.

With a rag dipped in cool water, she sponged the sweat from Alexandra's forehead. The skin seemed cooler now, as if the fever had already broken. And she was breathing evenly, without gasping for each gulp of air. The nervous thrashing, too, had stopped, and she slept soundly.

The small narrow window showed grey when Katrushka returned to find Tasha proudly attentive to her duties. She had half expected to find the child asleep, but Tasha smiled and announced that Alexandra had slept quietly all night without making a sound. With a nod of her head signifying her satisfaction, Katrushka closed the door once again.

A plaintive cry from Alexandra drew Tasha's attention. Though she could not understand the words, she felt the plea in that voice.

"Mischa, please come back. Don't leave me alone."

All Tasha's weariness disappeared as she returned to the chair beside the bed. With a broad and tender smile, she whispered in Russian, "I am here, and I won't leave you."

"I was afraid. It's so dark."

She rested again, and for a minute or two seemed to have fallen back to sleep, but when she spoke again, Tasha felt a chill go up her spine at the unmistakable heartbreak in Alexandra's trembling voice.

A dense cloud of blackness enshrouded Alexandra, a fog through which she felt her way as she searched, though she had no idea what her goal was. Somewhere ahead—she sensed rather than saw—there was light, and she heard someone calling to her from it. She called back, and when he answered, assuring her he would not leave her, she felt at peace. She recognized that the words were in his own tongue, and she tried to answer in the same.

"I never meant to hurt you," she apologized. "Will you never believe that I had nothing to do with it? I couldn't say anything to you that night because you were so angry at me and it didn't matter then."

As the tears trickled from her eyes, Tasha wiped them away. She wondered if this were a sign of the fever worsening. Perhaps she should call Katrushka. But when she touched Alexandra's forehead and found it cool and dry, she knew it was not the fever. And Alexandra spoke hesitantly, not deliriously. Her words came slowly at first, making it difficult for Tasha to follow, but she listened carefully.

And she felt a pang of guilt, as though overhearing a confession, for these words were meant for other ears than hers.

"I don't kow how many times since that night I've wanted to die. Without you I didn't want to go on. And when the soldiers came and I killed them, it was so horrible. The blood, the look on his face—" She shuddered and lifted a trembling hand to sweep away the vision. "I had to kill them, I had to. I didn't want to, and I knew what I was doing and what they would do to me,

249

but even though I didn't want to, I still killed them. *I killed them!*"

"It's all right now, it's all right," Tasha whispered. Now she was frightened as well, yet she no longer considered calling for help. Alexandra lay quietly.

Through the rest of the day, Alexandra slept soundly. Tasha, too, dozed. Katrushka brought her some bread and soup late in the afternoon and left an extra bowl by the fire for Alexandra, should she waken hungry. When Katrushka left, Tasha peeked out the door before it closed and saw Grigori standing just a few steps away.

"How is she?" he asked his mother.

"The girl will recover in no time at all, given rest and good food. Go on about your business and don't worry so about her. She isn't yours to worry about."

Tasha would have listened longer had not Alexandra called to her.

"Where is Vasili?" she asked in French.

"Vasili went back to the war," Tasha stammered in Russian, guessing by the sound of the familiar name what the girl had asked. "Are you feeling better? I have some soup if you are hungry. Do you want some tea?"

So it had been a dream after all. Mikhail was not here with her and even Vasili was gone. She remembered now.

The sense of unwelcome returned. There was hostility in this house; Alexandra felt it as certainly as one feels a draft upon opening a window. She wanted to scream, to run away. It was so frustrating to be tied to a body that did not meet one's needs, weak and frail and—. The last she could not face yet. Time enough later when she had rested more and gained back some of her strength. Katrushka came in and tried to persuade her to eat the soup, but she wanted none of it. The tea, hot and strong, satisfied what little hunger she had.

Though she slept nearly all day, Alexandra tired quickly, and soon her eyelids began to droop.

"Madame Tcheradzina, please. I must know what— what is to become of me."

Katrushka looked puzzled, almost hurt, but she

answered with her usual smile, "You are our guest, for as long as you wish to stay with us. This is your home and we are your family."

"But I am a stranger to you."

"We are all strangers when first we meet, even when we are born. While you are here, you will be one of us." She took the teacup from Alexandra's hand. "Is there anything else you need?"

Hesitant, afraid to ask so great a favor, she said, "Could you let Tasha sleep in this room with me? I won't keep her from her work, but at night, when it's dark and I'm alone, I would like her with me."

Katrushka's expression became even more puzzled, but she assented.

"Why you want her, I cannot imagine, but all right, she can sleep on the floor over there. Good night, child."

Alexandra did not watch Katrushka leave, even though the closing of the door left her in darkness. The fire, reduced to warm red coals, cast little light, and it took her eyes a while to adjust. Yet those moments of blindness held less terror than the sight of the man waiting patiently in the next room.

Grigori Tcheradzin, no more taciturn than usual, ate his meal without entering into the family conversation. He was not interested in Khardichev's new bull or the death of an old hermit on the mountain. He had heard Vasili call the girl Snowbird, and now the name kept running through his brain like the trill of a nightingale.

She was, without question, the most beautiful woman he had ever seen. Unlike the sturdy Cossack women he had known all his life, she was fragile, delicate as a snowflake, and the very difference of her was enough to make her attractive to him. Yet there was something altogether separate from her physical qualities that surrounded her and made him want her.

He knew that Valentina, sitting across the table from him, hated the girl with every fibre of her body. It was no wonder. Alexandra represented everything the proud and pampered Valentina could never be, but worse, she provided competition. The daughter of the village elder, wealthy by local standards, and easily the prettiest girl for miles, Valentina had never been challenged when she set her eyes on a man, until now, and Grigori had seen the jealousy in his sister's eyes the moment Vasili brought Alexandra into the house.

There would be trouble, and he could only guess how much.

"I think I shall go to bed early," Valentina said with an exaggerated yawn. "I didn't get much sleep last night."

She made it quite clear by the tone of her voice whom she blamed for her lack of rest. Katrushka frowned at her daughter but said nothing as the girl left the room.

In her room, Valentina undressed quickly, for it was chilly and she wished to crawl into her bed where it was warm and cozy. Before she pulled the woolen nightgown over her head, she looked down the length of her body and wondered just how it compared to *hers*.

She was proud of the long, well-muscled legs that had held her on many a wild ride across the valley. Her belly was flat and firm, her hips wide for the easy bearing of many sons, though she had never given childbirth much thought until today. She cupped her small breasts in her hands, the pale nipples hard in the cold room, and felt jealousy burn like a brand through her. The girl Vasili had brought was slender and fine-boned as a fawn, but she had the body of a woman.

Valentina's confidence slid for the first time in her life. Angry for having thought that the sickly creature really posed any threat, she set her chin defiantly as she shrugged the nightdress down over her shoulders. Before she climbed beneath the quilts, she searched under the bed for a small wooden box and set it on the pillow as she snuggled into the bed.

It was a strange assortment of bits of trash that she spilled out, hardly the things a girl would place like treasures in a box so carefully hidden. A bent and rusted horseshoe nail, a short linen strip dotted with dark stains, a stub of a thin cigar, a lock of hair pressed in a folded sheet of paper. After returning the other items to the box, she opened the paper to touch the thick dark curl.

"You're wasting your time."

She had left the door unlocked and became so absorbed in her thoughts that she failed to hear Grigori enter.

"What gives you the right to come in here without knocking? Get out and mind your own business."

He shook his head with sad frustration.

"I warn you, Valentina. It would be better if you forget this dream of yours. Five years is a long time, and you were only a child then."

"I was fifteen, the same age Mother was when she first married. And anyway, I'm not a child now." She tossed her thick, red-gold hair in proud defiance. "I'll be the judge whether it's a waste of time to wait for him. You'll see; he'll come back."

Anything more he could say would go as unheeded as all his previous admonitions. If Valentina wanted to spend the rest of her life mooning over a man who would never pay any attention to her, who would never even look at her the way a man looks at a woman, then that was her choice. Grigori believed her right about one thing, if nothing else. Her lover would come back, someday, but not for the reason she expected.

Chapter 25

IN THE growing light, the ruins of Smolensk took on a nightmare appearance. The French cannons had reduced it to rubble even before the fire took hold, and what remained was barely recognizable a city. Few buildings still stood, and those that did were empty shells, stripped of every item worth carrying away.

There would be no battle. General Kutuzov had gathered his army to advance on Smolensk and the French, and when word reached the retreating generals of the size of the Russian force, they accepted their emperor's orders to march. To the thousands of French soldiers, Smolensk was a double disappointment: Not only was their long and well-deserved rest denied and their suicidal retreat to continue, but the supplies they had expected to find, food, medicine, winter uniforms, all had disappeared. So, too, their hope. To them, battle and a quick death seemed another mercy they would not receive.

After prowling the streets since dusk, Mikhail staggered with exhaustion and his own disappointment. Neither condition was new to him. He found the stallion where he had left him and rode to join his adopted regiment. If they followed the French, as he fully expected them to do, he could sleep in the saddle. That would not be new either.

What sentries the French had posted slept as soundly as their comrades. The clatter of hooves woke some, but too late for them to stop him. Kutuzov had halted the army some five miles east of Smolensk, a distance Mikhail could traverse in time to get some breakfast before the day's march began. His stomach growled; he tried to remember when he had last eaten and could not.

He saw the approaching rider from his left, down a narrow street at once prosperous shops, but chose to ignore him. Probably a French officer in search of plunder or deserters or returning from a night spent in the arms of a whore.

"Damn!" Mikhail swore as the pistol ball whistled past his head. "What the hell do you think you're doing?"

He had hoped the half-light of dawn would provide enough cover that he could lie his way out of a confrontation.

"I might ask the same of you. By whose authority do you ride toward the Russian prisoners?"

In the clear morning air that reply caught Mikhail off guard, more because he recognized the voice than because it posed a question to which he had no immediate answer.

"I'm trying to find my company.," he stammered, trying to sound slightly drunk and guilty at leaving his men."

"A clever story, but one I am not inclined to believe." Mikhail saw that he carried a second pistol in his right hand.

The bluff had not succeeded; escape was out of the question with a gun aimed at his head.

"I've waited a long time for this, Count Ogrinov, and I am going to enjoy it," Trabert said as he brought his horse closer to the Russian. "I knew, given time, she'd bring you to me." The thin smile dissolved. "Dismount, leave your horse where it is, and you will walk where I tell you."

Mikhail surrendered without a fight, but he would not give the mad colonel the satisfaction of stealing his mount as well. As he handed the reins to Trabert, he let them fall, and the animal leapt to a wild gallop. Tempted for a moment to chase the beast, Trabert swore at his captive.

"Damn you, Ogrinov! You'll pay for that. You've cheated me for the last time. Now, move!"

Saving the stallion from whatever fate the colonel had in

255

mind gave little consolation to a man whose soul screamed with torment. He followed Trabert's instructions until, as the sun burst like a fireball over the eastern hills, they halted not far from the city gates.

It was a glorious morning, clear, crisp, frosty, with no hint of snow, yet all around him lay the most gruesome collection of misery Mikhail had ever seen.

"God in Heaven!" he muttered in Russian. "No Cossack barbarian can lay claim to causing this; every bit of the credit goes to the fat, mad Emperor of civilized France!"

He had seen men die of battle wounds, but many of these had never been injured. Frostbite had claimed more fingers than weapons had, and hunger was killing more than the cannon. It was worse, much worse, than he had guessed. Seen from a distance, as when he had struck with the Cossacks on their night raids, the French were no worse off than one might expect. Now, walking among them, he forgot the man riding behind him. Surrounded on all sides by such wretchedness, his own fate, though still unknown, seemed preferable in comparison. Any kind of death was to be wished over this mockery of life.

Trabert barked an order to halt and brought Mikhail back to reality. Another officer rode towards them; Mikhail tried to see his face but the sun behind him put his features in shadow.

"I've found a spy wandering about the prisoners' stockade," the colonel boasted. "If you need me, I shall be interrogating him in my tent."

"Yes, sir," a young but weary voice answered. "General Murat has given orders that we are to be underway by noon," he reminded Trabert.

"I know the orders, Lascaux!" he snapped back, then ordered Mikhail to move on.

The pitifully small heap of coals in the brazier brought the temperature in the tent to something barely above freezing, though this was considerably warmer than the outside air. Trabert kept his pistol trained on the back of the Russian's head as he dismounted and turned his horse over to a waiting groom. With an almost audible sigh of relief, Mikhail entered the tent and found it empty.

"Did you expect to find her here?" Trabert taunted. "Sorry to disappoint you." He sat down on the cot and fished a flask of brandy out of the canvas sack he used as a pillow. "Damned fine brandy," he commented after swallowing three or four large gulps. "I must compliment you Moscovites for having the perspicacity to stock your cellars with some of France's finest."

Mikhail chose to ignore him, to stand quietly defiant and say nothing. As long as Trabert held the pistol, escape was an impossibility. But the colonel was known for his weakness to drink and it had once come to another's aid. The scars were covered with his gloves now, but the obvious difficulty Trabert had with the stopper on the flask gave evidence to the permanent damage Alexandra's teeth had done to his hand.

"I know what you're thinking," he went on. "You are wishing I would pull the trigger and end this quickly. Again, I must disappoint you."

"I am afraid the disappointment is yours, Trabert," Mikhail replied easily. "I prefer to extend my life as long as possible, by whatever means." Why do I have the feeling I shall regret those words? he asked himself, but he continued, "Actually I was wishing you would drink the rest of that swill you call brandy and get drunk enough to let me escape."

"It would take a good deal more than the few drops left here to make me so drunk I couldn't stop you dead, and I do mean dead, in your tracks." He pulled out his watch, clicked it open. "Ten o'clock already. They will be ready when Murat wants them to be."

"If you think that when they are gone you will have me entirely at your mercy, perhaps you had best think again," Mikhail suggested. "Might it not be just the other way around?"

"By the time the army departs, you will be quite incapable of harming anyone." He laughed again, as though he had seen some alarm in the blue eyes. Yet there was none, and Trabert knew it. "You should have learned not to underestimate the French, Monsieur le Comte!"

With effort, Mikhail kept himself under control. Not a muscle moved to betray the boiling rage within. The eyes remained placidly blue, serene, but Alexandra's words had come back to haunt him.

"Let us not discuss such an unpleasant subject as your impending demise. Shall we talk about something far more sweet and lovely? The beautiful Mademoiselle Aubertien, perhaps?"

Mikhail remembered the almost sensual feeling of Bernard Choulier's throat breaking in his hands and wished he could feel it again. But Trabert still held the pistol steady.

"A spirited girl, not easily tamed, but well worth the effort, as I am sure you know. I don't believe I have ever enjoyed a woman quite as exciting as she is."

He said "is." Then she was still alive. If the colonel had her, she could not be far away. Keep the man talking, Mischa told himself. Get him to tell you everything, anything, most of all where she is now.

He was lying; he had to be. Alexandra would never cooperate with this beast.

"I believe she enjoys it."

Trabert stopped, searched the Russian's face for some sign of response. Nothing! Was the man made of stone? He needed Ogrinov's anger and would do anything, say anything, to arouse it.

"Perhaps you would like to see her one last time, before I take you to your execution. Let me warn you, however, she is not what she once was. I was obliged to defend myself against her one night, and unfortunately she now wears a rather long scar on her left cheek."

"I should prefer to remember her the way she was," came the still calm reply.

He would not have cared what she looked like if only he could see her again.

The man was unshakable. Guessing that the Russian

knew the truth and that continuing this charade would do no good, Trabert shouted for the guard.

Two ragged sergeants walked into the tent. One had a blind eye, Mikhail noticed, and the other limped badly. What sad days had fallen on the Grande Armee!

"This man has confessed to spying. It is my duty to see that he is properly punished and to set an example for others who may have similiar thoughts. Find a priest if you can, but with or without one, I'll see this bastard dead within the hour."

As usual, Manette was nowhere to be found. Lascaux shouted her name over and over, but above the tumult of panic, he could not be heard more than a few feet. Twice he saw her, only to lose her again in the crowd. And the nervous stallion often found his way blocked by a cart or wagon, making a thorough search even more difficult.

More than an hour slipped by before the lieutenant almost accidentally found her, tending as always to the wounded.

She recognized the urgency in his cry even before she located him in the throng. As soon as he had her attention, he drove the horse frantically to her.

"What has happened?"

He reached down his hand to her. At the panicked look in his eyes, she grabbed hold and let him pull her up in front of him.

"I can't shout any more," he gasped. "I don't know what it is about you, but you have inspired me to this, even though I know it is treason and mutiny and I deserve to be hung for it."

She looked over her shoulder at him and smiled.

"That can only mean a soldier is going to save a life instead of take one."

"If it isn't too late already."

Lascaux cursed each wagon that blocked their path, swore violently at the creeping army that made each step seem a mile.

"St. Croix was right when he told you he saw the Russian count yesterday wandering around the camp. I just saw him, too, or I think I did."

Manette held her breath a moment and prayed.

"Where?"

"With Trabert about an hour ago, no, more like two hours ago. He was the colonel's prisoner, and when he told me he was going to interrogate a suspected spy, I knew something was wrong."

They both knew Trabert's predilection for executions before interrogations.

"Are you certain it was Ogrinov?"

"No, how could I be? I've never laid eyes on the man. But Trabert's prisoner certainly fit your description."

Her heart pounded with fear, with hope, with dread. Tears welled up in her eyes and a sob stuck in her throat.

"Lascaux, how do I tell him she's dead?"

He put an arm around her waist to hold her as the horse dodged a squadron of soldiers in poor but recognizable formation. Tightening his embrace, he felt his own voice quaver as he scolded her.

"We agreed Alexandra didn't die. If that Russian servant hadn't found her, he would have come back and told us. You convinced me; don't tell me you never believed it yourself?"

It was impossible to tell whether they gained or lost ground. All around them the sea of human misery flowed, tossing them every way but that in which they wanted to go. Panic-stricken, Manette twice tried to slide from the saddle to make her way on foot. Finally she gave in to the painful sobs and the tears burning her eyes. Leaning against Lascaux, she cried for the first time in years.

They had bound his hands with a piece of coarse rope while still in Trabert's tent, and now, with a brisk wind numbing their fingers, he ordered them to untie the prisoner. Accustomed to misery as much as to incomprehensible orders, the two sergeants did as they were told.

"Now remove his coat and shirt."

A grin spread across Trabert's face, and he took another sip from his flask.

"The wagon over there, with the broken axle. It will do quite nicely."

The overturned wagon would serve as the wall against which he would be shot. Mikhail knew Trabert intended to appropriate the sable coat for himself and wished neither blood nor bullet holes to mar it. But why the shirt as well? What could the colonel want with a coarse peasant's smock?

He understood when the sergeant with the blind eye pushed him face first against the cart and began to tie his wrist to the broken front axle. His other wrist was encircled by the same rough cord as earlier and then secured to the rear axle. This was not the fate he had expected, and he was totally unprepared for it.

"You will have to make your own peace with God, Count Ogrinov. There is no priest available for spies." Why doesn't this man even shiver with the cold?

Trabert was frightened, though Mikhail could think of no reason why he should be. He pulled at his bonds, found them too strong to be broken easily. It was no easier to face the slow, painful death that awaited him.

Once, when his father had caught him pulling the wings off flies, he had been beaten with a leather strap. At the age of eight or nine, he had thought he would die of the agony, but in a few days the red welts had disappeared, and he was none the worse for having learned a lesson in cruelty. And he remembered he had not made a sound. Could he show the same courage now?

It struck him like lightning, white-hot against his numbed flesh. Lost in his memories he had let Trabert with his Spanish bullwhip sneak up and land the first lash without warning. Mikhail pressed his forehead to the rough boards and gritted his teeth until the fire in his back died. A deep breath when he heard the whistle of leather through the air and he thought he was ready for the second.

Trabert snaked the whip with clever skill, laid the

second blow an inch away from the first. The supple muscles of the Russian's back quivered convulsively as the current of agony spread through every nerve in his body. The colonel laughed high and long, then swallowed the rest of the brandy and shouted:

"The wrist is just getting warmed up. See if this feels any different."

The tip caught him between the shoulder blades, and while the searing pain still roared in his brain, he felt Trabert lay his full force into the next blow. Eyes screwed tightly shut and teeth clamped so hard his jaw trembled, Mikhail screamed in his head but let not a whisper pass his lips. Though he felt nothing but the branding iron agony, he kept his mind clear, tried to concentrate on something else. Yet with each lash, determination waned.

What the devil difference does it make? he asked himself. You'll be dead soon enough and pride won't change that.

Warm, sticky blood trickled down his side from the welts opened by the continuous beating. He had lost count after the thirteenth stripe, for now there was no respite between lashes long enough to tell when the pain of one ended and the next began. From his fingertips to his toes, there was no place on his body free of it, no nerve that did not scream with it. He had locked his knees to keep from sagging against the ropes around his wrists and possibly pulling his arms out of their sockets. The bindings had cut into his skin; little rivulets of blood snaked to his elbows. Despite the cold, he was dripping with sweat. It burned his eyes and in the open wounds.

"Scream, you bastard!" Trabert cried. "I know you can hear me! Scream, just once, and I'll stop."

Mikhail refused to answer. Gulping the cold air into his lungs, he listened to the colonel taunt him with empty promises and lies. As long as Trabert talked, he held the whip still. And Mikhail had seen him lay the pistol down in the snow. He tested the ropes again, found them loosened just a little.

"The brandy's gone," Trabert muttered, his voice loud in the afternoon quiet.

Mikhail heard the snap and the whistle, braced himself against the wood. The musketball in his thigh at Friedland had been a thorn prick compared to this. Another quick lash shocked the breath out of him, but still he refused in silence.

The Russian was weakening. Trabert rested his arm and searched for the flask he had forgotten was empty. He had wanted to see the proud count reduced to a screaming animal, but his death would be enough. He was losing a lot of blood now, and he had been exposed to the cold almost an hour. A few more carefully placed stripes and, if he still held his tongue, Trabert would just leave him to die. The army was an hour ahead of him, and Trabert had no wish to strain his horse. There would be an extra lash or two for having cheated him of the black stud.

The long bullwhip had grown heavy, yet it slithered accurately and coiled itself around the hard bulge of Mikhail's upper arm. He was losing consciousness now; each blow sent a fiery red flash through the blackness. Sweat and tears blinded him more than the sun on the snow.

Trabert sang drunkenly. "Oh, my sweet Alexandra, you have brought me such joy today. See what I've done to the pretty Count Ogrinov? What, don't you want to get a better look at him?"

Mikhai fought off the encroaching oblivion long enough to hear laughter as Trabert walked away. Hatred vanquished pain for a moment, and he turned his head a little so he could see, through the tears and sweat and torture and rage, two shadowy forms, close to each other as though they were one, stroll across the snow towards France.

The broken axle gave way, but not the rope. The crash turned the colonel around.

It was not possible. The Russian had freed himself, and armed with this crude but deadly weapon, he advanced, murder clear in every fibre of his being. Trabert searched for the carelessly discarded pistol, picked it up, but when he fired nothing happened. The powder was ruined by the snow that melted when the warm metal, held too long in his hand, lay too long on the ground.

In his haste to get away, Trabert dropped both the gun and the whip. Once he had mounted and started toward the protection of his comrades, he never looked back for fear the count, like some reborn monster, would be following on his heels. He did not see the man stagger under the weight of the weapon to which he was bound and finally, fall to the ground.

His whole body felt on fire though he lay in the snow, and he knew his hold on consciousness was slipping. One small part of his brain tried to remind him that Alexandra would rather die than consort with an animal like Trabert, but that quiet voice of reason could not compete with the bitter memories of another woman's treachery. He had loved Tamara, too, but she had broken his heart and then mocked him. Now he loved Alexandra only to see her betray him as well. Dear, sweet, beautiful Alexandra, whom he loved so much and whom he had hurt so much. He had made himself believe she would survive at any cost, but he never thought she valued her life over his and over his love for her.

He looked up, fighting to see her clearly one last time, but she was gone. Trabert rode alone, no laughing Alexandra behind him. As life itself faded, Mikhail cursed her for denying him that one last vision. She had cheated him again. He closed his eyes and did not weep.

The red stallion trotted briskly through the thinning ranks of stragglers. Manette shaded her eyes with her hand and strained to see beyond them. She saw only a large dark object that looked to be a disabled or overturned wagon. Not far to her left she made out Trabert's tent; the colonel had not broken camp.

Lascaux nudged the horse to an easy canter, then suddenly pulled him to a dead stop.

The body lay twenty or thirty yards ahead of them, the blood bright against the stark white of the snow. Stunned, Lascaux reacted too slowly. Manette, with a scream, slipped to the ground before he could stop her.

Feeling the cold but not caring, she took off her coat and laid it over him. Where the blood had run from his wounds to the ground it had frozen into crystals like finely cut rubies. She lifted his head and placed the hem of her skirt under his face. Though neither gesture brought any response from him, Manette felt the thin, fragile pulse beating in his neck.

"Is he dead?" Lascaux asked cautiously.

"No, not quite." There was a dreamy quality in her voice that made the young lieutenant uneasy. "There's no need for you to wait, Lascaux. I'll stay with him."

"Don't be a fool, Manette. He's going to die soon enough, and there's no sense sitting here freezing yourself. He's in no pain."

"I said I'll stay."

She smoothed the tangled curls away from Mikhail's forehead with a hand far steadier than her voice.

"For God's sake, Manette! If there were a way to take him, I would do it. You know that. But we can't do anything for him, unless you'd like me to put a bullet in his brain and end it now."

He knelt with her but kept his eyes away from the man lying in the snow. He had seen enough from a distance to know the Russian was beyond help as well as beyond suffering.

She never ceased her gentle caress. His breathing was shallow but steady, his pulse still beat rhythmically. Blood had soaked through her coat from his mangled back, yet when she lifted a corner to examine the wounds she saw the edges were drying and all the worst stripes had stopped bleeding altogether.

"You go back, Lascaux, and leave me here. Mischa gave me back my life once, and I owe him this much at least."

Tears like ribbons of silver streaked the face Lascaux turned to his, and her mouth was salty with them as he kissed her. He started to walk away.

"Damn it, I can't do it. Let me help you carry him to Trabert's tent. From the looks of it, the colonel himself is gone. At least your friend will be out of the wind."

"Leave him alone!" she ordered with the ferocity of a lioness defending her cubs.

He knew what he had to do and did it without remorse. Grabbing Manette with one hand, he jerked her to her feet while he drew his pistol. This time his reactions were quicker than hers. The sharp crack of the shot silenced a terrified scream in her throat and when she tired to throw herself on the body, Lascaux held her so that she could not even turn to look back.

He lifted her onto the red stallion once they were far enough away from the Russian's body that she could not see it. In a state of total numbness, she sat quietly. Lascaux was prepared for fainting or hysteria, but not this. Tonight, or perhaps in the morning, he would find time to explain why he had done it, why the sight of a rider on the horizon had told him he had no choice.

Chapter 26

AS SOON as they rejoined the retreat and Manette found Dr. Vaniche and the ambulance corps, Lascaux dismounted to help her down. With an angry motion she waved him aside and walked away without having said a single word.

He lost track of her during the busy afternoon hours when the march was still unorganized and chaos seemed the order of the day. The hills became steeper and more slippery, until the only way to descend them was on the seat of one's pants. Going up posed different but far more serious problems, especially for the horses. Twice within the space of fifteen minutes Lascaux called upon his corporal to put helpless beasts out of their agony. The corporal gave him an odd look, but did the job as ordered, though he thought it strange the lieutenant did not simply fire his own pistol into the animals' head himself and have done with it.

Wandering alone through the camp after dark, Lascaux searched for Manette. He carried a heavy coat he had removed from the body of a young soldier, a pathetic suicide, to replace the one she had so selflessly given to the dying Russian. Arriving at the main hospital tent, he was told by Dr. Yvan, Napoleon's personal surgeon, that Madame Duquesne had not been seen for hours.

He returned to his aimless wandering.

There was no gaiety in the camp tonight. Not that it had been an over-abundant commodity before Smolensk, but that disappointment had demoralized the troops even further. It affected the whores, too. One sidled up to Lascaux and asked in a thin voice if he needed someone to warm his bed. Warmth was as valuable a commodity as gold these days. He shook his head sadly and watched her walk away.

She approached another officer and, as Lascaux continued his search for Manette, he heard her make the same plaintive offer. It was the man's caustic refusal that caught his attention, however. He reached for the pistol, but Trabert had stepped out of the firelight before Lascaux could take him. His own cold-bloodedness, even towards a monster like Trabert, surprised him.

If he had followed Trabert, as he was inclined to do, his search for Manette would have been shortened considerably. He turned in the opposite direction and missed seeing her trail stealthily after the colonel.

She had, in fact, been stalking her prey for hours, since darkness had fallen to provide her cover. Her time would come, and she had all the patience in the world. If not tonight, then tomorrow, or the day after. She gripped the knife all the more tightly as she followed him toward his new quarters.

Major Sabac had died only a few hours ago, but Trabert found nothing at all ghoulish in appropriating the man's tent and supplies before his body was disposed of. Though not as large as the shelter he had abandoned earlier, this had fewer holes for the wind to enter and boasted a folding camp stool as well as a cot. The one-eyed sergeant, as ordered, had found enough wood to light a smoky fire, and Trabert entered with a look of satisfaction on his face. He had eaten rather better than usual, and with a full flask of brandy beside him, he lay down on the cot and pulled the blanket over him.

Protected from the worst of the wind by the tent itself, Manette huddled in the dark and tried to keep her teeth from chattering. She was cold and she was hungry, but she was also still patient. When the fire that had warmed the tent died, when it no longer cast dancing silhouettes on the canvas walls, then it would be time, not a moment sooner. She could wait that long.

Slowly, the camp settled into silence. Snoring and the occasional squeak of a sentry's boot on the snow soon became the only sounds. A gibbous moon, not full for another day or two, floated overhead in a clear sky. Manette did not sleep. She wondered if she would ever sleep again, if the memories of horrors old and new would let her close her eyes in peaceful rest. Touching the blade of the knife with her thumb, she did not resist the realization that thrust itself into her thoughts. Only death brought peace.

A pile of red embers still glowed when Manette lifted the tent flap and stepped inside, but they gave no light. The moon outside was brighter, and for several precious seconds she was blind in the sudden dark. Then finally, she made out the sleeping shape on the cot.

He lay on his left side, his face to the wall. The collar of his tunic protected his throat, the easiest target. Devoid of any emotion, Manette calculated the precise point and angle of entry before lifting the blanket to expose his neck. The fabric of his coat was stretched taut, making it a simple task to locate the spot between the fifth and sixth ribs. Poising the long blade no more than an inch or two above him, she muttered a meaningless and unfelt prayer for his soul.

She could not believe how easy it was, after all. Her hand didn't shake, even her heartbeat remained strong and steady. The point of the knife was against the fabric when she felt the warmth cover her hands. Slowly the blade moved away from the colonel's heart. Then she realized that the warmth came from another pair of hands, strong masculine hands that held hers gently imprisoned.

"I could not let you do it," Lascaux whispered in her ear. "He deserves it and worse, but not at your hands."

He led her outside and together they walked away from Trabert's tent. Several hundred yards away they found a place near a small fire and sat down. The colonel's brandy, which Lascaux had stolen, traced a fiery path down

Manette's throat and warmed the icy lump in her belly. Lascaux poured a second swallow into her cup and watched as she drank it.

"In a minute or two you'll feel a lot better," he promised. "Would you rather sleep or talk?"

She shook her head.

"I can't sleep. I can't even close my eyes without seeing it all over again."

"I can't either," he admitted.

But he did not admit that she was the cause of his sleeplessness. She had come so close to murdering Trabert, and indeed would have without his intervention, and the idea still haunted him. Whatever the Russian had been to her, the thought of his death had destroyed something in her. Lascaux knew that now was the time to tell her the truth, before she looked for another life to take.

He wrapped the coat around her and allowed her another sip of the brandy to warm her. Sitting as close to her as he dared, but not as close as he wanted, he took one of her cold hands and pressed his lips to it.

"Manette, I didn't kill the Russian."

"No, not really. Trabert did most of the job first." She pulled her hand away as though she had not forgiven him despite her words. "It's over and done; he's out of his misery. I don't want to talk any more about it, Lascaux. Not now, not ever. Maybe that way I can get it out of my mind and stop seeing—"

Grasping her shoulders sternly he entreated, "Please, Manette, you've got to understand. As God is my witness, I didn't kill him! The servant, the one we sent after Alexandra, he came back. I saw him riding toward us." He saw disbelief staring back at him from her soft brown eyes. He let go of her and stood to pace in frustration. He could not look at her and keep his mind clear.

"What the hell else was I to do? I couldn't leave you there, and I knew I didn't have the strength to pull you away from him. He'll be taken care of far better than we could. That's why I fired the shot, to signal Vasili, or whatever his name is, to hurry and not to go back."

"You're the one who doesn't understand!"

"Don't I? Give me credit for something, Manette. I saw the look in your eyes; it's still there. And I heard the crazy softness of your voice when you talked to him. But, damn it, Manette, he's not yours any more! Whether Alexandra is dead or alive, he's not yours!"

He had seen it so clearly, even when she had not, and she knew he was right.

"St. Croix told me, weeks ago, that she was a spy and that she worked for a Russian count. It has taken me all this time to piece it together, and I'm still not certain that you aren't in one way or another a spy yourself, but it doesn't matter any more. What does matter is that I want you to believe me, Manette, more than anything else."

"I believe you, Lascaux. Can you believe me when I tell you that, were I not nearly old enough to be your mother and an honorably married woman, too, I would take what I see offered in your eyes and give the same back gladly?"

In the morning they would see things differently, and perhaps then they might feel guilty. Remembering another night, on another battlefield, when another man had saved her, Manette took the lieutenant's face between her hands and kissed him softly.

"No, *ma cherie*," he whispered, "I cannot believe you. Prove it to me." He kissed her back, hungrily. "You are forty years old, and I am twenty-seven, so you are hardly old enough to be my mother." Another kiss, and his hand reached under her coat. "And your husband—"

"If you can forget my age, I will forget my husband," she interrupted. "I will forget everything."

Not until the report of the pistol shot carrying clearly in the cold air reached Vasili did he see the two nearer figures, for he had been concentrating on the distant army. Though he could not identify the man and woman, he recognized the red stud immediately. He touched his heels to his own grey and the animal jumped at once to a gallop. Vasili was so intent on keeping the other horse in sight that he paid no attention to the overturned wagon and very nearly charged past the corpse lying on the blood-spattered snow.

The gelding was thrown back on his haunches by the force of Vasili's jerk on the reins, and the animal had barely come to a halt before his rider dismounted.

Gingerly, Vasili lifted the coat from Mikhail's back. Sickened by the savagery that had done this, he swore in every tongue he knew and called down a thousand curses on the Corsican as he searched for the mark of Lascaux' merciful shot.

There was none.

And the lacerated flesh was still warm. Suddenly hopeful, Vasili lifted his master to his shoulder and, as though he were no more than a sleeping infant, carried him to the flimsy campaign tent left behind by the frantic Trabert. He laid Mikhail, unconscious but alive, on the cot, then set about preparing their quarters.

Using his anger as well as his axe, Vasili demolished the wooden cart and carried the pieces back to the tent. The timber burned hot and clean, with little smoke. Though he would have preferred a less conspicuous campsite, Vasili was grateful for the shelter. He could not even think of moving Mikhail until morning, and tonight showed every sign of being bitter, bitter cold.

Mikhail remained unconscious while Vasili pried the ruined coat loose from the wounds. Pieces of skin that had stuck to the cloth came away despite his caution, opening several of the welts afresh, but the bleeding subsided quickly. The stripes would heal, in time, to leave ugly scars but no other permanent damage, providing, of course, that the man lived.

At present, that was not to be taken for granted.

Vasili's first concern, after cleaning the lacerations and covering Mikhail with both quilts he had brought, was to secure a second horse. The journey from the mountain village had taken only two days; the return, with but one horse, would require five or six, and Vasili knew his master was in no condition for that kind of ordeal. Stealing from the French was the easy solution, as they were no more than two miles away. They were also fiercely protective of their mounts and the animals themselves were hardly worth the risk. He had not yet made up his mind whether to settle for whatever the French could be persuaded to part with or to try for quality at an even greater risk in the Russian camp slightly further to the north, when Mikhail called from the cot.

"I'll kill you," he mumbled in Russian. "You first, Trabert, not quickly, not easily. Let the girl watch you die."

"He's gone, Mischa. It is I, Vasili."

"Then you can help me, Vasili, old friend. Hold her for me, will you? while I slice the balls off this swine. I wonder how she'll like him as a eunuch after sharing his bed all these months."

He lay calmly, hardly moving except to breathe and to speak; only his voice betrayed his anger. Vasili felt his forehead, but there was no sign of fever. This was a fantasy born of torment, not a feverish delirium.

"Alexandra's not—"

"Shut up! Don't ever speak her name in my presence again, or I'll have your tongue out for it!"

He had risen too quickly, and the return of consciousness was soon followed by the return of pain. Choosing to hold his tongue rather than lose it forever, Vasili handed Mikhail a flask of brandy and said:

"I'm going to try to find another horse. The French are closer, but I think—"

"While you're there, see if you can't also find Mademoiselle Aubertien and her current stud, Augustin Trabert," he jeered. "Bring me back their heads."

The anger had taken too much energy, and the pain had grown intolerable. After another long swallow of the brandy, he lay back down on the cot and fell instantly sound asleep.

The black stallion had not gone far when he left Mikhail, and Vasili found the animal wandering just a mile or so away from Trabert's camp. He hoped a reunion with the horse would have a favorable effect, but Mikhail remained morose as ever. He looked the animal over closely before climbing rather awkwardly into the saddle and setting out towards Moscow.

Vasili said nothing, though he did allow himself a sigh of relief that he had no explanations to make, which would have been necessary had Mikhail headed towards the mountains.

Keeping to a steady pace, Vasili estimated that their journey would take four days, barring any new blizzard. By some miracle, the weather held clear but cold. Game was plentiful, and in the shelter of Trabert's tent, even a small fire sufficed to keep them warm. But on the second night, the brandy ran out.

Mikhail raised the flask and swallowed the last few drops. Looking puzzled and almost angry, he turned it upside down.

"It can't be gone," he muttered, the first words he had spoken in two days. "Where's the rest of it?"

"There is no more. You've drunk it all."

With sudden fury, Mikhail hurled the empty flask at the servant, then lay down to sleep, his face to the wall. Half an hour later, the nightmare began.

Laughter, sweet, soft, beautiful laughter. It surrounded him like the music of Moscow's church bells on Sunday morning, ringing in his soul until the vibrations threatened to shatter his sanity. He could not see her through the red haze of pain, but she was there, taunting, teasing, laughing, always laughing. When he reached for her throat to strangle her and silence the laughter forever, he found only a wooden chess piece in his hands, a pawn carved in his own likeness. His scream of rage threw her into a fit of hilarity.

"Stop it, stop it, *stop it*!" he roared, waking Vasili. "Shut up, you lying bitch! I'll find you, and when I do, so help me God, I'll make you wish you had died along with Moscow! You used me once like a pawn to get what you wanted but you won't do it again. This time I'll kill you, Tamara. I'll finish the job my brother started."

Vasili shook him violently, but it was some minutes before Mikhail threw off the mantle of sleep. He was bathed in sweat and strangely disoriented when he finally escaped the fading echoes. The horror of his dream would not leave him, and he knew sleep was impossible now. Attacked by a feverish chill, he sat wrapped in his quilts as close as he dared to the fire. He doubted he could hold off the fever. The brandy had helped; now that it was gone, he had nothing to sustain him for the rest of the journey. Without it, guilt for some unknown crime pressed down on him, and he could not stand the pain of the memories that came to him each time he closed his eyes.

By morning, he could hardly walk. He had spent most of the long, sleepless night staring at the fire, and exhaustion had opened the gate to fever. He refused to let Vasili examine his back, claiming that the chill would be his death. That was part of the truth. He could feel the infection, the hot tenderness that increased hourly as the poison concentrated. Every muscle, every joint, ached as he mounted his horse. The pale sun hurt his eyes, and he shivered while sweat dripped from his brow.

His hold on consciousness was tenuous at best. Only the sound of laughter, beckoning him from the other side, kept him from sliding into oblivion. The road took them now towards Kaluga, and everything was destroyed, ravaged, burned by the Russians in self-defense and then demolished by the panicked French. He blamed her for everything, though he suddenly realized he had no idea whom he was blaming.

What had once been a sizable town with a tavern where Mikhail had spent many a pleasant evening was now a snow-covered, silent memory. He saw it only hazily through his fever, but it burned in his brain with a bitter fire. So much was gone, so much destroyed that could never be rebuilt. Only the stone church remained in this town, empty, sepulchral, but in others they had passed there was nothing left.

The winter day was short, but the moon at its full shed clear light on the snow and they did not stop at sundown.

Much later, and only because Vasili insisted, they paused long enough to brew bitter tea and rest the horses. Then the servant's urgings to sleep went unheeded, and they remounted to ride on.

Old Vanya, half a century the Ogrinov head coachman, saw them first, eerie shadows against the last light of sunset. Age had taken the old man's teeth and hearing, but his eyes were all the keener for it, and as he walked from the stables, he glanced toward the western sky and saw the approaching riders. He entered the kitchen where his son Aram was cook and ordered:

"Bring Countess Anna here to me, and don't breathe a word of this to anyone else. The young master and Vasili Petrovitch are on their way."

Aram obeyed as though Vanya were the old count himself, and fifteen minutes later, Anna Petrovna appeared in the kitchen.

She wasted not a moment of time. Without hysteria or simpering, she dispatched two servants to meet her grandson with the sleigh, ordered his rooms prepared and dinner taken to them in case he should be hungry, then she swept out to the drawing room, after all the details were seen to, to inform the rest of the family.

She had restored sufficient calm by the time the sleigh pulled up to the door that Vasili was able to carry Mikhail through the foyer and up the stairs to his room without being stopped once. Still, Vasili did not breathe easy until he was inside the room and Anna had closed and locked the door behind him.

"For God's sake, Vasili, don't leave him like that. He'll suffocate lying on his face."

Mikahil lay on his stomach, his face buried in the pillow, just as Vasili had gently placed him. Anna started to roll him over.

"Don't touch him, Countess," Vasili warned.

She stepped back and looked at the quiet, authoritative serf who seemed no longer to be just a servant.

"I want the truth, you great bear," she demanded. "What has happened to my grandson?"

He had taken off his gloves and hat, then removed the fur coat so he could move more freely. She would settle for nothing less than what she had asked for, the truth, and she had the same talent for ferreting out lies that Mikhail had. Vasili knew he could not trick her.

She helped him untie the heavy fur cloak he had wrapped about Mikhail in the sleigh, and when they removed it, he shivered with the sudden chill. Under the cloak, his red tunic and white linen shirt were drenched with sweat, and, as Vasili had feared, the infected cuts had glued the shirt to his back.

"The French did this?" Anna asked without batting an eye.

"And then they left him to die in the snow."

Chapter 27

WITH WORK to occupy her time, Alexandra felt the days pass more rapidly than when she was confined to bed, yet still it seemed an eternity from dawn until evening. But if the days passed slowly, the nights were longer still, when she could not sleep and lay awake with her thoughts. Tossing and turning on her bed until sheer exhaustion took control, she dozed for an hour or two before daybreak and that was all.

Her unlikely friendship with Tasha deepened, which they both took great pains to hide from everyone else. It was not all that difficult to do. Katrushka was too busy to notice, Dmitri spent most of his days away from the house, and Valentina made it a point to ignore both of them. Only Grigori paid any attention to the servant or the guest, but he seldom said a word to either.

"I don't understand him at all," Alexandra said one morning while she and Tasha were kneading dough for Christmas breads. "In fact, I don't understand any of them."

Tasha sprinkled flour on the table and pushed a stray lock of curly brown hair out of her face.

"That's because you don't know what I know," she said.

"Is something wrong?"

"No, it's just that, well, you frighten me a little."

"*I* frighten you? In heaven's name, why?"

"Because you're different. You aren't like *them* at all.

278

When Vasili brought you here, I thought you were a very great lady, and I didn't know how to act around you. I've never been outside his village in my whole life. You were something I didn't know, and so I was afraid of you."

"Are you still afraid of me?"

"No, not as much. I know you better now. You really aren't so different from the rest of us as I thought."

"And you aren't as stupid as you let them think you are."

Tasha laughed and said, "Do you think I'd still be here if they guessed I had any brains?"

Alexandra found it hard to believe the girl was only sixteen.

"That first night, before Vasili left, I knew that something was wrong. Katrushka had told me all about you and how delighted she was to have you stay with us, but I couldn't believe all the things she told me. It just didn't make any sense at all."

"What did she say?"

"First, you have to understand that Katrushka adores Vasili Petrovitch. In her eyes he can do no wrong, so when he told her you were to stay here as our guest as long as you wanted to, she didn't like the idea, but she accepted it. She will do anything he asks her to, even smile and cuddle you, though she thinks you're a French whore."

"Does she really?"

In a very matter of fact tone, Tasha replied, "Oh, yes, but don't let it bother you. She believes a lot of things that aren't true, like that Vasili was the father of your baby."

Alexandra felt the blood drain from her face as she handed two round loaves to Tasha, who placed them in the oven to bake. Struggling to remain calm, Alexandra asked, "What makes you think he wasn't?"

"You talked a lot in your sleep that night, some even in Russian."

Alexandra's knees went weak; she sat down heavily on the wooden bench and wished for a glass of brandy, even vodka.

"No one else knows?"

"No one. Katrushka pampers you because she feels guilty about letting Vasili down after he left you in her care. But she isn't the one you have to worry about."

"Grigori?"

"No, not him either. It's Valentina you have to watch out for. If she even suspected, you'd be dead in a twinkling. She's been in love with Mikhail Pavlovitch for years."

That was why Vasili had not mentioned Mikhail's name the night of their arrival. It was a wonder Alexandra herself had not let it slip at least once or twice in the past weeks. She reminded herself she would have to watch everything she said very closely.

Grigori's untimely arrival put an end to their conversation, and Alexandra cursed him for it. She had the feeling it would be a long time before the opportunity to resume the discussion presented itself, and her curiosity had been piqued by this tiny revelation of the inner workings of the Tcheradzin family.

She did not feel comfortable with Grigori, especially when he maneuvered her out of the kitchen where Tasha chaperoned and led her into the quiet, dim parlor. Though the resemblance she had once imagined between him and Mikhail no longer existed, her thoughts always drifted to Mischa when she found herself alone with Grigori.

He had been outside and stood by the fire to warm his hands.

"There is a blizzard coming," he said after a long pause. "Tonight it will start and last three days, maybe four."

He still spoke in the same slow, simple Russian he had used since her arrival, though it was no longer necessary and in fact irritated her.

"We will be locked into this valley until spring. No one will come in or go out until the snow melts, in April, or maybe not until May."

If you are trying to make me feel trapped, you are doing a damn fine job of it, she thought angrily.

He was staring at her, his cool grey-green eyes boring through her. It was a sensation she experienced often yet never quite got used to.

"You are not a servant. Why do you mock us by working in the kitchen with Tasha?"

"I merely keep myself busy," she replied. "Would you prefer I sit around all day waiting for someone to bring champagne and cake on a silver tray?"

"You might feel more at home if you did." His sarcasm had a bitter edge to it.

It was an absurd remark, one she had no intention of honoring with a denial.

Unable to stand the silence or his stare any longer, she told him, "Whatever it is you think I was or should have been, forget it. I grew up the daughter of a perfectly ordinary tailor. I have sewn my own clothes since I was old enough to thread a needle, I have cooked my own suppers, and I have even scrubbed floors more than once in my life. I daresay I was less spoiled than—"

"Than my sister. You don't have to lie to me about her, or try to cover up for her."

As though the confession embarrassed him, he turned his eyes toward the fire and away from Alexandra.

"Why do you continue to play into her hands?" he asked.

"I didn't know that I was."

"Don't tell me you haven't heard the things she says about you."

"If you have any complaints about my conduct please say so and I will try to correct what deficiencies you may find. As for your sister, she is beyond my domain. I suggest you talk to your parents about her."

The storm Grigori had predicted struck that evening, blown from the highest reaches of the mountains on a wind that screamed in the chimneys and moaned at the windows. Alexandra sat by the fire, and found it hard to concentrate on embroidery when terrifying memories swirled through her thoughts like the snow outside the cottage. Already the window panes were edged in white.

Snow had fallen before and she had watched it without this feeling of panic. With stout timber walls around her and a fire roaring beside her, she knew she was safe from the storm's fury. Still she shivered each time her eye strayed to the window. She had accepted the long wait until spring as a time in which to rest, to forget, to heal the scars left by sorrow, and she faced it with patience. Grigori's warning changed it to something entirely different, as though the peace and solitude the lonely winter promised had become a prison sentence. It angered her to think he had that kind of power over her. Determined that he should not, she returned to her needlework with fresh energy.

There were more storms and more snow, and as the winter passed, each day exactly like another, Alexandra withdrew further and further from the hostile environment in which she was trapped. Everthing in this village was alien to her, and she knew its inhabitants looked at her the same way.

Only her memories and hopes sustained her. Mikhail would come; he had to come. When spring arrived, so would he, to take her away from this place of unspoken hatreds. She refused even to think about the way they had parted, because Vasili's presence assured her that whatever had caused Mikhail's fury that September night was now forgotten and therefore forgiven. Waiting for him, she set her hopes on springtime and the future. Nothing else existed.

The days grew longer, slowly, almost imperceptibly. The sun was brighter, too, and warmer, and finally there came a day when the icicles hanging from the edges of the roof melted and dripped frigid water onto the heads of all who passed under them. Birds began to sing on sparkling frosty mornings.

But not every aspect of the seasonal reawakening was to be looked upon as welcome. Grigori had changed, Alexandra noted with some alarm, his quiet, brooding politeness giving way to more attentive concern. He took time each morning to inquire about her sleep, which she always told him had been excellent, even if she had barely closed her eyes. During the evening meal, he did his best to bring her into the conversation despite her own reticence and the glaring looks from his sister. Though she tried at first to make herself believe he was being nothing more than a friendly host, she knew he had other motives.

He made no attempt to approach her when she was alone, though she usually had the house to herself for a while in the afternoon. Nor was there any hint of impropriety in his voice when he spoke to her. He gave her no obvious reason to feel the way she did, and yet the feeling persisted, as it had from the moment she met him, a feeling of being watched when she was alone and a nervousness when she was not. She had begun to fear him.

It made no difference that, as the weather continued to improve and the days lengthened, he spent less and less time at home. He left shortly after wolfing down an enormous breakfast and rarely returned before supper, when he ate like a man starved. Though he asked about everyone else's activities, he never volunteered a word concerning his own.

That very secretiveness was enough to arouse Alexandra's curiosity. She hoped that perhaps if she knew him better, understood the workings of his mind, she might lose some of her fear. What, she wondered, did he do all day that it left him so exhausted he fell asleep in the parlor as soon as he had finished supper? Why did he smile more often in the past two weeks than in all the months since she had come to the valley? To approach him with questions like those required courage she did not possess, but she needed the answers. She turned to Tasha, and on a blustery spring night, Alexandra learned what she did not want to know.

"A bad storm," she whispered as she snuggled under the blankets and blew out the candle. "You're not afraid of the thunder, are you?"

The house shivered as another tremendous explosion rocked it. Rain pelted the windows and the wind set the panes to rattling.

"No, I'm not, but Valentina is," Tasha replied, sitting up with her quilt tucked around her knees.

Alexandra, who harbored her own unreasonable fear of the dark, felt a twinge of pity for the girl's terror, yet she could not scold Tasha for taking cruel pleasure in another's distress. The Cossack girl had too often displayed senseless cruelty towards her servant to be deserving of anything better.

"Tomorrow she'll sleep most of the day and want nothing but tea and honey. You won't hardly know she's around. Unfortunately, Grigori will be just the opposite."

"Why? Is he afraid of storms, too?"

"Of course not! But if it is still raining tomorrow, he won't be able to work, and that means he will stay at home and bother us all day." She tried to suppress a giggle. "Not that I'll mind having him here!"

Remembering the long discussions she had held with Justine and Yvette in their room above the tailor shop and all the secrets they had shared, Alexandra rolled out of bed and dragged a quilt to join Tasha on the floor. She poked the carefully banked fire and added a few pieces of wood until it crackled merrily with warmth and dancing light.

"I want you to tell me about him," Alexandra asked. "You must know Grigori better than anyone else, and I want to know all there is to know about him."

"I ought to. I'm the only one who pays any attention to him. His sister despises him, his father barely tolerates him, and Katrushka doesn't care at all about him. All she talks about is Vasili!" Jealousy clenched her hands into fists. "I just can't wait until Katrushka finds out the truth, that you aren't Vasili's woman after all. She'll probably die on the spot, and it would serve her right."

"You really are in love with Grigori, aren't you?"

"And what's wrong with that?"

"Nothing at all."

Another clap of thunder shook the house and broke the sudden tension that had grown between them. In the silence that followed, Tasha lost her defiance.

"Well, it doesn't hurt anything, I suppose. I do what I'm told to do and I don't waste my time on useless dreams like Valentina does, and even if I can't have him, at least—"

"Who says you can't have him?"

"I'm not what he's looking for, and you know it as well as I do."

"Then he's a fool. Grigori, or any other man in this valley for that matter, would have to be a blind fool not to see beyond the flour on your nose or the apron around your waist."

"Then Grigori is a blind fool, because he will never see me as anything but a kitchen brat." How it hurt to admit it, but lies and believing in lies could only hurt more, and Tasha was too realistic to lie. "You don't understand."

"Then help me to understand."

Tasha lowered her eyes to the fire and dropped her voice to a whisper barely audible above the storm.

"I knew about it before anyone else, and even though no one made me promise anything, I never intended to tell you."

Alexandra knew this was the answer she had waited so long for.

"Grigori has found someone else. He is building a house for her and when he is done he is going to ask her to marry him. I'm not supposed to know anything about it, so how can I go to him and tell him you're in love with someone else? If I do, there'll be more explanations and everyone will be hurt and he'll hate me forever." Silent tears fell. "At first I wanted to hate you for coming here and ruining all our lives. But I'm not like Valentina. I can't even be jealous that he loves you and not me. I knew from the beginning it wasn't your fault and that you would rather have it different, too. Besides, you were my friend."

Alexandra had heard the worst of all her fears realized. As she put her arm around Tasha's shoulder and soothed her with quiet words, Alexandra scolded herself for not having seen the truth much sooner. It should have been so plain; in looking back, everything that had seemed so mysterious became perfectly clear. Only one question remained.

"How long until he finishes this house?"

"Six weeks, two months, depending on the weather."

"We won't do anything until then, and perhaps by the end of May something will happen to solve all our problems."

Chapter 28

AS THOUGH to make amends for the hard and cruel winter, spring lavished the valley with unexpected beauty. The oak and beech trees spun lacy webs of green to clothe their naked limbs, and at their feet the violets turned shy faces away from the warmth of the sun. The air was clear, the sky brilliant, and everything seemed in a rush to enjoy the renewal of life that came with the season. Birds filled every inch of air with song, from the first brightening of dawn until the stars twinkled at night above the shadows of the mountain. With the dark came different sounds, the muted call of owls, a fox's bark, the keen screeching of bats. Winter's silence was gone.

Yet this awakening passed virtually unnoticed by the woman who had waited so long and so patiently for it. Alexandra saw no flowers, heard no birds, felt none of the happiness of spring. As the months of May progressed, and still no stranger rode into the valley to whisk her away, she waxed more despondent. Tears came easily, too easily, and her mind sought desperately for release.

She was sitting, as usual, in her chair on the porch, with a bit of embroidery lying untouched in her lap when Grigori walked up the steps one superb afternoon. He called her name twice before she looked up.

''Are you busy?'' he asked.

''No, not really.''

''Good! Come with me; I have something to show you.''

His own joy blinded him, for in his overwhelming happiness he saw only the green beauty of her eyes, not the sorrow that dimmed them or the blue circles under them that told of sleepless nights. He held her hand in his lightly, as though her fingers were fragile porcelain that would break in his grasp, and he did not feel the trembling. With her at his side, he beamed as he led the way to the edge of the village and the home he had built for one reason only.

"Go in, go in," he urged. "It is yours."

She stepped into the parlor, a bright little room with white curtains fluttering at the open windows. Sunlight pouring through the panes streaked the floor with bands of pale gold.

"The kitchen is in here, and the bedroom through that door. And see, I put two fireplaces, one here and one in the kitchen, so it will never be cold in the winter. There is a spring not twenty paces from the kitchen door; you won't have to walk all the way to the village well."

"Grigori, please," she said, trying to turn away from him.

"I know, I know. I'm getting ahead of myself."

His exuberant smile gave way to a more serious mien, and taking both her hands in his, he looked directly into her eyes and with slow deliberation spoke the words she had so long dreaded.

"I want you to be my wife, Alexandra, to live with me in this house that I have built for you. When my mother finds out what I've done, I will no longer be welcome under her roof, but it makes no difference. You are the woman I want, no matter what Katrushka says or does."

Her mind was numb. She could not find the words to answer him, and she knew she must.

"I'm flattered, and deeply honored," she managed to whisper, "but I need time."

"You've had all winter!" he exploded, then calmed almost instantly when she drew away from him in fear. "Forgive me, my love, I didn't mean it. Of course you may have time."

There was impatience in his words. Alexandra knew he would demand a quick answer. How long could she hold him off?

"A month Grigori. Give me a month, until Midsummer, and I will tell you then. I promise."

It was a longer wait than he had anticipated, but to Alexandra's surprise, he smiled and agreed. Then, abruptly and without warning, he took her in his arms and kissed her.

Though her first impulse was to fight him, she suppressed it and forced herself to submit. In his clumsy passion he bruised her lips until she could hardly bear the pain, and even breathing was difficult against the crushing embrace of his arms. When he finally released her, she gasped with a sigh of relief, but there were tears already starting in the corners of her eyes.

He spoke quietly, and he did not ask for forgiveness.

"I couldn't help it. You are too beautiful and I am only a man, like Vasili, who must be a fool not to come back for you."

For a moment, her heart stopped beating. Someday she would have to tell him the truth, and as she walked with him back outside into the sunlight, she tried not to think of it. Four weeks remained to her, in which time much could happen. At the moment it was enough to try to erase the memory of Grigori's inept lovemaking and focus her mind on surviving one more day without Mikhail.

Valentina took her place at the table just as Dmitri began the devotion that preceded every meal. Ignoring his disapproving glance, she bowed her head with mock humility.

Only Alexandra noticed the gleam of wickedness in Valentina's eyes, and she did not like it. It warned of trouble soon to come. More nervous than usual because of it, Alexandra toyed with her food and ate little as she wondered just how much longer this tension could last. She had almost accustomed herself to it after two weeks of never knowing when Grigori would suddenly blurt out his announcement but she never relaxed for a second. Nothing could ever blot from her memory his hands, his mouth, his fierce demanding maleness. She did not trust him and knew that she never would.

"You aren't eating, Alexandra," Katrushka's voice intruded upon her thoughts. "Aren't you hungry?"

"I guess I was just daydreaming," she answered with a forced smile. "I thought the gardening would give me an appetite, but I'm too tired."

It was only half a lie, for the exertion of pulling weeds and cultivating the soil around the vegetables had left her muscles sore and weary, but she had no taste for food at all. She was aware, too, that Valentina continued to stare at her, and the evil in those eyes chilled her blood.

"Not too tired to take a walk in the moonlight with your lover, though, are you?"

The silence that followed Valentina's softly spoken accusation vibrated with expectancy. Alexandra rose and with regal grace faced her adversary across the table.

"I will not dignify that absurdity with a denial."

With Grigori at her heels, Alexandra strode from the room and headed for the door, but he grabbed her arm and dragged her back despite her angry protests.

"Let go of me," she hissed, but he paid no attention, and he was too strong for her to fight him off.

He held her in front of him and stated, "It's true, what Valentina said. I am Alexandra's lover, the one she meets every night."

It wasn't true; it couldn't be. She refused to believe what she had just heard him say. Astonished, she let him push her into a chair without resisting. Her knees had gone too weak to support her anyway.

"*Slut*!" Valentina shrieked. "You filthy French whore!"

Grigori tried but could not reach across the table to strike his sister.

"I told you from the very beginning she was a whore," Valentina went on. "You let her live in this house while all the time she was seducing him."

290

"I did nothing of the sort," Alexandra insisted in her own defense.

Dmitri called for order with a loud thump of his fist on the table, but no one heard or paid any attention to him. Katrushka began to cry.

"Alexandra and I fell in love months ago, but because of Vasili, she refused my attentions until it was no longer possible to deny the truth. And I knew that because of your promise to Vasili, you would throw her out if you discovered it." He looked at his mother with unmasked hatred and added, "Now it is out, and whether you like it or not, we are going to be married."

Valentina went white with rage, then exploded.

"No! I forbid it! I won't let you marry that scheming bitch!"

She pushed her chair back with a loud scrape and strode around the table towards Alexandra.

"You'll never be part of this family. I'll kill you before I'll let you take his name, you—"

Dmitri blocked her way and for a short space of time there was quiet again.

"Go to your room *now*," he ordered. "I will deal with you later, you foul-mouthed brat, and I may forget that you are my own daughter instead of a bawling fishwife." Then, not once looking at Alexandra, he turned to Grigori. "You are guilty of the most horrible deceit, not only towards your parents, whom you were taught to honor and obey, but towards a friend, a trusted and loved member of this family. You are no longer welcome in my house, and when you go, take the woman with you."

"But what about Vasili?" Kathrushka wailed through her tears. "What are we to tell him when he returns and finds how we have treated her?"

"We will tell him he should have come back sooner."

"I gave him my word," she sobbed. "Grigori, you must give it up. She is not meant for you. She belongs to someone else, and you must not take her away from him."

"She belongs to *me*! If Vasili wants her, he will have to fight for her."

"Don't be a fool, Grigori."

Unable to miss the climax of the little drama she had so cleverly set in motion, Valentina stood in the doorway.

"Take the harlot to your little love nest, dear brother, but don't expect her to marry you. She won't. Whores don't marry men; they just—"

Grigori's open hand caught her cheek full force, knocking her to the floor with a cry of real pain. When neither her father nor mother went to her aid, Alexandra took a cloth from the table and knelt to hold it to Valentina's bleeding nose.

"Get away from me, you French bitch," she growled through the blood, "before I strangle you here and now."

A little over an hour after Valentina had sulked off to her bed with a wet cloth pressed to the back of her neck to stop the nosebleed, Alexandra tied the last of her belongings into a neat bundle and prepared to leave. She accepted without hesitation that the only course open to her was to go with Grigori.

"You should have told them the truth," Tasha scolded.

"Why? It wouldn't have changed anything."

"Are you sure?"

"Yes, I'm sure. And even if it had, I doubt that it would have been for the better."

"But you could have destroyed Valentina."

"I have no wish to destroy anyone, not even her, though I suppose she deserves it as much as anyone. I can't have what I want; I can't stay here, I can't leave this valley. All I can do is go with Grigori."

"Valentina would have killed you if Grigori hadn't stopped her."

"I don't care. What's done is done." She looked around the little room one last time. "Is that everything?"

"I think so. But I still think you should have told them the truth."

Tasha knew that Alexandra was right, and she had no choice but to do as Grigori wished.

"I will miss you, Alexandra. Can I visit you?"

"Of course, you may. Heavens, Tasha, I'm not going away to—" She stopped, unable to go on. No, she thought sadly, I'm not going away to Paris or Moscow; I just wish I were.

Grigori took the large bundle of her clothing from Tasha and held the door while Alexandra stepped outside. She strode beside Grigori up the now moonlit road to the little house nestled close to the woods.

He said nothing to her until they were well away from his parents' house, and she mentally thanked him for those moments of silence. They gave her a chance to adjust to this sudden change of direction in her life, to contemplate what had happened and to prepare for the immediate future. Though moving into the new house had certain advantages, it also held certain drawbacks that she must take into consideration. Most notable was that they would be living together without the benefit of marriage, and while it was not uncommon for first-born children to arrive a mere five or six months after the wedding, the inflexible morality of the villagers would not tolerate open fornication.

She refused to face the alternative. Better to live accused of one crime than guilty of another, she reasoned with a mind remarkably clear after all the shocks of this evening.

Grigori interrupted her thoughts.

"I am sorry, Alexandra. I did not want it to happen this way."

"It wasn't your fault," she said, not quite certain she believed her own words.

"In the morning we will find the priest and be married before Valentina can spread the story. I know it's sudden and not what we planned, but we must make the best of it."

" 'Not what we planned'?" she echoed incredulously. "We never planned anything at all!"

"You wanted a celebration, and I feel terrible because I know how disappointed you must be. What Valentina did was unforgivable, but the damage has been done and all we can do is live with it."

Twice again she tried to make him listen to her, to remind him of his promise of time, but to no avail. He interrupted her every time she spoke, and the feeling of frustration soon turned to anger as she came to see the truth hiding behind his words.

He was not the least bit sorry for having deprived her of a wedding feast and celebration. His eagerness to ensconce her in his own home belied his apologies clearly. Not once did he stop to comfort her or hold her or even look into her eyes as he expressed his false regrets. If Valentina's outburst had not been planned, and Alexandra now doubted the spontaneity of her disclosure, Grigori had acted swiftly to take advantage of the situation. And Alexandra, the almost willing victim, had fallen easily into his trap.

"By this time tomorrow everything will be fine," he told her confidently. He opened the door and stepped into the house. Though the darkness obscured his face, Alexandra heard the smile of victory in his voice. She shuddered. "You will be my wife in the eyes of God and man, and nothing will ever separate us again as long as we live."

Chapter 29

MIKHAIL AWAKENED lazily and stretched his arms and legs with a loud yawn before he opened his eyes. The sun was still just a promise below the horizon but its glow turned the morning clouds coppery and touched all the countryside with brightness that heralded another fine day.

He ate leisurely, then watched the sun come up in a glorious blaze of gold and lavender while he saddled the black stallion and began the day's ride with his shadow stretching out before him. As the rising sun warmed his back, he noted with pleasure that the scars no longer prickled and itched the way they had at first. Only two of them gave him any discomfort at all now, the two that had nearly killed him.

He remembered only that one night out of the entire six week nightmare, but it was enough. Vasili alone had not been able to hold him; it took two other servants as well to keep him still while his grandmother drew the red-hot knife blade through the festering wounds. The rotten flesh had sizzled and filled his nostrils with the most horrible stench as it burned, and the pain made Trabert's lashes seem almost gentle in comparison. He had screamed once, then fell into the murky oblivion that held him captive until the year changed.

The lacerations on his back healed rather quickly after that, but his complete recovery took months, for the loss of so much blood had weakened him and the battle against the infection further sapped his strength. When he finally regained consciousness on the first of January, he needed help just to sit up in bed. All winter he allowed himself to be waited on, by his mother, by Anna Petrovna, Vasili, and by the suddenly ever present Irina Leevna Drubetskaya.

The thought of Irina brought a light chuckle from him as he turned the black off the main road and onto a narrow track leading still higher into the mountains. Poor Irina! He'd give a thousand rubles to see her face when she found out he wasn't waiting for her in Moscow as he had promised. He didn't mind lying to her, but his conscience pricked a little at deceiving the others. By the time they realized what he had done, he would be safely away from their well-intentioned nosiness. He needed more than anything time to be alone, and at the Ogrinov estate or in Moscow, where he had sent Vasili early in the spring, he had no hope for anything but continued pestering.

Though his body had recovered from the ordeal, not all his wounds were physical. Marina and Anna Petrovna ministered to his torn flesh and Vasili helped him regain his strength, but not even Irina's therapy could ease the mental anguish brought on by the memory of that final vision. All of them tried, perhaps too hard, to make him talk about it and get it out of his system, or in the case of the insistent young widow, to make him forget. He steadfastly refused to do the former, and he found the latter impossible.

He could not look at Irina without seeing green eyes in place of her blue ones. Her cool, sensuous body reminded him of another, warmer, softer, sweeter. He knew there would be no pleasure in making love to Irina, and despite her numerous invitations, he did not bother to prove his point. She could not respond as someone else had to his touch, his kiss, his voice; Irina performed because she was expected to, like a trained bitch in a circus.

In the mountain village where he planned to spend the entire summer, he could keep the past a secret. Alexandra was gone, lost forever, and the question of that illusion need never be asked or answered. He thought he had seen her, yet he could not believe it of her. He wanted to see her one last time before he died, but he had not wanted to see her with Trabert. He wanted her to live, but not at that cost. Torn between too many choices, he shoved them all to the back of his mind, because none of them had any meaning now. Alexandra was gone.

Twice before in his life he had found the simple life of the Cossacks a marvelous restorative, when his wounds had been of the body one time and of the spirit another. Perhaps it would work as well on both together.

The sun climbed higher and grew warmer, for not a single cloud marred the perfection of the sky. Mikhail stopped at each stream to let the horse drink and to splash himself with the refreshing water before continuing. Having eaten the last of his provisions for breakfast, he was resigned to missing lunch and hoped he would arrive in time for one of Katrushka's suppers. He let his memory conjure up visions of the long table in the Tcheradzin dining room covered with platters of roast lamb and spicy chicken and bowls of early strawberries in thick cream. He and Grigori had made whole meals of those berries as childhood companions, and he could taste them yet.

He wondered how much the village, and the Tcheradzins, had changed in the five years since his last visit. Dmitri would always be Dmitri, hard as iron, humorless, but honest and hard-working. Katrushka never lacked for energy when it came to having fun or helping someone else. He remembered how she had fussed over his other injury, and he hoped she would not take this one as seriously. Then, with the thigh wound still livid and dangerous, she had done everything but carry him around on her own shoulders. This time he was completely healed and shouldn't require much attention. But he never knew, not with Katrushka.

There had been a daughter, a gangly lass in her teens, whom he remembered as a stubborn, fierce-tempered tomboy with long braids flying behind her as she ran after her brother and his friend. She had been such a nuisance, tagging along when they went fishing or hunting or, even

297

worse, when they sought other forms of diversion. She was probably married now with at least one little tomboy daughter of her own.

By late afternoon Mikhail rode in the shadow of the mountain and the way was dim, but he was never lost. He guided the stallion into the last narrow pass that led into the forest and the valley and they moved through an eerie gloom that was neither daylight nor twilight.

On this, the last day of spring, the woods were alive with scent and song. Wildflowers bloomed in extravagant profusion, their blossoms little sparkles of white and pink and yellow against the carpet of grass, and mixed their delicate perfume with the freshness of oak and pine and new-turned earth. Overhead the air snapped with the scold of a squirrel and the hammering of a woodpecker.

There was no need to hurry now that he had only a mile or two before he arrived at his sanctuary, so he let the horse slow to a walk and savored the tranquility of the afternoon a bit longer. In a short while he would be surrounded by his old friends, clapped on the back, forced to drink a dozen or more toasts with fiery Cossack vodka, and kissed by every eligible or available woman in three villages. He needed the last few moments to prepare himself.

Still within the shadow of the trees he paused to drink in the beauty of the valley spread before him, and from the corner of his eye he saw a girl emerge from the trees not far away with a basket full of flowers she had picked. More interested in finding Grigori and a hot meal, Mikhail ignored the child and kicked his mount to a brisk canter down the road.

Little had changed in five years, he noted with satisfaction. The only houses he did not remember were the little cottages at the top of the road, which were obviously new, and one nearer to Tcheradzin's. He would ask Grigori about it, because he thought Grodatny the singer had once lived there, but in an old, dilapidated hovel, not the sturdy house standing there now.

The smoke rising from the chimneys drifted with the breeze and carried with it the luscious aroma of two dozen suppers. Mikhail's stomach rumbled rather loudly as he tied the black to the porch rail and climbed the steps to Grigori's house.

He knocked twice but received no answer, nor did his shouts bring anyone. He was about to open the door himself when the servant girl appeared, out of breath and rather angry at being disturbed.

"You must be Tasha. Do you remember me?" he asked when she had let him in the cool parlor.

"I am Tasha, my lord, and yes, I do remember you." She curtsied with as much dignity as possible with a dab of butter on her nose and flour up to her elbows. "Please excuse me while I find Valentina," she stammered, then dropped another bow and ran to escape through the kitchen door.

He laughed, not unkindly, at the girl's almost frightened excitement. One look at him had set her to trembling like an aspen leaf, and he swore he saw her lips quiver. He would have preferred to see Grigori first rather than his obnoxious younger sister, but since Tasha had disappeared too quickly for him to ask, he would have to wait and ask Valentina her brother's whereabouts.

Valentina entered the parlor with a scowl. She had no time to entertain a visitor when one of the horses needed grooming, and Tasha received a well-deserved tongue-lashing for interrupting her. She would have refused to go with the impudent brat but she needed something to bandage a cut on her hand. She wiped the blood on the seat of her black trousers as she grumbled her way through the kitchen. If the visitor did not approve her appearance, she would be more than happy to leave him to his own devices and return to her work.

That thought came back to her the instant she strode into the parlor and saw the well-remembered silhouette against the window. Her face turned as red as the scarf around her head when she realized how ludicrous a situation she had put herself into. It certainly was not proper for her to bow to him like a man, but neither could she very well make a decent curtsy in man's clothing.

"Please, forgive my lack of manners. I've been busy in the stables and—oh, where is that brat Tasha? She was supposed to get me a bandage for this."

She had no choice but to repeat her earlier action to keep the blood from dripping to the floor. Mikhail turned away, half embarrassed himself at her discomfiture.

"Perhaps she went to find Grigori," he suggested when it became apparent that Tasha was not in the house.

"It shouldn't take her long. He's never anywhere but one place this time of the day."

The sharpness of her retort startled him, and he wondered what had happened to make her so bitterly resentful toward the brother she had once almost worshipped. As quickly as it came, however, her anger died and she regained what little poise she had, enough to apologize once more.

"Please, please, sit down and let me get you something to drink. Wine? Vodka? I can get you a bite to eat, too, unless you want to wait until supper. Tasha has it all ready; we were just waiting for Mother."

"No wine on an empty stomach," he said, though he was thirsty and would have enjoyed a cool glass of wine.

"Then I'll fix some tea," she offered, and without waiting for his assent or refusal, she dashed into the kitchen. "Mother will be back very soon, I think. Old Karachnikov died this morning and she's gone to help the grieving widow lay him out."

Mikhail took a chair near the window and stared out at the lengthening shadows. Twilight came early to the valley, but it lasted for hours; not until long past supper would the sky finally darken and the first stars of summer appear. He felt at peace, listening to the chatter of the girl in the kitchen and watching the lazy summer afternoon outside.

She set the cup on the table beside him and stepped back, afraid to be too close to him. Dusty and dirty and unshaven, dressed in peasant's garb no different than that worn by the men in the village, he still wielded the power to enchant her.

"Karachnikov, Karachnikov," he muttered, trying by repetition to remember something about the man who had belonged to that name. "He was the cobbler with the ugly wife and all the ugly daughters."

Mikhail sipped his tea and closed his eyes, let weariness steal over him almost against his will while he listened to her. The wooden chair felt soft as a featherbed, and unlike the horse he had ridden for the greater part of the past week, it did not move beneath him. He could easily have fallen asleep were it not for the eyes staring so intently at him. Something beyond ordinary awe at the presence of a nobleman lurked behind those opalescent orbs, something which set him on his guard.

"If you're tired, you can use my bed," Valentina suggested, not caring if he thought it immodest or impertinent.

"No, thank you, but I'd appreciate another cup of tea."

Their hands touched for a fleeting second as she took the cup from him, and when she disappeared into the kitchen, she was trembling with anticipation.

It was Tasha who, a moment later, brought him his second cup of tea, not as strong as the first and sweetened just the way he liked it with wild honey.

"Valentina is washing up and changing her clothes, and when she is more presentable, she will be back," Tasha told him. "I have to go on an errand; if she asks, tell her I will be back soon."

She was out the door at a run before he had a chance to ask if she had found Grigori.

Alexandra sat at the table, her eyes closed, her head resting on hands folded as if in prayer, when Tasha walked into the cottage.

"Tell me where Grigori keep his vodka. I think you need some."

"No, I don't want any," Alexandra mumbled. "I intend to be in full control of myself when the shock hits me. I'm just glad you managed to get my husband out of

301

the house first."

"I'm sorry I couldn't warn you. I thought and thought, but there wasn't a way to tell him without telling you at the same time. And I couldn't stay, so I came back as fast as I could. I hated doing it, but what else could I do?"

Alexandra lifted her head slowly. "I knew he was here half an hour before you came through the door. I saw him ride through the woods as I was coming home with some flowers."

"Did he see you?"

"I don't think so. At least, he didn't recognize me."

"What are you going to do?"

Alexandra sighed and pushed the red babushka off her head before she answered, "For the moment, sit here and finish this cup of cold tea."

"But sooner or later you'll have to—"

"Yes, sooner or later, but not right now."

Worried but unable to pinpoint the source of her concern, Tasha left her friend very reluctantly. She knew that something must be desperately wrong with Alexandra for her to have maintained such calm in the face of this latest shock. It wasn't at all like her not to react.

But Tasha had no way to suspect the hell Alexandra had lived in for the past two weeks.

She had married Grigori in a daze the morning after their hasty departure from his parents' house, and news of the event travelled so quickly that the first well-wishers were waiting at the cottage when Grigori and his bride returned from the church. Alexandra found herself caught up in a nightmare that had begun with a jealous woman's spiteful accusation and an impassioned man's lie.

And after two full weeks, she had not awakened from that dream. Indeed, it grew more horrible each day, each night, not because of what happened, for nothing had, but because of the inevitability that it must. The wedding celebration had lasted until dawn, leaving Grigori too tired and too drunk that first night to do anything but crawl to his bed and collapse in a snoring heap. For the following week, Alexandra's own femaleness held him at bay. Only her very real fright and equally genuine tears continued to keep him from demanding his rights as her husband, and she knew he would not wait much longer.

She finished her tea, then prepared a bath. As she scrubbed her body and washed her hair, she tried not to hear the voice accusing her of primping for Mikhail. She felt a twinge of guilt, for the voice was right.

The twilight had deepened and the first stars twinkled faintly in the sky when Alexandra stepped onto the porch and sat down to brush her hair dry in the warm air. A bit of breeze blew up the valley carrying with it the distant wailing of Karachnikov's widow and daughters as they mourned, and the voice of a mother scolding her children. As hard as she tried to sort out the whispers of other sounds and distinguish one voice above all the others, Alexandra heard nothing from the house where she knew Mikhail was, just a few hundred yards away.

Such a short distance. She could walk it in the time it took to count twenty-five strokes with the brush. If she did, the nightmare would be over, one way or another. Yet at the back of her mind the thought lingered that he had not come for her, did not even want her. Was it right to destroy Grigori's dreams because her own had died? She brushed away tears and started another five hundred strokes while she watched the lights wink out in the houses below her and she did not move from her place. Mikhail must come to her, not to prove his love or to atone for any wrong he had done, but because she refused to hurt someone as innocent as Grigori. She had to know Mikhail no longer wanted her before she would give him up.

"I do not love my husband, nor will I ever, but if the worst happens, I will stay with him and be as good a wife to him as I can," she whispered half to herself, "and never let him know the truth." A lump formed in her throat, but she continued, struggling to keep her voice steady even though no one heard except the owls and the crickets. She thought of Therese and Armand, husband and wife out of necessity, and they seemed happy. Perhaps eventually she would find that kind of contentment with Grigori. "I cannot promise more than that, because I know that if Mikhail asks me, I will go with him regardless of any vows or promises, no matter how sacred."

As the moon's bright crescent floated over the ocean of the night sky, she waited. Though her arms ached from brushing the long cascade of her hair and her eyes itched with weariness, she did not enter the cottage to seek her bed. Sleep was impossible. From the moment she had looked up and seen him riding through the woods she had known how long this night would last. Every second seemed an eternity, and the irony brought a sad smile to her lips, for this was Midsummer's night, the shortest of the year.

Shadows moved, slowly but inexorably. The owl whose cry had kept her company returned to his roost and the night grew silent as all the valley slept. She hardly dared to breathe, afraid of breaking whatever spell had fallen in this final hour before the dawn. Peace and purity surrounded her, and the harmony of all Creation filled her with a serenity that gave her the strength to accept whatever the new day brought to her.

The soft twittering of a bird shattered the stillness. Wakened from a restful trance that bordered on sleep, Alexandra picked her brush from where it had fallen and stood for the first time in hours to stretch and yawn and smile at the signs of daybreak. The moon rested in its descent, but already the shadows it cast were fading. The incandescence preceding true dawn had begun to glow with the promise of another perfect summer's day. Just as Alexandra turned to go inside and catch an hour or two of sleep, she saw the figure walking unsteadily up the road, stumbling more than once and barely able to put one foot in front of the other. Closing her eyes to the sight, she made her way into the still dark bedroom and lay down.

Sleep came so swiftly, so miraculously, she did not hear her husband come in the door nor waken when he fell onto the bed beside her and began to snore.

Chapter 30

THE VOICES that wakened Alexandra were not echoes of a dream but real. She turned instinctively away from Grigori, but his pillow was empty. As she listened to the quiet whispers coming from somewhere outside, she pulled the blanket up to her chin. It was fear, not cold, that made her shiver, and the guilt could not warm the ice that gripped her soul. All the horror, all the pain, all the bitter memories she had so slowly buried sought their way back to her consciousness. The sound of his voice resurrected them.

Staring at the ceiling, she tried to black it out of her mind, and with her remaining strength battled to maintain her fragile hold on reality. If for a moment she dared to close her eyes, it was his image her brain conjured up and she could not bear it. She sought numbness, the relief from all sensation of body and mind and soul, the oblivion that was her only refuge. In the past it had come to her on nights when exhaustion closed her eyes in surrender to the dark void of sleep. Now the bright light of day shone around her and neither sleep nor its oblivion released her, because she could not blot out the sound of his voice.

She heard only whispers too faint to distinguish the words, but she knew when Mikhail paused and when Katrushka spoke. Alexandra caught her breath each time he stopped and did not breathe again until she heard his voice and knew he had not gone.

Time ceased. Whether a minute passed or an hour,

Alexandra neither knew nor cared. Every cell of her being was bound by the web of that muffled voice. She lay still, silent, eyes open but unseeing, so completely mesmerized that she heard nothing but what she wanted to hear, not even the slow footsteps mounting the porch stairs or the squeak of the front door as someone opened it and entered.

There was a long pause in the conversation, during which she believed she would die of the waiting, but when it resumed, the speakers were much closer, right under her kitchen window. She could hear every single word.

"I can tell you no more than I already have," Katrushka said. "Vasili brought her here half dead and said nothing but that we were to care for her."

"That isn't like him, especially after all we had gone through to find her."

"Do you accuse me of lying? I swear by the Blessed Virgin and all the Holy Saints that I believed she was Vasili's woman. Why did he say nothing, not a single word? It would have been so simple if only he had told me." The anger that had been so strong in her first words now changed to sadness.

"Yes, 'if only,'" Mikhail echoed.

"I am truly sorry, Mikhail Pavlovitch. Go in and see her, and I will send Grigori as soon as I can. Are you sure you won't stay another night at least?"

"No, I can't. I'll go as soon as I get this over with."

They said no more, and Alexandra felt her heart begin to pound within her chest as Katrushka's footsteps faded. At any moment he would come in, find her, and the whole ugly nightmare would be over. Alexandra waited with her breath burning in her lungs until she wanted to scream.

But it was Grigori's face, not Mikhail's, that suddenly appeared above her, so hideously distorted that she almost failed to recognize him.

"I should have known I'd find you here," he hissed. "You lying, deceitful French whore!"

He spat in her face. Petrified, she could not even raise

her hand to wipe off the saliva and felt it slither down her cheek like some slimy, evil slug.

"I gave you my honor, the security and protection of my home, I even gave you my love, and this is how you repay me!"

He grabbed the edge of the quilt covering her and ripped it off the bed, then reached for the white linen blouse she wore, tearing it easily.

"Night after night I have lain beside you, shared this bed with you, and I have never touched you because you said you were afraid of men. Why did you not look afraid when I came in here just now and found you waiting for him?"

As she drew back from him, she managed to whisper, "Grigori, for the love of God, don't do this! Let me explain!"

He did not give her the chance. He was on the bed, grabbing for her blindly.

"You aren't going to stop me this time with your lies. I saw it in your eyes while you were lying there, waiting for him, in my house, in my bed, the bed you are supposed to share with me."

Rage and jealousy and something else had taken him beyond the point of reason. One hand closed on her shoulder, and he dragged her away from the wall, pulled her to her knees and forced her to look at him.

"I am a man, just like him, but you are *my* wife, not his, and I am going to prove it!"

She was nearly naked, the scraps of her clothing scattered about the room, and the whiteness of her skin, the pallor of sheer terror, stopped him only for a moment while he let his eyes feast on the beauty that he had been so long denied.

All her strength was gone. She had not even the power to close her eyes to the sight of this man, now turned into a fiend from hell. The demon of lust possessed him as he tore off his own clothes; his body quivered with an unholy desire.

"You are my wife," he repeated without tenderness.

Like a beast he fell upon her, and when he forced his body between her thighs, the fragile thread, so patiently spun, broke. She had lost her tenuous contact with reality. Her only tie to sanity snapped under the strain of Grigori's savage brutality.

Her scream shattered the air. It stunned Grigori more than the sudden resistance she put up. Her nails clawed his back and shoulders, drawing blood. She slid her knee beneath his leg and rammed it into the tense muscle of his upper thigh, though he reacted quickly enough to prevent her reaching a more sensitive target. She beat at him with her fists, tried to sink her teeth into his arm. He had no choice, as his own sanity returned, but to ease away from her ferocious attack. His lust was gone; the raging desire, though unsatisfied, no longer consumed him.

The echoes of that scream still rang in Mikhail's ears when he stormed into the cottage, his sabre drawn and ready. The house was dim after the brightness outdoors, but what little he could see told him all he needed to know. On the bed, the unclad body of the woman men had gone to their deaths for. The thought suddenly stopped him, as he saw standing only a few steps away the man who had done what Mischa himself was guilty of, what he now regretted more than anything else he had ever done.

He heard nothing, not Grigori's quiet apology, Grigori, who had once been closer to him than his own brother, nor Katrushka's tearful pleas as she stood behind him and begged him not to do what she knew was inevitable. Above their voices, even above the pounding of his heart, all Mikhail heard was the memory of that scream. It had cut him like a knife, stabbing to his vitals until it caused physical pain.

He must end it now. Either avenge the suffering she had endured or pay for it himself. And there was but one way to do that. In an oddly calm voice he challenged Grigori to what they both knew was a senseless duel, and together they walked out of the house, into the street.

Katrushka ran after them, only to return to the bedroom a few moments later. Any attempt at dissuading these madmen was destined to be fruitless; they were bent on destruction and nothing less would satisfy them.

"They are going to kill each other," Alexandra announced. "Is there nothing we can do?"

The older woman shook her head as she handed Alexandra a glass of vodka.

"Nothing. It is the unfortunate lot of women to bring men into the world and then watch them hurry themselves out of it for no good reason at all." She swallowed her own vodka without tasting it, then sat down on the bed beside Alexandra. "Mikhail Pavlovitch is as much my child as Grigori. I have known him since he was a little boy, when his father brought him here to get him away from the soft life in Moscow. He and Grigori grew up together, always the best of friends. And I nursed his wounds, when the French shot him and when a woman's deception nearly killed him."

Afraid and feeling helpless, Alexandra wrapped herself in her quilt and wondered if he held her responsible this time, too. Had she, like some other woman before her, betrayed him? She downed the raw liquor in hopes it would bring her out of her numbness. It did, and she began to weep. And pray.

It took little time for a crowd to gather. Surrounded by the silently excited villagers, the two men faced each other grimly. The afternoon sun was warm, and since Grigori wore only his breeches and boots, Mikhail unbuttoned his shirt and slipped it off. There were gasps from the crowd at the sight of the still red scars that latticed his back. To prove he needed no pity, he raised his arms and flexed the muscles that rippled unharmed beneath the battered skin.

Of the same height and reach, they were evenly matched, Grigori's superior raw strength balanced by the speed and spring-steel resiliency of Mikhail's finely trained body. The tested each other with tentative thrusts and

310

mocking lunges, as though this were merely an exhibition of fencing skill. But each knew, though not a word had been spoken, that the reward to the victor was his life. The woman came second now, second to honor and to pride, for there was murder in their eyes, as well as regret.

They fought with determination, not fury, and the clang of steel on steel had a ghastly rhythm to it. Neither man seemed willing to take an offensive position; both remained cautious. First Grigori struck, his blade crashing against Mikhail's with such force that the vibrations carried on down his arm to his shoulder. Then Mischa countered with a thrust Grigori barely turned away in time. One and on, it went, and they drew not a single drop of blood.

Nor did they speak, and the villagers respected that silence. There were no raucous cheers, no applause for a clever feint or even a sharp intake of breath when one blade or another came close to its mark. All was tense concentration.

Gradually Grigori assumed the role of aggressor, becoming more active and relying on his strength to wear down his opponent. His honor in this village was at stake, and he felt rage growing in him again. But Mikhail, so relaxed he seemed almost to smile, took the defensive stand willingly. He let Grigori make all the moves and merely waited for the right opportunity. It would come, he knew, eventually, and he had the patience.

Dust settled on them, clinging to the sweat. Dirty little rivers of mud streaked their bodies as the afternoon wore on. Despite pain and exhaustion, neither man would lay down his weapon, for neither was ready to accept defeat. The constant attacking had taken much of Grigori's strength; he had not the stamina for a sustained battle such as this had become. But Mikhail, too, was wearied. The sabre grew heavy. He found it harder and harder to hold the blade at the proper angle, to bring it up or down to counter Grigori's slashes. And the tender scar tissue hurt. Burned by the sun, the wounds felt raw, as though freshly opened.

There was a savage beauty to their movements, as though they danced a macabre ballet, circling, crossing, meeting for an instant, then parting, a *pas de deux* to the death. Mikhail, still on the defensive, never stopped moving, for he knew Grigori was calling on his last reserve.

Then Grigori drew first blood, with a wild lunge Mikhail parried off balance. Grigori's blade just touched his arm, but the razor edge cut deep enough to send a red trickle to his elbow. He hardly felt it through all the other pain and did not take his eyes off his opponent to look at the wound. There would be time enough later, if he lived. And if he did not, this little scratch would not matter at all.

Grigori smelled triumph, and his momentary over-confidence gave Mikhail the opportunity to retaliate. He evened the score with a sharp jabbing thrust that put the tip of his sabre into the meat of Grigori's shoulder. As he lifted his hand to feel the extent of his injury, he realized how seriously out-classed he had been from the beginning. What he did not know was that he fought two opponents: Mikhail and the tangle of emotions within himself. The one was as deadly as the other.

When the end came, it was so sudden, so unexpected, that no one reacted for several seconds. The weapon slid from his hand and fell with a soft thud to the ground. As the victor threw his own bloodied blade atop it, a young woman broke through the crowd to kneel beside the defeated man's body.

She lifted his arm and looked at the ugly, gushing wound, a gash from wrist to elbow that had sliced through muscle to the bone. She paid no attention to the blood soaking her blouse and skirt; she concentrated on binding his arm with strips torn from her apron while he was still unconscious and unable to feel the pain.

"Go to her, Mikhail," Tasha said without looking up from her task. "She's been waiting a long time."

Dmitri stopped him before he had taken a dozen steps. "It would be better if someone else tells them.

Katrushka is there, too, and to see only you might make them think Grigori is dead,'' the old man whispered as he placed a trembling hand on Mikhail's arm. "I will go; you stay and help the girl with Grigori.''

Mikhail agreed. He was not certain he could even have walked all the way to the cottage at the edge of the woods.

"It is over,'' he said to a groggy but conscious opponent. He reached down to take Grigori's hand and help him to his feet.

Grigori waved off all other offers of assistance and leaned on Mischa until the momentary dizziness wore off and he stood, though unsteadily, alone.

"It has been a long time, Mikhail Pavlovitch, since you and I fought as children.'' He swallowed a lump in his throat and, with his uninjured arm, embraced his friend. "Today we fought as men. You have won; the woman is yours now, and we are even.''

"No, she is not mine. She is your wife, and I have no right.''

Grigori shook his head and was glad the crowd had dispersed. He did not care who heard what he had to say, though the words would have humiliated another man, but he wanted to salvage some pride.

"Alexandra was never my wife. If I had killed you, she would still be yours, never mine. Now go, you fool, and take what is yours. Don't keep me standing here in the sun or I will make a bigger fool of myself than I already have by fainting like a woman because of a little cut.''

Mikhail stood alone in the middle of the street and watched as Grigori slowly walked back to his father's house. Katrushka came running to help her son climb the stairs, but he brushed her away and let Tasha steady him. Not until the door closed behind them did Mischa turn and begin the long trek to the little cottage at the edge of the forest.

Of what Dmitri whispered to Katrushka, Alexandra only understood enough to know that Grigori had been wounded and needed his mother's attention. About Mikhail he said nothing, and when she tried to follow Katrushka, he held her back. The grave look in his eyes alarmed her. She wanted to know what had happened, no matter how horrible, but the anger in Dmitri's eyes held her mute, unable to utter a sound.

When he, too, had gone and she was alone, she closed her eyes and saw visions of Mikhail's body lying still and cold in the dust.

But she dared not go outside. She had to wait. Five minutes passed, then ten. Why had they not brought Grigori home? Why did Dmitri not want her to see her husband? Was he afraid she would try to avenge the death of her lover? She refused to let them think that of her, refused to think that Mischa could be dead. Unable to stand the silence any longer, she resolved to go to Grigori, nurse him, prove to all of them that she did not hold him to blame for Mikhail's death.

She stopped with her hand on the door latch. Once outside, on the porch, she would have an unobstructed view of the street and anything in it.

"What is the matter with me?" she wondered aloud. "Where are the tears I should be shedding? Oh, Mischa, have I waited all this time for you only to lose you again, this time forever? I can't believe I've accepted that you're dead, without seeing for myself. I have to go out there and face it, because I have to know and because I can't stand to stay in this house, in Grigori's house, another second."

But she could not face it, and she knew it. She sank to her knees on the hard floor to offer a prayer, and it was in asking for forgiveness of her sins that she finally accepted his death.

"Why?" she begged, tears now streaming down her face. "Everything is gone now. I loved you so, and I never even told you. They were right to keep Grigori away from me; I would kill him, and then I would kill myself, if it would take me to you."

And then she wept. Like droplets of blood, her tears splashed on the floor and she collapsed, sobbing.

She had fallen asleep but was still crying softly, the whimpers shaking her body convulsively, when Mikhail walked wearily into the house.

Chapter 31

ALEXANDRA STUMBLED through the dark cottage to the kitchen and struck a fire on the cold hearth. Her hands trembled as she cupped them around the small flame and blew on it until it caught. Then she sat back and let out a long sigh.

Her sleep had been troubled with dreams that left her confused even now she was awake. Who lay in the bed beside her? She thought, as she had crawled out trying not to disturb him, that it was Mikhail, but was he not dead? Refusing to give in to despair yet unable to believe there was still reason to hope, she went outside to fetch water.

The grass was dewy cool on her bare feet as she crossed to the spring. As she set the first bucket to fill, she sat down, ignoring the dew soaking her skirt, and tried to clear a path through the cobwebs sleep had spun in her mind.

"Good morning, Alexandra."

She jumped at the unexpected voice and turned to find Tasha standing a few feet away. In the moonlight the girl looked especially pale with deep lines of worry etched onto her young face.

"You scared the life out of me!" Alexandra exclaimed.

"I'm sorry. I just came to tell you he'll be all right now. I thought you would want to know."

"Yes, I did. Thank you."

Before Alexandra had a chance to ask who it was that was all right, Tasha went on. "He told me to tell you he was sorry for the things he had done and for blundering into the middle of your happiness the way he did.''

Now she knew, and it filled her with pain. It cut into her like a sword thrust, searing her heart and soul, tears hot on her cheeks. Mikhail had burst into her life and with a simple apology was bowing his way out, leaving her to Grigori, with whom he supposed she had found peace.

"I didn't want this to happen," she moaned. "It was wrong from the very beginning." She grabbed a handful of grass and tore it up by the roots just for the release of energy the action gave. "I should never have married Grigori, I should have found a way to refuse him, even if—but it doesn't matter now. Mischa never really cared."

"At least you had hope. What have I got? I'll take care of him, bind his wounds, sew him back together, but he'll never see me as anything but his servant, and even though he knows I—"

"Whose servant?" Alexandra interrupted sharply.

"Grigori Dmitrievitch Tcheradzin's. Who else?"

"But he—I thought he was—" She looked towards the cottage for an instant, then back to Tasha. Unable to believe what she now understood to be the truth, she whispered, "Mikhail is here?"

"You mean you really didn't know?"

Alexandra lay back in the grass. A sigh of relief escaped her. "I thought he was dead. Dmitri said nothing about Mischa, only that Grigori was hurt, and he wouldn't even let me ask. I was too afraid to go outside and look, so I waited and waited. I must have fallen asleep on the floor, because I vaguely remember someone coming in and putting me to bed." The stars above her had paled now; dawn was near. "Don't give up hope, Tasha. If you love him, don't give up hope."

"Thank you, Alexandra, and God bless you. Everything is going to be fine now, you just wait and see. God bless you both."

Standing in the shadows looking at Tasha's young face with its bright eyes and hopeful smile, Alexandra suddenly felt very, very cold.

The water in the cauldron had just begun to boil when she heard the first sound from the other room, a long yawn followed by a groan and some unintelligible mumbling. A few moments later, Mikhail appeared in the doorway, looking more dead than alive. He still wore his filthy breeches and had pulled on the shirt that had lain in the road while he fought Grigori. His face was haggard and covered with a half-grown beard, and his eyes stared from redrimmed sockets.

"Don't you like what you see?" he asked sarcastically. "Does a little blood and dirt upset your delicate sensibilities? You lousy bitch." He muttered that last in English, forgetting after so many months that he could not use it to hide his secrets from her.

It made no sense to fight him, and she hadn't the will anyway.

"There's plenty of hot water if you want to clean up," she told him. "And you know where the door is if you want to leave."

She turned her back on him and strode into the parlor, where she sat down and picked up the mending she had started two days ago. It didn't matter that the torn shirt was Grigori's or that she had set it aside to gather wildflowers in the woods and come home so changed. It kept her busy and out of his way.

I am in control, she said to herself. I've come through the horror and can see clearly what he still views from behind a cloud of dreams and anger and fear and—

"Damn you!" he swore. "For God's sake!"

He ended with more expletives in French, Russian, English, and other languages she had never heard before. The short, explosive syllables were filled with pain. She braved his wrath to offer her assistance.

She found him seated at the table with a basin of hot water and a filthy rag in front of him. He had ripped the sleeve from his shirt and torn it into strips, but his left hand was too uncoordinated to cleanse and bandage his other arm. He winced as she pressed a clean hot cloth against the cut, but he said nothing.

"I'll get some bandages and a clean shirt for you while you wash," she suggested.

"Don't bother. I want nothing from you, nor from your husband, *Madame Tcheradzina*.."

"You've no right to talk to me like that!"

"Haven't I?"

"What did I do to deserve it?"

"Grigori was my oldest and one of my dearest friends, and look what you've done to him. You used him, prostituted yourself to him, and it damn near cost him his life."

"I didn't do that. You were the one who challenged him, Mikhail Pavlovitch Ogrinov. *You* came into *his* house and—"

"*His* house? Then where is he? Why isn't he here now? Why is he with his mother and sister and why isn't his loving wife tending his wounds instead of some half-witted kitchen maid?"

The words hurt. She clamped her hands over her ears to shut them out, but he grabbed her wrists and made her listen.

"You'll bed anyone, won't you? Trabert, Grigori. Take whatever a man has to offer until someone better comes along. Well, I'm sorry, I don't want what you have to sell. I don't need a whore like you."

Calmly, when he had finished, she replied, "I am no whore, Mischa. I was once, though not by choice. You may think whatever else about me you wish, but that is one sin I am no longer guilty of."

"Do you deny seducing Grigori?"

"Stop accusing me of things I didn't do! Valentina accused me of meeting a lover. Grigori confessed because he was already in love with me and was taking advantage of the situation. What else could I do but go along with it? I was alone here and afraid; I had no other choice."

"And if I hadn't stumbled upon you yesterday, would you have continued with him as willingly as you have in the past?"

He remembered her scream and how it had stabbed him, but he remembered, too, the pain of seeing his

319

friend lying in the dust. A man betrayed by a woman, and it brought back other memories, when he had been the betrayed.

"I might have killed Grigori, Mischa. I've done it before, and I would do it again."

"What? Has the little Snowbird turned into a falcon? Now I know why the best birds are females. There is a certain viciousness about the way they kill, as if they enjoy the sight of their victim's blood, the futility of the struggle. Is that how it felt? Did you enjoy it?"

"No, I did not, but I had to survive. All three of them deserved—"

"Three of them, Little Falcon? But I finished one for you."

"They deserved what they got, at whoever's hand."

"But Grigori is your husband."

"Because an old man said some words and pronounced us married, yes, Grigori is my husband. That is all. I never, as you put it, bedded him. He is my husband in name only."

"Why? Wasn't he good enough for you? Or did you have another lover already waiting?"

Her reaction was pure instinct. She slapped him with every ounce of force within her, and through the dirt and stubble of beard his cheek turned red.

"Shut up, you filthy animal," she snarled before he had recovered from the shock and could retaliate. "This is my house and I order you out of it. I want no more of your insane accusations. Go back to Paris and ask Manette Duquesne the truth. Or Dr. Vaniche or Lascaux, the lieutenant who helped me get away from Trabert. Or, for that matter, ask Vasili what I went through."

She turned to avoid the blow, but his fingers grazed her cheek, and a second later the back of his hand struck the other side of her face. She saw him rub his hand; she refused to touch the place where his knuckles had bruised her jaw, for she would not let him know he had hurt her.

"That was stupid, Mischa. You've made your arm bleed again."

He glanced down and saw that the bandage was red with fresh blood.

"The hell with my arm! After what you watched Trabert do to me, do you really think I'd be bothered by a little scratch like this?"

"I don't know what you're talking about!"

"I'm sure you are quite disappointed that I survived. How you must have enjoyed the little scene with your brave lover, clinging to him like a fungus on rotten wood while you laughed."

"Stop it!" she screamed. "I never saw anything! I ran away from Trabert the minute I saw him, right after he shot that poor soldier in the head. He chased me, but Lascaux told me where the Russian army was camped and he thought I could find you and be safe that way, but the snow was so deep and it was so cold that I took too long to reach the encampment. By then, you were already gone and I was alone. I wanted to die."

"It's a shame you didn't."

"Perhaps you're right," she admitted with a sigh. "At least then I wouldn't have to listen to you accuse me of things I never did. Vasili should have left me out there."

There was no point in arguing with him further. She picked up the linen bandage and tossed it on the table, then walked away from him towards the bedroom to find him a clean shirt.

She had not heard him follow her, and suddenly she could feel the warmth of him close behind her. His arms encircled her, his hands cupping her breasts as he pulled her back against him gently.

"I'm sorry," he whispered against her cheek.

"Don't, Mischa, please don't," she begged as he began to caress her body. She wanted to fight him but couldn't; her emotions betrayed her, strangling a scream in her throat even before he turned her around and covered her mouth with a soft and sensuous kiss.

"No, please, not again," she moaned, remembering the last time she had seen him and the way he had tortured her amid the flames of Moscow. "You said it would have been better if I had died out there. How many times I wished the same thing! Have you any idea what it is to be a slave, a captive animal, used in the most vile and cruel ways ever imagined by creatures that claim to be human beings? Do you wonder that I feel no guilt about Jean's murder? Not even Manette argued my right to take his worthless life.

"I thought I had suffered enough with Guignon, that I had atoned for whatever sins I had committed, but it wasn't over. Napoleon's soldiers were no kinder in defeat than in triumph, and my personal purgatory wasn't ended when I fled Moscow with them."

"I saw the retreat. I know how you—"

"Oh, you saw it! Did you sit on a distant hilltop and watch the passing parade? How entertaining it must have been for you! Had I known we had an audience I would have waved to you while I starved and froze and sold my body for a crust of moldy bread."

Ignoring the pain it brought to his arm, he lifted her and sat down on the bed to cradle her against him while the words tumbled one after another in ghastly succession.

"I'd lie in the dark and cold with the smell of death all around me and I'd cry, not because the filthy bastards had cheated me out of a bit of food, but because I felt I *should* have died, killed myself, rather than let them touch me. They hurt me, Mischa, oh my God! How those beasts hurt me!"

She spared him no detail in describing the way Guignon and Henri had raped her while poor Bernard lay bleeding to death just a few feet away. Self-loathing grew in Mikhail as he realized he had forced her to relive all that horror, and the horror he himself had created.

His long fingers gently combed her hair back from her face, and he saw the discoloration of her jaw. To judge by the way she winced at his touch, he had hurt her more than he thought, but it was the deeper injury he had done that made him wish, as she recounted Guignon's death, that she had killed him, too. He cursed himself, damning himself to circles of Hell Dante had never imagined. And, like Manette, he marvelled that Alexandra had survived, even at so appalling a price.

She lay in his arms, warm and still shaking, her tears soaking through his torn shirt, and emptied her heart of all the pain she had held within it for so long. He listened to tales too horrible to believe, heard of her being passed around by the soldiers as if she were a jug of wine to be shared by all, then traded for the food so scarce along the entire line of the retreat. How, he wondered, did she live through the hell of the winter, that special hell he had so fervently prayed for? He had seen the bodies of strong soldiers lying in the quiet repose of a frozen death; what had kept this frail creature alive? Where had she found the strength?

Then she told him of her miraculous reunion with Manette, and he understood. He did not recognize the other name she used so frequently and could only guess that this Lascaux was a rare kindness in that world of brutality. She spoke the lieutenant's name often, and even through the distortion of her sobs, Mikhail heard the affection in her voice and felt instant jealousy. But that envy turned to gratitude when he learned of the Frenchman's aid in her escape from Trabert.

"Then it wasn't you," he breathed, holding her the more tightly to him. "You were gone before the French ever reached Smolensk. I always knew you would somehow survive, but when I saw you with Trabert, I couldn't believe you would go that far." He kissed her again to stop his own tears, but the taste of her brought back all the painful longing and he could not keep his eyes dry.

"Vasili could have told you that, if you bothered to ask him." She wiped her cheeks on her sleeve and looked at him half fearfully.

"I didn't. I swore instead I'd cut out his tongue if he so much as mentioned your name again," was his rueful reply. "Later, when I might have listened to him, it made no difference. I couldn't come to you in the winter and he thought you were safe here anyway. If I hadn't already freed the man, I would do so now."

Sliding off his lap and walking purposefully back to the kitchen, she told him firmly and suddenly, "We'll talk more after I've taken care of your arm." She had already told him too much, more than she wanted to, and she still was not sure about his attitude. He seemed to be holding something back. Much as she wanted an explanation, she was afraid, too, of the truth.

He followed her and sat down to rest his arm on the table. The wound was bleeding, and she intended to do what she could for it before any further discussion, or argument, ensued.

The water in the basin had grown cold, but that in the cauldron still steamed over the low-burning fire. Alexandra threw more wood on the coals then dipped the bowl full again and carried it back to the table.

"You might as well take that filthy shirt off," she suggested as she reached up to take a bottle of vodka from the shelf.

"It can wait until you're done." He had guessed her intentions correctly when she set the bottle down but brought no cups.

Cleansed of dried blood and dirt, the wound proved smaller and less ugly than Alexandra had expected, but was still deep and gaping and should have been sewn closed immediately. It was too late now, and she hadn't the stomach for that kind of needlework.

"There will be a nasty scar; I can't help that," she said. Talking seemed to keep her hand steady enough to pull the stopper from the vodka bottle. "Do you want a drink first?"

He shook his head. With his teeth already clenched too tightly for any other reply or questions, he felt her fingers spread the wound further open. He knew it was necessary, and he knew she did not relish the task, but cleansing with raw spirits hurt no less than cauterizing with a red-hot knife blade. Sweat beaded on his forehead and dripped down the sides of his face as he struggled against the agony, but at least he had not the stench of his own skin burning in his nostrils. Even closing his eyes could not hold back the tears.

Taking a pair of shears from the shelf, Alexandra began snipping at the tattered shirt until she could remove the filthy, sweat-damp rag before he recovered to protest.

Her cry of horror reached through the pain that, though slowly subsiding, blocked all other sensations, and he knew what had happened.

"Trabert?" she asked.

He nodded and managed a hoarse, "Now you know why one more scar doesn't matter," but he could say nothing more until the fire in his arm cooled enough for him to breathe rather than gasp. Even then he found that the words came slowly and with great difficulty.

"I knew from the beginning that you weren't there, that Trabert was lying, but I couldn't take the chance that perhaps he was telling the truth, that he had you somewhere alive and would kill you if I did something foolish. I had been fighting for weeks against thinking you were dead, and I wanted to so desperately to have found you. Then, when I knew he was going to kill me anyway, I wanted to see you one last time, and my imagination played a dastardly trick on me. I saw you with him, laughing as you rode off together while I lay dying in the snow."

Alexandra wrapped clean linen around his arm and tried to keep from looking at the scars on his back. They reminded her of too many other horrors. When she had finished with the bandage, he put his arm around her and tried to pull her down onto his lap, but she danced just out of his reach.

"None of that now," she scolded. "You've got to take care of that arm or it will start bleeding again. The water ought to be hot enough now for you to take a bath, if you want. I don't think Grigori would mind if you borrow a clean shirt and his razor this once."

He had been smiling until the mention of his rival's name. Now a look of sadness crossed his face, making him turn away from her. He had forgotten, and the reminder that she was married brought a fresh kind of pain.

"No, I've taken enough that belongs to him already." He stood up, waited until he was certain he could withstand both the searing pain in his arm and the worse ache in his heart. "Goodbye, Alexandra. I'm sorry, for what I've done here and for what I did in the past. I do not deserve your forgiveness, but I ask it nonetheless in hopes—"

"Stop it, Mischa. We have both suffered enough, and both suffered equally, so let us not bring on any more needless pain. No, I am not Grigori's wife. I belong to you, Mikhail Pavlovitch Ogrinov, and I always have."

Chapter 32

THE STREET was deserted; Alexandra walked toward the Tcheradzin house, having left Mikhail napping after his bath. She encountered no one, but she felt eyes peering at her from every window she passed. So uncomfortable was the feeling that she sighed with relief upon reaching her destination.

Tasha opened the door and gestured her inside.

"I've been expecting you," the girl said. "Come into the kitchen."

"I can't stay long," Alexandra insisted. She refused the offer of apple-filled pastry. "I only came to collect Mikhail's belongings and to ask about Grigori."

"He's fine. A little weak, but he lost a lot of blood. It wasn't nearly as bad as it looked at first. Right now he's resting, or I'm sure he'd want to see you."

Alexandra lowered her eyes.

"I wouldn't know what to say to him," she murmured. "Where is Katrushka? I wanted to ask her about Mikhail's wound."

"She and Dmitri went to petition for an annulment of your marriage. And Mikhail knows more about medicine than Katrushka; he would have told you if you did anything wrong."

"Does Grigori know?"

"Oh, yes. It was his idea. He told them that they were to waste no time getting it."

"It wasn't much of a marriage anyway," Alexandra

muttered half to herself. "How long will it take?"

As hard as she tried, she could not keep excitement from creeping into her voice.

"Not more than three or four weeks, I suppose."

"I never meant to cause him such sorrow, and I'm overwhelmed by his kindness. I can never thank him enough."

"What is it you are thanking me for now?" Grigori asked as he walked into the room.

As he came closer, she could see how weak he was. He grasped the back of Tasha's chair for support, and his face was deathly pale.

"For—for the annulment," Alexandra stammered.

"I was never your husband, not for a single minute, and I never would have been. Even if Mikhail Pavlovitch were dead and you never saw him again, you would always belong to him. I knew that as soon as I saw how you looked when you were waiting for him."

She saw no pain in his smile, nor sadness. A wave of relief swept over her with the understanding that he had never really loved her, had only seen her as an instrument of revenge.

When Alexandra returned to the cottage, she tried to explain her thoughts and feelings to Mikhail, but it was not easy.

"Grigori hated Vasili, though I don't think he ever really knew it, because Katrushka always compared him to Vasili. And because he thought I belonged to Vasili, he used me to hurt his enemy. When he discovered the truth, his disappointment manifested itself in violence."

"But why direct it against you? Why not at me, since I was the one who disrupted his dream?"

The ache in his arm made bending it difficult. He fumbled with the buttons of his shirt unsuccessfully and finally allowed Alexandra to help him.

"You were his friend; he would never willingly hurt you. And he didn't argue when you challenged him because he felt guilty over taking something that was yours. Telling us to stay here in the house that he built for me to lie in as his wife was one way he tried to make it all up to you.''

Her own guilt sent a shiver through her, but still she leaned instinctively towards Mikhail. As his arm tightened around her, she forgot everything else to become aware only of him. He was hers again, after all the months of waiting, all the suffering; she had her happiness.

He kissed the top of her head, then almost apologetically whispered, ''If you don't let me eat some of whatever Tasha has packed in that basket, I am very likely to faint from starvation while making love to you.''

The aroma of freshly baked bread and still-warm pastry floated about the room as Alexandra lifted the cloth covering Tasha's very welcome gift. Underneath lay a slab of roasted pork, a round cheese, and a crock filled with rich, steaming potato soup. Two long-neglected appetites sprang to life. Alexandra set the plates and bowls on the table and poured mugs full of wine while Mikhail awkwardly but stubbornly cut the meat into thick slices. Then they sat down to a meal they could not have enjoyed more had it been a royal banquet.

In spite of Mikhail's protestations, Alexandra wrapped her shawl about her against the chill of an evening threatened with storm to take her customary walk amongst the trees. Though she would have preferred solitude, she did not attempt to dissuade him from accompanying her. Had she not, after all, been watching just for him all those other evenings when she strolled alone?

She had not yet told him of Grigori's decision to annul their unconsummated marriage and knew that she must soon, but as they ambled through the darkening forest, she was content just to hold his hand and try to accept the reality of his presence. Nothing else mattered.

They walked without speaking, followed no certain path and seemed almost unaware which direction they took. Though the sky overhead remained clear, thunder rumbled a distant herald of the storm to come and in the damp, heavy air the scent of rain hung sweet. An ominous pall of silence settled over the woods and the entire valley; even the birds and crickets had ceased their nightly concert.

The first pale flashes of lightning sparkled through the treetops like fireworks.

"We'll get wet if we don't hurry back," Alexandra remarked as she turned to retrace her steps.

"Then let's not hurry. It's been a long time since I've been caught in a summer shower."

It was the dark, however, not the rain, that forced them to return to the cottage. Clouds rolling in from the west blotted out the sunset more quickly than expected, and by the time they reached the road leading back to the valley, the darkness was almost complete. Alexandra hardly noticed the enormous drops pelting her head and shoulders as she hastened to escape the enveloping night and the terror it brought. Once inside the kitchen, where the fire still glimmered on the hearth, she breathed a little easier, but her fingers trembled until she had lit the candles.

"We got wet after all," she laughed when the flickering light that instantly banished her fear revealed their bed-raggled appearance. "Do you remember the day we rode through that horrible storm to the inn and you invented that monstrous lie for the innkeeper?"

He smiled at the memory and replied, "Yes, I do, and extremely well." Water dribbled from his hair into his face as he sat down in front of the fire to dry, and he took his arm out of its sling when she handed him a towel. He said nothing more, causing her to wonder if she had stirred up a deadly brew of memories, but he was still smiling when he returned the towel to her. "I hated waking you that night. You looked so peaceful, so utterly exhausted, and I wanted so badly to lie down beside you and sleep for a day or two."

"No sense worrying about it now. We can't change the past."

"No, we can't. Whether ten seconds ago or ten years, it

is permanent." He rose slowly, gazed into her firelit green eyes, and said what he had to say. "Good night, Madame Tcheradzina."

"And where do you think you would go at this hour of the night and in the rain?" she asked him.

When he turned, reluctantly as though some force stronger than his own determination directed his footsteps, he faced her from a distance their outstretched arms could span, yet it felt as though miles separated them.

"I told you I was never Grigori's wife. He has petitioned for an annulment of a marriage that never existed. The past can't be changed, Mischa, but the future can." Her voice faded to a low whisper, husky with the hunger she could not conceal, but when she spoke again, after a pause of such intense silence that even the storm seem to abate, each word rang clear.

"I am yours, Mischa. I always was and I always will be, yours and yours alone."

Lacking the strength to take a single step, she reached out across the narrow gulf between them. At first only their fingertips touched, then their hands clasped as a magnetism greater than any lodestone drew them together. If his wound pained him at all, he ignored it.

His lips touched hers only briefly before travelling to her nose, her eyes, her chin and throat, then back again to her mouth with a thousand tiny kisses, as though one were not enough. He buried his face in the rain-damp tangle of her hair and drank in the scent of her while he nibbled at her ear, sending little cries of delight from her, and then, unable to hold it back any longer, he let the damned-up passion flood free, a torrent to tumble over everything in its path without heed.

He did not kiss her; he devoured her, and she did not protest as his tongue explored the inner corners of her mouth seeking the familiar sweetness he remembered so well. Her response was unlike anything he had ever experienced, demanding in her own way as well as giving.

They collapsed on the bed after leaving a trail of discarded clothing in their wake. There was no time for the caresses and soft words, the gentle prelude to physical rhapsody; the drumbeat of wildly pounding hearts already heralded the crashing finale. Mikhail felt his muscles tense as he pulled her trembling body atop his, then relaxed as she took him into the soft, wet warmth that closed around his hardness in a sensual embrace. Like him, she needed no arousal other than the need for him streaming through her. She wanted him and was ready for him, and when the convulsive explosion of his climax triggered her own, too soon to satisfy all the desire they shared, she knew this act was itself merely the overture.

She lay curled beside him, her head on his shoulder while her hand lay flat on his chest, rising and falling with each steadily slowing breath. His pulse too had calmed as had hers, but not even the gentle tattoo of rain on the windows could lull her to sleep, not yet. Not while his fingers gently caressed her arm, just as they had that night so long ago when he had taken her home after Rosalie de Beaumartin's party.

Trailing her fingers through the curly hairs on his chest, she tried to remember every detail of that evening. She had never dreamed, not for a moment, that that chance meeting would eventually put her in a peasant's cottage with him somewhere in the mountains of Russia.

"Jesus Christ, Xan, must you tickle me to death?"

She laughed then, but when his right hand closed over hers, she felt the weakness born of pain and resisted his attempt to place it on another part of his body.

"You need rest, not that," she scolded him, but already he had pushed her hand down to his belly. Her fingers involuntarily reached further until they curled possessively around him.

He groaned.

"I need you, Snowbird. I have hated you, despised you, cursed the very memory of you, but I have never stopped needing and wanting you. Tonight I will have my fill of you." He slid his hand between her thighs. "And you will have your fill of me."

He was kissing her again, covering her from forehead to belly with tender little mouthings. His lips lingered only a moment on hers, just long enough to tease her tongue past his teeth and then leave her gasping as he wandered down her chin and throat to her breasts. She shivered as his tongue caressed her swollen nipples, and when he covered one hard peak with his mouth and began to bite it gently, she could not suppress a little wail of pleasure that leapt free from her.

Like a grass fire, the heat in her loins spread to every part of her, even her toes, curling and uncurling them to some unknown rhythm. His fingers probed inside her now, skillfully stroking the places he knew would drive her past any point she had ever been to before. She arched against him langourously, enjoying with almost breathless delight the sensations he aroused in her, wanting only this moment, this feeling, to last forever, and yet at the same time seeking the culmination that would end it.

All the wildness of their first union was gone. He poised himself above her and let her quivering fingers guide him into her, slowly, with no frantic urgency to complete the deed. If there is a limit to one's pleasure, he thought, I will take her with me beyond it.

An hour later, he did.

Chapter 33

THE BREEZE that usually cooled the evening never materialized. Alexandra stood on the porch, her hair knotted carelessly atop her head, staring towards the darkening woods. She held a folded piece of parchment in her hand, used it now and then to fan her face against the stifling July heat.

Mikhail had promised her, when he set out at dawn with Grigori on their long-delayed fishing expedition, to return before dark. The earliest stars already glimmered in a grey and moonless sky and still there was no sign of him. In a very short while it would be too dark to see, but as long as there was even a hint of light, she would wait and watch. As the darkness intensified, so did her fear, and she felt a chill despite the warmth of the night. Glancing toward the window aglow with the bright flame of a candle, she tried in vain to quiet this apprehension.

It was silly, she knew, to bolt the door, but nonetheless she did it when she finally came inside. Her eyes ached with the strain of staring into the blackness; she rubbed them with her knuckles until they watered, blurring her vision even further. Once she was able to see again, she sat down and picked up the sealed document the priest had given her that afternoon. She had not bothered to open it because she could not read the Russian script, but she knew what it was; the priest had told her that much. The annulment had been granted. Both she and Grigori were free. Why then did she feel more afraid then ever?

"I'll be all right as soon as Mischa comes back," she said aloud and settled onto a chair within the candle's glow.

Talking helped some, but not enough, and there was little to talk with herself about. And inside the house the heat was stifling. No breath of air stirred the curtains hanging limply at the open window. As Alexandra pushed them aside to search once again, she heard a sound like a scurrying animal just outside the door. It sent a tremor through her. Laughing nervously, she chided herself for such timidity and turned back to the quiet and empty room. Yet she knew her ears, listening for hoofbeats on the soft, dusty road, strained to catch other sounds as well.

The paper in her lap, its official seal intact, gave her little comfort as she waited. Nervously she peered out the window again and listened for the faintest hint of horses coming down the mountain road. She heard nothing.

The night was silent, too silent. The owl nesting in the apple tree made no sound, nor the frogs, not even a distant wolf. Only the mindless crickets continued to chirp, yet they, too, seemed subdued. Whatever Alexandra had heard earlier was no starving cat hunting garbage for its supper. Something evil was out there, something that frightened even the night creatures into silence. She reached for the rosary lying beside the candle and fixed her eyes upon the shadowy icon hanging on the far wall.

Her fingers froze around the first bead and her lips could not utter even the opening *pater noster*. Out of the nightmare silence had come that sound again, the creeping or crawling of a large animal in the high, weedy grass between this cottage and the next. In the breathless air the swish of lush vegetation hung like an echo, but it was not repeated. Petrified, Alexandra dared not look out the window again, and it took all her courage to pick up the candle and walk into the kitchen for a knife, the only weapon she possessed. The reflection that she had had considerably less when she faced Jean Guignon helped to steady her trembling hands. She shivered, and yet her blouse, open as far as she dared because of the heat, clung

335

to her with the sweat born of terror.

With the candle in one hand, the long-bladed knife in the other, she stood, facing the locked door as bravely as she could. This was no ordinary beast lurking without; it was a fiend, human or otherwise, bent upon her destruction. She thought of all the fairy tales Baron Tchernikov had told her at a long ago dinner in Paris and all the hideous creatures he had described now seemed to be waiting, crouching, just beyond her door.

There are no such things, she told herself. This is the nineteenth century, not the ninth, and people don't believe in firebirds and witches who ride the skies in a flying mortar and pestle. I'm being a silly fool.

But nothing stilled the pounding of her heart, thundering in her ears until even the steady rustling of the weeds as the demon came closer was blotted out. She felt, rather than heard, the heavy footsteps approach, first up to the wooden stairs, then across the porch. The latch rattled as an unseen hand tried to enter. Alexandra raised the knife above her head.

"Xan, open the door! I've got my hands full of fish and you've locked me out!"

The knife clattered harmlessly to the floor as she jumped to lift the bar and let him in.

"Oh, Mischa, thank God it's you!" She threw her arms about him, ignoring the strings of gape-mouthed fish that kept him from responding in a like manner.

"Of course, it is I. Who were you expecting?"

Then, looking past her, he saw the gleam of the steel blade where it had fallen and realized that Alexandra clung to him in fear.

"For Heaven's sake, what has happened to you? Here, set the candle down before you set fire to my shirt and let me get some water for these fish."

Helping him unstring the dozen beautiful fat trout that would provide a scrumptious feast on the morrow, she felt a good part of her terror dissolve. She lit more candles to brighten the kitchen and stood at the door while Mikhail filled a bucket with icy water from the spring to keep the fish from spoiling.

"I'm sorry I didn't get back as early as I said I would," he apologized.

"You're here now; that's all that counts."

"Who were you planning to kill with the knife? Did someone threaten you or try to break in?"

Embarrassment over a childish fear made her laugh, but the memory of a too quiet darkness and the noise that had disturbed it left a nervous note in her laughter. She told him the truth, knowing she could not lie to him.

"I'll go outside and see if there is any sign of someone—or something—having been around the house. If it was as big as you say it sounded, the weeds should still show evidence of its passing." When he saw worry flicker in her eyes, he kissed her and reassured her. "I'll take the pistol and you can hang your rosary around my neck." He did not make fun of her, as though perhaps he shared some of her superstitions, and as he stepped out the kitchen door into the night, she saw him cross himself.

He came back much too soon.

"Whatever it was, it's gone now," he said, sliding the bolt into place across the door. "If it were a wolf or boar, you'd have heard more noise. I suspect your imagination carried you away and it was no more than a dog noising around."

"But I didn't imagine it. I swear I didn't!"

"No, I didn't say you imagined it. There was plenty of trampled grass to indicate something had been out there, but no sign of it now. I'm sure it's nothing to worry about anyway."

His nonchalance was infectious. By the time they had finished their very late supper, Alexandra was able to laugh at his description of Grigori falling into a pond in a fruitless attempt to retrieve a particularly sly old trout. While she washed the dishes and scrubbed the table, Mikhail removed his grimy clothes and poured water from the the kettle into a basin to wash the worst of the dust

337

from his skin before bed.

He reached for the towel hanging on a hook on the wall and suddenly froze, his hand in mid-air, at the sound. Snatching the pistol from the table where he had left it, he slid the bolt and walked once again into the silent night. The gentle plopping of soapsuds dripping from Alexandra's hands to the floor echoed loud in the quiet as she followed his signalled order to bar the door once he was outside.

His eyes, once accustomed to the dark, quickly made out the shapes of the apple tree and the lilacs that formed a border between the two cottages and he kept as close to this cover as possible. Only starlight, pale and deceptive, lit the night. He hoped it would be enough. He did not want to have to shoot in the dark and risk killing an innocent human being.

That the prowler was human he had no doubt. The nameless wolfhound old Avram Narodny, who lived next door, kept as a companion slept on his master's porch, barely visible as a sprawled lump in front of the door. Had there been an animal wandering through the village, the hound would have set up a howling fit to wake the dead. Humans he ignored as unworthy of his attention; if Alexandra had forgotten that, Mikhail had not. He held the primed pistol steady as he searched the weeds for his prey.

Amazed at her calm, Alexandra sat at the table and waited. The roof timbers groaned above her as though a weight had been lowered on them, and the sudden creak made her jump, but she quickly realized it was only the rising evening breeze that shifted the house and caused it to sigh. The stuffy air in the kitchen began to swirl as the wind blew through from the open parlor windows. Alexandra, too, sighed with relief; after days of almost tropical heat, she felt cool again. And there was the scent of rain on this breeze.

She was too intent on enjoying the change of the temperature. By the time she remembered the danger, it

338

was too late; the gust of storm-laden wind snuffed out the candles before she could set chimneys over them. The kitchen plunged into darkness, like a tomb or a dungeon, or the stable where Jean Guignon had tortured her.

She could not see a thing. The hearth was dark; the coals she had banked earlier were now covered with ash and shed not even a dull glow. She could hardly tell if her eyes were open or closed as she groped her way towards the fire, guided by its lingering warmth. Her fingers closed on the poker, grasped it tightly, but before she could push it into the pile of embers and stir them to flame, she felt the shock of revelation hit her.

She knew who had been lurking outside the cottage. There had been no animal, as Mikhail had probably guessed when he lied to ease her worry. The prowler was human, Alexandra felt certain, and it could only be one person.

Swallowing her fear, she lifted the poker and turned her back on the fireplace. If the wind had not brought clouds to obscure the stars, there would at least be some light outside. Something tripped her as she made her way to the door, a piece of fabric that her fingers identified as Mikhail's discarded shirt. She pushed the door open without a sound from hinges too new to have rusted.

There was less light than she had hoped for, barely enough to see even faintly. No sign of Mikhail or his quarry, and she did not dare to call out to him. The wind, stronger now and almost cold after the day's heat, whipped her skirt against her legs, making it difficult to walk to the gnarled apple tree that shaded the kitchen window. Concealed by its drooping limbs, she could wait and watch, the iron poker ready in her hand.

Mikhail cursed her foolhardiness when he saw her run to the apple tree, and he fervently hoped she would not shout to him. A second before she darted out the door, he had finally spotted his prey, a figure lying prone in the high grass not twenty feet from the corner of the porch. It moved with utmost stealth, crawling on its belly a few feet at a time. Once, when it crept over a rock or some such obstacle, it grunted with pain, and Mikhail recognized the voice.

Holding the pistol steadily, he emerged from his hiding place and called out to the creeping shadow.

A cloaked figure rose slowly to a crouched position, its back to him. He felt menace in its stance.

Though Alexandra could hear his voice, the wind distorted his words and swept them away from her. She knew not what he said nor to whom he spoke, and was barely able to distinguish his shadowy silhouette against the mottled background. A good thirty or forty paces separated her from him, so that she saw the flash as he fired the pistol before the sound reached her horrified ears.

He thought for a moment to follow the fleeing phantom, but it raced for the trees, where he would have no chance to find out or to protect himself from an ambush. His wild shot into the air had not had the desired effect, but he suspected it would be some time before the prowler returned. He had hoped for surrender and was disappointed not to have obtained even the slightest glimpse of the face behind the raised cowl, but the owner of the voice had gasped in surprise at the sight of the gun.

Chapter 34

ALEXANDRA HANDED the parchment to Mikhail shortly after breakfast. To maintain some show of calm despite her rapidly increasing excitement, she picked up the last of her mending and tried to keep the needle poking only into the fabric, not her finger. From the corner of her eye she watched him scrutinize the red wax with its impression of the bishop's ring, and then, finally, break the seal and unfold the letter.

When he had scanned the fine writing once, he reread slowly, carefully, before laying it on the table. He sighed.

"The Church has certainly taken her time," he said softly, "but at least the deed is done."

Without looking up from her sewing, which was proceeding poorly, Alexandra took a deep breath for courage and said, "I want to leave, Mischa. I don't care when you take me, but I cannot stay in this village any longer."

It was her first thought upon waking, and the remembrance of what had happened the night before had strengthened her resolve to tell him, not ask him.

"I suppose it's time we think about it. Winter is not that far away, and I don't want to be caught by it here," he mused casually. "Probably in a week or so we can start making plans."

"Not in a week, not even tomorrow. I don't want to spend so much as one more night here."

He looked at her, surprised at her vehemence. She had made up her mind, that was clear, and he knew how stubborn she could be when her temper was roused. Something had quite obviously aroused it now and he would have a time calming her enough to make her see reason.

"I can be ready to leave in less time than it takes you to saddle two horses," she boasted.

"All right, all right! Let's first settle down and decide what we must do before we leave. It isn't as simple as rolling a few clothes into a bundle and jumping on a horse. To begin with, I only have one horse. I'll have to buy one for you."

Waving her arms in frustration, Alexandra wailed, "There must be a thousand horses in this valley! How long can it possibly take to buy one? Mischa, I am afraid that if I am not out of this village before sundown today, I will never see tomorrow. I have to get out, because if I don't, she will come back and kill me tonight without fail."

" 'She'?" he echoed, his eyebrow raised. "What makes you think your visitor was a woman, and why would she want to kill you?"

He knew. He had shown too little surprise at her statement, and she sensed it was more because he had not expected her to guess than because of the news itself. She leaned back with a sigh.

"Valentina has hated me since the day I arrived. She played upon her brother's wish for revenge against Vasili to trick the two of us into marriage because she was smarter than he and knew it wasn't Vasili who had been my lover. How cleverly she manipulated us, like a master puppeteer, pulling all the right strings to make us dance for her pleasure! The one thing she couldn't control was Grigori's sense of honor, which turned out to be greater than she counted on."

"Because he never consummated the marriage?"

She nodded.

"He wanted only to hurt Vasili, not me, and she didn't understand that. To her there are no innocents. Once married to her brother, I was no longer a threat."

"A threat to what?"

"To her love for you."

He quashed his impulse to laugh, but could not help scoffing, "Valentina is only a child. Children get over this kind of infatuation."

"Valentina is not a child. You remember her as a girl of fourteen or fifteen, but she is a woman now, and her feelings are those of a woman."

As unpleasant as it was, the truth must be accepted, and Mikhail had no reason to doubt Alexandra. What he had only suspected about Valentina, Alexandra knew without question.

"It had to be Valentina. I'm free now and she has lost her advantage. The only alternative was to eliminate her competition."

There. She had told him the truth, and all that remained was to wait for his decision. The possibility that he would refuse her request hung like the broad blade of the guillotine in her mind; she dared not think he preferred a victory for her rival. His continued silence strained her already taut nerves. In vain she tried to read his thoughts, but the blue eyes stared beyond her and revealed nothing. The steady rain left behind by the storm had diminished to a drizzle while they talked and was being replaced, as the morning wore on, with a suffocating mugginess that added to Alexandra's nervous discomfort.

Impatience and frustration gradually turned to anger. Having lost her hope that he would agree to an immediate departure, Alexandra silently cursed him and made up her mind to force the issue. She walked to the door and stepped outside.

"Where the hell are you going?" Mikhail asked, jumping to follow her. "It's still raining."

Poised to descend the stairs to the muddy street, she turned and faced him with defiance tilting her chin.

"I don't know and I don't care, so long as it is away from here." She took the first step downward, left one foot on the porch as if waiting for a reply that would determine her course, but she continued almost immediately to tell him, "I never knew where I was to begin with. I've been lost since the day we left Paris. How can I know where I'm going when I don't even know where I am?''

When she took another step in the same direction as before, Mikhail crossed the porch in two strides, but she had already reached the bottom step and put one foot in the mud. She was just beyond his grasp and, like an actress waiting for her cue, she stopped but did not turn. The next move was up to him.

He spun her around with such violence that she slipped on the wet ground and would have fallen had he not gripped her arm so tightly.

"You little fool!" he snapped. "Why seek a slow, lonely death when Valentina offers a quick and easy one? If you think I cannot protect you from one jealous woman, why choose me to guide you out of the mountains? Go on, pack my things as well as yours, silly woman that you are, and do it quickly. Anatoli Arashchev has a chestnut mare I think I can talk him into selling, but we will have to be gone before he changes his mind.''

After only a moment's hesitation to be sure she had not misunderstood him, she fell into his arms and laughed with joy until he silenced her with a kiss and led her, for the last time, into the cottage.

They rested in Smolensk for a few days while Mikhail sent word ahead and made arrangements for a carriage and driver to transport them the rest of the way. After the long ride from the mountain village, Alexandra appreciated this concession to comfort, through it meant an extra day or two of travel.

In their small but comfortable quarters at an inn on the outskirts of Smolensk, they spent their nights and most of their days in peaceful enjoyment of each other. Loving, laughing, sometimes crying and then loving again.

"I will never stop being amazed at how beautiful you are," Mikhail said as he lay beside her. "No paint, no powder, no jewelry, ribbons, or curls, and you are still exquisite.''

"No clothes, either. Please, Mischa, you promised me

we would go shopping today. We're leaving for Moscow tomorrow and I still have nothing but the peasant clothes I brought with me from the village."

Embarrassed by his steady, appreciative gaze, she tried to draw the sheet over her nakedness, but he pulled it back down.

"When are you women ever going to learn that you are much lovelier without clothes?"

It did not matter that he had made love to her twice since waking and it was not yet noon. He wanted her again.

"I am so afraid of losing you," he whispered as he held her close to him, feeling the living warmth of her. "That vision of you with Trabert won't leave me alone, and I can't stand the thought."

She took his face between her trembling hands and met his eyes.

"It was a nightmare for both of us," she told him, "but now we are awake and together again, and all the pain is behind us."

Her eyelids dropped as she kissed him and her lashes fluttered against his cheek. They could go shopping later.

Rain plagued the entire journey from Smolensk. The hired carriage made slow progress on muddy roads, and the inns they spent each night at were frequently shabby affairs, offering musty beds and tasteless meals. After the fifth such day and night, Alexandra's mood turned as gloomy as the weather and she began to complain.

"How much longer?" she asked, stretching her neck to ease some of the cramp in her shoulders. "Do you think we can find somewhere that has decent food for a change? I don't think I can stand any more boiled cabbage."

"No boiled cabbage, I promise. In fact, I think you will find tonight's accommodations quite to your liking."

She looked at him suspiciously, wondering just what that hint of laughter in his voice meant.

"A bed without mildew and a *hot* bath, not lukewarm?"

"Most assuredly. You could probably have satin sheets, if you asked. But it will be a bit later tonight than usual, so perhaps you ought to nap for a while."

"I'd love to, but—"

The carriage hit another rut in the road and she was thrown rather violently against him, illustrating precisely the point she had tried to make. They both laughed uproariously.

Mikhail had been right about their late arrival. Added to her other discomforts, Alexandra fought gnawing hunger before he announced that they had turned off the main road and onto the lane leading to their night's lodging place. Soon, several pinpoints of light came into view that gradually brightened until she could see lanterns on the porch of a large building. Three people, two men and a woman, waited by the door, but through the rain Alexandra could not make a guess at their identity.

The carriage halted just as the sky opened its floodgates a bit wider. Alexandra ducked her head to dash between the raindrops, but before she had taken a single step, two strong arms lifted her off her feet and carried her to the veranda's shelter.

"You see, little bird, he kept my promise," Vasili whispered in her ear as he set her back on her feet. "You look much, much better than when last I saw you, Snowbird, but it is only an improvement on the most beautiful creature God ever made."

"I do believe the great bear is in love with her!" Princess Vera Ylbatskaya exclaimed as Mikhail ran up the stairs and out of the rain. "We've been waiting for hours. What happened to you?"

"The roads were a disaster," he explained, half out of breath. "Well, Uncle, this is indeed a surprise. I did not expect to see you here."

Andrei Tchernikov harumphed and hoped he wasn't blushing.

"It is sheer coincidence. But we can discuss all that over supper, which has been waiting a long, long time."

As Vera led Alexandra into the house, with Vasili

following closely, she clucked over the girl's appearance.

"I don't care what this oaf says, you look positively dreadful. If someone doesn't do something, you will fade away right before his eyes." And when that someone strode into the foyer, she leveled a long finger at him. "You ought to be ashamed, Mikhail Pavlovitch. This poor child is in no condition to spend a week traveling. If she didn't look so undernourished, I'd send her to bed this instant, before supper. But as soon as she has had a decent meal, it is off to bed."

She met with little resistance. Mikhail and Alexandra marched ahead of the princess into the dining room, where liveried servants waited to serve the meal. Vera immediately began urging food on Alexandra, exhorting her to eat veal and spiced chicken and baked pheasant and oysters, until Alexandra had to shout that another mouthful would make her burst.

To Mikhail's surprise and relief, the princess managed to curb her curiosity throughout dinner and refused to let Andrei ask any questions either. She promised everyone plenty of time in the morning, but as soon as dessert was over, she hustled Alexandra upstairs to a bath before bed, while the gentlemen relaxed with cigars and brandy.

The bathroom was a spacious chamber off an even larger bedroom decorated all in pink, hardly a color one would associate with the brash Vera. Everything about it was opulent, almost gaudy, from the lace-draped canopy bed and enormous chandelier in the sleeping chamber to the rose-colored marble bathtub.

"I told you, Snowbird, all those months ago in Paris, that he belonged to you. Was I not right?" Vera asked as she leaned back in her chair and puffed on her cheroot.

Soaking in rose-scented water, Alexandra blushed scarlet.

"Or perhaps you would prefer I put it the other way around? No matter, child, it is all the same. But it is very clear that Mikhail is your devoted slave, whether he belongs to you or you to him."

"Not Mischa! He is no one's slave. Whatever his

feelings for me, he is still his own master and quite beyond my control," Alexandra insisted as Vera's maid pushed her head under the water to wash her hair.

The princess' laugh rang with bitterness.

"Years ago I thought the same thing about a man very much like Mischa, and I learned to my eternal regret that every man has his weakness. His was honor. I loved him and I thought he loved me, but my friend seduced him and he married her out of honor."

Alexandra felt the princess' pain herself.

"Even after all these years, I still remember the touch of his hand, the color of his eyes." She sighed and shook tears away, then blew a lazy smoke ring toward the ceiling. "Alexandra, my dear, do not make the same mistake I did. Don't let him get away from you."

"I don't intend to, if I can help it."

"Good. I'll leave you to your rest now. If you need anything, just ring for Marta. Or call me. My room is at the end of the hall. I'll be going down to chat with the gentlemen for a while. Sleep well, Snowbird."

She walked out the door and closed it softly behind her, then poked her head back in.

"And just in case, Mikhail's room is right across from yours."

Andrei Tchernikov did not possess the same control Vera did; he began firing questions at Mikhail the instant they were alone. Though this meant the details of Alexandra's story came to him secondhand, he knew it also spared her much suffering. And Mikhail seemed eager to tell him.

"I do not know how she did it," he said when he had finished. "Thousands of men died who suffered less than she did. How did she survive?"

"You ought to know the answer, Mikhail. The girl loves you. And don't scoff."

"How can she after what I've done to her? I don't think I realized until tonight, until I saw how humiliated she was, that I have treated her like a common whore."

"Mikhail! I won't let you speak of her that way!"

"But it's true, Uncle. The night—the night I left her outside Moscow, she had said something to me about being afraid, and I didn't understand her. Now I do. She wasn't afraid; she was ashamed of herself because I had made her my mistress, my whore."

"You bastard! You ought to be horsewhipped!"

Mikhail poured himself another cognac and smiled over the rim of the glass.

"I was. And you warned me, Uncle. You said you'd see me skinned alive."

With a cough Andrei tried to apologize.

"I didn't mean it, not then and not tonight. But have a care for the girl, Mischa." A creak overhead drew his eyes to the ceiling. "That's your room above us, isn't it? I thought you sent your servant to bed hours ago."

"I did, but you know Vasili. He'll be down in a minute to tell me to go to bed. Worse than my grandmother he is at times."

He swallowed the rest of his brandy and got up to leave, but Tchernikov gestured him back to his chair.

"A bit of advice, Mischa. Give some thought to the girl's future. You owe her that much at least."

"What the hell am I *supposed* to do with her? I can't send her home very easily."

The baron harumphed again.

"Did you ever think of marrying her?"

When Mikhail tried to speak, Tchernikov went on without a pause.

"Why did you damn near kill yourself trying to find her? Why did you spend two months in the mountains with her? Why is she still with you? Why does your servant grin everytime he looks at the two of you together?" At that point he held his tongue and did not press the issue. He gave Mikhail the time to think, to come up with an answer.

He had none, not right away. He was remembering Paris and the night they had first loved, the night he had taken her virginity. And the night they had come to the edge of Moscow and loved so passionately before Napoleon burned the city. The pain Trabert had inflicted upon him was nothing compared to the anguish of thinking he saw her with the sadistic colonel and believing, if only for a moment, that she had betrayed him. And the murderous jealousy that had almost cost him Grigori's life.

"I don't know," he mumbled. "It's not like it was with Tamara."

"Oh, damn it, haven't you gotten over her yet? That's eight, nine years ago!"

"She's the only other woman I've ever loved." He did not like the taste the word left in his mouth. Too trite, too often used in vain. "Xan's not like Tamara, either. She's not quite like anyone."

"No, she's not."

Andrei was pressuring now, very gently, very cautiously.

Mikhail went on in a strange, quiet voice, "Grandmere would like her, don't you think? I know Father would have. She's a lot like him, you know, except that she tends to be very French in the way she shows her emotions. Father never did that, not even when Nikolai died. He was very English when it came to keeping his feelings to himself."

"Some men are like that. I don't recall you shedding a fountain of tears when your brother died, either."

"That was different. I hated Niki for what he had done to me. I could have forgiven Tamara, but not Niki. Now I can't forgive her, either." He drained the last of his brandy and shook off the melancholy. "Mother, of course, always wanted a daughter to plan a wedding for. She'll be happy now."

"You already know how I feel, and I'm sure Vera would approve, too."

"If Vera approves, then it is settled. And now, Uncle, I must bid you good night. I am very tired, and my bed awaits."

Alexandra felt her heart stop beating, and for a moment she wondered if it would ever start again. She had come to his bedroom because she could not stand being away from him, even for one night, when so few nights might remain. She wiped away tears of joy trickling from the corners of her eyes with the edge of his sheet and reminded herself to take nothing for granted. He had been known to lie his way out of an uncomfortable situation before. What he had told the baron could very easily be another escape maneuver. She stretched out flat on her back, clenching the sheet in her fists to steady herself as hope turned to despair.

I must not expect anything from him until he gives it to me, she warned herself.

With that in mind, she threw back the blankets and sat up to retrieve the nightdress she had removed before crawling naked into his bed. She could not stay here, but must wait for him to come to her. In the dim light afforded by the single candle, she had difficulty untangling the ribbons on the sheer garment, and before she could pull it on and rush across the hall to her own room again, she heard familiar footsteps.

She crept under the sheets again and lay still, hardly breathing, as he came in and closed the door behind him. With a weary yawn, he sat down to pull off his boots, resting after the first as if to gather his energy for the second. Then he rose to undress. Alexandra could not resist watching as he shrugged out of his coat and began to unbutton his shirt. Her fingers ached to do the task for him, to touch him as she pushed the shirt over his shoulders and down the length of his arms. The scar from the duel still stood out as a pinkish welt against his skin, but the marks on his back had faded to a ghostly white trellis. She had accustomed herself to it, more or less, but tonight it held all its old horror.

He yawned a second time and stretched his arms above his head as if to prove that nothing as insignificant as a few scars on his skin could diminish his strength. Then, as Alexandra continued to stare in rapt fascination, he unbuttoned his trousers and stepped out of them. She wondered if he would be so unconcerned about his nakedness had he known he was observed. When he turned to approach the bed, she had the answer to her question, and desire to match his flared like a tiny flame deep inside her at the sight of his arousal. She caught her breath and felt the sheet rub against her nipples.

He lay still for a moment or two, breathing evenly just inches away from her. He could not possibly be unaware of her, yet he had closed his eyes and thrown his arm above his head as he often did when he slept. Not until he reached his other hand across the bed to clasp hers did he break into a smile.

"You knew I was here!" she gasped when she saw how wickedly his blue eyes glittered.

He kissed her before answering, "Why do you think I left the candle burning? I sent Vasili to bed right after dinner because he was falling asleep on his feet. When I heard someone up here, it had to be you."

He thought of the half-promise he had given Andrei. Would it make any difference if this beautiful creature were his wife? Would he still want her the way he did now when even utter exhaustion failed to destroy his desire? It was not a question to be answered now. Only one thing was possible when he held her like this, warm and soft and hungry in his arms, and nothing could change that.

Chapter 35

BREAKFAST WAS a noisy affair, a veritable circus of questions, answers, sly winks and smiles, that Alexandra was most reluctant to leave behind. Yet when she and Mikhail were settled in the elegant carriage Vasili had brought from Moscow, she admitted to relief that they were alone again, for Mikhail had said they would reach the city no later than tomorrow morning.

Mile by muddy mile they drew closer. Night did not really fall on these gloomy days; it crept up quietly until the grey skies turned black. Long before darkness descended on this last evening of their journey, Mikhail ordered Vasili to stop at a roadside hostel.

The noise of the pounding rain on the roof forced him to raise his voice to Alexandra.

"I'm hungry!" he shouted. "We'll stop here for something to eat and then I think we can make it home yet tonight."

Inwardly she wailed, You can't do this to me! You promised me one more night.

Just as before, she wanted the journey to end, but not the night. She needed these last hours alone with him; without them, she knew she could not face whatever awaited her in Moscow. But unlike that night a year ago, she was forewarned and could make an effort to realign his plans.

It turned out to be easier, and slightly more painful, than she had expected.

Though the carriage was comfortable enough, long hours in it and bad roads had given her a backache that usually subsided an hour or two after leaving the rocking, jolting conveyance. She intended to use what was really a minor discomfort to insist they not continue until she had rested and recovered. To assuage any guilt that might discourage such subterfuge, she reminded herself that it was not entirely untrue. Her back did hurt.

Once Mikhail was filled with warm food and wine, he would be far more amenable to her suggestion. Holding her skirts up with both hands, she let him take her elbow to help her across the short yard to the inn. The downpour soon drenched her clothes, and thick mud tugged at her feet. She pulled her boots free only with a struggle at each step but finally reached the porch that ran the entire front of the long, low building. As she placed one foot on the wooden stair, the slippery mud still clinging to her boot caused it to slide from under her.

Mikhail's hold on her arm kept her from landing bottom first in a puddle, but her other ankle, trapped in the oozing mire, twisted before she could pull it loose. With a cry of real pain, she put all her weight on the other foot and almost lost her balance again. By then, Mikhail put his arm under her knees and swooped her up to carry her inside.

His diagnosis, after careful examination, was that she had suffered nothing more serious than a slight wrenching of the tendons. He brought her dinner on a tray and served it to her in bed, though she protested she could walk to the dining room, with a little help.

"You wanted to get to Moscow tonight," she reminded him. "I can't hurt the damn foot if I'm sitting in the coach."

"One bounce and you'd brace yourself with it, possibly injuring it seriously." He probed the slender ankle with gentle fingers. "There's very little swelling, and no bruise. You say it doesn't hurt too much? Try wriggling it a little once more, slowly."

She did, but it hurt more than she wanted to admit, and he knew it.

"I think it best we stay the night here and not try to travel any further until you've had some rest. By tomorrow you should be as good as new."

So she had her last night.

After several fruitless attempts to divest her of the wine-colored travelling dress without risking any further injury to her ankle, Mikhail finally let her stand while he unbuttoned it. She leaned on the bedpost to keep her weight off the joint, which felt better when she moved it now than it had just a few minutes ago. She was not about to tell him, however, and climbed dutifully back into bed dressed only in her chemise.

"Aren't you going to join me?" she asked, patting the space she had left for him on the narrow bed.

"Only if you promise not to assault me during the night." He already had his coat off.

"I make no promises at all," she giggled. "But I am an invalid, remember? How dangerous can I possibly be?"

"You, my dear, are always dangerous."

He snuffed the candle and lay down beside her, but not touching her.

"Tomorrow I'll have a doctor look at that foot, but for now I suggest sleep."

"I don't."

Her hand was warm on his flesh, caressing him gently as she rolled onto her side and lay her head on his shoulder. He needed no more arousing; he never did. He could have taken her the moment he saw her lying there with that silly transparent garment covering her yet not concealing a thing. He knew she would have been ready for him; she always was. But tonight there was a new urgency to her lovemaking. She was at once tender and ferocious, demanding and pleading.

He removed the thin chemise to leave her lying naked and beautiful in the half-dark. Her skin was gold in the firelight and it glistened with a sheen of perspiration. The rhythmic rise and fall of her breasts, their peaks hard and the color of burnished bronze, tempted him. He teased them with his thumb until she cried out in the agony of desire and he was forced to silence her with a kiss.

She did not wait, as she usually did, for the pressure of his lips to part hers; she took the tip of his tongue into her mouth almost before their lips met. The taste of him filled her, and as his tongue licked across the edge of her teeth, she wrapped her arms around him and pulled him down to her. The warmth of her, the pounding of her heart beneath hard nipples pressed against him, the eagerness of her mouth moving under his, he caught the fire of her mood.

His swift, effortless entry satisfied the immediate longing. He was part of her now. She lay still beneath him, relaxed, content. Then he began to move within her and with a few slow and gentle thrusts rekindled the blaze. He could, he knew, bring her quick release or draw out the delicious torture until all her passion was spent, all her hunger fed. He chose the latter.

Her nails dug into his shoulders as he withdrew almost to the point of leaving her body completely, only to drive once more inside her. Though she clasped her legs around him tightly, he did it again, and again, each time plunging deeper. She could not fight him, could only move with him until he brought ecstasy to her. Every nerve in her body tingled with it, it rang in her ears and sang in her blood, and when she felt she could stand no more, the sweet explosion ripped through her. She cried out, not once but a dozen times, as each wave crashed over her, drowning her in beautiful agony. The savage tide took him, too, and had they not clung tightly to each other, they might have been carried out to sea.

Mikhail pulled the blanket over Alexandra and walked to the window to look out upon a marvelously clear sky. He had almost forgotten what stars looked like and gazed with affection on the Great Bear and Orion, the Hunter.

"I'll not be sorry to have seen the last of this rain for a

while," he said. "It appears that the sun will shine on our arrival tomorrow."

"Well, it won't be up for quite a while yet, so come on back to bed." She yawned loudly. "I really am tired now."

The fire had gone out, but it wasn't really needed, and when Mikhail opened the window, cool clean rain-washed air swept into the room. He drew great gulps of it into his lungs and then, before Alexandra could complain of a chill, he lay back down beside her and drew her close to him for warmth.

She lay back, welcoming the hard reality of his body touching hers. He pushed the thick mane of her hair up so he could kiss her neck and shoulder, nip at her earlobe and the delicate line of her jaw. Like a kitten, she rubbed against him and made soft sounds like purring when he slid his arm under her breasts.

The memory of another night when they had lain thus haunted her each time she closed her eyes. She had slept then and wakened to a nightmare she had thought would never end. The promise of a very different future brought a hesitant smile to her lips, but she did not sleep without dreams, and not all of them were pleasant.

The day was too beautiful, too glorious, for Alexandra to mope very long.

"I wish we had an open carriage today," she said as Mikhail handed her into the still damp-smelling carriage. "I don't think sunshine has ever been so welcome."

He smiled, taking his seat beside her. She had spoken scarcely a dozen words to him during breakfast and had even turned away from his kiss. He remembered what he had told Andrei and knew what she was thinking.

"Tomorrow I promise you a tour of Moscow in my grandfather's phaeton, provided it doesn't rain, of course. We'll drive past the Kremlin and perhaps even catch a glimpse of the Tsar. We can take a picnic lunch to eat in the park and you will see all the sights in one day."

The carriage jerked into motion and quickly picked up

speed, as though the horses knew they were returning to their home stable. When Alexandra saw the city itself in the distance, she gasped, not with fright, but with awe. What she had remembered as a raging inferno, an ugly ruin, or a cold and bitter corner of hell, no longer existed. This was not the same city she had entered the night of the holocaust; it was a new and different world, bright and beautiful. Church spires and curious shaped domes glittered gold and silver against the pale early sky.

What had she, after all, expected? That Moscow would lie in the ashes as a monument to Napoleon's folly? No, nor could it remain as a shrine to her own suffering. She was but one of thousands who had known tragedy that winter, and others had lost much more than she.

That streets were busy with traffic: carriages, carts, horses and ponies everywhere, but Vasili knew his way through the snarl. They made steady progress at a pace that enabled Alexandra to see the shops and houses as they passed. Everything was so much larger, busier, gayer than Smolensk. She found herself growing more and more excited.

"It won't be much longer," Mikhail told her. "Look, there's Saint Basil's Cathedral, as sacred to every Muscovite as Notre Dame is to the Parisians."

Alexandra stared at the great church with its domes like gilded onions and at first thought it gaudy and ugly and lacking the graceful spirituality that suffused the gothic arches of Notre Dame de Paris. Then as they drove past it and she could see it closely, she felt the power, the primitive, glorious power of Mother Russia and her people, that surrounded the edifice with its unfamiliar style. In an awe-filled whisper, she said, "It is magnificent!" and could not take her eyes from it until the turned down another street and buildings blocked her view.

"This is Brozhansky Street, where my friend Ilarion Denisovitch Parofsky lives, in that brick house right there. We have to cross two more streets and then we turn left onto Saint Helena Street and we shall be home."

His eagerness glittered in his eyes and for once when she

tried to draw his gaze, she failed. She could almost hear him naming the occupants of each and every house they passed. They turned at last onto Saint Helena Street and a knot of apprehension tied itself in the pit of Alexandra's stomach as she watched Mikhail's face light with a smile. To her astonishment, he looked away from the window just as the horses slowed.

"We're home," he whispered.

He waited until Vasili had opened the door. And then, for a long minute, he stood very still, staring at the house but not moving toward it, until Vasili finally offered his hand to help a waiting Alexandra from the carriage.

Seen all at once, the Ogrinov house was more imposing than she had at first thought. It rose a full four stories of grey stone, the windows set symetrically along the length of the facade. The double doors of the main entrance sheltered under a portico of strict classical design. At either corner of the house smaller entries complemented the whole. As beautiful and elegant as any mansion in Paris, the house on Saint Helena Street appeared cold and forbidding.

"I miss the window seat in the library," Mikhail mused, "but this will do." He turned to Vasili and asked, "Is it all done? There was still so much to do when I left."

The servant grinned. "You must see for yourself. Or do you intend to stand outside and just look at it?"

Laughing, aware suddenly that he had spent too much time already, Mikhail took Alexandra's hand and linked it through his arm to lead her up the marble steps. At the instant they reached the top, the huge white doors swung inward.

"Good morning, sir. The Countess awaits you in the red drawing room."

That calm announcement in almost unintelligible English came from a tall, thin man, dressed in long outmoded livery and powdered wig who stood inside the door and bowed as Mikhail and Alexandra entered.

"Thank you, Edward," Mikhail replied. "Mother is in the morning room?"

The tall man shook his head. "No, sir, I believe she is in the music room."

"Tell her I am here, with Alexandra, and we will be visiting with Grandmere."

"Very good, sir. Shall I send some refreshments?"

When Mikhail declined the offer of a second breakfast, Edward bowed solemnly and turned sharply on his heel. Alexandra had no time to wonder what on earth an English butler was doing in Moscow, for he quickly led them down a short corridor to a sitting room decorated in blue and gold. Directly off it was another, visible through wide double doors. This room was done all in rich, warm red.

"That will be all, Edward," Mikhail said, his voice quiet and unsteady.

The servant bowed again, and exited without another word. Not until he had gone, however, did Mikhail move towards the next room, with Alexandra clutching his arm.

From the cool tones of the first room they entered the embrace of lush reds and dark woods. All around her swirled an air of vibrant sensuality that did not belong within the plain grey stone walls. It was hardly the atmosphere one would expect to find an elderly Russian countess comfortable in.

"So, Mikhail Pavlovitch, you are home."

Anna rose from a chair by the window and only when she stepped into a band of sunlight shining through the half-opened curtains did Alexandra see the Countess.

"Yes, Grandmere, I am home."

In their brief embrace, Alexandra saw the depth of their affection. Mikhail might blink back tears and cough on a half-swallowed sob, but Anna Petrovna let the glistening drops slide down her cheeks with no effort made to restrain them.

She was so unlike the matriarch Alexandra had imagined that she had to suppress a laugh. And she wondered if the dowager Countess wore black in mourning or because she looked exquisite in it. The heavy taffeta rustled with each step as if she were enticing an admirer to follow.

Mikhail began, once he had cleared his throat, to make formal introductions. Anna Petrovna stopped him.

"Ignore his foolishness. You are Alexandra, and you must call me Anna, unless you care to call me *Grandmere*, as this great hulking grandson of mine still does."

"Oh, no, Madame la Comtesse, I do not believe so," Alexandra replied, feeling her face burn. She knew Mikhail was grinning, taking amusement while she suffered.

"*La*, no one has called me that since we last entertained the Tsar!" Anna exclaimed. "I do like the sound of it, but five syllables are too many for pleasant conversation, I insist you call me Anna."

She refused to hear any arguments and took Alexandra by the hand.

"I love this room. The old house, the one the Italian bastard burned, had a red drawing room, but it was small and ugly, so when Mischa began to build this house, I made him promise me a lovely red room. What do you think of it?"

While Alexandra tried to find a polite but honest reply, Mikhail, who walked just behind them on this little tour of the room, said candidly, "It reminds me of the salon in the most expensive whorehouse in Paris."

"Exactly! That's why I like it!" Anna exclaimed.

She is as outrageous as Vera Ylbatskaya, Alexandra thought. Perhaps more so, because at least the Princess has the excuse of her upbringing. This woman is the widow of a count and a grandmother several times over. What does she know of French brothels?

But Anna's laughter was contagious, and Alexandra could not remain immune very long.

Chapter 36

IF ANNA Petrovna even saw the disapproving glance Mikhail sent her way, she completely ignored it and continued her effortless captivation of Alexandra. Her questions about Paris tumbled one after another, barely giving Alexandra time to answer between them. When Mikhail attempted to speak, he realized his grandmother did not want to know what had happened in the salons among the fashionable elite. Alexandra could draw pictures of the narrow lanes and alleys where the working people lived, suffered, and died, and these were the people Anna had come from.

They hardly noticed his departure. He excused himself to pay his respects to his mother, he said, and left the two women chattering in excited, emotional French. Save for the difference in their ages, they might have been school-girls in Paris discussing their beaux. Mikhail shook his head with a smile as he mounted the stairs of the house he had last seen when it was but an empty shell, unfinished and cold. He approached the open door to the second floor music room and stopped to listen to the Mozart sonatina his mother played on her harpsichord.

The instrument sat in front of the window to catch the light, and the sunbeams glittered as well on the crown of golden curls atop Marina's bent head. Music had always been her one true passion. Though she stared at the door where her son stood, she saw nothing, so firmly entranced was she by the music.

"I am home, Maman," he said quietly as the last notes faded twinkling into the sunlit silence. "I'm sorry to be so late. The weather, the roads, delayed us."

"Oh yes, yes, I know. It doesn't matter as long as you're here now."

He had to help her to her feet before she could embrace him, smother him with maternal kisses as though he were still a child, a lost little boy.

"Vasili assured us from the first time that you were all right, but I've worried so. You're going to stay home this time, aren't you?" she asked hopefully. "Promise me, please, Mischa, you won't run away again."

"I believe I am here to stay," he answered with a smile. "At least I can promise not to run off without a warning first." He gave her a reassuring kiss, though a bit of doubt remained in her eyes.

"When we heard you hadn't arrived in Moscow, that you had disappeared again, your grandmother screamed at me for days. Mischa, you cannot imagine how that woman, my own mother, tormented me with my guilt. I began to hate her, to blame her for everything, for Papa's death, for Niki's death, for your father's death." Mikhail shuddered at the mention of his brother and the memories it provoked. "I blamed her for the loss of everything and everyone I had ever cared about. It was a month before I understood how wrong I had been, and how right she was.

"I know I can never make up to you for the things I have done, nor can I expect you to forgive me for them. All I ask is that you give me a chance, please, to try to make it different now that—"

"What's done is done," he interrupted, "and it changes nothing to discuss it. Let us put our guilts and our grievances aside and concentrate on improving the future, for we cannot alter the past."

Alexandra's words fit the situation perfectly. He did not wish, now or at any other time, to renew old hurts, and burying the past as one buries the dead was the only way to keep the pain from returning.

He patted her hand and suggested, "Why don't we go

downstairs and I will introduce you to Alexandra, if Grandmere hasn't frightened her away yet.''

Ten minutes ago he had entered this room with the reluctance of years of distrust and a sense of unwanted and unpleasant obligation. He felt free of the burden for the first time in years, perhaps for the first time in his life, and he noticed that his mother's hand on his arm rested lightly, as though she, too, were relieved of a heavy weight.

Mikhail had not been gone for more than a few seconds when Anna's curiosity about Paris seemed suddenly satisfied. She sighed almost wearily and said, ''Paris will never change. She is as eternal as youth, and twice as seductive. I wonder, then, why we both left her?''

She did not need to look at Alexandra to know a mask of caution had fallen over the girl's face. She said nothing, and Anna quickly filled the silence.

''I don't expect Mikhail to return very soon,'' she said in a low voice tinged with foreboding. ''These audiences with his mother do not always go well.''

This bitterness felt for a daughter-in-law was not difficult for Alexandra to understand; mothers often retained an excessive protectiveness towards their sons. She nodded, relieved to have the conversation turned in another direction.

''Do you get on well with your parents?''

Alexandra jumped, startled and dismayed; she felt as though she were on trial and wanted desperately to be found innocent. She kept her wits about her enough to know that this casual question was merely the means to find out what kind of family she came from.

''I don't remember my real parents. I was raised by my Aunt Therese and her husband. We were a very close family,'' she said truthfully.

''No brothers and sisters?''

''Only two step-sisters, both older than I. Yvette was married to a lieutenant in the army just days before I left Paris, and Justine was engaged to a singer at the Opera.''

"Everyone *was*. Are they all dead?"

No, I am, Alexandra thought, at least to all of them.

"It has been so long since I've seen them or even had word of them; I really don't know. I certainly pray that they are not, but with Albert in the Army, and Justine's betrothed somehow connected with Mikhail, I can't help but worry."

"I was luckier, I suppose, than you, in that I left no one behind. My mother died when I was seven, leaving my father with two children. My brother had already decided to become a priest, though my father wanted him to be a baker, like the rest of the family. I had even more scandalous ideas; I wanted to dance."

"*Dance?*"

"You sound just like my father did then! But I thought life on the stage infinitely more attractive than the existence I saw my neighbors leading. Women were old at thirty and dead soon after, and they spent those few years in abject misery. Not I!

"I ran away from home when I was ten and attached myself to a very famous dancer whose vanity far outweighed her talent or her intelligence. By the time I had learned enough about her art to take her place, she had learned more about scheming and tried to get rid of me. I had no future in Paris after that, so before I reduced myself to beggary or worse, I took myself to Moscow. That my fortunes took a brighter turn here is, I hope, quite plain to see. I hope yours do, too."

"Thank you. I'm sure they will."

She's going to ask me what I plan to do here, Alexandra thought nervously and without an answer. Oh, Mischa, where are you? How could you leave me alone like this? What am I to say to her?

She had become adept at inconsequential small talk in the salons of Napoleon's Paris and now pulled that almost forgotten skill from her memory.

"I wish I could have seen Paris the way you did. There was little of beauty most of the time I was a child, and I think we all learned to live with a certain amount of fear.

At least there was always uncertainty."

"Sometimes even the horror of slavery is preferable to that," the Countess added. "Security and stability seem much more attractive once they are lost in the maelstrom of ambition."

Justine, Yvette, the peaceful rooms over Armand's shop: all my happiness sacrificed to my selfish desires! Alexandra wailed inwardly. How well I know whereof she speaks!

"And how bitter the taste when men achieve their goals at a price higher than they wished to pay. The Corsican took Moscow, but see how dearly it cost him. He will lose his Empire now. Did you ever meet him?"

She could switch her tone so quickly, but this time she did not catch Alexandra unawares.

"Only once, and I found him most unpleasant."

"I believe I should have spit in his eye had I been introduced to him," Anna said indignantly. "Such a monster!"

Alexandra had the impression of a very elegant little blackbird ruffling its feathers. Anna tossed her head and straightened her shoulders as if shrugging off something unclean.

"One hesitates even to imagine what might have happened had he made his attack on Russia during a more favorable season," Alexandra said, with a shudder of her own.

The very idea left them both cold and lost in thought for a moment until approaching footsteps disturbed them and released them from the momentary images of hell.

Alexandra immediately recognized the strong cadence of Mikhail's step and closed her eyes in a silent sigh of relief. Much as she dreaded meeting another member of his family, she felt she could face anything or anyone as long as he was with her. This interview with his grandmother had been almost too much.

Yet once she saw his mother enter the drawing room, she felt no dread at all. She calmly accepted Marina Fyodorovna's kisses of welcome.

"I'm sure you are tired after your long journey, so I will not tire you with more questions. Rest for a while, and we can talk later," Marina said softly.

Alexandra, for one, had no desire to argue. The prospect of a hot bath and a nap was far too inviting. Marina apologized that Alexandra's rooms on the second floor were small, but at least they were quiet, overlooking the courtyard rather than the street, and in the one completed wing of the house; she would not be disturbed by the noise of workmen trying to complete the rest before the Christmas holidays.

As they walked together up the stairs, Mikhail further informed her that his grandmother had put a maid at her disposal. Any complaints, he insisted, must be immediately directed to him.

"The old lady can sometimes be a bit perverse, and it's not beyond her to send up some ignorant bitch from the farm just to test your patience." He stopped with his hand on the door handle and looked down into her calm but obviously weary green eyes. "You need the rest, Snowbird; do as she says, and if you need me, I shall be right across the hall."

A few pounding heartbeats later, she stood alone on the other side of her door and watched as he closed it.

"I *am* tired, and as soon as I get out of these filthy clothes and have a bath, I am going to take his advice and sleep for at least three hours," she told herself firmly.

And her ankle had begun to throb, just a little. She hobbled to the nearest chair and slumped onto it.

Her sitting room was undoubtedly small, but its luxurious furnishings created a sense of intimacy. The soft grey silk walls enveloped her in a fog of tranquility; she yawned and slid into a more relaxed position with half a thought to doze in the chair.

"Mischa, you must have been right," she mumbled, forcing herself to her feet. "Ah, well, I've dressed and undressed myself often enough; I don't need some lazy scullery wench to bathe me."

With another yawn she made her way to the open door

leading to a bedchamber slightly larger than the sitting room and decorated in the same pale, soothing tones of grey. A vase of wine-red roses provided a touch of brilliant color beside the bed, but all else was shimmering, silvery, seductive grey.

The bed had been turned down, and it took all the strength of will she had left to stride past it towards the tub of steaming water in the tiny bath and dressing room.

Her lone trunk stood empty to one side of the tall wardrobe cabinet; the absent maid had at least unpacked before disappearing, though the hatboxes lay in an untidy pile, and her shoes were scattered on the floor. Struggling with one hand to unfasten the long row of buttons down her back, Alexandra began to sort through the slippers and boots with the other hand in hopes of finding a pair to match.

"Worthless slut!" she muttered. "I certainly shall complain about this."

But when at last she found two matching slippers and the final buttons slid from their loops, a good portion of her frustration left her. She stepped from the pile her gown made around her ankles and approached the wardrobe to choose a dress for the evening.

The doors were locked.

"Damn!" she swore, and she stomped her foot so hard a bolt of lightning shot up her leg to bring tears of pain as well as anger.

Favoring the injured ankle now with a pronounced limp, she stormed to the crumpled travelling dress and stepped into it once more. She turned the sleeves right side out and thrust her arms through them, but the impossibility of reaching the buttons defeated her. With a little moan of self-pity, she sank to the floor. Nothing mattered now but rest and the oblivion of sleep. She kicked away the dress that had fallen from her shoulders and pulled off her shoes and stockings. It was then just a matter of stumbling to the bed and collapsing upon it.

"But mademoiselle, surely you will have your bath first?"

Alexandra heard the words through the pillow she had covered her face with. She bleated out a pouting, "No, I'm going to sleep. Go away." But the voice continued.

"I have your favorite ecru satin all pressed for dinner, the one you like to wear with the sapphires and pearls."

Slowly the words and familiar voice penetrated the muffling pillow to her brain. Too shocked to move, Alexandra lay still and let other hands lift the pillow from her until through her tear-blurred eyes she saw the well-remembered face.

"Giselle! Oh, my God in Heaven, it *is* you!" Ignoring the pain it brought, Alexandra jumped to her feet and embraced the quivering maid frantically. Then, just as suddenly, she pushed Giselle away. A scowl of black anger clouded her face and she screamed as loudly as she could. "*Mikhail!*"

Giselle, speechless, her own smile gone, offered a handkerchief, but Alexandra refused it. She wiped her face on the back of her hand and called to him again, louder.

"I will kill him, with my own hands. He had no right to do this to me, to tease me and then nearly kill me with the shock of his cruel trick. It is the last time, the very last time."

"Please, mademoiselle, let me explain. You must not blame him; he—"

"Don't tell me what I may and may not do!" Alexandra snapped. "That miserable bastard, he has gone one step too far."

Then the object of her anger burst through the door to stand clad only in a towel, and dripping water on the polished floor.

"My God, Xan, what's wrong?" His hands reached to her as his eyes sought any sign of hurt. "Has the girl done something to harm you?"

He didn't know. She could tell that much from the way he stared at her, the way his hands trembled. He hadn't even seen Giselle cowering by the bed.

"I am so sorry, Mischa. I've frightened you," she

apologized. She did not mind the soapy water soaking through her chemise from his wet chest and arms as she fell against him and let his embrace tighten around her. "I thought you had played a dreadful trick on me, teasing me again, and I was ready to kill you with my bare hands."

Not even the absurdity of such a suggestion helped him to ignore the effect she was having on him, and he did not like the idea of it being so obvious to the servant girl hiding behind the bedpost. Whatever nonsense Alexandra babbled about this time was going to take a lengthy explanation he preferred to hear privately. In Russian he ordered the all but invisible maid out of the room. She didn't move, and Alexandra began now to quiver with laughter.

"Come here, Giselle. He won't hurt you, I promise."

It was Vasili who provided the complete explanation, in the library before supper.

Everything made perfect sense, of course, once they knew all the facts. What better way to lay a false trail for anyone chasing the escapees than to take Alexandra's maid and all her belongings to a secluded chateau on the Breton coast. The plan to remain at the chateau for at least a month disintegrated when Napoleon's invasion of Russia became imminent. Giselle was sent to St. Petersburg to wait for further instructions, which finally came when Vasili received word from Mikhail just a week ago that he was returning to Moscow.

"I wanted to surprise you," the serf mumbled. "I never wanted to scare you. I wrote to Giselle the day I got Mikhail's letter from Smolensk and told her she was to come here at once with all Alexandra's belongings and prepare for her arrival. It is all my fault," he admitted. "I should have told Mikhail and I didn't. I was wrong, and I am very, very sorry."

The shame in his eyes melted any anger remaining in her; she smiled and forgave him, as he probably knew she would. Then Mikhail jumped from his chair and crossed the room to stand toe to toe with his servant.

"Just one minute," he said sternly. "All the blame is not yours. How did you explain all this to my grandmother? Why did she say absolutely nothing to me about a lady's maid appearing at her door one day and demanding to be shown to Alexandra's room? I cannot believe she asked no questions, unless someone provided her with answers and she knew as much about this as anyone else."

The ensuing silence declared Anna Petrovna guilty. None of Vasili's later protests could reverse the conviction, but Mikhail's laughter pardoned her, and everyone raised glasses of quickly poured vodka to toast the sly Countess and her enthusiastic conspiracy.

There were little details to be filled in, a process which could take days or even weeks, but by the time she was dressed for dinner, Alexandra had heard more than the essentials of Giselle's long tale. Her experiences had changed her. Though she remained as timid as ever in the presence of strangers, and especially men, she had acquired considerable confidence in herself. And she had learned to listen and to watch.

"I am quite surprised at some of the things I've heard around this house."

Intrigued, Alexandra sat still as a statue and watched Giselle's fingers turn the long wavy locks into a superb coiffure with a cascade of ringlets at each shoulder.

"Such as?"

"First, there is no love lost between Countess Anna and her daughter, Princess Marina."

"You mean her daughter-in-law, don't you?"

"No, Princess Marina is her daughter, and not really a princess, either; they just call her that, though I don't know why. But Marina married a foreigner and kept her Russian name afterwards, which means her son isn't really a count after all. His grandfather was, and a very powerful one at that, but *he* has no title at all."

"So Mischa isn't a count, and not even an Ogrinov. How odd!" Alexandra mused aloud. "I wonder why he never told me?"

"Perhaps he thought you were after his title. Or maybe it was easier to get into the right places in Paris if he used it."

With a derisive snort Alexandra replied, "Telling me the truth would have been the easiest way to find out what I was interested in. If I'd only wanted his title, he could have been rid of me a lot sooner."

"Maybe he was afraid that is exactly what would happen and so he said nothing." Letting that thought sink in, Giselle went on quickly, "Anyway, Countess Anna doesn't get on well with Marina, and apparently he is the reason. Each wants him exclusively, or so the servants say, and neither will give him up. There was another son, too, who died several years ago, but they never fought over him."

"I thought I had put all the fighting behind me, that I would find peace and quiet and happiness in this house," Alexandra sighed. She stood up and walked over to the silver framed pier glass. She had almost forgotten what she looked like in a perfectly fit satin gown with the rich sparkle of sapphires against her skin. A smile of honest pride curved her lips, and the blue stones winked back at her. Only the sparkle of her emerald eyes shone brighter. "I don't want to enter a family squabble and perhaps be forced to choose for one side or the other. Do the servants say which side Mischa himself favors?"

Giselle shook her head. "They don't have to. You know as well as I that he went to his grandmother first and only later to his mother."

These were disturbing thoughts to take with her to dinner, but Alexandra could not force them out of her mind. It made no difference to her whether he were a prince or a shoemaker; what worried her was his secrecy. What else had he not told her? Good heavens, did he perhaps have a wife he planned to present to her at the dinner table? No, she could dismiss that fear; the conversation she had overheard at Vera's assured her he was not married, at least not yet.

From a gallery decorated with portraits of men and

women in the fashions of the past two centuries, Alexandra descended one marble step at a time, her hand gliding along the polished walnut balustrade. Suspended from the ceiling frescoed in imitation of a summer sky, a chandelier that rivaled the magnificence of any she had seen in Paris, even at Napoleon's palace, shed its glittery light. Here was brightness and beauty with almost Grecian simplicity.

As she reached the last step, Mikhail turned and left his companion to take her hand.

Kissing her cheek lightly, he whispered in English, ''My dear, only once before have I ever seen you look so beautiful. Now come, I want you to meet a very, very dear friend.''

He placed her hand quite proprietarily on his arm, as though to announce his ownership of her before leading her to the young man with whom he had been talking at her arrival.

This was Ilarion Denisovitch Parofsky, Mikhail's very best friend. She had heard many stories about him, but not once had Mikhail told her that the man was so beautiful. More than just handsome, he was unquestionably the most beautiful man she had ever seen, with pale gold hair that curled lazily over his collar and eyes that were neither blue nor green nor grey, but somewhere in between all three. Not quite as tall as Mikhail, he carried the supple grace of a dancer on his slender frame, and the wide shoulders beneath his carefully tailored uniform bespoke sinewy, cat-like strength. Yet his smile was gentle and serene, lighting his perfect features with happiness. And when he took Alexandra's hand in his and raised it to his lips, she could not control the shiver that raced down her spine.

''You must call me Ilya, as all my friends do,'' he insisted. Though his voice was soft and quiet, she knew he meant only sincere friendship, nothing more.

Because there was no escape, she allowed herself to be escorted into the dining room by both Ilya and Mikhail and felt only a small measure of relief when Ilya took a place across the table from her rather than beside her. She was aware of his constant smile and gentle but persistent gaze throughout the meal.

Mikhail, however, seemed unaware of either her discomfort or his friend's preoccupation.

"The celebration for Ilya's wedding lasted four days, but the disappointed women of Moscow mourned for over a month," he laughed, bringing a flush to Alexandra's face.

Ilya didn't seem to care and continued to smile at her.

"And where is your wife this evening?" she asked, and an accusing note crept into her voice without her even knowing it.

"She is at home, awaiting the birth of our first child. Or perhaps children," he answered easily, the smile never breaking, the eyes as steady as before. "Both the physician and Lydia's grandmother are predicting at least twins, so she does not leave the house for any reason at all."

Anna Petrovna nodded for approval. "She is a very delicate young woman, your Lydia, and wise not to take any unnecessary risks. I will pay her a visit tomorrow, I think."

"She will appreciate that, Countess."

Kindness brightened his voice, and Alexandra had the impression that he dearly loved his wife, perhaps even shared some of her concern. Why then did he continue to stare at her?

"Ilya and I have been friends for so long I can't even remember a time when he wasn't talking me out of trouble I couldn't handle or helping me with what we could handle together," Mikhail announced. He raised his glass in a toast and quickly downed the contents. "We have shared good times and bad, horses, meals, our last bottle of vodka, everything." He was more than a little drunk.

"No, not everything," the soft, incredibly gentle voice said. "We have never shared a woman."

Displaying the effects of a bit too much vodka, Mikhail

nodded in agreement. ''That is true, but only because we never had to!''

''This is not a tavern! If you wish to behave like drunken soldiers, you will remove yourselves from my dining room and my presence at once!''

Like small boys, they grinned sheepishly, offered apologies that they did not really mean, and settled down to complete their meal with no further outbursts.

Chapter 37

MADE ON impulse, Alexandra's suggestion that she accompany Anna on her visit to Ilya's wife was one she regretted as soon as the words were out of her mouth. She had already displayed unqualified boldness by taking her breakfast with the Countess, but inviting herself on a personal call took audacity that surprised and embarrassed her.

She had no time, however, to imagine what disaster would befall her as a result of such impoliteness because the Countess immediately agreed that it was an excellent idea. Half an hour later they left together in a small carriage.

"It's not far," Anna said as she straightened the folds of her skirt, "and usually I walk, but I fear we might see more rain this morning. That was quite a storm we had last night. It didn't waken you, did it?"

Glad that the subject was nothing more intimate than the weather, Alexandra replied, "No, I was too tired. I slept like a baby."

"Travelling can be exhausting, even though one does nothing but sit and watch the countryside pass by."

They chatted amiably during the short drive, and Alexandra forgot her nervousness completely. Every ounce of it returned, however, the moment she stood at the door of Ilarion Parofsky's house. She had not considered the possibility of seeing him and now shivered with dread.

There was no sign of him, and after Anna had introduced Alexandra as her guest, Lydia apologized that her husband had left only a short time before and was not expected home until evening.

Alexandra had been prepared to see a frail child propped on pillows, lounging like an invalid. Lydia was nothing of the sort. Young, not yet eighteen, she glowed with health; it shone like sunlight in her deep, lustrous eyes. Despite her awkard condition, she moved about the little parlor serving tea with unusual energy. and her smile instantly dispelled worry.

"Dr. Spirov says I'm healthy as a horse," she laughed, tossing her head of auburn curls. "He is betting with my grandmother that I'll have two boys; she insists it's a boy and a girl."

Alexandra found it impossible to agree with Anna's belief that the girl had manufactured the story of twins to cover a pregnancy further advanced than was proper for a bride of barely seven months. For all her youth and naiveté, Lydia must recognize the futility of such a ploy. The birth of a single nine-month infant six or eight weeks ahead of its time would destroy her fabrication and prove her a liar, which Alexandra doubted Ilya would tolerate.

Besides, she genuinely like his wife and could not think ill of her. She was sorry, too, to see the hour pass so quickly. When Anna insisted they not stay too long and tire their hostess, Lydia refused to let them leave without a promise to return in a day or two. For the third time that morning, Alexandra acted before thinking and gave her her word she would pay another visit no later than Friday.

"I don't know what plans Mikhail has made, but I'm sure I can find an hour or so somewhere," she quickly added. The only thing she really felt certain of was that she had made a complete fool of herself.

No sooner had the carriage door closed than the sky opened and rain descended like a waterfall, and though she disliked the weather, Alexandra muttered a tiny prayer of thanks that the noise effectively prohibited conversation. She had fifteen minutes to develop an excuse for her presumptiveness, but when the vehicle stopped and

Vasili's familiar hands reached up to help her down, she had no more idea how to defend her actions than when she uttered that stupid promise.

She walked through the door and gave her damp shawl to Edward before hurrying towards the stairs to seek, if not solace, at least privacy in her room.

"Wait a moment, Alexandra," Anna called to her.

Like a bee dripping honey before it stings, Alexandra thought. Her heart skipped a beat as she turned to face the smiling Countess.

"I just wanted to thank you for brightening Lydia's day, and mine, too. I can find an excuse for you to miss your appointment with her; don't worry about that."

Am I not good enough for her? Alexandra wanted to ask. She stood but an inch taller than the Countess, yet she drew herself up with injured pride that made her feel as though she looked down from a great height upon the older woman and replied, "But I gave my word, and I do not make promises lightly."

Instead of the cold superiority Alexandra expected, Anna responded with an affectionate hug and kissed her cheek.

"If it is not raining, we shall walk together Thursday afternoon and see her. Now, go and change into dry clothes, then come down and have some lunch with me."

Several cups of strong coffee, compliments of his grandmother, chased the last yawns, and Mikhail faced the enormous stack of papers alert and awake but still tormented by a thundering headache. He smiled at his own idiocy; as Vasili had told him earlier, he was too old to be acting like a young fool. Ah well, he thought with a sigh, it was worth it. He reached for his pen with one hand and the top paper with his other.

Slowly the large pile resolved itself until only a single piece of paper, a carefully scribed list of items purchased and their cost, sat in front of him while he stared at it.

"Damn the bitch!" he swore softly. He dipped the pen in the ink but did not touch it to the paper. "Not a kopek over, not a kopek under. Dear, precise Tamara.'' Then he scrawled his name with enough violence to break the nib.

His head felt no better now, and his eyes throbbed, too, and Edward chose that moment to enter bearing a letter on a silver tray. Mikhail recognized it immediately, not by the ornate steal but by the familiar handwriting. He dared not ignore it, for Alexandr Pavlovitch Romanov, Tsar of all the Russias, did not stand even his mail to be kept waiting.

Mikhail read the four short sentences and groaned. The inevitable was coming much sooner than expected, leaving damned little time to prepare for it. Only one person would be pleased to learn that his imperial majesty had invited himself to dinner on Friday, but Marina had nothing more to do than select a gown and choose which jewels to wear with it. Still, it was Tuesday already, and there was much to do before the end of the week. Deciding to get it over with as quickly and painlessly as possible, Mikhail took the note, for it was too short to be considered a letter, with him when he and Alexandra went to lunch. He made the announcement in the dining room.

He did not notice that his grandmother was too pre-occupied to complain.

When Alexandra paid her promised visit to Lydia Parofskaya on Thursday afternoon, the main topic of conversation was, of course, the Tsar's impending visit and Alexandra's nervousness. Lydia stamped her foot in frustration, almost spilling her tea.

''I would so *love* to go. Ilya offered to stay with me if I didn't want to come, but I told him I wouldn't for that. He must go, even though I can't.''

''And why can't you?'' Alexandra asked. She had come alone on this call, leaving Anna to supervise the plans for tomorrow evening's reception. The Ogrinov house was an asylum of hysterical activity she was only too glad to escape, and had even ventured to walk the half mile without an escort.

Lydia patted her bulging midsection.

''Grandma was here this morning and she insisted they

will come this week. I mustn't leave the house now."

"And if you send Ilya to the reception, you will be here with two servants, one to send for the doctor, who may be attending another patient, and only one to stay with you. Who will tell Ilya? No, I insist I will bar your husband if he does not bring you, too."

It was another bold and probably foolish statement, and Lydia consented only to asking her husband, without whose permission she did nothing. Alexandra accepted that, but when Lydia added that he ought to be returning home any moment, Alexandra's blood suddenly ran cold.

She had not been able to forget their first meeting, and his arrival at the Ogrinov house yesterday afternoon had intensified her unnamed fear. He had come to see Mikhail and merely passed Alexandra in the corridor, but his smile and those eyes froze her in midstride.

"Mademoiselle Aubertien, how good to see you again."

She nodded politely. "Good afternoon, Captain Parofsky. Mischa is in the library."

"Yes, I know." The smile faded and he leaned closer to murmur urgently, "I must speak with you. Later, in a day or two," and then snapped her a smart salute before striding down the hall.

She hoped never to see him again, though she knew it was unavoidable. Certainly, however, he dared not attempt anything improper in front of his wife, so perhaps she was safer here in his own home, and that thought calmed her until the sound of his boots in the foyer announced him. Much as she longed to run and greet her husband, Lydia waited for him to come to her.

Alexandra had the advantage. She knew he was on his way and could be ready, whereas he would be caught off guard. All she needed was one look at his eyes to know the truth.

He came into the parlor and, obviously unaware of his visitor, rushed to his wife. His lips brushed her cheeks, then lingered on her mouth, until her giggles broke the spell.

"Good afternoon, Captain," Alexandra said softly.

"Good afternoon. Lydia told me you had promised a visit, but with the preparations for tomorrow, we thought—"

"A promise is a promise," she interrupted. "Besides, I am only a guest there myself, and I felt both useless and in the way."

Small talk. Stupid, inane, boring—but safe. Discuss the menu, the flowers, the other guests. Remind Lydia she must come or her husband would not be allowed in. Laugh a little. Alexandra kept her voice light and her smile sparkling throughout the five minute eternity of Lydia's presence. His response to her suggestion had been a noncommital "we shall see," before he left the room. By then it was time for Alexandra to leave, too, but she gave another promise to return the following week.

"And I expect to see you tomorrow night," she said as she adjusted her short cape around her shoulders, "unless you have a very good excuse!"

The sigh of relief she had held when leaving the parlor turned to a gasp; Ilya was waiting for her at the door.

Voice and eyes cool, he tucked a scrap of paper into her hand as he held the door open. "Until tomorrow evening, Mademoiselle Aubertein."

Chapter 38

THE FIGURES blurred on the pages and not even vigorously rubbing his eyes helped him to focus any clearer. Pulling out his watch, Mikhail squinted and discovered what he had feared was true; he had been working for more than three hours, far too long for a man who hadn't slept in almost two days. Concentration eluded his best efforts. Regretfully admitting defeat, he closed the ledgers, then snuffed out the candles. He kept one to light his way and, with a bellowing yawn, turned his back on the desk to leave the library to darkness.

Alexandra, too, struggled to stay awake. She had sent Giselle to bed hours ago, thinking she herself would fall asleep quickly. Instead, she piled the pillows behind her and with a glass of brandy settled down to wait for Mikhail.

His knock, soft and tentative, came as no surprise, but rather later than she expected. She laughed as she called her permission to enter; he had given her no other sign than a long stare over dinner that he intended to visit her. Had she read his mind? Or had he read hers?

He closed the door and poured himself a bit of her brandy.

"Nervous?" he asked.

"Why should I be? This isn't the first time you've come to my room late at night," she laughed, and rose to kneel behind him as he sat on the edge of her bed to pull his boots off.

382

His eyes dropped closed. Softly, lightly, as gently as spring raindrops, her fingers travelled over his skin, up and down the tense cords at the back of his neck, across the muscles of his shoulders so tight they quivered beneath her touch. He sighed with pleasure.

"I didn't mean *this*," he chuckled. "Tomorrow, though, and the Tsar."

She pulled his shirt the rest of the way off and pressed her lips to the tangle of curls at his temple where his pulse beat, strong and steady.

"And what else did you spend so much time and money on if not to prepare me for such things? I don't expect Moscow to be very different from Paris in the matter of kings and emperors and tsars. Perhaps this Russian Alexandr of yours will take a fancy to me as Napoleon did."

"I'd not jest if I were you," he warned. "Alexandr is not Bonaparte."

Relaxed, ready now for sleep, he tried to ignore the softness of the body he leaned back against, but exhaustion fled in the face of her warmth and the seductive play of her fingers. They had loosened the knots of pain in his neck and shoulders; now they tied others elsewhere. He wanted her desperately.

"Are you so bored with me that you groan at the thought of making love to me?" she teased when he grunted trying to rise from the bed to remove the rest of his clothing.

He needed no spoken retort; that he was neither bored with her nor loathe to make love to her was clear from his unashamed display of arousal. Where his weary body found the strength, he did not know. He would have been content to lie beside her, exchange a kiss or two as they had on many other nights and then surrender to sleep until passion wakened them in the morning. Having spent all his energy fighting exhaustion, he had nothing to fend off an attack of desire and Alexandra made such an irresistible enemy. He joyfully accepted defeat at her hands.

She untied the ribbons of her nightgown and pulled her

arms free, leaving the garment beneath her to frame her nakedness with its pale blue sheen. Like a rare and precious jewel, her body glowed in the candlelight: warm ivory, jet and sapphire, emerald fire and ruby wine. Seeing her bathed in light, Mikhail thanked again her childish fear of the dark, for now all his senses enjoyed her.

Touching her, tasting her, burying his face in the mass of her tumbled hair to drink in the scent of her. The sound of her huskily whispered, barely intelligible words of passion. Her movements were as frantic as his, her hunger as fierce. She took him into her body the way a starving man gulps food. She wrapped her legs around his thighs, then around his hips, forcing him deeper within the luscious warmth. To meet his thrusts she must withdraw and lose him, and rather than suffer that emptiness, she moved with him, holding him tightly within her.

A mixture of agony and sweetness tore through him, and yet there was no relief, only a tremulous sobbing beneath him and release from the tight grip of her legs. One single thrust, though it brought a scream of torment from her, and his desire spent itself, pouring his seed and his pleasure into the depths of her.

He did not remember falling asleep, but it was impossible to forget anything else. Alexandra lay on her side with one arm stretched out to him. The sheet covered her only to her waist, and the sight of her breasts, their nipples soft and full, sent the fire to his loins once more. He had to leave—now. Or be drawn to spend another hour or two in her bed.

Not that he would have minded doing exactly that on any other day but this. If last night's frenzy had failed to satisfy all his desires, they must simply wait until another time when he had less work to do. Then he would lie abed all day, if necessary, or all night. For the moment, he would take one kiss and one only from those dream-smiling lips and set himself to the day's tasks.

God in Heaven she was beautiful, and the longer he stared the more he wished to remain with her. In winter he could have pleaded the chill in the room and buried himself under a mound of quilts with her yielding body for added warmth. But this was early September and autumn was still weeks away. He had no excuse at all save his desire for her and that, he reasoned, was not enough to keep him from his desk.

He took his kiss and quickly rolled away from her before his determination, weak after only a few hours sleep, waned. A languorous sigh behind him tempted him to return; he resisted and began collecting the clothes he had left scattered.

"Good morning, Mischa."

Keeping his back to the seductive voice he replied, "Good morning, Xan."

"Must you leave so soon? I hoped at least you could find the time to breakfast with me." The sheet rustled; he pictured her groping for the blue nightdress and scrambling to achieve a modicum of decency before he turned around.

"I have a great deal of work to do."

"Oh, *damn* you and your work. You haven't had five minutes with me since you brought me here."

He pulled up his breeches and buttoned them while apologizing.

"I'm sorry, I truly am, but I can't help it. Do you think I enjoy spending hours at that desk, losing a night's sleep because my grandmother doesn't trust anyone else to handle her finances and my mother is incapable of adding two and two? I distinctly hate it, but someone has to do it."

"Let it go for a day," she begged. "How will it look if you fall asleep in the middle of a conversation with the Tsar? Mischa, you need rest, not more work."

Half dressed, he felt safe in facing her. Legs folded, sitting on her heels, she extended loving arms to her.

"I fear I'd get little enough rest if I stayed with you!" he laughed, but he took her hands in his and let her pull him closer. "All right, all right. I'll share a bit of breakfast with you, but not here."

"In the library then, in an hour?"

He almost agreed, but asked her instead, "Would you prefer the garden?"

She would. Delighted at the prospect, she kissed him lightly and chased him from her chamber so she could summon Giselle and get dressed.

The sun shone warmly, but in the shade of the pavilion, Alexandra was glad for the light stole Giselle had thrown about her shoulders at the last minute. As it was almost noon, she discovered a sudden appetite and ate heartily, noting that Mikhail, too, seemed grateful for more than his usual black coffee.

When they had finished their meal but not before Mikhail could swallow the last of his coffee and depart, Alexandra ventured to ask, "Do you know the Tsar well?"

"Well enough."

"Well enough for what?"

"I know Alexandr well enough not to trust him. Perhaps that is why, no matter which crown he wears, he keeps me in his favor. He trusts me, just as I do not trust him."

It brought to mind other breakfasts in Paris when Mikhail had prepared her for balls and dinners by describing the people she would meet. Pointing out both strengths and weaknesses, he painted as accurate a portrait of the Russian emperor as he could.

"Like all kings, he is caught between two worlds. He is human, a man who must eat and drink and sleep, and yet he is expected to be something more, a kind of divinity. Most men would choose to be one or the other, or to find a compromise between the two. Alexandr must play both parts, and it is the uncertainty of which role he will take next that leaves his people confused.

"At times he is a man of surprising intelligence, considering the madness that afflicts the Romanovs. He realizes this is a country clinging to the institutions the rest of the civilized world discarded several centuries ago. Without the changes he has begun, Russia will never enter another century peacefully, but it is only a beginning, and not a good one at that. Still, if he keeps his promises, there is hope.''

He sipped at his coffee and looked across the little table at Alexandra.

''I was about to apologize for boring you, but you don't look very bored.''

''I'm not. Please, go on.''

''Alexandr's other side touches the fringe of insanity. He can sink into moods of religious fanaticism, sometimes for weeks, when he sees himself as a messenger of God. He keeps ambassadors and generals waiting for hours while he is at his devotions. When he is like that, those of us who try to serve him must wait until he returns to sanity.''

''Why does the country not rise up against him? Surely there are enough ambitious men ready and willing to take control, and you said the serfs are virtual slaves.''

''With one difference. They are slaves with religion, and to them Alexandr *is* God's holy messenger. When he is at his weakest, they provide the necessary strength to protect him, even though they do absolutely nothing. It is loyalty of the blindest kind, fostered by priests who are controlled by the monarchy, but it cannot be ignored.''

''I don't know whether to feel pity for him or to congratulate him on his monstrous good fortune.''

''Best simply to avoid him, especially in your case.''

Again a warning.

''I can hardly do that, can I?''

''No,'' he answered with a long sigh, ''but be as cautious tonight as ever you were in Paris, perhaps even more so. There are only two men in the world I cannot protect you from, and Alexandr Pavlovitch Romanov is one of them.''

Leaving her to wonder who the other might be, he abruptly excused himself and strode toward the house.

Caution, he had warned, and she felt as if she had indeed stepped back in time. An evening of intrigue stretched ahead of her. She finished her coffee and, setting the translucent cup down rather sharply, she too returned to the house.

387

The library was cool and quiet. Sunlight streamed golden through the tall windows, checkering the polished floor. The clock had struck the half hour some time ago; Mikhail guessed it now to be near five. Barely enough time to bathe and dress before his guests arrived, but he had received another letter and refused to leave the desk until he had done with it.

Sealed with a dollop of plain red wax that bore no mark, it had plainly seen much travel as evidenced by the stains and curled corners. But the seal had not been broken. The writing appeared feminine yet strong, not at all timid; he did not recognize the hand but then he had known many, many women in Paris, though it surprised him that one would write to him. With more time to spare he might have speculated as to the author, but could not afford the luxury now and hastily broke the seal.

Monsieur le Comte,

It has now been a year since you left Paris with my sister. Our worry has been great, as perhaps you can imagine. Yesterday Madame Duquesne came here and asked about Alexandra and told me much that I did not wish to know, though I believe she spared me even worse. The only comfort was that she had last seen Alexandra alive and well.

If you are able to give my sister a message, I have enclosed a short letter. Please, I pray you, see that it gets to her. My words to you on the occasion of our last meeting in Paris were not altogether kind, but you gave me reason to believe you would keep Alexandra from harm. As she trusted you, so did I. I hope that trust was not in vain.

The second letter, folded neatly and sealed as had been the outer, fell to the desk. For a moment he stared at it, trying to fathom the horror those people had endured. Theirs was a sorrow they could not share with the thousands who had lost sons and brothers and fathers as soldiers in the war. Alexandra had, in a way, simply ceased to exist the day she took up residence in the house Count

Ogrinov had provided for her. What happened to her after that was not part of their lives.

He swore loudly in English, stood up and paced around the desk several times before snatching the sealed letter and running from the room. He raced up the stairs three at a bound to save every precious second of what little time he had. Vasili, his instinct as accurate as always, met his master in the corridor.

"Your bath is—"

"The hell with my bath," Mikhail muttered, pushing the servant aside. Then he turned, his hand raised to knock on Alexandra's door.

Giselle responded almost instantly, opening the door just a crack and shushing him with a stern finger held on her lips.

"She's just gone to sleep, Monsieur," she whispered. "Please, she's had so little rest these past few nights, and I hate to wake her."

"No, it can wait. It will have to. Let her rest."

He gazed down at the paper held so tightly in his hand after Giselle had latched the door. It could wait a while longer; it had already waited so long.

Of the two hundred guests at the reception, less than twenty were also invited to the dinner following. Alexandra was relieved to take her seat at the table beside Andrei Tchernikov. Relegation to the role of silent observer did not bother her in the least, though it was one she had rarely played before. It gave her the chance to puzzle over the strange events of the evening and to wonder what the later hours held in store.

The note Ilya had pressed into her hand the day before had said nothing more than, "I will wait for you in the room off the library at eight o'clock tomorrow night." Though she entertained speculations, she doubted he intended her any harm or would do anything dishonorable. Caught in conversation, Alexandra could not escape the crowded ballroom until amost ten minutes past the appointed hour and then she fairly flew down the dim corridor, her skirts indecently picked up to speed her steps. No one had witnessed her departure, of that she was certain. Princess Marina sat in a far corner of the room chatting with her brother, Anna Petrovna and the Tchernikovs dominated a small circle of conversation in the center of the room, and Mischa had been trapped by a rather mercenary looking woman, a tall, coldly exquisite blonde.

Ilya waited, impatiently pacing the floor, when Alexandra entered. As she turned to lock the door, he stopped her and said, "It would look more suspicious if someone could not get in." She was forced to agree.

"Please, let's get to the point. I don't understand this at all."

He had already helped himself to a glass of brandy and now offered her one, which she refused.

"I wish only to tell you that if you should ever need a friend, please call on me."

The queer light of passion in his eyes warned her to proceed cautiously.

"Surely you didn't need to make such a production of an offer of friendship."

"No, perhaps not, but I find the other things I wanted to say very difficult." He gulped more of the brandy. "Alexandra, he is my very best friend. I love him dearly, would give my life a thousand times over for him, and you—forgive my boldness for saying so—are the most beautiful creature I have ever known. I fell in love with you instantly I saw you, and it is neither my respect for Mischa nor my affection for my wife that keeps me from taking you in my arms right now."

He had chosen this room well, she conceded. If she screamed, who would hear? Yet he moved no closer to her.

"What is it that you are trying to tell me?" she asked. "Has Mischa another woman, a mistress, perhaps even a wife, here in Moscow? If that is so, please tell me and get it over with."

"Oh, no, Mademoiselle Aubertien, he has no current

390

mistress that I know of. And as for a wife, until Tamara dies, he will never have one.''

Tamara. She had heard the name before, but it took several seconds for her to remember when: the night Mikhail and Baron Tchernikov had discussed marriage. Mikhail had said Tamara was the only other woman he had ever loved.

Alexandra's mind raced, thoughts forming like waves upon a stormy beach. Mikhail had agreed that night to ask her to marry him, but in the weeks since, he had said nothing. Was this Tamara the reason? Who was she, and how could she keep Mikhail from marrying someone else? Alexandra felt a cold foreboding as she asked, ''Please continue, Captain Parofsky. Who is Tamara?''

''At one time,'' Ilya began very slowly, ''Tamara Ivanovna Rulyatina was the loveliest woman in Moscow, or in all of Russia for that matter. Hair like old gold, eyes as green as—almost as green as yours. Mikhail fell crazily in love with her, though he knew she was only after the Ogrinov money. I tried to reason with him, but he was beyond reason. And then he found out she had bedded half the eligible men in Moscow. Have you ever seen him when he loses control of his temper?''

''Yes,'' she whispered, but he did not hear her.

''I thought he would kill her, or himself. I kept him drunk for a week, and then we went hunting. He spent a month or more in the mountains and to this day I don't know if he has truly forgotten her, though he acts as if she never existed. But not long afterward, just a few months, Mischa's brother Nikolai announced he was marrying Tamara. According to Mischa, there was a night-long discussion that turned into an argument, and the brothers never spoke to each other again. Three days later, Niki and Tamara were married and moved into the Ogrinov house. Mischa never said anything about the fact that he had to see her every day, but it was torture for him. He had his revenge, however. Married less than six months, Tamara was delivered of a baby girl. I do not know the reason, but Mischa knew that the child couldn't be Niki's, and when

Niki found out the truth, he made a feeble attempt to protect his wife's honor and his own pride.''

"I take it he failed."

"Miserably. And the child's death didn't help." At Alexandra's gasp, Ilya quickly assured her that at least that tragedy had been unavoidable; the child died of natural causes. "Nikolai attacked his wife the day her child was buried, and he beat her within an inch of her life. Mischa said he heard Niki's last words as he stormed out of the house, leaving his wife screaming in agony. 'Let the bitch try to play the whore now!' An hour later, Niki was dead.''

"Suicide?"

He wiped perspiration from his forehead and took another long swallow of the brandy.

"No one ever really knew; it was kept quiet. He was dead and that was the only important thing. Tamara, however, was alive, though her beauty was destroyed forever. She blamed Mischa, of course. He tried to buy her off, since it was money that she had wanted from the start. He granted her an income for the rest of her life if she would just leave him alone.''

"Isn't that blackmail of some kind or other?''

He shrugged. "I suppose so, but it didn't really work. She swore that no matter what he did, he owed her more than he could ever pay and she would call his debt due if he ever took a bride.''

She felt his eyes on her face and when his fingers touched her cheek she felt a shiver of fear slither through her.

"She meant it, Alexandra, and somehow I think she is capable of it.''

"Wouldn't Mischa protect me?'' She knew she had spoken without thinking, but the words were out.

"I'm sure he would try to. I don't know how much of this he has told you, if any, and I do not know what his intentions are toward you, so perhaps I have spoken when I should not. But if anything happens to you, or threatens, I am here, too, if you need me.''

"Perhaps you would not want me after Tamara has had her revenge."

"You have shown me more than the beauty in your face, Mademoiselle Aubertien, and that is something no one can destroy. Perhaps Mischa has seen it, too. Mischa has never even hinted that there would be another woman for him, a woman Tamara could threaten. But I think there is one now."

Leaving the little room, Alexandra felt strangely calm, as though she had expected a far more emotional scene and was relieved nothing untoward had happened. But that calm did not remain with her. The few minutes it took her to walk back to the ballroom gave her ample opportunity to imagine a score of possibilities, all of them unpleasant, and she returned to the reception obsessed with a need to confront Mikhail and demand answers to all the questions Ilya's warning had raised. She did not see him, however, or the predatory blonde with whom he had been talking. She was still searching for him when Anna Petrovna grasped her arm and pulled her off to introduce her to still more guests. There was no escape; Alexandra relied on instinct and her old training to maintain the conversation while her eyes scanned the crowd. Mikahil had disappeared.

Contrary to Alexandra's worst suspicions, he was not in the company of Irina Drubetskaya. Without so much as a polite goodbye, he had walked away from Irina and her absurdities just moments after Alexandra had left for her rendezvous with Ilya. Angry at himself for his rudeness but angrier at Irina, Mikhail went looking for Alexandra. He found Lydia instead.

He kissed her hand gallantly and then took the seat beside her when she begged for his company.

"Don't lie and tell me you've been alone all evening because I've been watching you and I know better," he said with a smile not altogether forced.

She blushed. "Everyone has been so kind. Even the Empress spoke to me for a while, and Countess Anna seems to ask me every ten minutes if I am all right or need anything."

"And are you all right?"

"I haven't felt so well for weeks. Alexandra must have been right when she said it would do me good to get out. I woke up this morning so excited and so happy. She is a wonderful person, your Alexandra."

He nodded in agreement though he had heard little of what she said; his attention had turned to her physical condition.

"Where is Ilya?" he asked suddenly, interrupting her glowing praise of Alexandra.

"I don't know. He got tired of all the company I was attracting and I haven't seen him for half an hour at least." Mikhail frowned and got to his feet. "Oh, please, Captain Ogrinov, don't worry so. Women have babies every day of the year, and I'm certainly no different from anyone else. Besides, where could I be in better hands than right here?"

He did not quite share her confidence and looked nervously about for her husband. Lydia quickly guessed the cause of his concern but did not betray any fear when she bluntly asked him, "Will it be tonight?"

"I don't know. Possibly. Within the next few days at least." He patted her hand reassuringly. "The wait is almost over, and soon you'll be presenting a new Parofsky to the world."

"Only one?"

He shrugged.

"It's hard for me to say. Of course, twins are possible. Anything is. But we will just have to wait and see."

It was some time before Ilya turned up, but by then Mikhail had seen for himself that Lydia did not want for attention, and he wandered off into the crowd to search for Alexandra.

He had no trouble finding her, but neither had his self-invited guest of honor. Mikhail's first reaction on seeing his emperor's smile beaming above the dark crown of Alexandra's hair was that she desperately needed rescuing, and under present circumstances he might be able to do what he couldn't in another place at another time. He made his way towards Alexandra and her admirer and at the last minute remembered to wipe the scowl off his face and put on a smile.

The Tsar appeared only slightly drunk, a sign that he was not suffering another fit of religious zeal. A few glasses of champagne, however, could hardly account for the brightness of his pale eyes, a flicker of the fanaticism that always lurked like a hungry tiger. Was he on the verge of returning to that state of passionate devotion that bordered so close on insanity, or had he just left it?

"Ah, there you are, my dear Mikhail Pavlovitch. We have missed you."

He used the royal plural not knowing how apt it was. Alexandra's relief showed plainly in the roll of her eyes.

It was boredom Mikhail had helped her to escape, but it would be a while before she could explain that to him, so with an amused smile lighting her face she walked to the refreshment table for a badly needed glass of champagne.

"Good evening, Alexandra. I've been looking for you."

She recognized that voice and turned her cheek up for Baron Tchernikov's kiss.

He had seen the tension in the way she held her glass and the fluttery, uncertain gestures she made with her fan, for the room was cool despite the crowd.

"I see you arrived safe and sound."

"Yes, though the trip was a nightmare. I didn't know you were on your way to Moscow."

He harumphed.

"I wasn't. But I knew that once Mikhail was back, the Tsar would want to see him, so I came back."

She credited the baron with her survival of the long, elaborate dinner that followed the reception. Without him to entertain her quietly, keeping her smile from fading, she doubted she could have remained at her place. She had known from the beginning that it would be the Tsarina Elisabeth who sat beside Mikhail, but nothing prevented the hot pang of jealousy when she saw them together. When she met his eyes, was it longing she saw in them, and if so, for her or for the drab imperial woman at his side? Alexandra passed a hand across her eyes to wipe away the image of intimacy that only envy could have created in her troubled mind.

Ilya's warning, too, bothered her, and served to confuse her even further. The wine, a different variety for each of the eleven courses, did nothing to clear her thoughts. Though she ate little, toying with the shrimp and oysters and venison, she sampled each wine. When the Tsar rose and proposed a toast, she could not hold back a giggling little hiccough, but tears were just as near the surface.

Fish gave way to pheasant, and the hours dragged on. Dessert was served shortly after a clock somewhere had chimed the midnight hour. Warned by a cautious hand on hers when she reached too often for her goblet, she regained a little control but still struggled against an embarrassing flood of tears. She kept them in check through the last of the fluffy confections and managed to reach the music room without succumbing, thanks in part to an instinct that drew her to Sonia Tchernikova. Gradually, the wine lost its power and Countess Anna's strong coffee took hold.

While the other women engaged in idle but often malicious gossip, Alexandra sat listening to Marina's skillful rendering of Scarlatti on the harpsichord. Lost in her enjoyment of the music, she heard none of the talk around her until the baroness dropped onto the settee beside her.

"Really, Alexandra, my dear, you needn't look so glum. To be honored by a ball at the Kremlin is hardly a thing to pout about, especially since Mikhail is almost certain to be granted a title for his heroics. And if what Andrei tells me is true, there might be a royal reward for a little Snowbird from Paris as well."

Chapter 39

"MISCHA! WAKE up, damn you! *Mischa!*"

Parofsky accompanied his shouted demands with a torrent of blows upon the locked door and jiggled the handle several times for emphasis, then bellowed again.

"Ogrinov, you bastard, get out of bed! Lydia's having the baby!"

He pounded his fist on the heavy door one more time, then stepped back to brace himself for a more physical assault of the portal.

"Save your shoulder, Ilya," came a groggy voice from the other side.

The scraping of a key in a lock and the door swung inward. Mikhail, clad only in a red dressing gown, ushered Ilya into the room and immediately offered him his choice of brandy or vodka.

"Don't try to talk until you've had a drink. And for God's sake, sit down. My head hurts enough without your stomping around here like a rogue elephant." He poured some vodka into a tumbler and waited until Ilya had swallowed most of it before continuing. "Just tell me when the pain started, how she's feeling, and where the hell is the faithful Dr. Spirov?"

His throat seared by the vodka, Ilya croaked, "Dr. Spirov is in bed with a broken leg. I saw him about an hour ago, which was about an hour after Lydia wakened me. She said she hadn't gone to sleep last night, and the pains started right after we returned."

"Then it's been a good twelve hours." Mikhail scratched his unshaven chin and wished he hadn't sent Vasili off on errands. "I should have guessed this would happen when she told me she felt so much better last night. That's the best warning. How is she now?"

"She seemed to be all right, but tired. And afraid. Olga is with her, and I sent Ivan for her grandmother."

"Olga will take good care of her, and she's not alone, but I still think it best we not waste a great deal of time. Have another drink while I dress."

As Mikhail disappeared into the adjoining room and closed the door, a sudden, very ominous silence descended. Though not particularly religious on most occasions, Ilya crossed himself and glanced about him for an icon. There was none, and he felt a shiver of dread pass through him. Even a quiet, tapping knock on the same door he had been prepared to break down was enough to make him jump to his feet and bark a nervous, "Who's there?"

Alexandra in rich blue velvet, her long hair tousled around her face and down her back, was more enchanting than Alexandra in lavender lace or sprigged muslin, and Parofsky wisely gulped down an exclamation as he opened the door to confront the unidentified caller.

"Mademoiselle Aubertien. I was just about to tell Mischa that Lydia asked for you. She's having the baby."

"Now? This morning?"

"Yes, and the doctor has conveniently broken his leg, so I came here."

"I don't know how much help I can be. I've no experience at all with childbirth, but I will do what I can."

"Lydia just wants you there because you're her friend; Mischa can handle the rest of it, but she's afraid and she wants you."

A little confused at his nonchalant confidence in Mikhail, Alexandra quietly excused herself with a promise to be ready in less than ten minutes. Though she was not at all sure she had the strength to watch Lydia in the agony of birth, she could not withhold the comfort of a hand to clasp.

Only two horses were waiting at the door, but Mikhail wasted no time and hoisted Alexandra up in front of him before spurring his mount to a full gallop. His rough handling and the short but furious ride left her too breathless to ask any questions, and when they arrived at the Parofsky house, the maid Olga was waiting at the door to lead them to Lydia's bedroom.

There was someone lying in the ornate four-poster bed, a pale and wasted creature whose hair lay in sweaty braids pinned atop her head. A sour taste flooded Alexandra's mouth when she realized it was Lydia. Her cheeks were ashen, the sharpness of the bones accentuated by gaunt hollows and dark circles beneath her closed eyes. Covered only by a crumpled sheet, her body looked grotesque and ugly and very, very still.

"Ilya, is that you?"

A pathetic whisper, audible only because everyone else seemed to hold their breath.

He pushed past Alexandra to enter the room and kneel at the side of the bed. Taking the limp hand in his, he kissed it gently.

"Yes, my love, it is I. Alexandra is here, too, and Captain Ogrinov. Everything is going to be just fine now."

An elderly woman none of them had noticed rose slowly from her chair by the window and hobbled with a gnarled cane to the door. A long finger pointed to the hallway; she took both Alexandra and Mikhail with her and closed the door.

"You know, Mikhail Pavlovitch, I don't hold with this," she croaked in raspy Russian. "If she weren't my only granddaughter, I'd not let you in that room. Bearing children is women's business and men are best left out of it. But she wants you."

"The pains. How far apart are they and how strong?" he asked, ignoring her censure.

"Sometimes five, sometimes ten minutes. For the last half hour they have been strong, too strong for a first child this early. She had the last one just as you rode up, so she'll be resting now for a while."

Ilya opened the door and gestured to Alexandra.

"She wants to talk to you," he whispered.

The window had been closed against any drafts and the room she entered reeked of sweat and suffering. Alexandra swallowed another knot of nausea and knelt where Ilya had.

"I'm here, Lydia."

A smile turned up the parched lips.

"I knew you would be. Grandmama thinks I'm so silly, but I wanted a friend here. And I needed to thank you for last night. I was so happy." She had to pause as if to search for bits of strength and string them together until she had enough to speak again. "And please, Alexandra, if I die, I want you to see that Ilya doesn't do anything foolish. Men are not as strong as they want us poor women to believe."

"Hush, now, hush! You mustn't talk like that. I refuse to listen to such nonsense."

Yet even as she spoke, Alexandra sensed the presence of Death very close to her. She had become too familiar with his handiwork in the French army camps, and an evil chill in the hot, motionless air told her he waited. She refused to give way to tears and resolved instead to fight. Lydia's eyes fluttered open briefly, and her hand reached out for Alexandra's, clasping it tightly.

Lydia's long, low moan had a half-human quality to it as her body stiffened against the torture it perpetrated upon itself. Alexandra was aware someone else had entered the room, walked to the other side of the bed, but she saw and heard nothing because all her attention centered on the twisting, screaming figure beneath the sheet. Her reactions came automatically; she used her free hand to stroke Lydia's wet hair back from her forehead while murmuring whatever words of comfort came to her lips. Like crooning to a baby, the words themselves meant nothing; only the voice and tone mattered. When the spasm had passed and Lydia lay panting but still, Alexandra let her own muscles, unconsciously tensed, relax.

"Are you going to sit there just holding her hand or are you going to help?"

Mikhail, his shirtsleeves rolled up past his elbows, stood scowling down at her from the other side of the bed.

"Help? Help do what?" She had never quite got used to his habit of slipping into English.

"Deliver this baby, what else?"

"I don't know anything about delivering babies," she said with a touch of desperation.

"You don't have to know much; Lydia will do all the really hard work." Then, in French, he addressed the patient. "Lydia, I am going to examine you, to see how close your baby is to being born. If I hurt you, don't be afraid to let me know."

Alexandra continued to caress the girl's dripping brow while asking, "Isn't there something you can do for her pain?"

"Nothing." He moved to the end of the bed and draped the sheet over Lydia's knees. "Opium would dull the pain but would also stop the contractions of her womb. The child, once it is ready, must be born in order to live. Lydia is no different from any other woman, Xan. I can't help it."

She had thought him heartless yet at the same time knew he was only telling her the truth.

"Everything is fine, Lydia," he murmured when he had completed his examination. "Are you thirsty? Here, let's put another pillow behind you and Alexandra will bring you some water."

She found the pitcher and a goblet and held the cold liquid to Lydia's lips while Mikhail urged her to drink slowly, in small sips. She had to lie back frequently—the effort of swallowing drained her meager resources of strength quickly—but drank every drop and asked for more. Mikhail shook his head.

"Not just yet, but in a while," Alexandra soothed.

"Here's my hand again; you hold on and I'll wipe your face with a cool rag."

Exhausted by the pains that now came only a minute or two apart, Lydia fell into a semi-conscious oblivion between them. Her hand never let go Alexandra's.

"It won't be much longer now, Xan." How reassuring his voice could be, as though it were she who needed comforting rather than Lydia. "Another hour, maybe two, and it will be over."

His words had a finality to them she did not like.

"Is Lydia dying?" she asked bluntly.

"No, I don't think so. This is not unusual for a first child. Many women labor two or three days before theirs are born, and Lydia is young, healthy, well taken care of."

"But it is possible she may still die?"

Wearily, he admitted, "Yes, it is possible."

Another spasm, long and very hard, pulled a yowling scream from Lydia. When it subsided, Mikhail returned to the chair he had drawn close to the bed.

"Unless something goes wrong, I fully expect her to be up and about again very, very soon. Please, Xan, stop worrying."

"How can you be so calm about it? Doesn't her suffering mean anything to you?" She was concerned but not hysterical; her steadiness impressed him.

"Xan, I have watched a hundred children come into the world and each of them arrives the same way. Would you rather cut her belly open and take the child that way, running ten times the risk both mother and babe will die?"

"It just seems so unfair for her, for any woman, to be tortured that way. Men never are."

A low, bitter laugh, then, "You should know better than that. Women do not fight their kings' battles and die in slow, lonely agony on some foreign battlefield or freeze to death in a country they never wished to see. Does it really matter if—"

The incomplete question hung in the fetid air, meaningless and forgotten as Lydia whimpered to signal

402

the onset of another contraction. Shaking off his own exhaustion, Mikhail got to his feet, and the moan became a wail. Methodically, Alexandra mopped the perspiration away and watched Mikhail place his hand on Lydia's abdomen.

"It will be over soon," he said quietly.

She offered him a glass of water; he took it and tried to wipe his forehead of the sweat that dripped into his eyes but his sleeve was too wet already. Alexandra handed him a dry towel.

He tossed the towel to the floor. "Thank you. Are you frightened?"

"Yes, I mean, no." She *was* frightened, but she dared not let him know or he might guess the reason. Perhaps, she thought as her eyes met his, he already has.

A split second of silence, and the sickening sound of tearing flesh could be heard even above Lydia's wail. Alexandra looked down the length of the bed to see Mikhail pull an ugly, bloody lump from Lydia's body. Her own stomach revolted, but because she had eaten nothing all day, she forced down the nausea and watched as the lump squirmed and emitted a feeble cry.

"The first one'a a girl," he announced. "Is Lydia conscious?"

"I don't think so."

"I think I can finish without her help, though it would have been easier. One more little push and we'll have the job done."

She took the squalling infant from his hands and before she had washed the blood and mucus from it, she heard the second cry.

"I am not surprised," Ilya said quietly. "I'll send someone for a priest right away."

"I'm sorry, my friend. I did everything I could."

Exhausted and angry, Mikhail lost control. The glass he had just toasted Ilya's daughters with seemed to mock him, and he threw it with all his strength against the wall. Parofsky, his face drawn but calm, left the room, and when the door had closed, Mikhail collapsed on the sofa and wept.

It was clear that at least one child would die, possibly both. Born too early, they were tiny, barely complete. The eldest had difficulty breathing; Ilya had been warned not to expect her to live past morning. As for the other, Mikhail admitted he had little hope.

When Alexandra found him, he had dozed off slumped against the arm of the sofa. The sharp staccato of her heels on the bare floor wakened him.

"Come, Mischa, the priest is here and everyone is waiting." She stretched her hand toward him as though she meant to pull him to his feet. "Lydia is awake, too, and she won't let them start without us."

The priest used his deep voice to comfort as well as to exhort as he performed the baptismal ceremony in as little time as could be considered respectful of both the Church and the pale new mother. When it was over, Mikhail laid his god-daughters, Maria and Alexandra, in their cradle rather than face the others just yet. He had not regained full control over himself and knew he must not let the others see it.

Maria, the elder child, already showed signs of weakening. Watching her struggle for each breath, he felt the anger rising again along with hot tears he could not check. A hand on his brought around to face a pair of wide green eyes.

"How long?"

An expectant question such a short time ago, now filled with dread.

"An hour, maybe more, possibly less."

"Can Lydia hold her for a while?"

He nodded his assent but could not look at her when she picked up the infant and carried it to its mother. Lydia should have been sleeping after her ordeal, but under these circumstances he did not try to dissuade her staying up nor urge her to take the mild dose of opium he had left for her. There would be time enough later for sleep.

Nor did he argue when Ilya sent him home.

"They are in God's hands now, not yours, Mischa. Olga and I can take care of Lydia, and if necessary, we will send for you," Parofsky insisted. "Go home and rest; there is nothing more you can do here."

Leave us alone with our grief. Mikhail heard the words that no one said, read them in averted eyes and masked faces that revealed none of their emotions. He felt it, too, in the way Ilya's hand rested heavily on his shoulder. Such a commonplace gesture, yet it embodied both his desire for the company of a friend and his need for solitude.

"I will stop by tomorrow," Mikhail promised and stepped out the door into a warm, clear night.

Two long strides took him away from the pale glow around the doorway and he filled his lungs with fresh air for the first time all day. Though it relieved him of none of the weariness or sadness, the night gave him a measure of peace he needed desperately.

The house was dark when he arrived, and respectfully silent. In his rooms he found Vasili had prepared his bath, laid out clean clothes, and then disappeared with his usual discretion. Mikhail glanced at the full decanter of brandy; it was temptation easy for once to resist. The room across the hall, however, posed another enticement, one of far stronger attraction.

She had been so strong, so beautiful in the face of brutality and ugliness and tragedy, and he had no right to burden her with more. But he wanted her. Not the sensuous Alexandra whose body delighted him, but the Alexandra who had smiled when asked if one of the children might be named for her and only later, in a lonely corner, let a tear fall. He alone had seen her, and she hastened to stop the tears at once. Sending her away from the Parofsky house had been necessary; he saw how close she was to complete collapse, and he wanted those few minutes to himself anyway. Still, he had missed her companionship on that quiet stroll through the streets, and he missed her more now that she was so few steps away.

He cursed his carelessness in not giving her a sedative that would have put her effectively a million miles from him. Did she have trouble sleeping? Had she turned to the brandy bottle as a source of forgetfulness, or did pure exhaustion take command? He grabbed at a towel and stood up out of the cooling water wondering if perhaps she lay awake in her bed and waited for him to chase the demons of sorrow so she could sleep. No, he thought, she would come to him if that were the case.

"But what if she's afraid to come because you said you wanted some time to yourself?" a voice inside nagged at him. "You told her that when you put her on a horse and sent her home."

With those and other worries plaguing him, sleep was impossible. He blotted the water from his body and pulled on trousers and shirt but didn't bother with the details of combing his hair or shaving before slipping stockingless feet into a pair of velvet houseslippers and heading for the only sanctuary left to him.

After the stench of Lydia's bedroom and the pure clean night air, the fragrance of wood and old leather curled about him like a courtesan's perfume. It made no difference that the library was new, the books so recently set on their shelves that they hadn't time to collect dust. It had the feeling of age, of security, of staid permanence. Vasili must have known he would come here, for two candles burned on the mantel, lit not half an hour ago to judge by their length.

There was no window seat as there had been in the old house, or he would have chosen to watch the night pass on Saint Helena Street. Next to the settee by the fireplace was a table where he could put the candles if he wished to read, but he thought instead of his father's old leather chair, now situated in the far corner of the room near the window. As he approached it in the uncertain light, he slowly grew aware of another scent, fragile beneath the heavy perfume of books and woodwork. Lilacs in September, soft, sweet, innocent.

Almost invisible in the shadow of a bookcase that formed a small alcove in that corner of the room, she stood beside the chair, waiting.

Shortly before dawn, when the light outside the window was no more than a murky haze, Vasili entered the library and found them exactly where he had expected. Alexandra was curled on Mikhail's lap, her head resting comfortably on his shoulder. Though their eyes were closed, neither had slept, holding a silent vigil of their own.

Maria Ilarionovna's funeral was a quiet affair on a soft September morning. Mikhail, Alexandra, and Countess Anna comprised fully half the mourners who watched as the tiny casket was lowered into the earth.

Afterwards, Mikhail knocked on Alexandra's door to make certain, or so he reasoned with himself, that she had gone to bed as he had ordered her to. She had been through too many traumatic shocks in the past few days, and with so little sleep, she was in a weakened condition that offered an easy target for fever or pneumonia.

When her door opened and he found her waiting, he discovered he was neither angry nor surprised that she had totally ignored his commands.

"It is very simple," she explained. "I can't sleep. Last night I tossed and turned until I ached, but as soon as I slept, I started dreaming and woke up. It is easier to struggle against the weariness than to live through it all again."

"That's a sign of guilt, Xan, and I can't imagine why you'd feel guilty. The whole thing was my fault."

"Yours? I was the one who insisted she come to the accursed party. None of this would have happened if I had kept my mouth shut." The green eyes filled with tears that overflowed quickly. "I felt so sorry for her shut up in that little house day after day. I wanted to make her happy, and look what I've done to her instead."

"That's absolute nonsense, Xan. No, don't argue with me; just sit down and listen."

He took her arm and led her to the loveseat facing the fireplace where today there was no fire, only a cold stone hearth. She sat stiffly, nervously twisted the sash that tied her gold robe about her waist.

"Lydia went into labor because it was time for her to, not because you persuaded her to get off her backside and do something."

"But the walk afterwards—hadn't her doctor told her to stay off her feet and not exert herself any more than necessary?"

"Yes, which is precisely why she had such a bad time. Under the circumstances, I was amazed she took less than twenty-four hours to get through it. Two days would not have surprised me at all. I've seen women her age, in her condition, go as long as three days, and in the end both they and their children die all too often."

She turned away, horrified.

"If I had been here from the beginning, I would have advised Lydia to take long, vigorous walks, to keep her activities as normal as possible. The easiest birth I've ever witnessed was a young girl in the mountains at harvest time. Every hand was needed to gather the crops, so she kept up with the others and in the late afternoon delivered a healthy baby boy. The next day, she tucked him into a sling so he could suckle while she went back to work. Peasants breed the way they do because they do not allow themselves to become lazy and soft, the way Dr. Spirov lets his aristocratic patients."

Puzzlement had, for the moment, stopped her tears, and she gazed at him with a kind of caution, as though she feared further revelations. She remembered wondering, in that horror-filled little room where Death had stalked, why Mikhail had been so confident. He knew exactly what to do and when, had never even at the worst moments of crisis lost his grip or let anyone else. But curiosity had fled in the face of more pressing considerations and now she fought belated modesty to stammer her question.

"How did you learn so much about women having babies?"

It was his turn to stare, laughing with disbelief, until he asked, "You really don't know, do you? And all this time I assumed you did."

"Knew what?"

408

"My father was a physician."

"Oh!"

With that quiet exclamation she slumped against the back of the settee.

"He wanted very much for me to follow him, but I couldn't. I even studied medicine at Oxford, but I didn't have the strength to endure the frustration that totally dominates a doctor's life. He had it; he could watch people die every day and go out the next morning with his faith and hope undiminished, thankful for the few lives he could save. I wanted to save them all; I hated death and fought it with everything I had, but it was never enough. It still isn't."

He slammed his fist angrily into his palm to vent some of his anger and for once it seemed to work. The stinging of his hand could not match the deeper, fiercer pain inside, but as it eased, it reminded him that all pain subsides with time.

"If Lydia and her babe live, it will be because God wishes them to," he said softly. "Little Maria died, not because of what you did or what I could not do, but because twins are usually born prematurely and are therefore not fully developed. She was unable to breathe properly and she died. It was God's will."

"Are you telling *me* this, or yourself?"

He smiled with tenderness.

"Both of us. We both need it, just as we both need some rest."

Simply because it was closer, they fell exhausted onto Alexandra's bed and in less than an hour surrendered to dreamless, undisturbed sleep.

Chapter 40

TIME WORKED its usual miracle to ease the pain and lighten the burden of grief so the survivors could resume the lives tragedy had interrupted. Though the days passed slowly, they did nonetheless pass, and with each one the memory hurt a little less.

Alexandra spent much of her time in the library, reading or just sitting with Mikhail. Sometimes they talked, but most often they sat in silence, especially in the afternoon when he returned from his daily visits to examine Lydia and check on the progress of the little girl everyone affectionately called Zanushka.

When he suggested on Saturday morning that they take advantage of incredibly perfect weather and spend the day driving in the old phaeton, Alexandra never considered letting propriety or grief stand in their way. Mikhail was smiling for the first time in days and she knew the change of scenery and atmosphere would do him good, regardless whether such entertainment offended others so soon after a close friend's loss.

Wearing a wide-brimmed hat to shade her face and long mitts to keep the sun from burning her arms, Alexandra adjusted the skirt of her apple-green dress and leaned against the cushions. On the opposite seat rested the enormous picnic hamper and several rugs for spreading on the grass when, as Mikhail put it, he found the perfect spot and the perfect moment. The sparkle in his eyes, bluer today than the cloudless sky above, set her to wondering if this might be the day he finally kept his promise and asked her to marry him.

"You must remember that Moscow is a very, very old city," he explained as the horses started off at a leisurely trot. "For centuries it has been a trading center where East and West meet and sometimes mingle. There is much about Moscow you will recognize as no different from Paris or Rome or London, because European influence is strong, especially in the last century or so. But there is more than a touch of the Orient here also. Moscow sits on a bridge between the two worlds, linking them, touching them, and yet remaining unique, because she is neither of them."

At first she thought he was merely being poetic, but as they made their way through the city, she came to understand how true his description really was. Many of the newer buildings, including nearly all constructed within the last year, looked like those in any other European capital, yet in the older sections, areas untouched by the flames, she felt as though she had entered another world. Dark, narrow alleyways somehow quite unlike those of Paris fascinated and yet frightened her, and she was half glad the phaeton was too large to negotiate them. Later, her curiosity did not go unfulfilled when they passed a small but noisy bazaar of strictly Turkish origin; Mikhail led her through the maze of stalls and helped her bargain for a few trinkets. The excitement of haggling prices with the merchants, who traditionally asked at least thrice an item's value in hopes of getting twice, made her long to stay, but the aroma of exotic food aroused her appetite and she did not argue when Mikhail suggested it was time for their picnic.

By the time they finally reached a suitable place along the river, she felt starved, but admitted that the wait had been worthwhile, for Vasili stopped the phaeton just inside a circle of trees providing welcome shade after hours in the unseasonably hot sun and also a measure of privacy.

While the servant unhitched the horses, Mikhail spread the rugs under a gnarled cherry tree. Several cushions gave

411

an extra measure of comfort. Alexandra had taken charge of the picnic hamper and after Mikhail settled himself into a relaxed, half reclining position, she handed him a tall goblet of cool wine.

"Are you enjoying yourself?" he asked, refreshed by a long swallow.

"Immensely. Why shouldn't I?"

"I had the feeling this morning that you were merely humoring me."

She unwrapped a platter of thinly sliced meat and set it between them before answering, "The opposite would be closer to the truth, except that I thought you needed some diversion, too."

"You've been talking to my grandmother, haven't you?" He laughed and took a piece of the cheese she had cut into chunks. "Which reminds me." His voice changed, more serious now, almost worried. "Did you see whom she was with this morning? When I came down for breakfast I noticed she had closed the doors to her drawing room."

"I have no idea."

"I asked Edward but he didn't know. He described a tall, heavy woman dressed in mourning, with her face completely covered by a veil."

"It sounds rather mysterious to me."

"It isn't unusual for a woman Grandmere's age to have friends who are recently widowed, and I suppose a woman who has been through the shock of her husband's death and the ensuing formalities of funeral and burial might want to escape the scene of her grief for a while."

"But you're still curious, aren't you?"

"A little. I'm sure if it is something serious, she'll tell me." He reached behind him for the wine bottle and filled both glasses. As he handed Alexandra's back to her, he noticed her brow had furrowed with concern. "I've frightened you now, haven't I. Please, Xan, forgive me. I wanted today to be wonderful for you, and I've ruined it already. Take my word for it, you mustn't let the old lady bother you."

How could she tell him it wasn't his grandmother that worried her? At the first mention of the unidentified woman, only one person came to Alexandra's mind. If it were indeed Tamara, what would happen? What kind of influence did the disfigured Ogrinov widow have with Anna Petrovna?

"No, of course I won't. As you said, more than likely it is only a bereaved friend, nothing to lose sleep over."

She smiled again, took another sip of wine. Even with Vasili's help, they had barely touched the feast the cook had packed in the basket, though they all had tried. Vasili tethered the horses under a tree on the other side of the carriage and then found a comfortable tree against which to take a nap himself. Alexandra heard his snores and felt a bit sleepy, too. Wine, the warm afternoon, tidbits of lunch to snack on, the nearness of the man she loved in this idyllic place: she lay her head on his shoulder and yawned contentedly.

"Wouldn't you be more comfortable lying down?" he asked with a yawn of his own. "Let me take off my coat and you can use it as a pillow. Put your head on my lap and close your eyes."

He folded the coat carefully so that the buttons were all inside, but she no sooner lay her head on it than she was up again, frowning.

"You've left something in the pockets that crackles every time I blink an eye."

"That's odd. Vasili usually checks my pockets when he puts my clothes away," he muttered, but he unfolded the coat and fished into the pocket.

The moment his fingers touched it, he knew why Vasili had not found it. Mikhail had hung the coat away himself the night of the reception for the Tsar, leaving Justine's letter forgotten in the pocket. He drew it forth, still sealed.

"I'm sorry, Xan," he apologized, handing it to her. She saw the name printed in Justine's precise hand, familiar even after all this time. "It came last Friday. I meant to give it to you then, but Giselle said you were napping, and in the confusion of the next few days, I simply forgot.''

"It's just as well," she sighed with a forgiving smile. "There is a limit to how much bad news I can take."

"Shall I leave you alone with it?"

She shook her head, then, because her fingers trembled so, she handed it to him to break the seal. With her eyes closed in hurried prayer, she opened the carefully folded sheet.

Dearest Alexandra,

I hope that if and when this reaches you it finds you happy and well. A visit from Madame Duquesne has encouraged my hope. She gave me the address to which I might send this.

We are all well. Albert returned in January, luckier than many in that he returned at all. He lost two fingers and several toes to the cold and nearly died of a bullet wound to the neck. Though he credits Madame Duquesne with saving his life, Yvette has proved quite skillful at nursing, too, and he is very much back to his old self. They are expecting a child in November, if that is any proof of his recovery.

Following your departure, Guy found it necessary to leave France and spent some time in England. He came back with the money to open a cafe near the Opera, and we were married just three weeks ago.

It has all been very hard on Papa, but he kept his wits about him as always. For Therese it was not so easy. I cannot count the times I have come upon her crying in the middle of the day, and I know she seldom falls asleep without tears. She blames herself for much of what has happened, and there is nothing we can do to help because she loves you so very, very much. You are all that is left to her of what she once knew.

If you can send word to us, I am sure it will help her as much as anything can. I have reason to believe she may be with child, not an easy thing for a woman of thirty-seven to face on top of all her other worries.

Manette told me much of what you had been through, though I am certain she left out the worst of it rather than bring more pain to us. When I asked her about Count Ogrinov, she wept, and I did too, at the story she told.

414

It is hard for me to write, not knowing if or when this will reach you. I do know, however, that the Count would do anything in his power to find you, to keep you safe. He is not the kind of man easily given to the tears I saw when we said farewell in Paris so long ago. I have wanted for over a year to tell you that, no matter what has happened, no matter what will happen in the future, he loves you. I hope it is not another year before you learn of it.

God bless you, dearest little sister,

Justine

Alexandra clasped Mikhail's hand unconsciously and folded the letter with her free hand rather than let go of his. She lay the paper on the rug beside her. Her throat was as dry as her eyes were moist; she sipped at the now warm wine and tasted her own tears. Mikhail waited, saying nothing, but his hand tightened around hers in a gesture that was anything but unconscious.

"They are well," she managed to announce. "Albert survived, minus a few fingers and toes, but he is well enough that Yvette expects a child in November. Justine married her opera singer." The sentences came slowly, with long silences between while she struggled against the sobs. "And Manette is well, too."

"Thank God," he whispered.

She looked at him and found him staring blankly into the canopy of leaves. He drew her closer, his gaze remaining upward, and pillowed her head on his coat as originally intended so he could stroke the wispy little tendrils of her hair back from her forehead.

"We met on the battlefield of Friedland. I had been hit by a French musketball, and expected either to die or, if lucky, crawl back to my own regiment. Manette found me and, on the edge of the battlefield, in poor twilight, with only my knife and an ordinary needle, she removed the ball and saved my life. Then her husband found us."

"Claude, the butcher?"

"No, she was married to a surgeon, a great hulking beast of a man who threatened to kill her if she didn't get out of the way so he could kill me. She didn't move, and for the second time that day, I expected to die. The man was insane, a raving lunatic, and while he screamed at her, I had time to draw my pistol. Can you believe she actually begged me not to kill him?''

''I can, and I can also believe that you killed him anyway.''

''I did. He was so intent on her that he never saw me take aim. I was shaking, partly in panic, partly in the first stages of shock, partly from the cold, but at such short range I knew I couldn't miss. She never even screamed when he fell. It was as if she had done all she could and now it was over, time to get back to the business of dealing with the living. She saved my life a second time that night by helping me escape back to my own regiment, holding me on the horse she had stolen and getting me alive through that first night.''

The roots of the cherry tree were not made for lazy reclining; Alexandra sat up and stretched the muscles of her back to loosen the aching cramp.

''Did you make love to her?''

He stammered, ''Did I what? To whom?''

She needed no other answer.

''I thought perhaps you had been lovers once, and I'm glad that at least one of the women in your past is someone as kind and beautiful as she. I consider myself honored to be in her company.''

Mikhail could not meet her eyes, but as he got to his feet, he managed to say, ''We were never lovers, not in the usual sense. She had been through a terrible ordeal, that day and for a long time before, married to a man who beat her, daughter of a profligate aristocrat who deserved his own death on the guillotine but dragged nearly every member of his family with him, then she goes off to war because she couldn't stand the thought of men dying. She needed some comforting that night, and I gave it to her, nothing more. Later, in Paris when we had met again, she had a new husband and her children and she didn't need me, not the way she had needed me that one night. So we became friends.'' He unfolded the coat and shook out the wrinkles before he slipped it around Alexandra's shoulders. "I'm sorry. This should have been a lovely day, and I've spoiled it."

In the early autumn twilight it was difficult to see his face, but she reached up to touch his cheek.

"It has been wonderful. I've learned that my family is well and that eases a great deal of worry from my mind. The day could not have been better."

As they climbed into the phaeton and rode back to the house in growing darkness and unbroken silence, she realized that the day could have been better, if only he had spoken those long-awaited words.

Chapter 41

THE SITTING room next to the library, despite her memory of the meeting with Ilya several weeks ago, had become Alexandra's favorite refuge. On the afternoon of the Kremlin ball, she slipped quietly into the empty room, lit her own fire, and curled up with a novel she really had no intention of reading. Escape was her only goal; Anna's questions, Marina's suggestions, and Giselle's lamentations made demands on her sanity beyond anything she had encountered in several months.

Warmed by the crackling fire, she stretched out on the sofa and wondered what havoc Giselle was at that moment wreaking in her latest attempt to choose her mistress' wardrobe. Giselle was determined that no one, not even the Tsarina, should outshine Alexandra tonight. Gowns had been laid out on the bed with appropriate necklaces and eardrops to see which costume would bear the most lavish display of diamonds, rubies, pearls, or combination thereof. It made no difference to Giselle that Alexandra insisted on wearing a modest cream-colored satin gown she had had made just last week especially for this occasion, to be worn with several ropes of exquisite pearls. The maid only wailed at the lack of glitter in that choice and continued her effort to persuade Alexandra otherwise.

How welcome, then was the solitude especially today, when she knew she must face certain questions and make certain decisions she had postponed far too long.

Though she had tried to ignore it, or excuse it when

ignoring failed, the problem of Mikhail's marriage proposal nagged more and more at her. He was extremely busy; social engagements claimed nearly every evening. Putting affairs in order after nearly three years of neglect took not only time but a great deal of mental effort. No doubt he felt he had to get this taken care of before he ventured on any new matters, such as marriage.

It did, on occasion, occur to her that he might have changed his mind, at least about marriage, if not about her. With no false conceit, she firmly believed his affection and his admiration for her had increased since their arrival in Moscow. Rarely did a night pass that he did not spend some time in her room, or invite her to his.

What did worry her was the mysterious woman in black.

Alexandra had seen the woman with the Countess just that morning, and this was not the first time. She came at least twice a week, sometimes more often, always dressed exactly as Mikhail had described. This morning Alexandra had watched as she entered the front door, handed Edward a note and then followed him into the red drawing room where Anna Petrovna was just being brought her coffee. Alexandra suppressed her panic long enough to take careful note of the strange visitor, her walk, her gestures, anything that might be a clue to her identity.

The woman was, Alexandra decided, neither elderly nor widowed. Though she walked unsteadily and appeared to be quite stout under her old-fashioned and voluminous widow's weeds, her carriage bespoke a much younger woman. Once the doors to the red drawing room had closed, Alexandra pattered down the stairs to see if she might pick up a scrap of conversation as she passed by on her way to the dining room. Not a whisper penetrated the solid walnut doors, only a ghostly hint of perfume. Countess Anna never used any scent but a touch of rose; the fragrance Alexandra sniffed was a musky jasmine, hardly suitable for mourning.

The only possible solution to this mystery was that Tamara, disfigured and outcast, had come to renew her threat. Careful analysis put all the facts in support of that theory, and as unpleasant as it was, Alexandra accepted it.

When she had asked Mikhail if he had learned any more about his grandmother's caller, he gave her a puzzled look before shrugging it off as unimportant. She had not believed him at the time and certainly did not now, some three weeks later. Who else could cause such a strange reaction in him? Only someone he feared, or who at least caused him some worry. His relationship with Alexandra was public knowledge, with the gossipers providing details often closer to the truth than they imagined. Any or all of it could easily have reached the ears of the lonely, bitter woman living only for revenge.

Such a woman could hardly go directly to the victim of her bitterness; she had to work through another, someone with whom she felt safe. Early morning unannounced visits to an elderly countess offered less risk than confronting Mikhail, who might have been tempted to do away with her himself.

Examining that point led to others, and set Alexandra to wondering about the conversation she had overheard at Vera's. Weeks had passed, true, but she told herself over and over again she remembered quite well that Mischa had told the baron he would marry her. But he also said he had loved Tamara. She shook the idea away and with it another, equally foolish. It made no sense to accuse him of teasing, of issuing that promise when he knew, as he admitted later, that she lay in the room above waiting for him. The hoax had gone on too long to be just a hoax.

But she would not go another night without some word, one way or another, from him. Indeed, it had gone on so long that she *could* not.

Having made that decision, she opened her book and tried to concentrate on the first sentence.

Mikhail ushered his grandmother into the library and closed the doors. They would not be disturbed here. Silently, he moved a chair in front of the desk for her before taking his customary seat behind it.

"Irina was here again, I take it." He did not ask; he knew.

"This morning, while you were out. That is the fourth time this week, and I believe Edward is beginning to have his suspicions."

He sighed, picked up the penknife and poised it between his fingers.

"She hasn't changed her story?"

"Not a word. And who's to say it isn't true? We know when you left here and when you came back, but in between then not even Vasili can vouch for you. No one can."

"Except Alexandra, and Grigori."

"My dear, do you really think anyone will believe the word of your French mistress against Irina's? Anyone but me, that is, so calm yourself. I am only being pragmatic."

He kept his blue eyes steady, though she had already seen the fire spark in them. He was becoming more and more like his father every day, and that was not perhaps such a bad thing after all.

"And if I refuse her ridiculous demands?"

Anna Petrovna shrugged.

"That is up to you."

Slowly, he pushed his chair back and rose, but instead of pacing, as she expected him to do, he walked around the desk and leaned on it. Though there were decanters of brandy and vodka within his reach, he ignored them.

"You know, Grandmere, that I can scandalize her far worse than she ever could me."

"I do, and I also know it could get you into very serious trouble. The Church takes a very dim view of what you did, no matter what your reasons, and/or hers."

"Even when the mother has threatened to kill the child herself the instant it is born?"

"Even then. At least then the sin would be on her soul, not yours."

"I do not consider what I did to be a sin."

"But the Church will, and it is a great deal more powerful than Mikhail Pavlovitch Ogrinov.''

She never paused, always had an answer as though she read his thoughts. He had a strange sensation of being maneuvered, driven down a road with no outlet.

"I will not do it," he said quietly. "I refuse to go through hell the way my father did for the same stupid reason."

Anna gaped at him, speechless for once. His anger was very old and very bitter and she did not like it. It frightened her, but she had to hear what he said.

"No one kept it a secret that I was born six months after my parents married. I don't care one way or another myself, except for what it did to Father. He didn't love her, and she used me to trap him."

Anna interrupted. "Mischa, you mustn't think that. Your parents loved each other very much. And if you think you are the only reason they married, you are sadly mistaken."

Leaning forward so his eyes were level with hers, he hissed, "He *never* loved her. He loved her best friend."

The Countess gasped. *"Vera Ylbatskaya?"*

"She met us everywhere, and I wasn't always the chaperon everyone thought I was. *They* were the two who loved each other. And because she loved him, she made certain no one ever knew, not even Mother. That friendship was Vera's only link to Father."

Utterly stunned, Anna motioned towards the glasses on the desk. Mikhail poured her some vodka, but still nothing for himself. She had not been prepared for this outburst and certainly not for the revelation. She might have accused him of making it all up, but she had never known Mikhail to lie.

"One more thing, since we're on the subject. They had a child."

She was beyond shock now.

"He was born while I was at Oxford, and he died a week later. I thought it would kill Father. I left University then, partly to take care of Father and Vera, partly because I couldn't stand the frustration. How could that perfect, beautiful little child, conceived in such love, just close his eyes and die in his father's arms?'' He was totally unaware of the tears dripping down his cheeks. ''I hated everyone that night, you, Mother, everyone, but it wasn't until Niki died that I understood what real torture it was for Father.

''He came to my room that night, and I knew he had been with Mother. She begged him for a sedative, something to make her sleep until she could cope with it, but he refused. He wanted her to suffer as he had, only he wouldn't tell her that. And he had always had to hide his grief, as Vera did. 'If I can't mourn a child I loved and wanted,' he told me the day we buried Niki, 'how can I mourn one I didn't?'

''After all that, after the scheming of my own mother, after the mess Tamara made of all our lives, after seeing my father, whom I absolutely worshipped, broken by a six or seven year old memory, is it any wonder I've vowed not to let the same thing happen to me?''

None of the Ogrinovs had given him this temper, and he could not have got it from the quiet, controlled Englishman who was his father; Anna had only herself to blame for putting Gallic fire into his blood. Calming him was a waste of time, and he paid no heed to warnings that, although his mother had retired for the afternoon, servants still roamed about the house, quick to listen and quicker to tell tales.

''I don't care!'' he shouted in Russian. ''Let them! I will not marry the bitch just because she claims to be carrying my child!'' Then, to be sure his grandmother had understood him clearly, he screamed again, in French, ''I'll marry whom I damned well please, and not some slinking pregnant whore!''

Unable to become interested in her book and so bored she feared falling asleep, Alexandra stood up and stretched. She thought she heard voices in the library, and after listening a moment identified one as Mikhail's.

''It's about time he got back,'' she said quietly to the empty room. ''He must have stopped to see Lydia on the

423

way home. I'll try to catch him before he goes upstairs and ask him how she is.''

She had her hand on the door handle when his declaration thundered through the partitioning wall. She had no time to doubt her translation, for his own came almost instantly. A flush of embarrassment left her face hot, but then ice seemed to fill her veins and the sweat on her brow froze.

The little speech she had rehearsed for tonight immediately upon their return from the Kremlin had just become unnecessary. Mischa already knew her secret.

Chapter 42

BARON TCHERNIKOV knew some manner of mischief was afoot when he caught Mikhail secretly smiling to himself behind a glass of champagne. The blue eyes sparkled with devilment and perhaps a touch of madness.

"By tomorrow she will be the walk of Moscow," Andrei whispered to him.

Mikhail jumped.

"Damn you, Uncle, don't sneak up on me like that." He set down the empty glass but did not take another. "Yes, she will be the talk of the city, all right. I will see to that."

Anyone else would have called the feeling a premonition of disaster, but Tchernikov was too practical, too realistic, to pay any attention to the chill creeping down his spine. A draft caused it, or perhaps the wine was too cold. At any rate, he shrugged it off and followed Mikhail's gaze.

Surrounded by a dozen admirers, Alexandra still stood out in the crowd. The shimmering silk as sparkling as the snow that had almost killed her shed an aura around her, dimming even the king's ransom of emeralds she wore around her neck, at her ears, on her wrists and pinned in her hair. Ice and green fire, the Snowbird resurrected, she dominated the assemblage of the highest Russian aristocracy. No man escaped her allure, yet no one ventured to touch her except on the dance floor. Even the Tsar himself kept to a respectful distance. Mikhail contented himself for now with watching her, never letting her out of his sight.

A certain captain of the guards had been watching her, too. Though he detested the role of commissioned lackey, Ilya had accepted assignment to the palace as a means of easing himself back into an active life after a rather lengthy leave. He could not grieve forever.

Behind him, in the corridor, he heard his replacement, Captain Novlesky, issuing orders and reprimanding those of his men who had even the tiniest speck of dust on their uniforms or smudge on their boots. Ilya wondered how many more minutes until he could escape far enough for a cigar.

According to the agenda Alexandr himself had set, the announcement of honors was to begin precisely at midnight. The incoming guard would relieve their comrades half an hour before that. Novlesky stepped smartly into position exactly on time, freeing Ilya to secret himself in some shadowed balcony from which to observe the proceedings, if he wished to. As he was about to find just such a spot and a cigar as well, he discovered a more pressing need. Mikhail was entangled by his uncles, a couple of cousins, and old Baron Tchernikov, all congratulating him in anticipation of the announcement, and he could not see that Alexandra had disappeared.

She made no effort to resist, knowing any attempt either to fight or to flee was useless. Despite his gently coaxing tone and friendly smile, the Tsar was no different from the others. She had recognized the madness immediately, and knowing Mikhail could do nothing even had he wanted to, she accepted this most cruel of fates.

"You are superb," he praised her, placing her hand on his arm and then covering it possessively while he leaned to whisper in her ear, "I may grant Ogrinov a second estate to go with his title if you fulfill all that you promise."

His first order, mumbled just as she broke free from a constricting circle of gaping young nobles, had merely been "Come with me, my dear," and she had had no choice but to follow where he led. Resignation banished her fear and she calmly took note of rooms and corridors they passed through. If given the opportunity for escape, however slight, she did not wish to lose her way back to the ballroom—and Mischa.

Wearing the beloved white gown that she herself had helped to sew and the emeralds Mikhail had given her because they matched her eyes had been a trick to manipulate him, to lure him back after his screaming denunciation. And it seemed to have worked. He doted on her, kissed her often enough to set tongues wagging, and clasped her hand throughout the long dinner. Though he danced very few dances with her, when he did it was as if the rest of the crowd had vanished. Now she was indeed alone, but instead of with Mikhail, she walked beside the one man he had warned her he could not protect her from.

After so many months of feeling safe in Mikhail's care, she discovered she had not lost the ability to force irrelevant thoughts from her mind and concentrate on the facts pertinent to her survival. Passing down dimly lit corridors, she ignored the details of exquisite decor, the frescoes and paintings, except to use them as signposts. For a brief moment she considered reminding this man he had barely half an hour until his scheduled speech, but what did it matter to him if he were an hour or two hours late? Who would complain to him of the delay?

The Tsar said nothing further until he pulled her into a large, brilliantly lit chamber and kicked the massive, gilded door shut. There was a soft thud and the click of a latch falling into place, but he did not lock it.

"Vodka, my dear?" he asked in his peculiarly accented Russian.

She shook her head. The long coiled ringlets lying against the back of her neck danced and yellow candlelight turned to green fire as it struck the jewels dangling from her ears. Her eyes burned with a different flame, as cold as Siberian ice.

"Too much light, I believe," he went on, and without letting go her hand, he strolled around the room snuffing most of the candles.

The room's original purpose might have been anything, but it was clearly intended for only one purpose tonight. The furnishings consisted of a large divan covered with red and blue brocade and several low tables, nothing but those items necessary for a romantic conquest.

"Your Majesty, may I ask why you have brought me here?"

"I should think the answer to that quite obvious." His eyes tried to lead hers to the divan; she stared steadily at his leering, half-drunken face. "And really, my dear, it will be so much easier if you let yourself enjoy it."

She succeeded in extricating her arm from his before saying, "I do not enjoy rape, and I will not allow this to be anything else."

He laughed, but she did not think he appreciated her defiance. "Nor I! Why not make this a pleasurable experience for us both and not force me to resort to unpleasant means. I want you and I mean to have you one way or another, Snowbird, so please, let us not waste time discussing a matter already resolved."

She must stall as long as possible, no matter how certain he was of the outcome. What was not yet might never be, if she could delay it long enough. Surely Mikhail, who had been so attentive to her all evening, would soon notice her absence and come looking for her.

"No, I refuse. And I cannot believe you would dishonor yourself by taking me against my will. What would such a disgrace do to Mikhail and his friendship for you?"

"Ogrinov will say nothing. He'll have his title, a secure income, and after all, it is not as though you were his wife. He has shared his women before."

He spun her around and began unbuttoning the white dress. Angry enough not to be frightened, though she knew she should be, she stepped away and whirled to face him again.

"I have no way of knowing whether what you say is true or not. If Mischa thinks to trade my favors for yours, then he had best look for another whore. And if you are lying, I can assure you he will never forgive you. Nor, Your Majesty," she spat, "will I!"

His pale eyes looked down into hers and she thought she saw confusion behind the lust, but when he grabbed her, crushing the breath out of her in his embrace, she knew he cared only about satisfying his desire, nothing else.

"Silence," he ordered, and covered her mouth with a wet, hungry kiss.

The double row of gold buttons on his coat dug into her through the thin silk, bruising tender flesh. Breathing became impossible; the blackness of oblivion clouded the edges of her vision as she fought off his strangling embrace. Coherent thought, her only weapon, slipped away slowly as the dark closed in.

He pushed her backward onto the bed, and while he knelt at her feet, she had the chance to catch her breath and regain her senses.

"You see, there is no escape," he cooed, removing first one slipper and then the other. "You can surrender to me and allow me to pleasure you, or you can face a less desirable but equally certain fate. The destination will be the same, regardless which route you choose."

His fingers caressed her ankles, slithered up her calves, squeezed gently at her knees, but she was aware of it, fully in control of her thoughts again.

"I do not surrender," she said in a low, cold voice. "Not to you, not to anyone."

He pushed her skirt higher and stroked the inside of her thighs. She kicked at him, only to have her feet clamped together, the ankles encircled by the long fingers of his left hand. Pain shot through her, but the possibility that he might break her bones could not break her spirit.

"What about Ogrinov?" When she reddened, he laughed. "So, you *do* surrender now and then! I can do much more for you, so why not surrender to me?" His fingers squeezed tighter; she held her breath waiting for the crack of splintering bone.

"No," she moaned as he lowered his body atop hers. She felt the hard bulge of his manhood against her thigh and knew that time was running out. He wanted her and would take her, and she dared not defend herself against the Tsar. "No, I will never surrender to you. You can cripple me or maim me or rape me a thousand times over, but I will always fight you. I will die fighting you, as God is my witness."

The face above hers changed with horrifying swiftness. Gone was the lust, the ugly but human passion of a man. Now she saw a monster.

"*Whore!*" he spat in her face. There was liquor on his breath, but the insanity in his eyes came not from drink. "Filthy French harlot!" Nor was it the jealousy that had enraged Grigori Tcheradzin. This was something incredibly evil, and it terrorized her as nothing else ever had. "You cannot seduce me as easily as you do those other fools. I will not crawl to you, begging for your unholy favors. Service those rutting foreign swine, but I will not soil my hands nor tarnish my immortal soul with you. Get out, heathen temptress."

He did not move off her, but neither did he impede her struggle to get out from under his weight. Limping, clutching her slippers in shaking hands, Alexandra staggered to the door while the man who had defied Napoleon sank to his knees in fervent prayer.

Once in the corridor, with the door securely closed behind her, she took a moment, no more, to fit her swollen feet into her slippers and to hook the buttons he had unfastened at the back of her dress. Fear and anger and a thousand horrible memories suddenly battered down her weakened defenses, and had it not been for a pair of strong arms that caught her, she would have collapsed on the cold marble floor.

"Go on, cry, let the tears wash away the sorrow. No one is going to hurt you now," Ilya soothed as he carried her to a cushioned bench set into a niche between two pillars where they could be shielded from prying eyes. "Don't try to talk yet, just cry."

He had been too late. He had failed utterly.

"Everything will be all right, don't worry. The worst is over now."

"Is it?" she asked, lifting that beautiful, tear-streaked face. "What if he tries again? And what will he do to Mischa?"

"Don't worry about Mischa. He can take care of himself. Right now we have to think of you."

"I'm all right," she sniffled, but still she trembled with terror. Though she remembered those last moments clearly, she had no idea what had triggered the Tsar's dramatic transformation. For the moment, it was enough to be free of him, and even Ilya's caresses were to be preferred over Alexandr's lust.

But where was Mikhail? Surely by now he must have found her if he had indeed sought her. No, she must not doubt him. After all, the Kremlin was an enormous maze of corridors and rooms, and perhaps she had been taken to an unlikely portion of the palace. Mischa might even now be searching somewhere for her. She wanted to believe that, tried desperately to push aside the insidious little voice that reminded her of the Tsar's hurtful words, but the idea that Mikhail had traded her body for a title combined with the memory of his angry words in the library, and doubt grew. Perhaps he had watched her so carefully all evening only to be sure the assignation was kept.

Strangling the last sob and wiping away the tears, she slid off Parofsky's lap to sit beside him and felt better to have only one of his arms around her.

"Give me another minute and I'll be ready to go back. Do I look terribly ravaged?"

What spirit she had! He let his eyes roam over her face and hair, pushed in a few pins that threatened to loosen her curls, and straightened the heavy gold necklace with its green stones. When she stood up, using one of the pillars for support until she was certain her bruised ankles would hold her, she even managed a weak smile. Only the puffiness around her eyes and her slightly red nose

431

testified to her weeping.

"One button wants buttoning," Ilya said. "Turn around and I'll get it."

She started to turn and then stopped. Her eyes opened wide and stared at the blank wall behind the bench. A smile of pure, radiant joy curved her lips and spread a luminous glow across her features. Gently, almost reverently, she pressed her palms to her stomach and whispered, "It moved."

He had too recently become a father to misunderstand. "Have you told Mischa?" he asked, not really surprised.

"I didn't tell him myself, but he knows."

The rapture faded, the smile vanished, and she sat down at his side to tell him the whole ugly, unhappy story.

Mikhail shouldered his way through the crowd, jostling some and treading on several feet. Black anger furrowed his brow and struck steel-colored sparks from his eyes whenever someone tried to stop him. He did not care if they thought his rage was caused by the Tsar's tardiness in announcing that Mikhail Pavlovitch Ogrinov was henceforth to be known as Baron Ogrinov. The title and the estates that went with it hardly compensated for the months and years of living with the fear of discovery that always hangs over the head of a spy. He considered his reward little more than an insult and cared not at all if the delay became permanent.

It was Alexandra's disappearance that brought on his stormy mood. He had done his best to guard her, to keep her within his sight since the moment they arrived at the palace, and also to watch his emperor for any signs of mischief. All went well, and the hour of midnight approached without incident. But Mikhail could not feel relief until the night was over and he had her safely to himself once more.

Then, in the time it took him to receive his Uncle Dmitri's congratulations, she was gone. His eyes swept the immense room, found neither Alexandra nor the Tsar, and all the fires of hell suddenly exploded in him. The fury he had unleashed upon learning Irina Drubetskaya claimed to be pregnant with his child was but a flickering candle in comparison.

His long, purposeful strides quickly took him away from the sounds of music and into the familiar labyrinth of the palace. Alexandr had hundreds of rooms from which to choose his trysting place and had probably selected a chamber remote from the busy ballroom, leaving Mikhail miles and miles of corridors to search while the Tsar enjoyed his prize.

So little time, so few minutes. Running to conserve each precious second, he tried to put himself in Alexandr's place, to think as the lust-maddened Romanov thought. His blood pounded in his ears like the ticking of a monstrous clock, marking off the seconds with each beat of his heart.

Stupid fool! he cursed himself as he turned down a well-lit corridor and listened for a voice, a sound, even sniffed the air for the scent of her perfume. No lilacs here, only damp and dust. Pride had done this, the pride of a man who should know better. As little as the word "Baron" in front of his name meant to Mikhail, he had thought Alexandra would want it. True, he'd not be the count who had charmed her in Paris, but at least it was a title, *his* title, and asking her to be his baroness seemed a more fitting proposal than merely asking her to be his wife. Again, as he had done so often in the past, he had underestimated her. Xan was no opportunist like Irina; Xan would have been content to live with him in the mountain village, baking his bread, cleaning his fish, washing and mending his clothes.

He slammed another door shut and turned to race back down the dead-end hallway. All the time he had wasted haunted him now that he had such desperate need of it. Loosening his cravat to breathe easier, he cursed himself and swore that if she would still have him in spite of his foolish and tragic misjudgements, they'd be married within the week. Tamara with her ancient threats could rot in hell and Irina could bear her brat in an alley if she wanted to keep her indiscretions discreet. None of them mattered to him.

If Alexandra desired, he would take her out of Moscow, out of Russia. To England, where she claimed she had been born and where his father's family still lived. Or to America, Argentina, the South Seas. He would offer her the world—if he could find her.

He paused to catch his breath and decide which way to go next. In the light from a silver wall sconce he fished his watch from his pocket and snapped it open. Five minutes past twelve. Time had run out. Even if the Tsar were late, it would not do for the newest member of his nobility to arrive tardy for the ceremony. Weary, disgusted, and with all his anger intact, he began the lonely trek back to the ballroom.

He heard voices and quickly realized he had come upon a private conversation, not the chatter of a crowd. Suspecting lovers, he halted where he was to listen before continuing on his way and possibly disturbing a tryst.

"Sentimental imbecile!" he muttered to himself, but he waited nonetheless.

Soft and gentle, a masculine voice murmured, "There, there, little one, now it is over and he won't ever hurt you again."

Ilya! Mikahil caught his breath, alarmed that his friend had dishonored himself so soon after his wife's sorrow.

"I don't know what I'd have done without you tonight."

Her voice, as tender and loving as Parofsky's, cut like the edge of a sword through Mikhail. In the silence that followed, he imagined their kiss, arms entwining, bodies melting together.

"You promise you will tell him?"

"Yes," she laughed. "I will confront him tomorrow and tell him what happened here tonight and that I cannot go on like this. Does that meet your approval?"

"I can't ask for more. I'm just glad I don't have to be there when he finds out. He'll be murderous."

Another silence, and then Alexandra spoke haltingly.

434

"It's true, you know. I can't take it any longer. If he can't understand that, then . . ."

"Come, we won't talk about it any more. Everything will be so different tomorrow. You'll laugh at all this foolishness then."

Bathed in a cold sweat, shaking as with fever, Mikhail listened as they got to their feet and slowly walked back to the ballroom.

Chapter 43

THE TWO questions that had plagued Alexandra for the past two weeks lost their relevancy the moment she closed the last of her trunks. What was to become of her now became her own decision to make, and she had made it. Why Mikhail had suddenly changed his attitude toward her no longer mattered.

He had, as usual these days, left the house early. He would have to learn of her departure after the deed was accomplished, but she doubted he would even notice her absence. In the two weeks since the Kremlin ball, the new Baron Ogrinov had ignored her so completely that she began at times to wonder if she had not died and now simply haunted the great house as an invisible spirit. He had not spoken a single word to her nor even answered the frantic questions about her his mother and grandmother hurled at him during the few meals he shared with them. It was as though she had ceased to exist from the moment she rejoined him in the Tsar's ballroom.

After the excitement immediately following the formal announcement that he had been elevated to the rank of baron for his years of faithful service, she had expected they would slip away together for a more private celebration. She planned to tell him then of the disaster she had so narrowly escaped just minutes before. Instead, Mikhail turned his back on her and she did not see him again for three days. Upon his return—from where, he did not say, not even to Vasili—he pointedly ignored her. He locked his door to her, sent back her notes unopened, refused even to look at her.

She endured this treatment for a full week before showing any sign that it affected her at all, but by then she was near hysteria, and it was to Anna Petrovna she turned.

"I do not know what to do," Alexandra said. An hour of sobbing into her coffee had done nothing but swell her eyes and make her nose run. "I don't know why he is doing this to me, what I have done to deserve it, or what I can do to end it, short of killing myself."

Anna handed her a dry handkerchief.

"You mustn't speak such blasphemy," she scolded gently. "Besides, Mischa will be out of his mood in another day or two, just wait and see. Be a little patient with him."

"But I have been!" Alexandra wailed, and a new rush of tears spilled down her cheeks. "What more can I do? He treats me as though I am a piece of statuary, or worse, because he never even looks at me."

"Just a little more time. He has a terrible temper, but it always wears off."

No less bewildered than Alexandra at her grandson's behavior, Anna did everything she could in the next few days to confront the miscreant and drag an answer from him. For the first time in his life, she failed, and yet she knew from the smouldering fire in his eyes that he suffered as deeply, in his own way, as Alexandra. Why he refused to discuss the matter with anyone remained the mystery.

At the end of two weeks, Alexandra realized she could no longer tolerate the situation. She was unable to sleep, had no appetite, and it came to her that she had not been out of the house since what she simply referred to as "that night." And she admitted to Giselle that she had begun to fear for her safety. Mikhail was mad, insane, and his very presence now terrified her.

Vasili confirmed her belief in Mikhail's madness when he returned, unopened as always, another of her notes, one she had slid under his door in the hope it would catch him unaware.

437

"I no longer know him, Snowbird. I have never seen him act like this, never. He is a man in a nightmare, and I can't seem to wake him up."

"Has he said anything that would tell you what I've done or what he thinks I've done?"

He shook his head. The despair in her voice touched him, but he had no answer for her.

"When I brought him back from Smolensk last winter, he forbade me to mention your name else he'd cut out my tongue. He was angry then, and ill, and hurt, and I could handle it because I knew the truth. Now, he merely reminded me once that if I didn't watch my tongue I'd soon be wearing it on a string around my neck. He does not raise his voice, shows no anger, no hate, no feeling at all. But the feelings are there somewhere, and they are killing him inside."

"Do you think it would help if I left here?"

His face paled under his beard. "Oh, no, you mustn't do that! No, Snowbird, you can't even think of leaving."

"You're not answering me, Vasili. Would it help Mischa if I got out of his life?"

"I don't know," he said honestly. "But I do not think it would help you. Where would you go? How would you live?"

She shrugged.

"I'd manage somehow."

They both knew she had already made her decision.

Other factors, however, played a part in setting her course for the immediate future. One was her pregnancy, now extremely difficult to conceal. And she was tired. She had had her fill of adventure and royal intrigue; neither ever proved to be as glamorous or romantic as Therese's stories had led her to believe. Without Mikhail she could not hope for happiness, but perhaps she could find some peace.

She loved him and knew that life would be meaningless without him, but she could not kill herself, not with his child growing within her. For the baby she had to live. If she lost Mikhail, at least she would have his child, but if

438

she stayed here, she was certain she would have nothing. He hated her, though she did not know why. After his angry outburst in the library she had thought he would be ready to strangle her, and yet he had never been so loving. Until the moment she walked up to him after Ilya had shown her the way back to the ballroom. The blue eyes were daggers, and he had never looked at her again.

In desperation, remembering what he had told her so many times, she wrote to Ilya and asked for his help.

"I must leave," she told him. "I need your help to get me to St. Petersburg, and then I will be able to manage by myself."

Unlike Vasili and the Countess, Ilya did not try to change her mind.

"I can take you there myself, but only if you will tell me what it is you are going to do. One of these days Mikhail is going to come to his senses and realize what he's done. He'll want to come after you."

"I don't want him to," she lied. "And I don't want you to, either."

"But he loves you! And you're going to have his child! You can't just walk away from him with that and leave him no clue."

"Yes, I can. He has given me no clue as to why he suddenly hates me, and I shall do the same."

So here she sat, surrounded by trunks, hat boxes, several smaller bags and valises, waiting for the carriage. Giselle checked the wardrobe and all the drawers again to be certain nothing had been missed, and then Alexandra sent her to fetch someone to carry everything downstairs.

Anna Petrovna materialized like a spectre in the open doorway, but her voice held only sadness, no anger.

"The least you can do is tell me where you are going."

Torn between a desire to close all the doors behind her and yet another to leave a trail Mischa might follow if indeed Ilya's words were true and he came after her, Alexandra looked at the Countess and found she could not speak at all.

"Can you not then even promise me you will let me

know when you get there?''

Alexandra nodded and let herself be embraced by this dear, sweet little tyrant whom she had come to love so well.

"I shall worry about you, little bird. And if he kills me for it, I will find out why that miserable grandson of mine is behaving like a lunatic. He has no right, no right at all, to treat you like this, or me either, for that matter. Perhaps, though it is hard, this is the best thing to do. It may open his eyes, for a change."

Fighting down a painful lump in her throat and blinking away tears, Alexandra murmured, "I will be all right. I will survive, as I always have. Don't worry about me, please. I'll write as soon as I've found a place to settle for a while. You know I blame you for none of this and wish you no sorrow."

Anna kissed her and then the servant was at the door to carry down the trunks. Ilya's carriage had arrived.

Chapter 44

THE WIND sweeping across Fowey harbor set the boats to dancing on their anchor lines and whipped the surface of the water to a froth of little whitecapped waves. Sheltered by the tall hedges lining the road, Alexandra felt none of the November chill, for without the breeze, the sun shone quite warmly. She had learned in her few weeks in Cornwall how suddenly a storm could brew and glanced seaward again. As it had been when she set out, the sky was cloudless, a pale autumn blue.

She had left the lodging house nearly two hours ago, never guessing the walk to Vinewood would be more than a mile or two. Alexandra had a lovely view of the house in the distance from her window on the second floor of the lodging house where she and Giselle had taken rooms. She wasted more than two weeks sitting at that window, staring blindly at the white pillared facade of the Tregarth home, before finally gathering enough courage to pay a long delayed visit.

The road twisted and turned with the contours of the hill and though this lengthened the distance from town, it also kept the climb much easier, a point Alexandra noted with gratitude. She passed no one on her way and realized this was the first time she had been alone, truly alone, for several weeks. The joy of solitude on a bright, clear afternoon made up for the long walk; she found herself almost disappointed when she came to the gateway that marked the end of her trek.

It was no more than an iron arch suspended between two brick pillars; there were no gates, probably never had been. The low stone wall stretched on into the woods and Alexandra suspected it enclosed rather spacious grounds. The Tregarths, she had been told, had the land, the money, the lineage of the nobility and lacked only the title. Now, stepping a bit timidly under the scrollwork arch, she wondered just what right she had to do what she was doing.

It was not too late to turn around. She could go back to town, pack her things, and be on the morning mail coach back to London without anyone in Fowey ever guessing why she had come here in the first place. She would be swallowed up by the city and live out the rest of her life peacefully, undisturbed by kings and tsars and spies who only wanted to use her. She had suggested such a future to Giselle the night before and received an unexpected response.

"Or perhaps we could sail to America and make our fortunes there," Alexandra added.

"Absolutely not!" Giselle shrieked. "I will kill myself before I set foot of any kind of boat again! First it is that Swedish ship with a crew of Viking cutthroats, then a leaky washtub from Dieppe to Portsmouth, and just when I was getting used to solid earth under me again, you make us spend two more days on the *Roxanne Clark*, probably named after an ugly old whore if ther is any justice in the world, to come to this place. No, mademoiselle, I am going nowhere else. You put me through a dozen kinds of hell and I do not want my suffering to heave been for nothing. You will go see those Tregarth people tomorrow."

That Giselle had suffered was no understatement. She had made some recovery since they had arrived in Fowey, but it would be at least another week before Alexandra allowed her to resume her full duties. She had become sick within hours of their departure from St. Petersburg even though the weather throughout the voyage was superb. The Swedish ship could not have been equalled for smooth sailing. If Captain Olaf Lund and his crew of the *Gustav Kjarne* resembled the fabled Norse warriors with their red beards and stern devotion to duty, they also provided spotlessly clean quarters for their passengers and delicious meals for those who had not lost their appetites. Giselle, after a week of almost total starvation, ate a small bowl of soup every day, while Alexandra feasted on fresh fish and poultry, delectable pastries, and the finest French wines.

The sea itself seemed to charm her. Day after day she stood at the rail and watched the ice blue waters slip past the hull, squinted at the sun sparkling on the ripples, and let the tangy spray sting her face and mat her hair. At night she slept dreamlessly, rocked like a baby by the gentle roll of the waves.

Once again, she was staring out to sea, past the harbor to the treacherous waters of the Channel and the empty reaches of the Atlantic beyond. Vinewood was behind her, the road away from it stretched out before her, and she searched the horizon for a glimpse of her future. She saw only the sky and the sea and a few puffs of cloud, then turned and trudged up the gravelled drive.

The wood that edged the estate like a frame on a painting gave way to immaculately kept lawn in front of the house and gardens on either side. The house itself remained exactly what it appeared to be from a distance: built for the comfort and tastes of a respectable country squire rather than a powerful feudal lord. A pillared porch extended across the entire front and reached the full three stories, with a small balcony for the second floor. The windows were large and numerous; Vinewood would be light and airy inside, and full of flowers. Even this late in the year, roses and chrysanthemums still bloomed in the gardens.

I could like this house, she thought. It is a comfortable house, a home, a warm place to live.

That house was now in front of her. She had only to mount the steps and cross the porch to be at the door. She could see lights behind the lacy curtains at some of the windows and therefore knew that someone at least was home, even if only servants. Her heart pounded and her palms were damp, yet she discovered a smile on her lips and a feeling of exhiliration in her soul.

She lifted the anchor-shaped knocker and held the cold bronze in her hand for a single breathless moment to feel the reality of it before rapping it sharply on the door. After what seemed at least an hour's wait, she was about to knock again when the door slowly opened. A middle-aged woman, the housekeeper to judge by her cap and stiff apron, stood just inside, careful not to let the wind blow a draft through the house.

"Good afternoon. May I help you, Miss—?" One raised eyebrow made the woman appear more suspicious than her voice indicated.

"Miss Valenceau," Alexandra said easily, to her own surprise. "I would like very much to see Miss Constance Tregarth, or if that isn't possible, to leave this message for her."

From beneath her cloak she produced a plain white envelope, and offered it to the housekeeper. She seemed reluctant to take it.

"Please, just give her this and I'll be on my way. I don't wish to disturb her if she's busy, or cause any trouble."

She tried to see past the woman into the house, but the foyer was too dark and the housekeeper too tall. Her dreams of this moment, all her fantasies and imaginings, had never included this kind of rejection. Always there had been at the very least a meeting with Constance Tregarth, and if sometimes the reunion was less than joyful—Alexandra always tried to prepare herself for the worst—she was able to walk away with a few questions answered at least. Facing a blatantly antagonistic servant, she doubted she would ever even learn what her mother looked like.

"You said you're Miss Valenceau?"

Alexandra nodded.

"You're French then, I take it."

Another nod, and she felt her smile fade. Then the memory of Giselle's words and of the long miles they had travelled together came back to her. She had come too far to give up on the very doorstep of her quest.

"Yes, I'm French. And I ask for nothing more than that you give my letter to Miss Tregarth. If you'll just promise me—"

She stopped, her sentence and her thoughts interrupted by the voice from inside the house.

"Mrs. Chance, is that someone at the door? I thought I heard a knock."

The housekeeper stepped back, closing the door and almost shutting Alexandra out completely, but there was so little space between them that she could still hear the hasty conversation, though not see the speakers.

"It's a young woman calling herself Miss Valenceau, Miss Constance. She wanted you to have this letter."

A rustle of paper as Mrs. Chance pulled the letter from her apron pocket. Then there was silence for a moment; Alexandra imagined Constance Tregarth turning the blank envelope over in her hand several times.

"It is not polite to keep a visitor waiting."

"Yes, Miss Constance."

Alexandra felt a stab of disappointment when she heard retreating footsteps before the door swung in again, but once Mrs. Chance gestured her inside, all the hope and excitement she had suppressed blossomed once again.

A quick glance around the small entrance hall told Alexandra this was an informal household despite the manorial setting. A pair of mud-covered walking boots occupied a corner beside a battered deacon's bench strewn with well-worn coats, hats, and gloves, as though the hikers had only just returned, except that the mud was too dry to be of recent accumulation. It made Alexandra wonder if the impression she had received of the Tregarth fortune were true or not.

Mrs. Chance shut the door and returned to take Alexandra's cloak. Her grey eyes stared with a boldness Alexandra found unsettling, especially when that eyebrow lifted again at the figure revealed without the concealing cloak. As if in defense, a tiny foot kicked out and drew a gentle pat. Alexandra kept her smile steady and tried not to think about the unspoken accusation in Mrs. Chance's sneer. She could almost hear the housekeeper snorting, " 'Miss' Valenceau, indeed!"

Immediately off the foyer was a sitting room, comfortably but haphazardly furnished with ill-matched pieces and cluttered with dozens of knick-knacks. A roaring fire in the massive stone fireplace gave the room an atmosphere more fitting a middle-class farmer's parlor, an impression strengthened by the three setters sprawled on the hearth. At the approach of unfamiliar footsteps, two of the dogs raised their heads, but it was the third that emitted a throaty woof. Presented with such a scene, Alexandra could feel no threat at all; she felt at home.

"Miss Constance? Miss Valenceau to see you."

"Thank you, Mrs. Chance. You may go."

And she went, too quickly, as though she was fleeing.

But Alexandra did not notice the housekeeper's hasty departure; she was completely occupied with grasping the reality of the moment. The speech she had rehearsed a hundred times while she stood at the rail of the *Gustav Kjarne* or paced the little deck of the *Roxanne Clark* or lay awake in her room at the boarding house evaporated from her memory. The woman seated by the fire, her hands and eyes busy with a bit of embroidery, was Constance Tregarth, who once loved a French aristocrat named Charles Aubertien and eventually bore him a daughter who now stood, unable to speak, just ten feet away.

"I have not read your letter, Miss Valenceau," Constance said, never looking up from her work. "If you have come concerning promises made to you by one or the other of my late brothers, there are a dozen young women ahead of you in the queue."

Alexandra noticed then that Constance's dress was heavy black crepe; she was in recent mourning.

"I'm afraid I don't quite understand, Miss Tregarth, but I assure you, my visit has nothing to do with your brothers."

She wished the woman would put down the damned

446

embroidery and at least look at her. She felt foolish standing there, tired after her long walk and made more uncomfortable by repeated squirmings of the child in her womb.

A bit angry, Alexandra took a few steps towards Constance and even stamped her foot in an attempt to gain the woman's attention. Only the dogs responded, one growling and another cocking its head to one side quizzically.

"I don't want anything, except perhaps a few minutes of your time," she said slowly, deliberately enunciating each word carefully to hide the shakiness of her voice. "And an answer or two, nothing more. If you can give me that, I'll go away and never bother you again, You may my word."

Unperturbed by her caller's quiet outburst, Constance reached for her scissors and snipped her thread with an air of superiority and waning impatience.

"I do not have a great deal of time to waste in idle conversation." She laid the embroidery on the table beside her and Alexandra held her breath as her mother finally looked in her direction. "Let's get to the point, Miss—"

She could not speak. The young Frenchwoman's tear-filled green eyes met hers and froze her to the very core of her soul. It wasn't possible, not after twenty years, to recognize a child she had last seen as an infant and was now grown to womanhood. Certainly not at a single glance. It simply was not possible. But then why the tears? And why the horrible pain Constance felt suddenly tightening in her own throat? Could a mother's memory truly be that strong?

With an effort, she whispered, "Alexandra? Is it really you?"

"It is I."

Constance rose and opened her arms to the child she had never expected to see again, and as she walked closer to her mother, Alexandra saw through the blur of her own tears that Constance's eyes, too, were wet, and their color was that of flawless emeralds.

They had tea in the cozy but cluttered room Constance called the winter parlor. Mrs. Chance brought the cart and left it for Constance to serve from, but before she departed, the housekeeper cast a suspicious glance on her mistress' visitor. They both noticed it and chose to ignore it rather than betray their secret. For a while, for an hour or two at most, this heady excitement was theirs alone.

"I am not surprised," Constance said when she learned of Charles Aubertien's death. "I think he wanted it that way. He was too much a part of the old way to live after it all collapsed around him. He would not have been happy as a penniless emigrè."

"But Therese was happy. At least, I always thought she was."

"Yes, but your aunt adored her brother and would do anything to please him. Women can do remarkable things when love is involved. For men the motivating force is honor, which is why men make such a mess of things." She spread some strawberry preserves on a still warm scone. "But to get back to your story. After Charles died, Therese did marry the tailor?"

"She did, and they were wonderful parents to me. Armand had two other daughters, Justine and Yvette, who are as much my sisters as if we had had the same parents."

With no trace of jealousy, Constance said, "I can see that you were loved, and that means very much to me. Don't be ashamed to admit, even to me, that you love them, too. I cannot hate them, though I may envy them a little for having you all these years. Now, tell me how you survived the Revolution."

The room had grown slowly dim as the sun moved westward with the afternoon, and Alexandra knew she must not stay. She set down her cup and rose to leave.

"I must go," she insisted when Constance begged her to stay. "My maid, Giselle, speaks very little English and she hasn't recovered yet from the sea voyage. I promised her I'd be back, and she'll be sick with worry if I'm not."

"Then I shall have Mrs. Chance send one of the boys to her with a message that you'll be staying the night. No, that won't do at all." She strode to the bell cord and summoned the housekeeper. "You write a note to Giselle and have her send all your things here. I will not present my father with his only grandchild and then tell him you're staying at Pansy Archer's boarding house." Then she walked back to Alexandra and took her in her arms once more. "I couldn't bear to see you walk out that door. Please, stay here. Stay with me, Alexandra."

Sir George Tregarth knew his daughter was up to some mischief the moment he saw her strolling out to meet him as he came in from the moors. She wore a girlish grin he hadn't seen for months, and there was something different about the way she walked, as though she were a girl and not a woman of almost forty years.

"Don't hurry, Father. Dinner has been delayed a while. Do you mind if I walk a way with you? It's such a lovely afternoon."

It was a beautiful afternoon, cool and golden as the sun lingered just above the moorland. Vinewood lay half a mile away, farther if they kept to the winding path.

"Have we visitors or something?" he grumbled. He disliked having his routine interrupted even by so trivial a matter as a late dinner.

"Let me see what you've been drawing today." She took his sketch pad from under his arm and held up the beginnings of another landscape. He loved these moors and never tired of sketching them. "I don't know how you do it; I swear I can almost hear the birds and smell the breeze."

"Enough of your compliments, Daughter," he said gruffly, grabbing back the pad. "Hurry and tell me why you are grinning like a well-fed cat so I know why to be angry with you."

His brusqueness was a habit developed over the years of dealing with people who bored him, and in a moment or two the iron grey eyes would soften to a misty green. He ran his long fingers through his hair, which, after almost seventy years, had turned snow white. Nothing else about him even hinted that he was approaching his eighth decade. His frame was as tall and spare as ever, his step strong and sure. He had started back up the hill when Constance put her hand on his arm to slow him just a little.

"Yes, Father, we have a visitor."

"Damn! You know how I hate unannounced and uninvited guests, especially at dinner. They are always unwelcome, but even more so then."

"Unannounced and uninvited she may be, but certainly not unwelcome."

" 'She'? Another predatory bitch to feed on my grief. Constance, I won't have it any more, I tell you. Never again."

She did not bother to interrupt him but let him rage for a few seconds and then, when he paused for breath, she said very quietly, very slowly, "Father, Alexandra has come home."

He did not need to think; he knew instantly that she spoke of the grandchild he had never seen. Understanding now the cause of her giddy smile, he frowned more out of seriousness than displeasure. To ruin her joy was the last thing he wished to do and yet he knew he must ask her questions that would hurt.

"Are you certain? It has been so long, and she could be just another fraud like all those women who claimed to be my daughter-in-law."

Constance shook her head.

"She is no fraud."

Sir George halted at the crest of the hill and turned to look at his daughter, his only surviving child. He stared at her the way an artist contemplates the subject of a portrait. Such appraisal was not unusual and she had years ago grown accustomed to it, but this afternoon she was overly conscious of the unerasable smile that not only curved her lips but sparkled in her eyes. A faint blush tinged her throat and cheeks.

"She's been staying in Fowey, at Pansy Archer's. I told her to have her luggage brought here."

"I suppose she leapt at that suggestion."

"On the contrary. She had a servant waiting for her there, so I think she is quite secure financially. Her clothes were of excellent quality, not flashy, but expensive. And she walked here from town."

"I see. But just what is it that makes you so sure she is who she says she is?"

"When you see her, you'll know."

The wind was pulling at her clothes and hair, and she walked into it with eagerness, leaving her father to hurry to catch up. This was most unusual for her; she did not like the moors around Vinewood, for they held so many memories, and her coming out to get him worried him as he hadn't worried in years.

"Don't give me any women's intuition poppycock. I want to know how she intends to prove she's the child you bore to Charles Aubertien twenty-two years ago."

"Do you remember the portrait that hung in the drawing room at Penloren?"

"Damn it, of course I do. Every brushstroke."

"It's her. Even Mrs. Chance saw it. She couldn't stop staring at the girl the whole time I was ordering a room made up for her. I sent Tim into town for her maidservant; they should be back shortly after dinner."

"You're going too fast, Constance. Don't let resemblance to an old picture fool you. After all, anyone intent on getting his hands on the Tregarth money could have found a girl who looks like that painting. Or the girl might have seen it herself and decided to cash in on her looks."

"I can't explain it, Father, but it is more than just a resemblance. You'll know what I mean as soon as you see her. I've put her in the front bedroom upstairs. Tomorrow we'll make the sewing room over for her maid."

"I hope this comes out well, Constance, but I am very afraid you are going to be disappointed. I do not wish to see you suffer all over again."

"I won't, Father, believe me."

"The room is perfect!" Alexandra exclaimed when Constance walked through the door. "And the view! I wish I could paint; the scenery deserves an artist."

"My father paints a bit. If you even hint that you like the landscape, he will drag you with him all over the county to show it to you."

"I don't think I'd complain. It looks lovely."

Though this room, unlike the parlor downstairs, was rather sparsely furnished, Mrs. Chance had placed two comfortable chairs in front of the fireplace screen and now the two women seated themselves, enjoying the warmth from the roaring blaze. The nervousness of their first hours together had vanished; they both tried to talk at once and ended up laughing hysterically. Finally, wiping tears from her eyes, Constance spoke first, but when she did, the subject was hardly humorous.

"I broke the news to my father, your grandfather, and I'm afraid he was a little less enthusiastic than I have been."

"And probably more suspicious."

"Yes, that too, but I suppose it's to be expected. Once he sees you and talks to you, I'm sure he'll accept the truth. It's just that he's been through so much the past few years, since my brothers died." Alexandra's gasp reminded Constance that the girl knew nothing of the family she had been separated from for so long. "We weren't the only family to lose sons to the war, but it is hard for him because they were the last Tregarths."

"I'm sorry. I had no idea."

"It was worse when the young women came claiming to be their widows, but Father keeps a good head about him always, and he asked for proof, which none of them had. You can understand what your arrival has done to him."

"Then perhaps it would be better if I didn't stay. I do not want to cause any sorrow or trouble, for you or for him. I left the last place I lived for just that reason."

Horrified, Constance reached out to her.

"No, I won't hear of it. Father remains suspicious and

he wishes I would do the same only to save myself disappointment. He said I am hoping for too much and that I refuse to believe you could be lying. It's true. Every time I look at you, I know the truth.''

When Sir George opened the door, his knock unheard, he saw what neither Constance nor Alexandra could see entirely. The sight of them together brought a rush of tears to his eyes.

Constance had been right; Alexandra was the portrait he had painted of his daughter nearly a quarter century ago. With an artist's eye, he sought the details, the line of jaw, the tilt to a nose, the convolutions of an ear framed by wispy jet-black curls. There were certain mannerisms, such as Alexandra's cocking her head to one side, that could not be caught by a brush and so could not be copied by an impostor. But it was the eyes, those great green jewels that glimmered with the soul's light, that stamped the girl as her mother's child. Without them he might still have believed, for the resemblance was strong, but had any doubt at all remained, it was gone now. The eyes could not be denied.

''Good morning, Alexandra.'' Constance restrained her embrace with difficulty, but she managed to avoid crushing her daughter. ''Did you sleep well?''

''Marvelously.'' And it was not a lie.

''I'm surprised. The wind came up shortly after midnight and we had quite a storm.''

''Storms have never bothered me. Actually, I'm rather fond of them. I always have been.''

Constance poured a cup of strong tea for herself and coffee for Alexandra.

''It must be your Cornish blood. You were born on a very stormy night not too far from here.'' She caught herself with a laugh. ''But I'm getting ahead of the story; you must tell me your tale first.''

Any lies Alexandra could have created to provide a decorous excuse for her actions would never have been believed, nor did she have the power of concentration to keep a long string of falsehoods consistent. The truth, however damning, however ugly, was the only answer she gave.

And much of it was painful, opening old wounds and touching buried memories to bring fresh tears, until she realized that speaking of the events did not hurt so much as the memory of one man. She had pushed him out of her life and out of her mind; his re-entry even as a memory burned like a flame.

It was late afternoon before Alexandra reached the final month of her history, the journey to England, and by then she had regained some composure, though describing the episode with the Tsar and her subsequent treatment threatened to start another spell of weeping. Her eyes were red and her throat sore as much from sobbing as from all the talking she had done since ten o'clock in the morning.

Refusing the lavish tea Mrs. Chance had prepared, she said, "I think I'd do better with a nap," and quietly excused herself to seek the solitude of her room.

She ran up the stairs and down the hallway, shoved the door open and then slammed it shut behind her. Leaning her shoulder against it, she struggled with the lock and cursed each time her trembling fingers failed to fit the key into its slot. When the sharp click assured her she was secure against any invasion, she staggered to the bed to collapse upon it and surrender to uncontrollable tears.

"I miss him so much. Every time I speak his name, it hurts me inside. Oh, Giselle, what have I done? Why have I walked away from the man I love so much I'd rather die than be without him? What a fool I've been!"

Giselle rushed at once to the writing table by the window and took out a flask of brandy. Pouring a little into the bottom of a tumbler, she carried it to Alexandra. It was French and very good, probably smuggled in long before the Revolution, and it kindled a warm little fire inside her. Her hand shook a little less when she handed the glass back to Giselle.

"I've ordered a dinner tray sent up and explained to

Madame Chance you'll be in your room for the rest of the night," Giselle informed her.

"When did you do that?"

"This morning, when I got the brandy. Did I do wrong?"

A pitiful smile, but a smile nonetheless, and one infused with affection and gratitude lit Alexandra's face beneath the tears.

"No," she said, "You did absolutely right. Now, if you'll just pour me another sip of this golden elixir and then help me into more comfortable clothes, we can get started on this unpacking. I'm damned sick and tired of living like a gypsy."

"Then we are staying?"

"We are staying."

Yet even as she said it, she had a desire to turn around and go back, all the way to Moscow. She missed him that much.

Chapter 45

THE STAIRWAY was poorly lit, but as Mikhail reached the landing he saw the spill of warm light from the open door to his room welcoming him.

"What in hell?" he exclaimed, halting just inside the doorway. "Grandmere, it's damn near four o'clock in the morning. What are you doing up at this hour?"

"Waiting for you."

Anna Petrovna made no move to rise to greet him, nor did she so much as smile at seeing her grandson for the first time in three weeks. The iciness of her expression held him in his tracks.

"Well, here I am."

He attempted a chuckle, but her expression failed to thaw, and he could not even force a smile when the snow on his hair began to melt and send an icy dribble down the back of his neck. His coat and boots, too, were leaving puddles.

"Where's Vasili?" he asked, unbuttoning the coat and draping it over a chair.

"I sent him to bed. If you're hungry, there's some cold chicken by the fire."

It wasn't what he had hoped for, but it would do, and after struggling to remove his sodden boots, he padded across the carpet in his stockinged feet to pick up the tray she indicated. Anna's presence in his rooms so late at night and the stern set to her features made him ill at ease. His hunger, however, demanded satisfaction before his

456

curiosity, and he settled down to a small feast and a bottle of excellent chablis. After tearing the leg off a fat, well-roasted capon, he was so absorbed in eating that Anna's first words quite startled him.

"I believe I have you, at last, in my power," she announced eerily.

He looked up, unable to reply because of a mouthful of chicken.

"I could not have planned it better myself, and yet it has all been mere chance." She moved, reached for a glass of vodka from which she took a tiny sip. "I have something to tell you, Mikhail Pavlovitch Ogrinov, and you are going to listen to me because you are too cold, too tired, and too hungry to do otherwise."

He didn't like the feeling of helplessness her voice created in him. He chewed warily, keeping at least one eye on her even while he broke a chunk from the loaf of bread or poured more wine into his goblet. He must not let his caution fall victim to fatigue.

She plainly intended to upbraid him for some misdeed or other, probably some forgotten insult or social oversight. Since his elevation to the nobility, he had been bombarded with far more invitations than any one man could possibly accept, so he turned down nearly all of them. No doubt he had slighted the wrong person.

Then he began thinking. Would Anna wait up three-fourths the night just to scold him for snubbing some influential personage or current royal favorite? He immediately answered his question with a firm no. Social propriety was hardly a matter to lose sleep over; she gave it no more thought than he did, and that was damned little.

Her behavior differed from normal, too, in that she rarely wasted time with preliminaries. Whatever needed to be said was said and the matter ended. Why then, he asked himself, has she been staring at me without a word for the last ten minutes? He knew her too well to think she had not rehearsed exactly what she intended to tell him. She was too clever to be caught unprepared.

He wiped his fingers and mouth on a linen napkin and

finished a second glass of wine. On one score, at least, his mind was clear. Her complaint could not have anything to do with any trouble he had been in with women, for he had avoided all entanglements, even those of a fleeting, professional nature, for months. Irina had married, happily or not, a fat but fairly wealthy banker several weeks ago and had made no more outrageous claims about the paternity of her child.

Tamara would not have entered his mind except that her quarterly payment was due on the morrow. Still, he shrugged at the thought. She had ceased to be a real threat.

Anna waited until he had set the glass down. His immediate needs for food and warmth had been met, and he was comfortable, relaxed, vulnerable. She felt no guilt at all in striking him under those circumstances. Indeed, she felt he deserved it, and probably more.

"Christ, I'm tired!" he yawned,

She leaned forward just a little, just enough to catch his attention, to open his drooping eyelids for a vital second.

"Alexandra is pregnant with your bastard," she whispered triumphantly.

The two or three seconds of silence that followed were a tangible thing that shattered with the goblet he flung across the room. The crystal shards had barely stopped falling when he swept aside the dinner tray, crashing china and silver and chicken bones to the floor. But his fury ended as quickly as it had begun. With a short sigh, almost a sob, he lay his head back and closed his eyes tightly.

"Where is she?" he asked, his voice as full of defeat as if he had asked the location of her grave.

"I don't know."

It wasn't completely true, but neither did she lie enough to feel guilty about it. And he was caught totally off guard. She saw that and allowed herself a little smile. He hadn't been so utterly at her mercy for years.

She walked over to him, daintily stepping around the mess he had made, to kiss his forehead and whisper, "Go to bed, Mischa, and we'll talk later, when you've had some rest. I'll get word to Vasili that you're not to be wakened."

He could only nod his head in assent. When she had gone, closing the door with a tidy click, he groaned and struggled to his feet, then staggered to the adjoining room and collapsed on his bed.

If he slept at all, and he doubted that he had, it was only in short snatches of a minute or two here and there. When he finally dragged himself out of bed two hours later, he was as exhausted as before, but he knew real sleep was impossible until he had answers to the questions keeping him awake.

They were not new questions, and this was not the first time he had lost sleep puzzling over them, but always before he had kept them to himself. Now Anna confronted him, forcing him to face the problem, and until it was resolved one way or another, he would have no rest.

While he peeled off his clothes, he walked around the room trying to shake the lethargy his fitful dozing had created. He dropped his shirt at the foot of the bed, hung his trousers over the arm of a chair, and left his stockings on the floor by the window, where he stopped for a moment to stare at the bleak grey dawn. The sight of unending snow, so thick he could not see the buildings on the other side of the street, threw him into despair. He picked up the nearest object, a book he had started several weeks ago and had then forgotten to finish, and heaved it across the room. As soon as the volume crashed with a satisfying thud against a bedpost, his rage died, quickly and silently, to leave him shaking with cold and something akin to terror.

Dressed and fortified with a glass of cognac, he wandered down the stairs and eventually found himself in the red drawing room without any conscious memory of having gone there. Anna was waiting for him, expecting him.

"I couldn't sleep," he explained rather weakly and walked toward the window to avoid her accusing eyes. The curtains were drawn against the cold; he held them back and felt all his senses freeze at the memories that rushed over him. Numbness was his only defense against it. Better to feel nothing than to feel only pain.

"I know. I couldn't either, but at my age I don't worry about it," she replied. "I'll have plenty of time soon enough to rest. It's you I'm worried about."

He didn't turn around, though he was no longer staring at the snow. Blinded by uncontrollable rage, he saw nothing that was real, only a vague image, like a shadow against the grey, of a delicate cameo face with sad green eyes.

"Damn you, Anna, where is she? And if you don't know where she is, why the hell did you bother to tell me anything at all?" he roared. His hand, clenched tightly on the red velvet, threatened to pull the drapery down around him. "I couldn't go to her now anyway, not in this storm. It will be days before I can get as far as the Kremlin, and if she's left Moscow, it may be weeks, or even months."

"Mischa, please, sit down. I will tell you what I know, but it isn't much."

"Don't bother! It makes no difference now. You should have told me a month ago, two months ago, when I might have been able to do something." He let go the drapery and slammed his fist against the window frame. As furious as he was, he still had enough control to keep himself from committing some act of foolish destruction, like driving his hand through the glass itself. "What in God's name can I do now?"

He didn't feel the tears until they spattered on his hands resting on the window sill. The warmth startled him into silence.

"To begin with, come over here and sit down. And lower your voice. There's no need to wake the dead with your screaming."

He wanted to ignore her, to shout even louder, but he knew if he opened his mouth only half strangled sobs would come forth. Tears were bad enough; he refused to give in to weeping for no other reason than self-pity, and so far that was the only reason he had. Before facing his grandmother, he poured himself another small dose of cognac, a healthy swallow and no more. Swirling the golden liquor in the bottom of the glass focused his concentration, and when he had gulped it down, feeling every inch of the path it burned down his throat, he turned dry eyes and steady features to her.

"I prefer to stand."

"As you wish."

"Just tell me where she is; I don't care about the rest."

His voice was on the verge of breaking again. Somehow he managed to hold himself together, but Anna read the signs of strain in his carefully veiled eyes, the nervous drumming of his fingers on the back of a chair.

"I don't know exactly where she is, but I do know she left Russia."

"*Left Russia!*" he thundered, almost overturning the chair he had gripped until his knuckles went white. "Where in hell could she go?"

"Ilya Parofsky took her to St. Petersburg, and she sailed from there."

The words scorched bitterly on his tongue as he spat out, "How kind of Ilya! First he seduces my—my—first he seduces her while his wife is mourning the death of their child and then he carts her off to St. Petersburg for a more private fling, away from me and his poor dear wife. I'm sure Madame Parofskaya will be just delighted to hear this bit of news about her husband and her erstwhile friend."

He was halfway to the door, striding slowly but with a hint of vengeful swagger, before Anna stopped him with a firm, "Lydia already knows."

"I suppose her loving husband confessed all to her after his amour left?"

"There was nothing to confess, Mischa. After all these years, you ought to know Ilya better than that. In the first place, he is devoted to Lydia, and in the second place, he would never take anything he thought belonged to you."

"What do you mean by *he thought*? He knew damned well Alexandra was mine."

"You let her go, Mischa," she reminded him. "You

abandoned her and that set her free to choose someone else.''

"But *he* wasn't free. He had no right to her, none at all.'' For a split second tears washed away the veil over his eyes, giving Anna a glimpse of the torment in his soul, but with a blink the tears were gone and the curtain descended once again. "She was mine.''

He poured another glass of cognac to swirl lazily and let the hypnotic action of the fluid calm these passions he couldn't seem to control. He had to stop thinking about her, because every time he did, he wanted to scream with the pain of wanting her and the anger at himself for ever letting her go. It was pride again, stupid, stupid pride. When would he ever be free of it? He stared at the liquor and the technique worked, though slowly; it was quite some time before he trusted himself to speak without shouting or to touch something without breaking or throwing it. Even his thought processes returned to more rational functioning.

He had to think, to put all these nagging questions in some kind of order so that the answers, if there were any, made sense. Still twirling his brandy, he sat down in a chair some distance from his grandmother, for the chair she had placed most convenient to her own was straight backed, armless, and uncomfortable, more suited to interrogation than conversation. Perhaps, he reflected groggily, that is what she had in mind.

"When did Alexandra leave?" It was a struggle just to say her name after all these months of trying to shut her out of his thoughts.

"I'm not certain, but I would guess late October, perhaps a little earlier. Ilya probably knows the exact date, and he's expected back in Moscow any day.''

They both looked toward the window, and though the closed curtains kept them from seeing the snow, its presence was no less real. Parofsky's return would be delayed, possibly indefinitely, by a storm of this magnitude.

"Damn this weather!" Mikhail cursed as frustration ate

away his tenuous control. Yet even as he spoke he remembered that a year ago this same paralyzing climate had saved Russia. Even the greatest curses contain a tiny blessing.

Sinking once again into contemplation of his current dilemma, he found himself in a renewed struggle against the old enemy, fatigue. If he closed his eyes to concentrate, he had severe difficulty opening them again, and staring into a whirlpool of cognac made him even drowsier.

"Have you no idea where she might have gone?" he begged. "I can't believe she'd try to go back to France, but anything is possible, and with the jewelry she took, she could afford to go anywhere."

Anna eyed him suspiciously.

"How do you know what she took?"

"I searched her rooms," he admitted, too tired now to lie or even feel embarrassed at the confession. "Everything was gone, absolutely everything. She didn't leave so much as a damned hair pin."

He was awake enough to set the glass on the table next to him before it dropped from his hand, but he had given up trying to keep his eyes open. He didn't care that sleeping in a chair would probably put a dozen cramps in his neck, back, and leg muscles, because at this moment his entire body cried out for rest, in any position, on any surface.

Anna watched him, waiting for the moment he was more asleep than awake and yet still conscious enough to hear her. After a long, loud yawn, he twisted in the chair to find a more comfortable position, arms bent at the elbows and resting on the chair, legs stretched straight out in front of him and crossed at the ankles. When the scowl on his face began finally to soften, she knew the time had come.

"I received a letter from her."

The blue eyes snapped open.

"It was written before she left St. Petersburg and then posted the day she sailed."

Mikhail groaned and sat up. He had come to the conclusion that Anna was tormenting him deliberately, which he undoubtedly deserved, but he was approaching the limit of his endurance.

"Are you going to tell me what she wrote, or do you plan to spend what's left of this wasted morning staring at me?" he asked.

From under a cushion on the sofa she retrieved the note and carried it to him, placing it in his hand when he found the strength to raise it. His fingers caressed the single sheet of paper, but he made no attempt to open it or read it. Though he shut his eyes against them, tears trickled out to run in salty rivulets down the side of his face.

When Anna spoke again, the old softness had returned; she had spent all the bitterness and only tenderness and love remained.

"Shall I read it to you?" she offered in a gentle whisper. Her hand touched his forehead and pushed back a curly lock of hair.

She did not expect such strong resistance when she tried to take the letter from him; his trembling fingers clutched desperately at it, threatening to tear it in two if she persisted.

"Just tell me what she wrote," he whispered and tightened his grip on the note when Anna released it.

"She said she was well, and there was nothing for you to worry about. She apologized for whatever it was she had done and hoped you'd forgive her."

"Nothing about her plans, her destination after she had left St. Petersburg?"

Anna's gentle caressing of his forehead had soothed him enough to close his eyes, but he was far from sleepy. Already he was making plans of his own.

"Only that she was going to her mother, but I don't know how she can possibly return to France."

A slow smile curved his lips.

"She can't, and she's not. She's gone to England."

"England!" Anna snorted. "Why in hell would a civilized girl like Alexandra go to England?"

"To find her mother." The smile was broadening. He stretched lazily, like a cat before a fire, and tucked the now rather crumpled letter into his pocket. "According to her story, she hasn't seen her mother since her father abducted her, or some such thing, when she was a small child and took her back to France. Her mother is English, and as far as I know still lives there."

"I remember now she told me she had been raised by an aunt, but of course I assumed that meant her parents were dead."

Mikhail stood up, stretched and yawned again, then took Anna in his arms and kissed first one cheek, then the other.

"I'm going to bed, Grandmère. I intend to sleep until I can't sleep any more. If Alexandra is in England, she's safe until I can get there, and until then there is nothing else I can do but wait and try to be patient."

He kissed her again and without another word left the room, leaving her perplexed but at least a little relieved. Before she was quite out of her sight, she saw him take Alexandra's letter from his pocket and open it.

Late in the afternoon, after a long nap, Mikhail summoned Vasili, who entered the room and proceeded to his usual tasks of preparing a bath, laying out clean clothes, sharpening the silver-handled razor. He did not speak unless spoken to and he refused to meet those hard blue eyes under any circumstances.

"Have you spoken to my grandmother today?" Mikhail asked in a voice Vasili hadn't heard in months. The tension and hatred were miraculously gone.

"No, I have not."

"What about yesterday? Did she talk to you or give you any special instructions while I was gone?"

Afraid to lie, Vasili carefully answered with the truth.

"She came to me in the evening and said she would wait up for you and call me if anything else was needed." And an afterthought, he added, "There was a note today, though. Edward brought it to me this morning."

"From the Countess?"

"Yes, telling me you were not to be awakened. I thought it should have come from you yourself, but I didn't question it."

"Nothing else?"

"Nothing else."

Against what he thought was his better judgement, Vasili turned around to face his master and found himself staring instead at an old friend.

"Then you know nothing about Alexandra."

Vasili had started to smile, but quickly erased all sign of emotion and kept to his role as servant.

"Am I supposed to?"

Mikhail shook his head and slipped into silence as he pulled a piece of paper from the pocket of his dressing gown and began to read it.

He had read her note twice before falling asleep and at least a dozen times more since waking, but if it contained any clue, any message, he had not found it. The few sentences conveyed no feelings, no regrets, no hints to help him understand why she had done what he saw her do. And more than ever, he now wanted to understand.

Sliding into a tub of scalding water, he pushed all thoughts, all questions, feelings and worries out of his mind to enjoy the pleasure of being alive again. There had been other times in his life when the simple comfort of a hot bath was more welcome than the Russian spring, but today the thrill came from appreciating that which he had taken for granted only a day or two before. The soft lather of soap, the slick of a finely honed razor across his cheeks and chin, the rough softness of a heavy towel rubbing him dry and tingling.

"Do you know if there is any supper left?" he asked while pulling on a clean white shirt that felt seductively cool against his warm skin.

"They were waiting it for you when I came upstairs."

"*They*? Is Mother joining us this evening?" He stepped into a pair of dark brown trousers.

"Yes, and Captain Parofsky's wife."

"Lydia? How the hell did she get here through all the snow? It must be waist deep by now." He pulled on a fawn-colored coat and stood still, staring ahead with a frown slightly furrowing his brow while Vasili smoothed the fabric over his shoulders. Some of his earlier mood had vanished; a touch of anger colored his voice and he walked out of the room without another word. Alexandra's letter, however, was once more safely tucked into his pocket.

The Lydia Antonievna he saw upon entering the blue parlor was quite different from the grieving young mother of almost three months ago, but if motherhood and tragedy had matured her, they had also left her lovelier than ever. The Countess eyed Mikhail warily as he greeted Lydia with a gallantry that bordered on the vulgar, bowing, kissing her hand, smothering her with compliments until she blushed as crimson as her velvet gown.

"How did you manage to get here through all this weather?" he asked with the same over-polite mockery.

Anna informed him, "I sent Pyotr for her this afternoon."

With a smile, Mikhail acknowledged the warning her bright eyes flashed at him. This is still my house, she was telling him, and I will invite whomever I please to visit me in it, regardless whom you wish to forbid. Accepting a momentary truce, he drew a chair beside Lydia and sat down. She turned to him at once.

"I'm afraid I never really thanked you for giving me my daughter, Captain Ogrinov. She has been the greatest blessing of my life, and I owe you a debt I can never hope to repay. If you ever have the opportunity to hold your own child your arms, I'm sure you'll know what I mean."

Except for the quiet crackling of the fire, the room was silent, and Mikhail was too stunned to think of a single word to break that silence, which became more and more oppressive. Twice when he opened his mouth, he bit back angry, ugly accusations without even knowing why he did it.

And what had happened, he wondered, to all those delightful feelings he had experienced upon wakening? Why, when he had thrown off all his own bitterness, did these women insist on animosity and a confrontation bound to leave someone hurt? He had been hurt enough; now was the time to stop it, for good. Too often in the past he had acted, as he almost had now, without first learning the facts, a mistake he must never repeat.

He turned to Anna and demanded the truth, all of it.

"Let me tell him," Lydia insisted. "I started it; I may as well finish it."

Anna looked first at Lydia and then at her grandson. As much as he tried to hide it, he was still feeling the effects of Lydia's remarks about his child. His reaction surprised Anna only because he made no comment on Alexandra's pregnancy when she first announced it to him. She had begun to think he might not have heard her, that perhaps the mere mention of Alexandra's name had deafened him to the rest of her rather blunt statement. His speechlessness in response to Lydia's taunt assured her that he knew.

"I have been sitting at home worrying ever since Alexandra left, and I simply can't stand it any more. I can't believe you turned your back on her just because she's going to have a baby. Other men might do that, but not you." She still remembered the anguish on his face when he realized one of her own children was dying. "There had to be another reason, some horrible mistake or misunderstanding that no one took the time to straighten out. Alexandra is gone, so I can't find out her side of the story. The other half of the story is yours, however, and I do intend to get that."

"Did your husband tell you he seduced Alexandra? Are you even certain he isn't nestled in some cozy flat with her right now?"

She couldn't sit still. Rage she had never known before forced her to her feet and she stood shaking with fury in front of him. In a seething whisper she continued.

"I know Ilya was in love with her, but I also know he would never touch her. Do you think I'm such a fool that I'd send my husband off with another woman and not

468

trust them both? Well, I'm not a fool, though you certainly are. Alexandra loved you, for what reason I don't know, and she would rather die than shame or dishonor you. Did you ever stop to ask yourself why a woman carrying one man's child would suddenly run off with another?''

''Damn it, I didn't know she was with child!'' he bellowed. Jumping to his feet, he pushed past Lydia roughly and strode across the room to stand by the fire. Placing his hands on the mantel, he rested his head between his arms and stared down at the flames. ''I didn't know anything until Grandmere told me today.''

''Then Alexandra was wrong to think you knew about the child. She said she heard you and the Countess arguing bout it the day of the Tsar's ball.''

He glanced over his shoulder and found Anna looking as confused as he.

''I swear I knew nothing,'' he insisted.

And yet he had to laugh at the irony that he, of all of them, was the last to know. He should have been the first. His laughter rang cold and bitter as one ugly revelation after another burst in his brain. Whirling around, he faced his opponents and smiled in anticipation of his ultimate victory. He understood their tactics now, and he was no longer vulnerable.

''I'm sorry, ladies, but I refuse to be manipulated like this. Two other women have tried to trap me into legitimizing their bastards, and I will not be caught by a third, though I am surprised, Madame Parofskaya, that you would go so far for your own husband's casual offspring.''

Lydia counted each of the twelve steps it took her reach him, but even counting again after she stood just inches in front of him could not calm her. There was nothing impulsive about the way she lifted her hand and struck his cheek with all the force of insulted dignity.

''You pig! You don't deserve her. You don't deserve anyone but the lowest, filthiest slut.'' The marks of all four fingers stood out red on his face and she felt an urge

469

to hit him again until the imprint was permanent. The urge overwhelmed her; she slapped him again. "I'm glad she left you. Alexandra may be miserable without you, but it will be better than spending the rest of her life with a self-righteous hypocrite. Ilya was wrong to think you loved her; you aren't capable of loving anyone."

She raised her hand as if to deal him a third blow, but it never came.

"You aren't worth it," she said as her hand fell. "Any man who would trade a woman who adored him for a title isn't worth the rope he ought to be hung with."

"*What?*"

Three voices gasped the question at once, startling Lydia enough that she jumped, and when Mikhail grasped her arms and held her prisoner, she could not stop a little scream of surprise and fear. His eyes, cold and fiery, bored into her; she was powerless against that mesmerising stare.

"I have listened to all this nonsense," he told her through clenched teeth, well aware that his mother and Anna Petrovna were ready to summon servants if he became too violent. "You almost had me convinced, but this—this garbage of trading Alexandra for a title I never even wanted! Who gave you such a ridiculous idea? And to whom am I supposed to have traded her?"

His fingers bruised her arms, but it didn't matter. Lydia thought of the pain he had inflicted on Alexandra and the pain she saw in his own eyes, and this was nothing compared to it.

"To the Tsar, of course. He told her himself while he was trying to rape her. If Ilya hadn't been there to rescue her, heaven only knows what might have happened."

It wasn't until he released her that both of them realized he had been holding her several inches off the floor.

"The child is Alexandr's then? He sent you to—"

"No, you stupid fool, it's yours! What do we have to do to make you see that?"

He had almost forgotten his mother, but now Marina approached him with as much fury in her eyes as he had in his.

"Alexandra was pregnant when you brought her to Moscow, though I'm not sure she knew it at the time."

"If you knew, why didn't you tell me?"

"That was her responsibility, not mine. Under no circumstances was I going to help her manipulate you the way I manipulated your father, or that other slut did Niki. It wasn't until she left that I realized she wasn't another Tamara, but I thought you had gotten over both of them."

Oh, God, he thought, she's so right, and I was so wrong. We both were.

"I blamed her, because I didn't want to accept the blame myself. It was easier to say that she had hurt me, betrayed me as Tamara had, than to admit I even could be hurt."

"Don't be blinded, Mischa, the way your father was, by pride or some stupid sense of honor. Do what you want to do, not what you think you ought to do."

He took his mother in his arms and understood for the first time that she had loved him.

"It has taken me a long, long time," he whispered in her ear, "to learn from my mistakes, but I think I have learned the lesson well."

Chapter 46

SPRING CAME stormily to the north coast of Cornwall, blown in on relentless winds off the Atlantic that whipped the sea at the cliff bottoms to a foamy cauldron. Even at low tide the beach below Penloren all but disappeared beneath the seething waves. The few flowers that dared to bloom in this weather were soon ripped to shreds by the furious storms. The lightning-brilliant night skies were hardly darker than the gloomy overcast days.

Sir George substituted ritual pacing of the long gallery for his usual morning walk along the cliffs, but otherwise he hardly seemed to notice the weather. Since returning to Penloren in early December, he had made several dozen sketches of the wild landscape that on these inclement days he used to create large, emotional paintings. The ink stains on his fingers faded or were covered with daubs and smears of paint, and he ruined a number of new shirts before Constance finally found his old, well-spattered smocks. By then, he pointed out, the shirts were in no better shape.

He loved Penloren with an artist's passion that had absolutely nothing to do with his family pride, which was considerable in its own right. The Tregarth name had been allied with Penloren for over two hundred years and with the land on which the house was built for six or seven hundred years before that, but he cared just as much about the architectural beauty of the late Tudor mansion and the exquisitely untamed countryside around it. He often spent hours on the rocky cliffs to watch the action of the sea, to study the set of the sail on a smuggler's bark, to glory in the colors of the sunset. The barren moors were as familiar to him as the neatly arranged brushes and pots of paint in his studio, and he knew the rocky faces of the cliffs as intimately as a lover, as in truth he was.

Beauty was the object of his affection, whether it lay in the sensuous curve of a woman's body, the velvet petal of a dew-kissed rose, or the ragged coastline of his beloved Cornwall, and he found that winter that he was surrounded by beauty. When he reluctantly admitted to Constance just before they removed from Vinewood that he had accepted Alexandra as his granddaughter, he only barely kept secret to himself the additional fact that he had come to enjoy the girl's companionship.

She frequently spent the afternoon with him in his studio, and on fine days when the sky showed bright blue and the wind died to a breeze, they walked together. Wrapped in a heavy cloak against the frosty air, she strode beside him, sometimes in silence, sometimes talking in quiet voices. It was on these walks that she learned the history of the Tregarths and of Cornwall and fell passionately in love with both. She felt as at home here as ever she had in Paris. Sir George, who violently opposed any suggestion that she call him Grandfather, adored her, and Constance had twenty years of maternal love waiting to be showered on her daughter. Frequent letters to and from France added to Alexandra's feeling of security and happiness, leaving only one thing missing to make her life complete.

Not a day went by that she did not think of Mikhail. Her child, due in late March by her calculations, provided a constant reminder that she could not possibly ignore. On several occasions after particularly vivid dreams of him wakened her and left her lying unable to sleep until dawn, she had started letters to him. All her explanations, all her apologies, her tirades, ended smeared with tears in the wastebasket beside her desk. She kept her promise to Anna Petrovna, however, and posted a brief letter to her in February that merely explained she was well and had

473

found what she was looking for. She gave no address, but suggested she could be reached through her sister in Paris. It was more hint than she really wanted to give, but by then it was too late to retract it. Worrying caused more of the dreams, and losing sleep was not something she could afford to do.

Her health continued magnificent, despite the uncomfortable weather and her advancing pregnancy. To Constance's disbelief and against Giselle's daily warnings, Alexandra maintained as active a routine as possible. As the days and weeks passed, even Sir George, who tried to ignore the subject entirely, conceded that his granddaughter suffered none of the usual complaints of women approaching a confinement. His indelicate comparison of her to a healthy draft horse drew a thoroughly disgusted stare from Constance, but Alexandra smiled.

There was never any discussion of Alexandra's future; both her mother and her grandfather acknowledged her right to do and to choose as she pleased. Sir George had let it be known that he considered Alexandra and her unborn child as his heirs after Constance, and legitimized his granddaughter at least to the extent of recording her birth and her father's name in the parish registry. The vicar was speechless and quite prepared to resist, but Sir George assured the man that it would be done, one way or another, and it was. This laid both an honor and a responsibility on Alexandra that she did not quite know how to handle. As with nearly everything else of any importance, she set it aside to be contemplated after the baby was born.

Staying busy helped to pass the long, dreary months of winter, but nothing kept her from dreaming, almost nightly, either of Mikhail or of Lydia. The closer her time approached, the more she worried, and Constance's assurance that such worry was normal did little to alleviate her fears. It was merely a matter of waiting and hoping and praying.

Winter went out, at long last, on a mild note with several clear, sunny days perfect for hikes over the moors or along the cliffs, but by then Alexandra knew it wasn't safe for her to engage in such strenuous activity. She was able to pace the long gallery for a few minutes at a time, however, until a nagging ache in the small of her back reminded her to sit down and rest for a while. Each afternoon, though she longed to be outside, she found it necessary to take a nap or she fell asleep before supper. It irritated her to be so much at the mercy of her body, to have it rather than her own wishes in command. Enforced laziness put her temper completely out of her control as well. She had no patience with anything or anyone, least of all herself, and gave in to every excuse for tears.

"I will be so glad when this is over," she sighed one night as Giselle plumped the pillows behind her. The pain in her back was so great she could not even bear to sit in a chair; reclining in bed helped some, but the pain refused to go away.

"It won't be much longer, a few days at most. Isn't that what the doctor said this afternoon?"

"Yes, but he said that last week, too. I am so afraid he doesn't really know what he's doing. I wish Mischa were here." It was a desire she had had for the past several weeks but had only now dared to put into words. "When Lydia had her babies, he knew exactly what to do, and if he were here, I know I wouldn't be half so afraid as I am."

She picked up the book she had been reading, hoping that it would bore her enough to fall asleep without thinking any more about the man she had walked away from, because she knew that if she let these thoughts continue, she would begin blaming herself for her awkward situation, not him.

The book did help, and she fell asleep as another howling storm blew in to lash the coast. Thunder still rolled in the distance when she wakened shortly after daybreak, but by the time she had bathed and walked, or rather waddled, downstairs for breakfast, patches of blue sky broke through the clouds and joined with each other to form a solid canopy. Sunshine streamed through the diamond-paned windows that, when Constance opened them, let in the sound of birdsong as well as fresh, rain-washed air.

"I do hope this means we're done with gloom and rain," Constance remarked. "I could do with some decent weather for a change. Father is driving me quite insane with his complaints; I need to get him out of doors for a while."

Alexandra sighed and helped herself to a croissant and a cup of coffee from the sideboard before taking her place at the table. It was impossible to move her chair close enough to make eating comfortable; she ended up with crumbs on her distended belly and twice spilled coffee on the table-cloth as she tried to replace the cup on its saucer.

"I'm afraid it is going to take more than a change in the weather to do me much good," she said dismally.

Constance smiled sympathetically.

"I know the feeling well. Is your back still bothering you?"

"It's better, I think. I feel almost good enough to take a stroll along the beach."

"If you feel *that* good, it's a sure sign the end is near. I'd suggest you not go any further than the terrace or the garden, and I'll send word to Dr. Colvin to stop in this afternoon."

Alexandra really did not care if the doctor came or not, but she took her mother's advice and stayed close to the house. Though her back had improved and now ached only slightly, she still felt too awkward to move about much and took her exercise ambling about what would be the garden, if the weather ever permitted anything to grow. The lilacs hedges had started to green, but it would be weeks yet before their clusters of purple and white blossoms appeared. Alexandra hoped her increasingly cumbersome wait would be over by then.

What few benches the garden boasted were grouped around the empty carp pool, but she located a wooden potting bench that she pulled to a sunny spot by a breach in the hedge. From there she looked out over the lawn to the edge of the cliffs. She could tell by the sound as the waves broke on the rocks and rolled up the gravelly beach before they slithered back down again that the tide was out. Listening to the endless rhythm so soothed and relaxed her that she dozed, waking only when she began to lose her balance and almost fell. As she stood up and stretched, she discovered the pain in her back had returned, worse than ever, and she decided to forego the rest of a very pleasant afternoon in the garden and find something indoors more comfortable to sit on.

She had taken half a dozen extremely painful steps when the first contraction seized her. Braced for the same agony that had preceded her miscarriage, she was quite surprised that this passed so quickly and so easily. Though it left her heart beating a little faster and her breath coming in little gasps, the pain was actually less than the annoyance she had endured in her back all these long months. With a feeling of relief that it was all nearly over, she wasted no time walking steadily back to the house.

Despite Sir George's insistence that there was plenty of time, Constance sent one of the stableboys on a horse to fetch Dr. Colvin as soon as she had Alexandra tucked into bed. It might be two days or more before the child was born, but Constance refused to take any unnecessary risks.

Alexandra wished the physician had been less dedicated, but he came the moment he received the message, much to her dismay. After a cursory examination of his patient, he announced that the child was in the proper position for birth and it was only a matter of time.

"I could have told him that myself," Alexandra muttered in French to Giselle, and she wished, not for the first time nor for the last, that Mikhail were with her.

By sundown, a glorious hour of golden light and rose-colored clouds against a lavender sky, Alexandra's pains were stronger and came more frequently. She maintained a cheerful outlook between them, but each spasm brought back clearer and more horrifying the memory of Lydia in a shadowy room with Death watching and waiting. Though she had done everything she could remember Mikhail telling her Lydia should have done, Alexandra still worried.

Darkness fell and yet another storm brewed. Wind moaned in the chimneys, adding an eerie echo to Alexandra's muffled cries, and each flash of lightning seemed to trigger another contraction. But she did not scream, as Lydia had, nor sink into the sweet oblivion of unconsciousness. She wept, as though the tears would wash away the pain and sorrow and loneliness that engulfed her. She felt like a pebble tossed on a beach, battered by the waves that never drowned her yet never lifted her far enough out of their reach to avoid their ceaseless torture.

She lay panting but otherwise still after a particularly strong spasm that had lasted, by her own unreliable counting, more than a full minute.

"Mother, go get Dr. Colvin," she ordered between gasps. "I don't care if he said half an hour ago that nothing would happen until morning. Tell him to come—*now!*"

She had not yet caught her breath before another pain seized her, wrenching out a small wail that the thunder drowned. Constance ran from the room without a word of protest.

Alone with Giselle, Alexandra squeezed the hand that had never let go hers.

"If anything happens to me—"

"Nothing is going to happen," Giselle soothed, wiping a cool cloth across a sweaty brow. "Everything will be just fine. In a little while—"

"Stop it and listen to me," Alexandra interrupted impatiently. "A dozen things can go wrong, and I want you to know what to do if I die."

This time the agony proved too great for the woman who had survived the holocaust of Moscow and the bitter Russian winter. She screamed just once, loud and long. Her voice was strange and weak afterward, but she murmured as tears of heartbreak, not pain, rolled down the sides of her face, "Tell Mischa. Write to him or to Justine;

she will know how to get word to him. I want him to know where his child is. I owe him that much.''

Constance burst into the room, literally dragging the middle-aged physician behind her, and above Alexandra's second scream, Giselle heard him insist that the child could not possibly be born so soon. He was still trying to explain the various reasons for his opinion when Alexandra clenched her teeth together and with an anguished, clearly audible cry of ''Damn you to hell, Mischa!'' gave birth to her son.

Chapter 47

TRISTAN MICHAEL was two weeks old before Alexandra felt confident enough to leave him in someone else's care while she wandered beyond the garden for a solitary walk along the cliffs. Though she intended to be gone no more than an hour, the time slipped by quickly, and she needed the solitude too desperately to return as she had promised.

The question of the boy's christening had been raised, and she knew that the matter involved a far more complicated decision than selecting a date. As she sat on a granite boulder overlooking a serene expanse of ocean, she forced her mind to concentrate on the issue at hand rather than letting other thoughts invade the tranquility of the afternoon.

There was no quarrel with either her choice of the child's name—Sir George had in fact been delighted that she chose an old Cornish name—or with her grandfather's insistence on the parish church at St. Teath as the place. It remained, however, to decide upon a surname for the boy, and with so many to choose from, Alexandra nearly threw her hands up in frustration.

She had herself used the Valenceau name most of her life, but it was not hers. Neither, legally, was Aubertien. Tregarth had every right, if bastards have any rights at all, especially second generation bastards, and Alexandra knew Sir George wouldn't quibble about legality. He fully intended Tristan to be his heir.

The idea of giving the boy his father's name was,

though a fond wish, utterly impossible. A wistful sigh turned to ironic laughter as Alexandra recalled that she did not even know his name herself; Mikhail had admitted to using Ogrinov out of convience because his father was a foreigner. For all she knew, he might have been Chinese or Egyptian or even a Jew. How strange, she thought, and yet how appropriate, that my son should literally have no name.

Perhaps, for his sake, it would be best to use the name she had adopted. There was no dishonor either to the boy or to Armand, whom Alexandra would always think of as her father, but certain attendant difficulties forced her to reject the idea once and for all. It would mean, as the boy grew up, either making his life a perpetual hell the truth of his bastardy or covering the dishonor with deceit. Continuing the fiction, year after year, always with the threat of error, of a flaw in the carefully woven tapestry of falsehoods, was not the future she wanted for herself or for Tristan. Was the facade of legitimacy worth living with the eternal risk of discovery? Could she—and this would be the hardest task of all—maintain the life by keeping the truth from Tristan? She knew she could not deny the child the truth; she and he must live with the knowledge that they were and always would be, no matter what lies they told or anyone else believed, bastards, and they might as well be honest about it.

Though Alexandra had not gone far from the house, the half-mile walk back to the garden gate suddenly seemed a very, very long way. She knew by the length of her shadow that she had stayed out longer than planned, but with this dilemma more or less solved, she could not regret the time taken for herself. She had needed it.

Giselle waited for her, not with Tristan in his basket screaming for food as his mother expected, but waving furiously a letter held high in her hand.

"It's from London!" she called as soon as Alexandra was within hearing.

Alexandra took the paper and asked, "Uncle Roland? I only wrote to him ten days ago; the English post is

481

certainly to be praised for its efficiency.''

The breeze coming off the Atlantic made reading the fluttery pieces of paper impossible, and indoors Tristan demanded to be fed. Settled into a comfortable chair, Alexandra unbuttoned her bodice and the starving, squalling creature in her arms set about satisfying his hunger. For a moment or two he continued to squirm as though he could not believe he was at last getting something to fill his belly, but eventually he calmed and lay still, and Alexandra unfolded her uncle's long letter.

Sir George had made the long effort, through his friends in London, to locate Roland Aubertien, her father's only brother. Writing to him after Tristan's birth, Alexandra had outlined only part of her history and expressed the hope that she might someday have the opportunity to come to London to see him. She mentioned Therese, but left out any reference to Charles, for she had no idea if Roland knew his brother had been dead these past twenty years. Though she had been almost embarrassed to send a full six pages to an uncle she had no memory of, he replied with an even dozen, the large sheets covered with fine, beautiful handwriting.

''He wants me to delay Tristan's christening, if I can, so that he may attend,'' she announced to Giselle after re-reading the entire letter. Tristan himself had fallen asleep. ''He's an attorney and has an important case coming to trial next week. 'I expect it to last until the middle of May,' he writes here, 'and the moment it is over I shall be on my way to Cornwall.' I think we can wait another month, don't you?''

Giselle crossed herself and touched the crucifix she wore around her neck. ''I'll pray nothing happens in the meantime.''

''Nothing is going to happen. Here, help me with him; he's drenched again.''

Removing his wet clothes wakened him, and he lay, stark naked and perfectly content to be that way, on Alexandra's bed. While Giselle gathered his clean, dry clothes, Alexandra talked and tickled the baby who was everything to her.

He was, even to her prejudiced eyes, an extraordinarily pretty child. Though the doctor insisted that children were unable to see clearly for the first month of life, Alexandra knew Tristan's sharp blue eyes missed nothing. He recognized the people around him, and if he could not quite manage a smile yet, he wore a delighted expression every time he saw his mother. His fine dark hair already showed signs of being curly and thick. He rarely cried, except when hungry and that was often enough, but neither was he dull and placid. He seemed full of curiosity, and his sense of adventure developed daily.

"I think your Great-uncle Roland is going to like you," she told her son. "He has three boys of his own—Charles, Thomas, and Stephen—and a little girl Elizabeth who looks just like my Aunt Therese. You, you little darling," she kissed his nose, then his forehead, and finished the sentence in Russian. "You look just like your father."

With news to share with the rest of the family, Alexandra left Tristan in Giselle's care and rushed down to dinner in a gown of springtime yellow trimmed with flounces of apple-green lace at cuffs and bodice.

A gentleman was standing in the foyer outside the dining room. But he turned at the sound of her footsteps on the stair.

She felt each drop of blood drain from her face, and she had to grasp the bannister to keep from falling. Before she could find her tongue and demand an explanation, Sir George introduced her.

"My dear Alexandra, I'm just getting acquainted myself with our new neighbor, Mr. Augustine Trabert."

"How do you do, Mr. Trabert." She kept her voice cool.

Bending rather too low over her hand and just touching it with his lips, the former colonel said, "I am pleased to meet you. I was not even aware Sir George had such a lovely granddaughter.''

The war had treated him harshly; he looked old and worn, much changed from the dashing soldier he had been before Russia. But the evil in his unlashed eyes glowed undiminished. He held her hand so that she had to see the scars and be reminded. She heard her grandfather invite Trabert to dinner, but she was too numb with shock to argue.

Constance, waiting in the dining room, read the anguish in her daughter's eyes. She steered the guest to the opposite side of the table. A small smile was the only thanks Alexandra was able to give, but Constance seemed to understand.

"You're from what part of France, Mr. Trabert? Near Paris?'' Constance asked as she took her own seat.

"No, I am from Brittany, but I have lived in London for more than ten years.''

Liar! Alexandra wanted to scream, but something in the way he looked at her kept her silent.

"I have just bought the house at Polstan, on the other side of St. Teath,'' he explained directing his words at Alexandra. "It is not as grand as Penloren, but after London, it is the peace and quiet I enjoy and the green countryside.''

She knew he meant her to contrast it to the cold and barren Russian wasteland where she had last seen him.

"I know the property of Polstan quite well,'' Sir George said. "A nice estate, with only one drawback. The gypsies camp there every summer for several weeks and hold a small fair.''

"Yes, the agent told me. He said it never bothered the previous owners, but I believe I may be less tolerant. They can be such nuisances.''

"Aye, that they can. When they aren't robbing the villagers of their chickens or scaring the children half to death, they steal in more subtle ways; telling fortunes, making useless love potions, casting spells.''

"No worse than a Cornish witch,'' Constance muttered under her breath. Then in a more conversational tone, she

484

asked, "Isn't there an old gypsy woman living on the Polstan land? I seem to recall—"

"She is an outcast of some kind. She lives in an abandoned cottage along the highway given to her years and years ago. She's quite old now, and makes some kind of living as gypsies always do, begging, stealing, telling fortunes."

He laughed, as though the old gypsy were of no consequence but his gulping of Sir George's excellent madeira betrayed a peculiar nervousness Alexandra had not noticed before.

He was smiling with the same confidence she remembered from that night in Paris. More chilling to Alexandra's blood was the challenge he seemed to have thrown at her. Without a word, he dared her to expose him. She knew he would not be so bold if he had not some hidden advantage. Until she knew his secret, she kept her own to herself.

When dessert was almost over, she broke her silence to answer Sir George's question about her letter. She spoke with care to see that her words had the proper effect on Trabert.

"Uncle Roland asked me to postpone the christening so that he might attend. I can't see any reason not to put it off a few weeks. I'm sure Tristan won't mind."

Trabert did not try to hide his surprise, or perhaps it was not genuine.

"You've recently had a child?" he asked incredulously. When she nodded, he stammered, with a touch of disappointment as false as his astonishment, "I was not even aware you were married."

"I'm not. Now, if you will all excuse me, I have my son to take care of and a letter to write."

She did not look behind her as she swept out of the room. If she remained in his presence one second longer, she would scream—or worse.

Giselle produced a pale green silk wrapper that Alexandra tied over her nightdress when the maid had finished braiding her hair for the night. Giselle was worried, and she took no pains to hide it.

"You think he came here deliberately?" Alexandra asked.

"I do. You said he was not surprised to see you when you came down the stairs. That alone should mean he expected to find you here."

"But how could he? He knew me as Alexandra Aubertien; here I have used only Valenceau."

The maid shrugged as she walked to the bed to turn down the spread and plump the pillows. Tristan slept in his cradle beside Alexandra's bed, and Giselle leaned down to kiss the snoring infant.

"Perhaps it was the gypsies."

Giselle had always been superstitious, but to believe that gypsies on the Cornish moors could have told him where Alexandra was—no, it was impossible.

"I think it far more likely he obtained the information in Paris. Not that Therese or Justine or Manette would have told him, but perhaps they inadvertently told someone else and he then found out."

She checked the candle burning on the mantel to be sure it would last the night and then crossed back to her bed and climbed in. She was tired, and she thanked God that she was, or she would never fall asleep. Not with these new worries to plague her.

"Don't worry, Giselle. With or without gypsy curses, Augustin Trabert will not get what he wants from me. I have defeated him before, and I will defeat him again."

Two weeks later, she began to doubt some of that confidence. Trabert had called twice, casually, but he used the opportunities to point out to Sir George that he and Alexandra had much in common and, even more casually, that he was a widower with no children. Alexandra knew exactly where this was leading, but Sir George, who had classified the Frenchman as merely another boring visitor, paid him little attention. And as the weather continued to improve, Sir George had nothing to keep him indoors with spring sunshine flooding the moors with golden light. He escaped with his canvas and oils to an isolated corner of the

Penloren estate where only the scream of an occasional gull disturbed his concentration and his peace and quiet.

Alexandra had less freedom, and she worried more and more as each day went by. Sitting in the garden with Tristan in his basket at her feet or browsing through Sir George's well-stocked library, or busying her fingers with needlework, she could not keep the hated colonel out of her mind. Giselle knew this, and she did her best to help find a resolution.

"You should tell Sir George," she insisted nightly. "He will know what to do."

"Giselle, there is nothing he can do. The man had committed no crime, not here in England at any rate."

"But your grandfather could keep him from visiting you."

Alexandra shook her head. She was particularly tired this evening and yet she wondered if she would be able to fall asleep or would lie frightened in her bed for hours as she had last night.

"I'm not sure that would be the best thing to do. Trabert has something in mind, some scheme he is hatching like a patient hen on an egg. When he looks at me, he is daring me to fight him. If I do, I know he will retaliate in some horrible way. Remember, he is a man who killed another man simply out of boredom. He would not hesitate to murder again for a *better* reason. And I am not alone now, either. I have Tristan and Mother and Sir George and you to think about. He could strike against any one of you."

Giselle crossed herself and raised her crucifix to her lips.

"I think it is the gypsies," she whispered.

Alexandra pulled the pins out of her hair and tossed them on the dressing table before she sat down. She did not look in the mirror now.

"Don't be silly. You can't possibly believe in gypsy curses."

"You believe in God, don't you?"

Alexandra nodded, looking puzzled.

"Did you ever see Him? Or one of the Saints? Perhaps

gypsy magic is real, too. The colonel has gypsies living with him, and that is not the kind of thing one would expect from a civilized, rational businessman.''

"Well, we know he isn't a businessman, no matter what he claims.''

"He may not be rational, either, then. I think he has had them put a curse on you and he is just waiting to see it work. Maybe you will take sick and slowly die, or worse.''

"And maybe I will fall in love with him and marry him, too. Don't be absurd, Giselle. Brush my hair so I can feed Tristan and get myself to bed.''

But the next morning, when Alexandra set out across the moors alone, she could not shake the suggestions Giselle had planted. She firmly told herself she did not believe in curses, but what if Trabert did?

She enjoyed these morning walks, and after the first shock of seeing Trabert had worn off, she no longer feared meeting him. Each day she walked farther, though never leaving the precincts of Penloren. If anything happened to her, as she fully intended to warn the colonel should they meet, Giselle would tell everyone the truth about him.

She was looking for Sir George, to tell him that the vicar was coming to afternoon tea, but she had no idea which isolated spot her grandfather had chosen to paint today. He had been on the beach yesterday and the day before, and in the little grove of wind-twisted oaks most of last week. She wandered aimlessly for an hour, checking all his favorite haunts, then turned back to the coastline. At the edge of the Penloren land was a wild ravine she had never visited before, and she clambered down the rocky sides until she came to the swollen stream rushing to the cliffs, where it cascaded in a narrow white ribbon to the sea. Lost in contemplation of this discovery, she did not hear approaching hoofbeats. When a shadow crossed hers, however, she looked up and was not surprised to see a familiar but unwelcome face staring down at her.

Sitting on a dark grey horse, Trabert, too, was dressed in grey; charcoal trousers, lighter coat, silvery brocade waistcoat. He looked the very image of a retired merchant, and in the shadows of the ravine, Alexandra noticed that he looked even older than before. He could not be fifty yet, not by several years, and yet he looked older than her grandfather. His pale eyes had taken on a dusty, grave-like hue.

"Good afternoon, Miss Valenceau," he greeted, dismounting and offering his hand to help her climb up the ravine. "You are well, I hope?"

"Quite."

As though there were no ice in her simple reply, he continued, "You certainly look lovely today, but then you always do. And how is Tristan today? I look forward to making the young man's acquaintance soon."

"You need not perform for me, Colonel. Tell me what it is you want and let us have it over with."

"Let me accompany you back to Penloren, and I will give you all the details."

"No, you will tell me here and now. I will not go along with your charade."

He smiled that same knowing, evil smile that had chilled her before. She clutched her shawl tighter around her shoulders and wished she was standing in the bright sunlight rather than at the bottom of this shady ravine.

"It is not out of my way to walk with you, and it is what I want most to do this afternoon. Come, I will even let you ride my horse."

"I prefer to walk," she insisted, but the Colonel had already taken her arm and began heading in the direction of Penloren house. She shook his hand off her arm and strode strongly down the coastal path.

"What more do you hear from your uncle?" he asked.

She wanted to scream. Walking beside him was torture.

"He will be here when his case is settled."

"And the date for your son's christening has not been decided upon?"

"No."

They walked for some distance again in silence, and she cautiously increased the pace. Unlike her, the colonel was not accustomed to strenuous exercise and began breathing heavily before they had more than half climbed the next hill.

She did not wait for him when she reached the crest, but she did not have to. He mounted his horse and rode ahead of her, blocking her path. She could see Penloren less than a mile away, but she knew no one could see her, and she felt a tiny spot of fear grow.

"You have been wise, Alexandra. Any warning to that senile old artist grandfather of yours would have meant sterner action from me. I want the same thing I have wanted for years: you. And now more than ever. I lost my fortune after the war, thanks to you. They stripped me of my rank, and when I returned to Paris, Napoleon had confiscated everything I owned. I escaped with barely my life. But I found out you were here, wealthy, comfortable, and alone."

"I will not give you anything."

"You will give me everything. You have a young son, my dear, and I suspect you would not like to see anything happen to him. I know that you walk in your garden with him, and I know that sometimes you take him with you down to the beach below Penloren. I am a fine marksman, my dear."

She almost screamed "You wouldn't dare!" but she knew that he would.

They had begun walking down the path again, which led now into a shallow valley, but there was no other way back to the house. The grey horse plodded steadily behind her, and over his quiet hoofbeats, Trabert's voice continued his threats.

"Your grandfather has several favorite spots to paint: a grove of trees, the waterfall, the cove above Trengarry Beach. He, too, would be an easy target. Your mother, as befits the lady of the manor, visits the sick and the old rather frequently. She walks or rides a chestnut mare named Gillie, and she always stops to visit her mother's grave in the cementery at St. Teath."

She felt physically sick, but she knew she had guessed at

490

least part of this long ago. And she had nothing to say to him that would effectively counter this threat.

"I will leave you to think on this matter, my dear. And remember that you have an uncle coming to visit you very soon, too."

Whether it was the look in her eyes that stopped him or something else, she did not know. He was plainly about to add another item to his list of unholy promises when suddenly he drew back. He gave her one last smile and then turned his horse sharply around and kicked it viciously.

She saw beyond him that there was a rider at the far end of the little valley, perhaps a mile distant, where the road crossed. She could not guess who the person might be; shadows and the distance would have made positive identification impossible. But the rider did not move, not even when Trabert came closer. Someone, for some reason, had been watching him and now waited for him. Alexandra shivered and ran toward Penloren, letting the wind whip her hair and pull painful tears from her eyes.

Augustine Trabert let his horse pick its own path down the long winding stretch of highway and didn't bother to spur the animal out of an easy canter when it headed for home. But when they reached the lane that forked toward Polstan, he kept the horse to the main road. As they crested a low hill, he paused to look down toward the stone-walled cottage at the bottom of the valley. A thin spiral of smoke drifted from the chimney and then blew away in the breeze.

The ring on the post was rusty and left stains on his gloves as he slipped the reins through it, but he didn't notice. Already he had heard a familiar voice humming inside the dark cottage.

"Tina?" he called. He never set foot into the place, though legally he owned it, until she invited him.

"Enter."

A little shiver ran through his veins as he ducked

491

beneath the low doorway. That one word greeting indicated she was alone, not an uncommon situation but still infrequent enough to be taken advantage of whenever it occurred.

She was tall, nearly his own height when he removed his boots, and her thick, red-gold hair seemed odd for a gypsy, but the old woman Rayda was certainly a Romany, and Trabert never doubted that the two strangers she had taken in some months ago were at that same race. He had met the other women, the veiled creature known as Madame Mara, only once, but that was sufficient. Something about her made his skin crawl, something in that low husky voice muffled by the concealing drapery of her black, shroud-like veil. Tina, on the other hand, made his flesh warm.

Bending over the crude table to set out plates for the evening meal, Tina watched her visitor come into the main room of the house. She had been expecting him and was dressed accordingly in a loose white blouse and full skirt of multi-shaded red stripes. A blue kerchief bound the mass of her hair back from her face and loops of heavy gold dangled from her ears.

"Good afternoon," she said. Her accent forced him to listen carefully to what she said, but her English had improved a great deal since he had first met her. "You have come from the Frenchwoman?"

There was no jealousy in Tina's question.

"Yes. I made it clear to her what I wanted and what I would do to get it." He sniffed the aroma of the stew bubbling over the fire. The gypsies had been poaching again; he smelled rabbit. "And if your potion works, I am sure I can persuade her to set a June wedding date."

"Don't worry. The potion always works. Have I not always told you the truth?"

"Indeed you have, though I do not know how you do it. When you came to me in London, I admit I did not believe you, but now I have no doubts at all. You are going to make us both very, very happy."

Alexandra, with her exquisite cameo beauty and her

492

fiery denial of him, aroused him much more than Tina, but the gypsy girl was willing. He had satisfied his lust in Tina's eager body all too frequently to deny the advantages of their relationship. He needed her desperately now, after more than an hour spent with Alexandra.

"Mara and the old one will be back soon," Tina said, but she was already walking toward the other room.

Trabert followed her, his heart pounding. He had his coat off and his shirt unbuttoned before he reached the door. He closed the curtain hanging after Tina lit a candle.

The tiny flame did little to banish the darkness of the windowless chamber, but he knew her body well enough without light. His hunger had become pain by the time he pulled her into his arms and dragged her to the pallet with him. Her small, hard-nippled breasts taunted him; he suckled first one, then the other, before covering her entire body with his and sliding his swollen organ into the steamy warmth.

His desire spent itself quickly, as it always did when Alexandra had fired it. Tina knew ways, strange techniques he had never experienced, to arouse him again and again, but as he submitted to her ministrations, he knew she could never, for all her seductive secrets, satisfy him the way Alexandra would. Soon, he thought as he shuddered in the throes of yet another climax, I will have them both.

Chapter 48

A LETTER from Roland Aubertien had arrived at Penloren that day, and the news that her uncle would be in Cornwall in less than a week did much to cheer Alexandra. Safe in her own room again, she shared the letter with Giselle, and then, declining supper, she sat down at her desk to compose a letter to the one man who might help her out of this horrible situation. At least she might feel better to have told him.

She knew sleep would not come until she was utterly exhausted, and so she worked well into the night, scratching out phrases that did not convey just the right thought and throwing away page after page in dissatisfaction. Giselle puttered about the room, putting things away that were already put away, taking things out no one had any need for.

"You must go to bed," she finally ordered. "It is past midnight already."

"If I did, I would only lie there and worry for hours."

"Then why don't you tell me what happened today? I know you met him. What did he do to you?"

"He threatened me, that's all. He wants money."

"He wants more than that," Giselle insisted.

And so Alexandra told Giselle everything Trabert had told her that afternoon. It did not help to share her fears with someone; it only made them worse, because now she had to worry about Giselle, too.

But there were no dreams that night, neither good nor

bad. It was the following night Alexandra wakened screaming.

She lay in the half dark, not yet sure if she had wakened or still lived in the nightmare's world. Slowly familiarity sank in. This was her room, Tristan lay snoring softly in his cradle, and a dishevelled Giselle stood by the bed with a candle in her shaking hand.

It was the same the next night and the next. Alexandra fought sleep for hours but when she finally closed her eyes, the horror returned. She saw a French soldier shot in the head, and when she went to him, he was an old man with silver hair and paint splatters on his shirt.

"It is a curse," Giselle whispered, tracing the sign of the cross in the air. Even the sunny morning could not dispel the atmosphere of dread in this room.

"Nonsense. I won't believe in that foolishness."

Alexandra had finished nursing Tristan and, feeling drowsy, lay back down on the bed. "I can't keep my eyes open. Tell Mother I'll be down for luncheon, but I need sleep more than I need breakfast today." She yawned and snuggled into the thick mattress while Giselle covered her with a quilt. "And you must forget this curse nonsense."

Giselle might have been persuaded to accept her mistress' confidence if Alexandra had had a peaceful morning's rest, but the nightmare returned almost the instant she had fallen asleep. When, with the assistance of several glasses of brandy, she dozed again and seemed destined finally to rest, Giselle took matters into her own hands. She had seen Satan in this torment and knew that gypsies were the devil's own servants.

Not daring to visit the Romanies herself and be gone when Alexandra might need her, Giselle enlisted a kitchen maid, Betsy Lytle, to run the errand. She listened carefully to Giselle's instructions then left, promising to be back at Penloren before noon.

Betsy Lytle knew every inch of the moors. Flower-decked now in the height of spring, they could be cruel and forbidding in the winter, yet they never daunted her. With

495

her curls tucked under a bonnet, she set out jauntily down the drive to the main road and then swung east toward the house where the old gypsy lived. A staunch Methodist, Betsy instinctively put her trust in the Lord and feared no evil as she trudged up one hill and then descended into the shallow valley, at the bottom of which stood the little cottage. Smoke rose from the chimney and the door stood open. Betsy guessed the two horses tethered at the side of the hovel belonged to the two newcomers to the valley, the young woman called Tina and the other, Madame Mara.

As she came closer, Betsy remembered to put on an expression of uncertainty before the gypsies saw her. She must not let them think they did not frighten her.

Rayda, who had been a fixture of the moors for most of Betsy's life, came to the door at the sound of a timid knock.

"Ye be Betsy Lytle, ben't ye? Old Tom's daughter," the hag greeted her.

"Aye, that I am."

"Come ter have yer fortune told? Or a love potion ter give one of them boys up at the Tregarth house?"

"Neither." She looked around her, scanning the surrounding hills. "Can't we go inside? Someone might see me here."

Rayda moved out of the way and ushered Betsy into the cottage. It was dark and smelled of old meat and stale smoke.

"I want a curse," the girl said bluntly.

"There be Cornish witches aplenty for that."

"I don't want their spells. I want the same curse you put on Tregarth's granddaughter, the one that give her them awful nightmares. She can't sleep at all now, and they do say she's going to die of it."

The old gypsy scratched her chin with a chipped and broken thumbnail.

"I know nought of any curse, unless it be some that my *guests* have cast. They have dealings with the new man at Polstan, not I. But I have others—"

"No, I want t'same as on Miss Alexandra. How do I get it?"

Greed flashed in the crone's eyes as she whispered, "Bring me three silver shillings tomorrow night when the moon is full, and I'll get yer curse for ye."

Betsy agreed, and let Rayda edge her toward the door, but as she was about to step outside again, Betsy heard sounds coming from the other room. She quelled her curiosity and did not look back until she was well up the road, almost to the top of the hill. Excitement sped her steps, and the sun brought perspiration to her forehead. Pausing to catch her breath, she sat down on one of the granite boulders that littered the hilltop.

Unware that they were watched, three women came out of the cottage. Though Betsy had never seen the other two, she knew them well enough from local gossip to recognize Madame Mara as the woman veiled in unrelieved black, unusual garb for a gypsy. The other woman, younger and much taller, lifted Mara into the saddle and then mounted the other horse astride. From this distance, Betsy could hear none of their conversation, but anger was obvious in the way Tina dug her heels into her horse and headed in the general direction of Polstan Manor.

True to her word, Betsy arrived back at the kitchen half an hour before the clock struck twelve.

"I weren't afraid of her at all," she explained after relating every detail of her expedition. "Leastaways not because of her bein' a gypsy. I don't believe none o' their spells and curses, neither, not even after what I heard."

"But can't you see what it has done to Alexandra?" Giselle wailed in protest. She *did* believe.

Betsy shook her head. "I know she been havin' bad dreams, but I don't lay that to no curse. That Trabert fellow scares her, that's all, and the more she do dwell on't, the more 'tis bound to scare her. I think there's more to all this than she wants to tell."

Giselle couldn't meet the girl's eyes and mumbled a prayer in French as she crossed herself again. But Betsy had more to say.

"To begin with, old Rayda is the only gypsy. The other two be foreigners, no doubt, but they ben't Romanies. And I think they are up to something with that Mr. Trabert."

Mrs. Chance looked at her quizzically. "How can you be so sure? You said the one who calls herself Madame Mara was all covered with veils so you couldn't see her face."

"Didn't need to. She rode sidesaddle, like a countess or something. I never saw a gypsy hardly ever use a saddle. And that Tina, the tall one, she's as blonde as a new sovereign. No one ever told me about her hair and I never saw her afore today, so I reckoned they were both gypsies, like Rayda. They ain't."

"And why do you think they have anything to do with Trabert, other than living on his land?"

"Because I accused them of it, and when I was gone, they headed straight for his place."

Feeling a bit guilty about acting without Alexandra's consent, Giselle confessed all while she dressed her mistress for dinner.

"Something had to be done," the maid explained tearfully. "I couldn't stand by and watch what was happening to you without trying to help."

"I know, I know." Alexandra had slept fitfully most of the afternoon yet hardly felt better for it. "Perhaps, as Betsy seemed to think, time will take care of it. Or perhaps he will now be forced to act instead of merely threaten. I dread the thought of what he might do, but I can't go on like this either."

Dinner was livened by the discussion of Betsy Lytle's adventure, the tale of which had spread rather rapidly through the household. Sir George had heard only fragments and listened with interest to Alexandra's more detailed version. Unlike her father, Constance did not scoff at the power of the gypsies.

"No, I have no faith in their curses, but they are

dangerous people," she insisted, "and therefore not to be shrugged off so easily. And if they are allied with this Trabert fellow, then they are doubly not to be trusted."

"You'll get no argument from me there," Sir George agreed. "The fellow had the nerve to come to me this afternoon while I was painting and ask to marry her!" He poked his fork into a piece of beef and raised it to his mouth. He stopped when he saw Alexandra turn whiter than the linen cloth on the table. "Good heavens, girl, what is it?"

"I'm—I'm just tired, that's all. And surprised. Why did you say nothing earlier?"

She could not let him suspect how terrified she was now. Trabert had indeed been warned by Betsy's visit to the gypsies, and now he was making his move.

"Because I told him he must ask you himself, that I was not going to be his go-between." He put the beef in his mouth and chewed slowly, thoughtfully, then asked, "If these other two women aren't Romanies, I wonder just what the hell they are?"

Before he had time to ponder that question to a possible solution, Mrs. Chance entered the dining room with profuse apologies for the interruption.

"There's a boy from the King Charles Inn at Fowey with a message for Miss Alexandra," she whispered to Sir George.

"For God sake, give it to her," he ordered. "I don't want her messages."

Alexandra's heart stopped beating for a second and she held her breath, terrified, but at the sight of the neat, tight writing, a smile spread across her face.

"It's from Uncle Roland," she announced as her eyes raced over the few lines. "He's in Fowey, says they had a terrible journey today and decided to rest the night before setting out for Penloren in the morning. 'I should hate very much to arrive too late to enjoy a long reunion. I intend to monopolize tomorrow with getting acquainted.' " She set the paper down beside her plate and rested her hand atop it to steady the uncontrollable shaking. Even as her smile grew, tears dripped from the corners of her eyes.

Constance motioned to the housekeeper and softly instructed, "See that the boy is well paid for his errand. Give him supper if he's not had any, and make a place for him to sleep."

But later, when Alexandra asked to talk to the messenger, Mrs. Chance informed her he had gone back to Fowey, as the night was clear and the near-full moon bright as day. Disappointed that she had lost the opportunity to ask what her uncle was like, how he looked, whether his wife was pretty or fat or silly, Alexandra had a sudden hunger for solitude. She found it in the garden for a while, until the deeper peace of the cliffs beckoned.

A breeze just strong enough to rustle her skirts brought the scent of the sea to her. The tide was in, obliterating the narrow shingle beach with foaming breakers that sent spray glittering like diamond dust in the moonlight. Somewhere overhead, flitting like a shadow from the spirit world, a nightjar called softly, but there were no other sounds.

She stood, for half an hour perhaps, staring out over the water, letting all the tension seep out of her. Drained, too, of every ounce of energy, she lay down in the cool, dry grass. Stars wheeled above her, winking like a billion teasing eyes. In the past few days, and especially in the past few hours, she had known too much excitement and fear and apprehension even to think during this wonderful period of utter peace, but certain thoughts required no effort.

She wondered where Mikhail was, if he saw the same stars she did, what he was doing on this warm, quiet evening. Loneliness closed in around her even as she was surrounded by open sky and sea and moorland.

She returned to her room without bidding good night to the other members of her family, though she knew Constance and Sir George were going over the arrangements for housing their guests due to arrive in the morning. Alexandra had no interest in discussing where her aunt and uncle and cousins—Good God, she thought halfway up the final flight of stairs, I'm to be overwhelmed with relatives after all these years an orphan—would sleep during their two week visit. All she did care about was her own sleep. Her rest on the cliff had not refreshed her, but it had cleansed her mind and then left her more exhausted than ever.

A noise tore her from a vaguely pleasant dream, and she was startled to find her room bathed in brilliant light. She remembered it had been dim only a moment ago, when she settled into the chair to feed Tristan. But she wasn't in the chair any more. She was lying in her bed, and sunlight poured through the windows.

"There, you see? I told you your mama would be awake in just a minute," Giselle whispered to Alexandra's son as she walked around the room and bounced him gently on her shoulder.

"What time is it?"

"Half past ten."

The bedclothes flew. Alexandra jumped to her feet with the realization that she had somehow fallen asleep twelve hours ago with Tristan at her breast.

He was hungry again, too. His lusty cry was what had wakened her, and he was no longer content with Giselle's bouncing and cooing. Once in the familiar embrace of his mother's arms, he set up a most unpleasant wailing and began to pummel her with his tiny fists. They got in the way when she tried to unlace the bodice of her nightgown, but finally he found what he was looking for and stopped his struggling.

With Tristan busy at his breakfast, Alexandra sat down at her dressing table and began snapping orders to Giselle.

"Don't fuss too much with my hair; I haven't got time. No breakfast for me either. And put away that green poplin. I want the embroidered white muslin from Paris. I can get my own stockings and shoes and—now what is this?" she picked up a folded piece of paper lying under a bottle of scent.

"It—it came about an hour ago. I was going to throw it away, but I couldn't read it and I didn't know if throwing it away might not be worse than letting you read it."

Alexandra's growing scowl made Giselle think that destroying Trabert's note would indeed have been the right thing to do, but Alexandra quickly put her fears to rest. She was angry, but only with Trabert.

"He actually had the audacity to tell me—not ask me but *tell* me—that he will pay me a visit this afternoon to set the date for our wedding." With a frightening calm, she laid the paper back on the table and took a deep breath. "Where was I? Oh, yes. I can get my own stockings and shoes, and I think I can get into the white dress without any help, so as soon as you've finished my hair, run downstairs and tell Mrs. Chance I need someone, one of the boys, to run over to Polstan with a message."

"You're not going to accept his proposal, are you?" Giselle asked in horrified disbelief. Her mistress' calm made her wonder if the woman had not finally lost her mind under all this pressure.

"Good God, no! I'm going to tell him I forbid him to see me any more. I am going to call his bluff. It may cost me, but I think he has underestimated me. I don't think he'll do anything at all."

Giselle departed, closing the door gently. As soon as the maid was gone, Alexandra went to her desk, took out pen and paper to compose the brief letter she hoped would end Trabert's torture. Few of her words were kind. If he needed her money so desperately, she suspected he would soon be forced to leave Polstan. He could not afford to push her too far. Or perhaps he had already gone too far, and now he would have to make a fatal move. She challenged him, knowing full well what she had put at stake.

Writing the letter with one hand had been easy enough, but sealing it required two hands, so she set it aside until Giselle returned and could help her. Tristan was hungry and didn't mind a little jostling as she moved around the room, opening a drawer to take out a pair of silk stockings, fumbling in a jewelry box for a necklace. By the time Giselle returned, Alexandra had managed to pull on her stockings and slip on her shoes, but her son showed no sign of relinquishing his hold and she had no choice but to wait until he was satisfied before she could dress.

"The letter I want sent is over there; I want it delivered at once. No reply is necessary, so tell the boy not to wait. I hate to think what Trabert might do to him when he finds out what the message is," she said, adding that last in a half fearful undertone. "Is there any word from my uncle yet?"

"No, but Nat Trenowe is watching from the gatehouse, so we'll have word the minute someone is spotted on the road."

"It won't be much longer, and if this glutton doesn't hurry, I'll still be in my nightclothes. Why didn't you wake me earlier?"

Giselle answered firmly, "Because you were sleeping and you needed that more than anything else. I wouldn't have wakened you even if your uncle were already here. Have you taken a look at yourself lately? You needed rest."

Almost to herself Alexandra said, "I didn't dream last night at all."

Luncheon was delayed an hour by the arrival of Roland Aubertien and his family, but no one, except perhaps the cook, seemed to care. When Nat Trenowe, who usually spent his time carrying water to, from, and around the kitchen, announced that a carriage had just turned off the highroad and into the drive, Alexandra took a long deep breath to still the wild beating of her heart. With Tristan in one arm and holding onto her grandfather with the other, she walked out into the courtyard to greet her uncle.

The eldest boy, Charles, stepped from the post chaise first. Alexandra guessed he must take after his mother, for he did not look like Therese at all. At eighteen, he was tall and very slim, his brown hair thick and ruffled by the

503

breeze. He smiled to Alexandra as he helped his younger brothers and finally his sister to the ground. Thomas and Stephen were junior images of their brother, but twelve year old Elizabeth was a golden blossom on this branch of the Aubertien family tree. Wide blue eyes sparkled in a smiling face framed by a froth of flaxen curls. Alexandra knew she was looking at her beloved Aunt Therese before the horror of the Revolution.

Roland Aubertien emerged almost reluctantly and quickly turned to take his wife's hand. That they were in love after all these years of marriage and still looked to each other for strength and comfort was obvious in the way they smiled at each other, ignoring everyone else.

For a brief moment the two families stood a few feet apart and said nothing. It was left to Elizabeth to break the spell by whispering, "Mama, please, may I hold the baby if Cousin Alexandra will let me?"

Through tears of joy, Alexandra exclaimed, "You certainly may, little cousin," and there was no more silence.

While her uncle took charge of the introductions, Alexandra studied both him and the effect he had upon her mother. At forty-two, Roland Aubertien hardly looked the part of a middle-aged lawyer. His sharp-featured face was unlined, his bright hair touched only with a frosting of silver at the temples. His years in the courtroom had given his voice a solemnity that his lighthearted banter kept from becoming dull. Though he was gracious in his greeting to Constance, he displayed none of the ebullient charm Alexandra had expected, and it was perhaps that very seriousness that set him apart from his brother and kept Constance from seeing too much of Charles in Roland.

There was still enough to remind her. Roland was taller, thinner, his shoulders not quite so broad, but his eyes still held that same mystery in their foggy blue depths. He lacked only that hint of the rogue. In many ways he typified the dutiful younger son, and Constance still thrilled to Charles' sense of adventure.

504

Will I be like this in twenty years? Alexandra wondered. *Taking pleasure only in my memories?*

Roland's wife Nancy presented an entirely different problem. How was this daughter of a country parson going to react to an environment of old wealth and two generations of bastardy?

Using formality to cover her nervousness, Constance said, "I hope you will enjoy your stay. Please be sure to tell me if there is anything you need to make you comfortable."

"I already have everything I need to make this a wonderful holiday: clean, fresh air, plenty of quiet, and room to move," Nancy beamed. "After growing up in a Dorset village, I find twenty years in London haven't altered my preference for country living."

She had hit upon the one thing she knew they would have in common, and from then on their differences seemed inconsequential.

Chapter 49

"I'M AFRAID my daughter has led a very sheltered life," Nancy commented as she watched Elizabeth's unabashed delight at being permitted to hold Tristan. With a full belly and surrounded by adoring females, he cooed and practiced his latest accomplishment, a full-blown smile. "At her age I had done a great deal more than just hold infants. That's what comes from being the second oldest of ten children," she laughed. "Sometimes it was nothing but work, yet I look back on it with memories only of the happiness. That's why I was overjoyed when Roland received your letter. All our married life he had been drowning in my relatives; he needs at least a few of his own."

"I know the feeling," Alexandra replied as she stepped behind a lacquered screen to change into a turquoise peau-de-soie gown for the evening.

Her room was in quiet contrast to the dining room. With Constance, Nancy, and Elizabeth, she had retired when word came after lunch that Tristan's appetite again demanded appeasing. The older boys had enthusiastically accepted exile to the stables, Roland and Sir George discovered they had political beliefs to discuss, so the women marched upstairs to sip chilled sherry, gossip, and discuss the matter of raising children.

"When Roland explained the details of Alexandra's circumstances, I felt almost too guilty to face you," Nancy admitted to Constance. "Of course, I knew about his sister and brother and Alexandra, too, long ago, but it still came as quite a shock to learn she was here.''

''But why would you feel guilty?''

Nancy shrugged. ''I was embarrassed by my happiness. My children and my husband and my entire life have been nothing but happiness.''

She lost her engaging smile for the first time.

''Did Charles' death bring you your good fortune?'' Constance asked. ''Did the births of your children cause the war that took my brothers' lives?'' When Nancy shook her head, Constance went on, ''Then you are not to blame and you must not feel guilty. Besides, all is well now and what is done cannot be undone.''

Alexandra, emerging from behind the screen, suppressed a little gasp at hearing those oh so familiar words.

Roland accepted George's offer of a pipe of rich, smooth Virginia tobacco, and when it was lit, he eased himself into a leather chair facing the window that gave an excellent view of the parkland stretching toward the highroad.

''I never missed the old life, not even the luxuries.'' He puffed slowly, savoring the aroma swirling about him. ''Oh, true, I've done my best to return to a comfortable life, but I think it is the challenge, the work itself, that has driven me, more than the goal of wealth.''

''Your brother wasn't like that. He and Constance lived in a hovel for more than two years waiting for me to relent and give my permission for them to marry, and I don't doubt he was happy because he was with her, but he remained an aristocrat to the end.''

''And it cost him dearly. Not just his life; he lost the woman he loved because of his stubborn sense of honor. Oh, look. You're about to have another guest.''

With a puzzled frown, Sir George went to the window, wondering who was calling, for he had invited no one. Recognizing the horse cantering up the gravel, he masked his anger but could not prevent some of it touching his voice.

"I'll get rid of him. Augustin Trabert is not welcome in this house."

He strode from the room without any other excuse. Roland, wondering what made this Trabert *persona non grata* at Penloren, continued to enjoy his pipe and the view of the late afternoon. Green lawn, dotted with trees centuries old, narrow ribbon of driveway, all bathed in the clear light of lowering sun. Nancy was right, he mused. There is a kind of peace one finds in the country that simply does not exist within the walls of the city.

That peace was shattered by the sounds of a distant argument, voices raised and then lowered in anger. Roland's first reaction was to investigate and he rose from the comfort of his chair. Three strides toward the open door and he paused, just inside the room but now able to hear what was said, or or rather what was shouted, in the foyer at the end of the hallway.

"For the last time, Trabert, my granddaughter is not seeing anyone today."

"Yet just a moment ago you said she was entertaining relatives from London. Surely she can spare ten minutes to speak with her fiancé?"

Acid dripped from that voice. The words as much as the venom in them shocked Roland. He had had no idea Alexandra entertained thoughts of marriage and wondered why, if the man's claims were genuine, Sir George refused him entrance. Was he genuine? Was Tregarth jealous or over-protective or was he justified in keeping a potential menace from her? Roland quickly decided Sir George loved his granddaughter very much, but not to the point of denying her something she truly wanted, even an unacceptable suitor.

"Alexandra will never marry you, you detestable serpent," Tregarth insisted. "I'll see to that myself."

Trabert laughed. "You said once that her life was hers to live. Are you reneging? Are you going to make her decisions for her?"

"She has made this decision herself. Now, get out!"

The silence hung in the air like an icy fog. Roland could wait no longer. Alexandra was his brother's daughter, as much his blood as Tregarth's. He crossed the threshold and walked into the wide corridor.

"You're lying!" the acid voice boasted. "I have a note from her asking me to come see her today. To meet her relatives, I presumed."

"Let me see it."

"Really, George, I'm not in the habit of carrying my casual correspondence about on my person." He assumed a slightly more conciliatory tone when he said, "Surely it would be just as easy to let her tell us both the truth."

Roland's entrance surprised both men into frozen smiles, but the atmosphere of cold hatred lingered.

"Go ahead, George," Roland said softly. "I'm sure Alexandra is thoroughly bored by my Nancy's gossip now anyway. You go rescue her and I'll stay with this gentleman."

"Augustine Trabert, of Polstan Manor," he introduced himself, bowing slightly, mockingly.

"Roland Francois d'Aubertien, Marquis de Toulombe." Trabert could hardly know that the estate belonging to that title had long ago been cut into little parcels for the peasants or the chateau burned by looters, but Roland took only small satisfaction in the amazement his words brought to his fellow exile's face, for the man's greed had been quickened by this new knowledge. "I am Alexandra's uncle."

Sir George hesitated for an instant. Aubertien was more than a match for Trabert, verbally or physically. Alexandra could certainly be in no danger facing Trabert with such protection.

Constance entered the drawing room with Nancy half an hour later. Both women were subdued as they greeted the men. Sir George paced nervously and wished he had a brandy but, being a gentleman, he would not drink without offering similar comfort to his companions, and

509

he would not give a drop of horse urine to Trabert. Roland, on the other hand, puffed calmly on his borrowed pipe.

"Alexandra will be down in a minute," Constance announced quietly.

No one spoke; there was nothing to say. Roland took his wife's hand and gave her a calm smile before leading her to a more private corner where they gazed out the window as he had done earlier. He wanted to talk to her, to ask her what had been said in Alexandra's room and to tell her of his own thoughts, but he could not here. Not with the man standing near the door as though he were holding them all prisoner. And when Roland thought about it, he realized that that was indeed what this Augustin Trabert had in mind.

Shadows had lengthened perceptibly, but the light remained clear, the images sharp. A doe and her fawn strolled across the lower park, followed cautiously by a handsome stag, his antlers hanging shreds of velvet. Roland watched, fascinated, until the trio of wild creatures disappeared into a shallow ravine that bordered the lawn. Only then did he notice a horse trotting up the drive, a magnificent black stud.

"Another guest," he announced with a touch of sardonic humor.

In the absence of other instructions, Mrs. Chance admitted the caller to the foyer, though not without reservations. She had heard every word of Sir George's discussion with Mr. Trabert and she now wondered if another such discussion was about to occur.

She glanced at the card the tall stranger had given her.

"Is Sir George expecting you, Mr. Hawthorne?"

"No, I'm afraid not. And my business is really with his granddaughter. She is at home today, is she not?"

"She is. She's just come downstairs." She hadn't meant to tell him that; the words just came as though he willed them from her.

She left him in the foyer and went herself to the drawing room, where silence lay like a pall at her entrance.

"Sir, there's a Mr. Hawthorne to see Miss Alexandra."

"You may tell him she's not seeing anyone today," Trabert ordered her sharply.

Mrs. Chance looked from him to Sir George, who sighed wearily and then said, "Tell Mr. Hawthorne we are busy with family matters, Mrs. Chance. It would be best for him to call some other time."

She did not like the attitude Sir George had taken. He hadn't seemed so defeated since his sons were killed. Mrs. Chance bowed and intended to do as she was told, but she did not like it. Even less did she like returning to the stranger with the compelling blue eyes and informing him Miss Alexandra would not see him.

When Mrs. Chance had gone, Alexandra let Trabert close the doors again and then she turned on him.

"I would call you names, but there are none to describe a piece of filth like you," she hissed, held back from him by her grandfather's hand on her arm.

"Now, now my dear, that is hardly any way to talk to your betrothed. We have already agreed, have we not, that your only salvation lies in becoming my wife. Or do you really want me to eliminate the members of your family one by one? I can do it, you know. Would you like more proof? What if I describe to you the café your step-sister and her husband have purchased near the Opera? And Yvette's little daughter Michelline, who goes strolling with her mother every Wednesday to visit the cemetery where Armand's first wife is buried? You see, my dear, I know all about them, and I have only to begin writing letters and they will be taken care of, one at a time, until you give in."

She had listened to him for half an hour, giving her the details not only of her own life, but of Manette's and Justine's and Armand's and even a former lieutenant, Pierre Lascaux. He even knew about Roland, about his office and his clerks and where Nancy's cook bought vegetables.

And now who was this Mr. Hawthorne? Was he some henchman come to give her more nightmares? At least

Tristan was safe, for the moment, but she knew he would not be for long. Something had to be done, and there was only one thing she could do now.

But as she took her first steps toward the leering colonel, he did what she had never expected him to do. From inside his coat he pulled a pistol. It might have been the same one he shot the poor sergeant with, but in any event she knew he would not hesitate to use it.

She stood no more than three feet away from him when the doors behind him began to swing open. The pistol was pointed at her belly, and Trabert's smile had turned to an insane grin. But then she saw the man approaching the door. Mrs. Chance was still trying to dissuade him but he gently pushed her ahead of him and made his way onward.

No! Alexandra tried to tell him. The last thing she wanted was for him to find her now, with Trabert. And yet she could not bear to tell him to leave. But if he did not, Trabert would kill him, and Alexandra could not bear that either.

It was too much for her. The blackness started at the very edges of her vision and then slowly moved in closer. She knew it was going to happen and there was nothing she could do to stop it. But when the last light finally winked out, she did not want to fall where she did.

Trabert turned at the sound of the man's voice, and the only thing Mikhail could see was the tumbled heap of turqoise silk and tousled black hair the colonel held in his arms.

She wakened to shadows and the stink of smelling salts, and Constance bending over her.

"You gave us quite a fright, my dear."

Alexandra sat up. She pushed away the rug that someone had covered her with as she lay on the sofa and started to stand but dizziness assailed her. She sank down again.

"Where is he?" she asked.

"Where is who?"

"Mischa, of course. He was here a minute ago."

"You mean Mr. Hawthorne?" Constance asked quietly, knowing exactly what Alexandra meant and not wanting to answer her question.

"Yes, Mr. Hawthorne, or whatever he said his name was."

"He left, Alexandra." Constance wanted to comfort her but knew there was no comfort to be given. "We tried to stop him, but he was gone before your grandfather or uncle could do anything. Even Mrs. Chance tried, but he just muttered something in some strange language and ran for the door."

"And Trabert, what about him?"

"Gone, too."

"But the gun? He had a gun, pointed it right at me. What happened?"

"We can tell you that later. Be grateful at least that he's gone, and we can deal with the rest of it later."

"No, Mother, I have to know now. And then I must go after him."

Sir George had come back into the room with the brandy and handed a glass to Alexandra.

"Forget him. He's gone and I don't think he'll be back," he told her.

She took the brandy and gulped it down. Not ready for it, she choked, but when the spasm passed, she found her head clearer and her legs steadier.

"It isn't Trabert I have to go after. I'd leave him to the wolves, if there were any. But I have to find Mischa. You don't understand, do you, any of you?"

She had got to her feet and was weaving her way towards the door when Roland stopped her. She tore free of his grasp and fled.

By the time Alexandra reached her room, she was out of breath and beginning to feel weak-kneed again. Panting, she ordered as astonished Giselle to shut up and listen.

"Get me out of this dress and into something I can ride a horse in. Astride, not sidesaddle. And I'll need something so I can carry Tristan with me. I don't know how long I'll be gone, and I can't leave him here alone."

513

Water splashed on her face helped restore her, so she could stand while Giselle fumbled with the long row of buttons.

"But where are you going that you—"

"She's going to find her little boy's father." Nancy opened the door and came in without knocking. "Here, try these on. Thomas is about your size; if you roll the bottoms up they ought to fit." Alexandra caught the trousers and shirt Nancy tossed to her.

"How did you know about Mischa? Did Mother tell you?"

"No, it's the striking resemblance between them. Especially their eyes. I suspected the minute Mr. Hawthorne entered the room. And the way he said your name, just once, before he left. There, those don't fit too badly. Better a bit loose than too tight. Now, get me a sheet and I'll make a sling for the baby."

Giselle, still trying to puzzle out what had happened, brought the required linen which Nancy expertly tore to the proper size.

"You'll find it quite comfortable once you get used to it," Nancy commented as she tied the carrier around Alexandra's neck and shoulders. "But don't expect to ride at a gallop. Mr. Hawthorne has no more than half an hour's lead on you, and his horse was dead tired when he rode it in. Do you know the country between here and Fowey?"

"Fairly well. Well enough to find my way."

"I don't think he does. He is staying at the King Charles, and I overheard him at dinner last night asking directions here. Until today, of course, I didn't give it a second thought, but he is not a man one forgets easily."

Nancy threw her arms around her niece and wished her Godspeed.

The courtyard was entirely in shadow when the stable-boy brought Alexandra's horse, but the sky above still held the sun's glow. Against the evening chill, she fastened a heavy cloak about her shoulders so that it covered Tristan, who slept in his snug little pouch against her breast.

"I have no more time to waste," she told her grandfather impatiently. "He's damn hear an hour ahead of me now, and it is almost dark. Go in and stay with Mother."

Sir George held the reins for her to mount but did not immediately release them when she was in the saddle.

"Is there nothing I can say that will keep you from chasing after this man as though you were—"

"Don't say it. You can't call me names I haven't already called myself. Just let me go, please, before it is too late."

From the corner of her eye she saw Roland striding toward her. His face mirrored with concern. She could not look at him.

"At least leave the boy here," Sir George begged. "Why expose him to possible danger?"

"He'll be perfectly safe. If I left him here, there's no wet nurse to feed him. Besides, I want him to have one look at his father." She jerked on the reins, pulling them from his hands. "I've got to go."

Then Roland called to her. She stared straight ahead, over her horse's twitching ears, rather than face her uncle and risk more tears.

"If it's a matter of Tristan's birth, his illegitimacy, you mustn't do anything foolish. I know you feel your pride and honor are at stake, but—"

Her laughter echoed off the stone walls surrounding them, wild brittle laughter that sent shivers through both men's hearts. She took full control of her horse now, wheeling him around to face the open gateway.

"It was never a question of honor," she said. "I've had my fill of what men call honor. You, George, who refused to acknowledge your daughter's love for a penniless emigre. My father's assinine vanity over the equally ridiculous preconditions you set for their marriage. Did you really think a Marquis would allow his daughter to be raised as another man's unwanted bastard? Did you believe Mother would go along with it, simply for the sake of *your* honor, not hers? And then there is Mischa, foolishly thinking he needed a title to prove he was as good as the rest of the Ogrinovs. Worse still, he thought he needed it to earn my love. I want no more to do with that kind of honor. All it creates is pain and hatred and broken hearts, and I've seen more than enough of that in my life. I have a chance to undo the damage and find the man I love. You won't take that chance away from me, because it is the only honor I care about. You'd do best to try to find the man who has threatened all our lives and deal with him; he is more a threat than my chasing after a man.''

She kicked the horse viciously. The animal, tired of standing, leapt to a headlong gallop Alexandra had some difficulty slowing to an easier pace down the winding trail of gravel to the highroad, but once on the firm, level track, she gave him his head and let him stretch out his strides.

The road was familiar enough in daylight, but as the last twilight faded, Alexandra began to worry that she might have made the wrong decision. Though the full moon banished true dark, shadows took on strange shapes and altered even the most commonplace objects. Passing through St. Teath village, she breathed a little easier knowing she had so far encountered no difficulty keeping to her course. Outside the village, she turned her mount off the road they had followed since leaving Penloren. Though the new track was wider and easier to follow, it led across the emptiness of Bodmin Moor.

There were no villages between St. Teath and Bodmin, and very, very few cottages. Half the houses she passed were abandoned shells, walls without roofs and vacant windows through which the eerie moonlight streamed. A flock of sheep on a distant hillside were the only living creatures she saw.

Lights from Bodmin town twinkled a greeting as she crested the last hill. With no watch, she could not guess at the time, but at least a few lamps still burned. It could not be terribly late.

The horse's hooves clattered on the cobbles as he trotted through the town. Passing a tavern, he whinnied to the animals tethered outside. Alexandra looked, but she saw no black stallion. Two miles or so down the road she swore

at her stupidity in not stopping at the inn to ask if any
had seen a traveller fitting Mikhail's description. He might
even have stopped there for the night. She kicked her
horse to a canter and continued toward Fowey.

At the bridge crossing the Fowey river, she paused long
enough to let the horse drink and to check on Tristan. The
jolting had not bothered him at all; he slept with an
innocent smile on his little mouth. Alexandra tucked him
back into the sling and fastened the long cloak, then
mounted again and crossed the river.

The moon that had just risen when she set out from
Penloren sailed high overhead as she neared Fowey.
Several ships rode at anchor in the harbor, their lanterns
bobbing as the waves rocked them gently. Alexandra
passed the road leading to Vinewood; after she had found
Mikhail, there would be time to go back, with or without
him, but first she must find him.

She soon found herself lost and alone on the waterfront.
The taverns were full of sailors, too frightening for her to
enter, but she knew she must ask directions of someone.
She could not wander the streets all night; she must, no
matter how uninviting, go into the next grogshop.

Now far ahead, she discerned a glimmer of light from
another tavern. As unpleasant as it was, she had to do it for
Tristan. Her heart jumped with hope when she saw a
figure come out the open door. He walked with a
steadiness that hinted he might not be terribly drunk, and
if he could direct her, she'd be spared going into the
tavern herself.

"Pardon me," she called, slowing the horse to a walk as
she drew alongside the man. "I'm looking for the King
Charles Inn. Can you tell me how to find it?"

He turned slowly.

"I'll take you there myself, Snowbird."

"*Vasili*! Oh, thank God!"

Chapter 50

FOR ALL its loneliness, Alexandra preferred Vinewood's comforts and its privacy to the cramped quarters of a tiny room at the King Charles Inn, and rode there alone after Vasili went in search of Mikhail. She had given him careful instructions to find the house, but once she showed him its white facade shining above the town, he laughed and called it a lighthouse the poorest sailor could not lose.

Both she and the horse were exhausted by the time they reached the house, and Tristan was awake, looking for his supper. Before anything else, she had to feed him, and walked about lighting candles in her old room while he suckled. She set the mantel clock with her best estimate of the time to measure the passage of the hours while she waited. As it struck midnight and marked the end of one day and the beginning of another, she knew she had been in the house half an hour. It seemed like weeks.

After making Tristan safe on the bed by surrounding him with pillows and a folded quilt so he couldn't fall off, she took a lamp to light her way to the kitchen, where she hoped to find water to wash with. It was there, but she had to struggle to get it. The pump creaked and groaned and nearly wore her arm out before an icy stream of water gushed forth to fill her pitcher. She assembled a collection of such useful items as a pan, a cup, and a small tin half filled with tea, some kindling and a few larger sticks to build a fire, and another dozen candles to supplement the meager supply in her room. She carried it all up the stairs without sloshing a single cup of water, and then hurried back to find more wood for her fire.

Quite proud that she had not lost the ability to take care of herself, she built a tidy little blaze and set her pan of water on the grate to warm. While she brushed her hair and gathered towels and soap, Tristan gurgled happily. She wondered what Mikhail's reaction would be to seeing his son. If nothing else, she hoped he at least would not deny his paternity.

She washed with the first pan of hot water, then set more on for tea. Though there was brandy on the dressing table, she decided to save it for Mikhail. She was drunk enough on excitement, and once she changed her riding clothes for the comfort of the nightgown she had found in the wardrobe, it was all she could do to keep from dozing in her chair.

Falling asleep was one of the last things she wanted to do. She wanted to be awake to greet Mikhail the instant he arrived. In her excitement at meeting with Vasili, she had forgotten all the questions she wanted to ask. Now, when it was too late, she realized she knew absolutely nothing about his sudden appearance at Penloren.

How had he found her? Why had he come and why had he let Trabert's presence chase him away? Did he know about Tristan? Pouring her tea, she tried to stop the avalanche of questions, but they swept over her. Why had he used the name Hawthorne? Would he listen to Vasili and come here for her?

The fire popped, waking her from a light slumber. Glancing at the clock, she knew she had not slept more than a few minutes; it was not yet one o'clock. Though she suddenly felt more alert for that bit of rest, she knew she dared not sit down or she would fall asleep in an instant. She busied herself with what tasks she could, such as banking the fire and changing Tristan's saturated clothes for dry ones. Then she grew drowsy again, and the bed looked inviting indeed. Tristan squeaked and yawned; he had succumbed. Alexandra yawned, too, and knew that further resistance was useless. She snuffed out the candles and moved the lamp so it shone in the window facing the driveway as an extra beacon, and then made a place for herself on the bed beside her son.

Mikhail had told Vasili nothing on his return to the King Charles, but he supposed that very silence spoke for him. He rejected Vasili's suggestion that they have some supper and had gone out alone to walk the streets and to think. And he warned the servant not to come looking for him. So far he had seen no sign that Vasili had disobeyed.

He tossed a coin on the table and got to his feet without tasting a drop of the liquor. He had stared at the pale liquid for half an hour, growing more certain with each passing minite that the solution to his problem lay elsewhere. A ton of better brandy than this would not wipe away the image of her horrified face when she saw him standing in her drawing room door. And all the brandy in the world could not make him forget whose arms had held her.

Outside the tavern he found some measure of quiet and realized it was the noise within that had made him uncomfortable. He walked some distance down the quay until the sounds of drunken sailors and their women had died completely. The harbor was still, the moon spreading a sheen of silver on the gentle ripples. The breeze off the water brought faint the creak of rigging, the lap of water against hull, the groan of timbers adjusting to each ship's motion. A bell clanged and the scurrying of feet marked the change of the watch.

The touch of a hand on his arm startled him; he turned angrily, expecting to see Vasili.

"Coo, luv, I didn't mean to scare ye."

The woman jumped back half a step and pulled her shawl closer about her.

He turned away from her and muttered, "Get out of here."

"An' why should I?" she drawled. "It's a public thoroughfare, ain't it? Besides, you look like a man what wants a little comp'ny. C'mon, a big, han'some cove like

520

you oughtn't ter be alone on such a fine night as this. It's damned romantic, it is, wi' the moon an' all.''

Except for the tawdry dress and the artificial copper of her hair, she was pretty enough, but he wanted no whore tonight. He wanted Alexandra, more than ever now that he had seen her again, traitorous bitch that she was.

"I prefer to be alone," he lied politely.

She eyed his clothes, saw that under a coating of dust they were of the latest style and most expensive make. There was money here, and she would see none of if if she gave up so easily.

"I can make ye ferget yer troubles, Cap'n. If they be money ones, I'll give ye a bargain. All night wi' me fer on'y two shillin's. That's a bed, too, mind ye, fer on'y two shillin's.''

He threw back his head and let the laughter roll from him, wave after wave of it. Frightened, the harlot moved away again, but not too far.

"One shillin'?" she whispered.

One part of his anger wanted to pick the trollop up and toss her into the scummy waters of Fowey harbor. But she had no way of knowing his pain, and she was only plying her trade, probably the only one she knew. It wasn't her greed that caused him to laugh, though he suspected she had never charged over tuppence before.

Grabbing her wrist, he dropped a fistful of coins into the upturned palm. Before her fingers closed over the hoard, she caught the wink of at least one gold sovereign.

"Thank ye, milord," Her voice quivered with awe as she dropped what she supposed was a graceful curtsy. "God bless ye, milord." Then, afraid his generosity was a symptom of more dangerous madness, she ran back in the direction of the pub.

If he could not find any solitude here in the streets, perhaps the privacy of the little room with only Vasili for company was preferable. In any case, he must avoid further encounters with dockside trulls. A sovereign was still a sovereign, and he did not have an unlimited supply.

The winding, hilly streets of Fowey confused him no

more than the familiar avenues of Moscow or Paris. Though he had wandered aimlessly for several hours, his unerring sense of direction brought him to the King Charles Inn just as a clock somewhere chimed once. He walked under the swinging sign of the King with his head tucked under his arm and stopped in the bar room when he saw someone moving around. That someone proved to be the innkeeper's wife, sweeping up the floor. She gave him the bottle of brandy he requested only because she knew he would pay twice its worth. He did, throwing the coins carelessly onto the counter. He hadn't even looked at them.

The room was dark and empty, which did not surprise him. He knew Vasili was out looking for him, but it didn't matter. Nothing did, except Alexandra, and she had turned against him again. He set the bottle on the table and began to take off his clothes, not bothering to light the candle. He didn't remember exactly where it was, and anyway he didn't need it. This was not the first time he had undressed in the dark.

And he had his solitude. Here he could lie in bed and drink his brandy until either sleep or alcohol gave him a few hours of forgetfulness.

He had never expected it to end this way. When Lydia cornered him with the truth about Alexandra's actions, a little morsel of doubt still remained, to be exorcised with the letter he received from Manette in reply to his own. Everyone around him, from his grandmother to Vera Ylbatskaya, from Vasili to Ilya, assured him that Alexandra had left him only because she loved him too much to hurt him. The possibility that she had lied to all of them, too, never entered his mind.

Now it was all he could think about, and it hurt. He climbed into the narrow bed that was too short for his legs and reached for the brandy.

Something was wrong. The pillow, a scrawny sack of feathers that had poked him the night before, was missing. So was the thin woolen blanket. And someone had sprinkled coarse salt on the sheet.

"If this is your idea of a damned joke, Vasili, I'll see you drawn and quartered for it," he swore.

He stumbled around the room in search of a light. He found the blanket first, tripping over it and stubbing his toe. More curses followed when he stepped on the pillow and nearly fell, but he finally found the candle, a stub but enough for the moment, and then fumbled through his discarded clothing for his tinderbox.

The room revealed by the flickering light was a shambles, yet as Mikhail stared about him in amazement, he detected a strange kind of order to the chaos. The valises and two trunks had been dragged to the center of the room; it was a miracle he hadn't banged his shin on one of them. The bedclothes were strewn about and a chair lay on its side, but nothing was damaged. His suspicions of trickery grew, as did his anger.

He righted the chair and moved the trunks out of the way, then turned to the task of remaking the bed. Where the pillow belonged lay a note. Furious, he snatched it up and would have ripped it to shreds had he not seen the writing and recognized Alexandra's delicate hand.

"Forgive the mess," she wrote, "but Vasili feared you might fall on top of this if we didn't do something to catch your attention. I am at Vinewood, the white house north of the city on the hill overlooking the river. If you go out into Copper Lane and look past the church spire, you'll see it."

It contained neither invitation nor explanation, but he knew, thanks to his unintentional sobriety, that telling him where she was constituted her invitation. He had only to go to her and ask for an explanation, if he wanted it.

The clatter of hooves on the gravel driveway wakened Alexandra from an eerie dream of gypsies dancing in the snow. Shaking off grogginess, she slipped out of the bed and padded expectantly to the window.

The drive below her was in shadow now that the moon hung in the western sky, but she saw three riders dismount, two men and a woman. A feminine voice hushed

523

the others as they mounted to the porch and opened the unlocked door. Alexandra's first thought, that her uncle, grandfather and mother had ridden at this ungodly hour across the moor to see that she was safe lasted only a second. Without the slightest panic, she knew that these strangers, possibly thieves attracted by the light in the window, meant no good.

The passage of the moon had put the foyer into darkness as well, and she used the delay that this presented the intruders to do what she could to protect Tristan. Scooping him off the bed, she prayed he would not waken, which he rarely did during the night any more, and then carried him to what had been Giselle's little room. So far she had not heard footsteps on the stairs, but she did not tarry. One kiss on the precious little cheek and she locked the door. If something happened to her, if the thieves killed or injured her but left Tristan unharmed, someone would find him. Sir George would probably set out at dawn himself, with the others in tow.

For the moment she could only wait. The room was void of any obvious weapons; she did not even hear a poker for the fire. Against three attackers she had no chance with only a cooking pot or a broken brandy decanter, but she put both close to the bed.

The door opened firmly, without hesitation, and Augustine Trabert stepped into the room.

"Good evening, Alexandra. Or should I say good morning?"

He left the door open, but no one else came in as he crossed to her bedside and drew a chair closer.

"You don't look very happy to see me. Or, I must admit, very surprised."

She sat with the pillows propped behind her, the quilts drawn up over her legs. As calm as her voice was, the green eyes blazed.

"I'm not."

"Happy or surprised?"

"Neither."

He laughed and reached for the brandy she had so conveniently provided.

"I should think after your strident denial of my courtship you'd be surprised to find me undaunted."

"Not in the least."

"And you're not afraid of me?"

"It would be a waste of time."

"Yes, it would, wouldn't it."

He clapped his hands, and a woman entered. Her whole body was smothered in black veils, and she limped grotesquely, half dragging one leg. From amongst the folds of her skirt she produced a slender brass flagon which she handed to Trabert without a word. After removing his gloves, he pulled out the stopper and poured the contents of the flagon into the brandy.

"Forgive my manners, Alexandra. This is Madame Mara, a most learned lady."

The creature bowed awkwardly, mockingly, then Trabert continued, "Madame Mara has created a soothing elixir for you, my dear. Her people are very skilled in these matters, and she assures me this medicinal potion will calm your nerves and put you into a, shall we say, more pliable frame of mind."

"I'll kill you afterward," she said coldly. "I promise you that."

"No, you won't my love. Madame Mara will be your constant companion from now on, to be sure that you continue this medication until we are married and for as long as necessary after that."

I am afraid, Alexandra thought. I am terrified and yet I sit here and do nothing to stop him. What is wrong with me?

He took two glasses from the table and slowly poured each half full. Handing one to Alexandra, he swirled the drugged liquor in his own while he contemplated the beauty he was soon to possess. The unbound hair mantled her shoulders and lay in disordered curls on her breasts. He lifted one thick tress, rubbed its luxurious strands between his scar-stiffened fingers with lascivious delight. Against the plain white lawn nightdress, her skin glowed warm and golden, inviting his touch. His hand grazed her chin, turned the smoldering green eyes to his.

"You won't hate me much longer," he murmured. "No one can resist this potion. You'll drink it, my sweet Alexandra, and in half an hour you'll be mine, all mine. Body, soul, and fortune."

She spat in his face.

"I will hate you through every second of my life and for all eternity afterward," she hissed. The temper was rising in her, sending her blood racing through her veins, ringing in her ears. It didn't matter that she was one against three; a valiant death held more attraction than the living hell Trabert offered.

He wiped the spray of saliva from his face, but the smile remained. Alexandra ignored it as meaningless, for she had seen his pale eyes come to a boil. As his anger grew, hers died. Serenity and hope returned to her clearing mind.

Her clock chimed thrice; Vasili had had plenty of time to scour the streets and alleys and waterfront taprooms to find Mischa. Even if Mikhail wanted nothing more to do with her, Vasili's loyalty was something she never doubted. He at least would come to let her know, to comfort her, to rescue her as he had so many times before. The sight of three strange horses tied at the entrance would warn him. Or Mikhail. If she could just find a way to stall Trabert without arousing his suspicions, help might arrive in time.

"I'm afraid one part of your scheme has come to fruition too late," she told him. "I inherit nothing of the Tregarth estate except an income, and a small one at that. Everything goes to my son."

Trabert leaned back with a satisfied grin. "And as his stepfather, I will control it. I suspected old George would make that kind of arrangement. It doesn't alter my plans one whit."

"Sir George didn't make the arrangements; I did. Just this morning. My uncle is a lawyer, you know, every aspect is perfectly legal."

His brow furrowed; she had cracked the stone wall of his confidence.

"Very carefully signed legal," she went on, barely controlling her voice as excitement, terror, and hope all warred within. "No matter whom I marry, *if* I marry, my husband will never touch a single farthing of Tristan's inheritance."

"That can be changed," he said. "I have lawyers, too."

He shifted nervously, and his natural pallor deepened. The brandy in his glass continued to swirl, round and round, as his thoughts, so clear just a moment ago, became jumbled. Was the bitch bluffing? Would such an agreement hold in a court of law? He didn't know.

It had gone so well until today, until she dared to defy him, and until that bastard Ogrinov showed up. Trabert had almost been afraid he would fid the Russian here with her and felt sure he dared waste no more time just in case the man showed up. But Alexandra had said nothing about him, and the colonel thought she surely would have if she expected him. Or perhaps she did not want to give her enemy warning.

The seconds ticked by inexorably. The longer Trabert remained silent and brooding, the better her chances that someone would come to her aid.

A shadow of motion caught her attention. Madame Mara eased one silent step at a time toward the door and slipped without a sound into the hallway, leaving Alexandra alone with Trabert, who had noticed nothing. Now the odds were even.

Her mind laughed at the idea, yet she did not change her belief in the equality of this pairing. For once she had the advantage of time to prepare for his attack.

He had not brought the gun, the only weeapon she had no defense against, and he carried no sword, but a knife was easily concealed and could not be ignored. The brandy bottle remained within her reach. Once she possessed it, she had only to strike it against the bedpost to arm herself. Even the pillows piled behind her could be thrown at him or used as a shield to fend off an attack.

"I will take my chances," he announced so sharply Alexandra lost her tight control. She swallowed a lump of fear and hauled her sagging confidence back to its feet. "Now, a toast to our future." He raised his glass and touched the rim to his lips but did not drink. "Come, my love, drink with me and then join with me in a supreme rapture."

"You will have to pour this potion down my throat," Alexandra answered with a devilish smile as she dumped the contents of her glass on the floor.

The knife materialized before the last drop of brandy splashed on the rug. He levelled it at her for only a fraction of a heartbeat before he dove onto the bed, plunging the blade where her throat had been. It encountered only feathers, but Alexandra rolled out of the way too quickly, tangling the sheet about her legs so that she was trapped when Trabert's weight pinned her to the mattress.

"I am not averse to that," he whispered.

His lips poised just above hers, he extricated the slender blade from the tattered pillow and held it at her throat. She dared not move or even speak. Only her eyes refused to hold still and darted from the leering face so close she could hardly focus on it to the decanter he groped for. He did not look away but kept fumbling blindly, his fingers knocking a book, a handkerchief, an empty vase to the floor without finding what they sought. Alexandra regretfully accepted that she had no hope of getting her own hands on the decanter before Trabert did, but she had not lost all expectations of victory.

He could not reach the brandy without moving off her, without adjusting his position. As the pulse in her throat bounded against the cold, razor-sharp steel, she waited for him to move. A year ticked by, then a decade. Her lungs burned, but she feared to draw a deep breath. Tensed to take advantage of the opportunity whenever it came, her legs began to cramp and quiver. A century passed before the pressure of his body on her lightened. Still the blade threatened; she could not move.

He stretched, and the tips of his fingers brushed cool crystal. A second effort only pushed it another half inch beyond his grasp. Cursing, he slid a few inches closer. That was all Alexandra needed.

He lunged for her, but the knife caught in the fabric of her nightgown and was ripped from his hand. Alexandra ignored the clatter of the weapon on the floor behind her and ran for the door, hoping to elude capture in the dark of a house Trabert had never been in.

Strong arms caught her in the corridor and slung her back towards the bedroom. Before she could see the man's face, those arms sent her sprawling on the floor.

"Idiot!" a woman's voice spat. "Must I hold her for you?" Her foot rested on the back of Alexandra's neck.

"I'll take care of her, don't worry. And I thought I told you to take that crazy old woman out of here."

"Madama Mara wishes to stay until the deed is done." The third voice came from the doorway. Alexandra could see only the hem of her black gown.

Trabert laughed nervously. "I don't need an audience."

"I will stay. Let the girl up, Tina."

So it was the other gypsy, a woman built as tall and hard as a man. As she felt the hard-heeled boot lifted from her neck, Alexandra remembered that Betsy Lytle had insisted Tina was no gypsy. An old fear, almost forgotten, came back instantly, and she got slowly to her feet.

"Valentina. I should have known," she sighed, facing the girl who had once been her sister-in-law.

Hatred had aged Valentina twenty years in ten months, and harshly. Bitter lines were etched on her face, marks of unrelieved anger. Vengeance stirred the once clear eyes to a murky, muddy grey.

"Give him the potion," she commanded Mara, who

still stood in the doorway.

"I already have it, mixed here with the brandy."

A subtle change came over Valentina's features. She bit her lip to still its trembling.

"Then give it to her. Hurry up. I want to know if it works."

"Surely you don't doubt the efficacy of Madame Mara's elixir. Have we not sipped this nectar ourselves, my little gypsy?"

Her face reddened.

"Just give it to her and stop wasting time."

He poured some into the one unbroken glass and handed it to Alexandra.

"I am almost sorry your Mr. Hawthorne isn't here to watch how—"

"Hawthorne!" Valentina shrieked.

"For God's sake, Tina, what the matter with you? You wouldn't know him; he's a Russian."

But she did not hear him. She grabbed for Mara as the veiled woman slunk from the room. The cripple was no match for Valentina's strength, and she was easily pulled back into the room.

"You knew, didn't you!" Valentina hissed in Russian.

A cackle emerged from under the shrouding veil. "Of course, I knew. That's why I didn't just give our colonel the potion and let him come alone. Mikhail will be here soon enough; I cannot wait to see the look on his face."

"What the hell is going on here?" Trabert demanded. He was losing his patience with these two madwoman. Alexandra was too close to being his, her arm soft within his grasp, her tousled hair filling his nostrils with the scent of flowers. He might not need the elixir after all.

Mara said softly, "Drink and you will soon forget we are even here."

Mikhail leaned against the bole of an ancient oak to ease the throbbing in his foot. He had worn out the stallion on his furious charge across the moors back to Fowey and knew that to take the beast out again would kill it. His riding boots were not made for walking up steep, cobbled streets and had raised agonizing blisters, but the pain provided a kind of penance.

He should have known she would not betray him. She had proven herself so many times before, and he had not learned. There was still the memory of Tamara lingering to sour all the sweetness Alexandra had given him, but no more.

As he stepped back onto the road, he glanced up at the moon. It had dropped further, but the corner windows of Vinewood still shone brilliantly. He thought he saw the gateposts Alexandra had described in her note not more than a hundred paces ahead, and surely the house itself was not above a quarter mile distant from the gate. He plodded onward, turned in at the gate, and began the final climb up the driveway. When a woman's scream pierced the night, he broke into a tortured run.

Emboldened by Mara's words, Trabert tipped the decanter up to drink. Though Valentina gasped, it was the creak of a door opening that lowered his hand. With a silent gesture, he ordered Valentina to pick up the knife still lying on the floor and then hand it to him. Alexandra watched, wanted to scream with the horror mounting at every thud of her heart, but it happened too fast. The knife glittered, heavy footsteps raced from the foyer up the stairs, and then a broad familiar figure filled the open doorway.

"Xan!" What in the name of Christ—?"

"Not so fast, *Mr. Hawthorne!*"

Mikhail felt the sting of the knife against his neck, knew that any movement could prove fatal. He froze.

"Very good. Very wise. You're just in time for the evening's entertainment."

Cold nausea rose at the back of Mikhail's throat. The first shock wore off and he saw more than just the pale oval of her face. The glorious waves of blue-black hair hung in matted tangles; the perfect features strained with horror. Only the jewel-like eyes had not changed from his

531

treasured memories. He knew, without seeing, that some-where very close to Alexandra stood a Valentina much altered from the young woman he had last seen skulking away into the dark of a summer night, and further into the shadows of this room he sensed another figure hiding. But his eyes never left Alexandra.

"I don't normally stand for interruptions, Count Ogrinov. Yours this afternoon was particularly irritating. Tonight, however, I shall make an exception. Tonight you are my most welcome guest. And as every good host is required to provide amusement for his guests, I shall proceed to do just that."

The silken voice quivered with insanity. Mikhail felt the knife dig deeper into the cords of his neck, too far from the carotid artery to guarantee a quick and easy death.

"Now, my dear Alexandra, will you drink? Or, if you prefer, I will begin carving pieces out of Monsieur le Comte." A tiny spot of red appeared on the taut skin as the blade punctured a capillary. To Mikhail, Trabert said, "You may not find my entertainment exactly to your liking, but I'm sure it will be unique. I am going to make love to that pretty little woman, and you are going to watch. Don't worry; I won't hurt her. Unless she wants me to, of course. Sometimes the elixir makes women do strange, wild things. Doesn't it, Tina?"

Valentina spat at him.

"Tut, my dear. That's so common. But when you aren't anything but a common gypsy slut, are you, Tina?"

She spat again.

"You must forgive her, Mr. Hawthorne. Gypsies have no manners. Now, as I was saying. Alexandra will thoroughly enjoy everything I do with her, or to her, for that matter. She will not cry out for you to save her or for God to send her death. Her ecstasy will be uncontrollable, her desire unquenchable." He squirmed delightfully at the thought and traced a fine red line down Mikhail's neck from ear to collar. "As will be yours. I fully intend you to taste of the marvelous drug, to enjoy the heightening of the normal urges. You must forgive me if I don't allow

532

you to satisfy them, of course. When it becomes too much for you, when you can no longer stand the sight of your mistress sprawled hungrily beneath another man's body, when your own desires tear you to pieces with pain and frustration, then I will show a touch of mercy. As soon as Alexandra is conscious enough to understand what she witnesses, I will honor her wishes to end your torment with death.''

''No!'' Valentina cried. ''Do to her what you want, but you are not to touch him!''

''Shut up, you stupid whore. I'll do as I please, with her and with him.''

''You kill him, and there will never be another drop of the potion for you.'' Valentina's voice was dry, choking.

''Would you prefer I give him to you after he's shared the brandy with my fiancee and me?'' He cackled again. Another line appeared, an inch behind the first. ''No? Then hold your tongue and let us proceed.'' He raised the decanter again to toast his madness. ''To my bride, Alexandra. I shall drink first, then you, my dear. I rather like the idea of using a bit of force to subdue you before the drug takes hold. Mr. Hawthorne will have to wait just a bit longer. I do hope he isn't terribly thirsty!''

Sick laughter bubbled from him, but the blade never moved. Mikhail waited, suppressed the hatred that seared his vitals, waited.

Valentina leaned against the bedpost for support as though she had become suddenly ill. Her face blanched, her eyes widened with horror as Trabert put the decanter to his lips. The brandy burned like a white flame, then an explosion ripped through him. Valentina's gloved hand shot out to smash the decanter, but it was too late. Pieces of glass buried themselves in his face and hand; blood spurted from a dozen lacerations, splattering Alexandra's nightgown as he pitched forward. The knife slid from his undamaged hand, but Mikhail didn't pay any attention. Trabert was dying at his feet.

''It was poison,'' Valentina wept as she lifted Trabert's mangled head onto her lap. ''I meant it for her. I couldn't bear to see her win again." It did not matter now that she fell into her native tongue; Trabert heard nothing. "I knew you'd leave me, never keep your promises to me, if you married her," she murmured to him, plucking fragments of crystal from his face without any real tenderness. Blood still oozed from the wounds but no longer gushed; the poison had done its work. "I didn't want you to die until you said you would kill Mikhail. If you hadn't threatened him, I would have taken the bottle away sooner. It was only *her* I wanted dead."

"You greedy slut. You would have robbed me of the one pleasure I had in life and all for the sake of your petty jealousy."

Neither Valentina nor Alexandra looked at the veiled figure stalking from its corner, but Mikhail did. Even through the thick shroud he recognized her voice.

"I really don't need to hide from you, Mischa, do I?"

Her words vibrated with malignant hate, but in her unveiled face all the corruption of unmitigated evil glowed like the fires of hell.

Alexandra gagged at what she saw coming toward her. A mouth so twisted by scars that the lips barely moved when Tamara talked. One vacant eye socket gaping above a cheekbone caved in like a dented tin cup. The remaining eye flashed, but it, too bore the marks of disfigurement. A single scar running from brow to jaw drew the lid down as though that eye always dozed.

"This what he did to me. You see my arm? He broke it in six places." What she held out had the appearance of a gnarled tree limb covered with pale human flesh. "I must sleep in a chair, never lie in a bed, for the flap of skin that was once my nose falls shut when I lie down. I walk only with constant, excruciating pain because his kicks shattered my hip."

One by one she shed the black garments until she stood, a twisted wreckage in an unadorned chemise.

"But now I will have my revenge. You spurned Valentina, Mischa, so she came to me after following you to Moscow. She remembered all the times you had talked about me to her brother, and she knew I would help her. She was right. I would do anything to avenge what you did to me.''

"Mischa didn't do this; Nikolai did," Alexandra heard herself say. "You lied to him to get his name and his money."

The grotesque face reddened. Tamara hadn't faced the truth in years and she did not like doing so now.

"So I used him? So what? Niki used me, too, to get even with his brother. If Mischa hadn't been so damned proud, so damned *honorable*. . . . But that's over now, except for the debt he owes me."

"I owe you nothing. I saved your life; I've kept you in secluded luxury. You've had more from me than you ever would have had from my brother."

"*You owe me your love*! And so does she. She stole what was mine. I watched her every day in Moscow, her visits with Parofsky's wife, her shopping sprees, even your little picnic by the river. She was so easy to follow, all the way to St. Petersburg and then here. Not very clever, for a spy. You were no harder, Mischa. I had only to wait for you, and you came."

"So *you* told Trabert where I was!" Alexandra gasped.

"No, my dear, I found him and brought him here. You left plenty of enemies in Paris, and he happened to be the one with the greatest desire for revenge. I have been a lonely widow with little to occupy my time all these years, and so I have written letters. The colonel did not learn by himself where your sister's cafe is or how Manette Duquesne spends her days. *I* did that. And you were so easily frightened! Just like a little bird!" The broken woman laughed hideously at her own joke.

Numbed by all the horror around her, Alexandra could not move fast enough to evade Tamara's sudden assault. A strong, incredibly beautiful hand grasped her long black hair, and Trabert's knife flashed in a gnarled claw. Alexandra froze just as Mischa had, for the same blade now threatened her throat.

"I won't let that imbecile Valentina kill her, Mischa. I

want her to live, as I have lived, a monster hidden in the clothing of the grave. I'll slice off an ear, gouge out an eye, burn a lovely cheek to a reddened, puckered scar. Will you want her then?''

"Yes," he whispered, but she did not hear, nor did she see his tears.

"A few slashes along her pretty jaw, a piece of flesh carved from one of those exquisite breasts. Perhaps a hand severed, or a foot, so she dies with every step, as I have.

"I would want her even then."

"Kill her!" Valentina screamed above his loving murmur. "Kill the French whore! I didn't come all this way to watch you coo to him. I want the slut dead!''

"No, you fool. That is too easy, even for a whore.''

But Valentina was not to be turned away so easily. Brandy dripped from the broken neck of the decanter she clutched like a dagger. One quivering step at a time she edged nearer.

"My dearest love, she is a *whore!*" She wept to Mikhail as she advanced on Alexandra, still held tightly in Tamara's mad grip. "She does not love you. She carried a child in her womb when she came to us that winter, and she wept for it as she has never wept for you.''

The blue eyes turned black. Oh, God, no, Alexandra wanted to scream, but a rope of dread tightened around her throat. He would believe this lie as he had believed all the others.

"You lying, stinking slut." he whispered hoarsely.

Valentina stood directly in front of her, the weapon poised to strike at her belly. And Tamara pressed the knife against her cheek. She didn't care any more. Not if he didn't love her.

Then Valentina lunged, not counting on the years and years of Tamara's patience. In spite of her deformities, she possessed the strength of the insane. She jerked Alexandra out of the way and let Valentina crash ineffectually into the bed. Only partially stunned, she swung the bottle in a wide arc. Involuntarily, impelled by some instinct for survival, Alexandra jumped clear without even thinking. Not even her nightgown was touched.

There was a groan behind her, as Tamara lost her balance, forced by Alexandra's escape maneuver to put most of her weight on her damaged hip. To grab the bedpost for support, she dropped the knife, but to no avail. The wooden pillar remained just out of her reach, and she fell as the knife bounced on its ebony hilt.

Slowly, Tamara staggered to her feet. Mikhail saw the pool of fresh blood on the floor where she had fallen, but the knife was not there.

"I do not die so easily, Mischa, as you well know." Now blood trickled from her gruesome mouth, and as she advanced on Valentina, backing the terrified girl towards the man's body on the floor, Mikhail saw that the blade was buried in Tamara's back.

"You will die," Valentina said defiantly. "First you, and then the French whore."

She swung again, just as Alexandra once had but without the same results. Tamara persisted, came closer and closer, though now her chemise was soaked with blood and she left a trail of scarlet drops. Valentina backed off, waiting for the inevitable. The woman could not live much longer with steel in her lungs and the life pumping out of her. One more step, then another. But her boot had caught on something, and when she looked down, Valentina saw Trabert's stiffening hand, the fingers curling as though to grasp her slender heel. With a cry of fright, she jumped.

The bare floor was slippery with blood and spilled brandy. Arms flailing, Valentina tried to save herself. As her feet flew out from under her, she threw the bottle at Tamara, then landed with a wail of pure terror in the pool of poisoned brandy, littered with the shards of crystal.

Dodging Valentina's missile took the last of Tamara's failing strength. She slipped to her knees, then collapsed, lying on her side.

"Don't bother to help the Cossack bitch," she told

Mikhail, who had gone to Valentina. Splinters of glass had cut her thigh in several places; blood ran in bright streaks to mix with the deadly golden liquor on the floor. "She'll be dead before I am. The poison works quickly when it enters the blood directly. Swallowed, it takes three or four minutes. This way, a minute, no more."

Mikhail backed away from the pathetic figure. Already Valentina's eyes had glazed. She stared but saw nothing. Tamara erred only in predicting her own survival; she never took another breath. Valentina's eyes finally closed a few seconds later.

Chapter 51

ALEXANDRA LAY still, too numb to move, while Mikhail tore the sheet from the bed to cover what had once been a beautiful woman, a woman he had loved. The froth of rich golden hair, Tamara's only remaining glory, lay just inches from Alexandra's feet. Mikhail shut his eyes to the sight, but no memories rose to haunt him; the present did that well enough.

Stepping carefully to avoid any contact with the poison-drenched glass, he picked up a quilt that had fallen to the floor and threw it over Valentina and the man she had murdered.

It took the last of his strength to gather Alexandra into his arms and carry her down the corridor, far from the sight and smell of slaughter. Exhausted, he leaned his back against the wall and slid to the floor. She lay her head on his shoulder and a sigh shuddered through her as the tears of relief finally came.

"It's over, and I'm here," he crooned. "Go on and cry it all out."

His constant singsong and the gentle caress of his fingers pushing tangled little tendrils of hair from her forehead soothed her until she rested still and quiet, almost as if she slept.

But she could not sleep. Already the ghastly horror of this night was fading from her mind as the reality of her rescue came clear. His arms were around her, his voice whispered in her ear, his heart thudded beneath her

539

cheek. Trabert was nothing but a bad dream from which she had wakened to the secure safety and loving warmth of Mikhail's embrace.

He kissed her, ignoring the salty tang of tears, blood, and sweat to taste only the sweetness of her lips.

"I'm going back in there," he said softly. "No, don't worry; I won't be but a minute. I have to get the lamp, that's all. Will you be all right?"

"Yes," she managed to whisper. He could almost hear the smile that was invisible in the darkness. "But hurry, please."

She shivered, partly with cold, partly with nervous relief, when he eased her off his lap. Though his coat smelled of dust and sweat, he took it off and slipped it around her shoulders. It would do until he found something else.

"I promise I'll hurry. A minute or two, no more, and I'll be back." Another kiss and he got to his feet, the blisters bringing pain he hardly noticed. But for his pauses along the walk to ease his feet and he might have been able to avert this tragedy. He shook the thought from his head; it was done and there was no sense worrying about what might have been. "I'm going to lock the door when I come out so nothing is disturbed before the authorities get here." He took her hand in his, but he honestly did not know if it was to give her reassurance before he left her alone in the dark or to take some strength from her. "Is there anything beside the lamp you want me bring out?"

Her hand tightened; he felt her whole body stiffen.

"Oh, my God, he's still in there!" she gasped. "I locked him in Giselle's room."

"The key. Where's the key, Xan?"

He thought at first that she had not heard him, that this new and inexplicable fear had frozen her senses, but she whispered so quietly that though he was only inches away he barely heard, "On top of the dresser."

After a few breaths of the relatively fresh air in the hallway, the charnel-house stench hit him like a cannonball. Already he had forgotten the extent of the carnage.

Though the bodies were covered, their death-masks hidden, great spills of blood stained the sheet over Tamara's twisted form. He wanted to close his eyes and walk past it blindly; with death waiting for any misstep, he dared not.

But what new horror waited in the maid's locked chamber? Remembering the fear in Alexandra's voice, he swallowed rising nausea. Another corpse? He thought, too, of Vasili. A chill brushed his heart as he wondered where his friend could be.

He found the key and beside it a candle sputtered in a pewter holder. He took them both, then hoped he would not need two hands to shoot the lock, the one to steady the other.

The latch clicked with a sharp sound, the door swung silently outward. Mikhail thrust the candle into the darkness and wished he had the foresight—and the stomach—to arm himself with the knife still buried in Tamara's back.

There was no blood, no body sprawled lifeless on the oval rug. Only a small wardrobe, an unpainted wooden chair, a narrow unmade cot on which lay a wadded quilt, and a dressing table. Mikhail tried the wardrobe doors. They opened to reveal a worn dressing gown hung on a peg. The drawers of the dressing table were empty, too, and not so much as a pin littered the top. The room was immaculate, except for the sloppy lump of blanket.

He turned back to the cot and understood. Very gently, he lifted a corner of the blanket. The sight of a curly-haired infant sleeping as though he had not a care in the world seemed perfectly natural, yet in striking, almost allegorical contrast to what filled the other room. Mikhail picked the child up and cradled him in one arm, with the candle stub in his other hand. He would have kissed his son but for the irritating stubble of beard on his own cheeks.

"I'll get the lamp by the window, and then we'll get you back to your mother. I think she is—"

He looked up to pick his way through the deadly rubble

and found himself facing two cocked pistols levelled at his chest.

"For God's sake, Vasili, put those damned things away!" he ordered in an angry whisper. "And why weren't you here half an hour ago?"

Vasili shrugged. "I didn't know I was needed." He crossed himself with a hand still holding a pistol. "Holy Mother of God, what happened? Is the Snowbird—?" He couldn't finish the question, could only stare at the remains of the tragedy.

"Alexandra's fine. You probably walked right past her in the hall. I'll explain everything later, if I can, but right now I need that lamp from the window. Whatever you do, don't fall. This glass is full of some kind of poison that kills instantly. I have to get this little boy back to his mother."

Leaving Vasili to fetch the lamp, Mikhail strode briskly down the corridor towards the huddled figure with her arms clasped forlornly about her knees. The candle was nothing now but a scrap of wick floating in a thimbleful of melted wax, but it brought light where before there had been only dark. Alexandra turned to him.

"Is this who you wanted?" Mikhail asked as he placed the bundle into her outstretched arms. "He must have slept through everything."

Alexandra held her son close, then looked up again at Mikhail, at the glittering blue eyes now warm with pride and love, the dark curls falling over his forehead, the gentle smile playing about his lips. A face she had never hoped to see again outside her cherished memories and dreams. He knelt beside her, setting the dying candle in front of them. Through the spatters of blood on her cheeks, tears traced shining streaks; with loving fingers, he wiped them away.

"Excuse me," Vasili coughed, looming over them like a great golden bear. "I have found some tea and some hot water, but only one cup."

The triviality of his dilemma brought laughter, and if a

moment of tenderness had been destroyed, so had the tension.

"There are more in the kitchen downstairs," Alexandra told him.

"Light us into another room first, and then you may go hunt for teacups," Mikhail ordered. "It is late already, and our new mother must get her rest."

He did not wait for her to try to walk on her own. With a single sweeping motion, he gathered both mother and child into his arms.

"Which of these doors leads to a bedroom?" he asked her.

"At the far end is my mother's room. I don't think she'll mind."

"Good. Now, hold on tight."

How silly. He doubted he could have cut her loose with an axe.

Vasili lit candles and turned down Constance's bed while Alexandra changed the ruined nightdress for another. The little bit of water in the pot went for washing both her face and the scratches on Mikhail's neck.

"They're nothing," he protested, when she became insistent about cleaning them. "I've taken worse injuries and lived."

"It's the poison I'm worried about. I'm going to have Vasili heat a bath for me later on before I even think about feeding Tristan."

"That's the boy's name?"

"Yes. I called him Tristan Michael."

"Tristan Michael what?"

Oh, no, she thought. He's testing me, trying to make me admit the boy isn't his. And I have no answer for him.

"Just Tristan Michael." She held her breath as she blotted the scratches dry with a soft towel.

"Good. I was afraid you'd have strung a dozen names on him the way the French have a habit of doing. Tristan Michael Hawthorne will do very nicely. I like the ring of it."

543

She echoed the name slowly, tasting each syllable as though it were a rare and very fine wine.

"Tristan. Michael. Hawthorne."

"Do I detect a note of uncertainty? You chose the name yourself."

Was he testing her again?

"No, of course not. It's just that I meant what I said literally. He is just Tristan Michael. He's a bastard and has no name. For that matter, neither do I."

She walked away from him to hide the first shame she had ever felt, but in an instant his hands were on her shoulders, turning her around. There was fire in his eyes, but his voice stayed calm.

"He is my son, Xan, and he will bear my name, if you wish him to. My father gave in to my mother's wishes that their children take her name as long as we lived in Russia. Hawthorne is a very old and honorable English name, one I should have been proud to call my own years ago. I hope I do not dishonor it now."

"You mean you're English? and French? and Russian?"

"As English as you, my dear."

"Oh, goodness, I believe I do need to lie down now. And where's Vasili with the tea?"

She climbed onto the bed and let Mikhail put an extra pillow behind her. When she assured him she was comfortable and needed nothing else except the tea Vasili was dallying over, Mikhail sat on the edge of the bed and pulled off the boots that had been torturing his feet. His stockings were stained with blood.

"I'm going to burn these now, before I forget," he said, holding the new boots aloft and carrying them to the fireplace.

"Because they hurt your feet? Isn't that a monstrous waste?"

"No. It isn't because they rubbed a few blisters; that was my own fault. But I've been walking in liquid death, and I want every bit of it burned."

Even that carefully worded statement reminded them of what had happened and of what had yet to be done.

Though they had far more pleasant topics to discuss, Mikhail knew what must be decided first.

"I'm going to send Vasili for the constable as soon as he's had a cup of tea with us. I won't deny him that little pleasure. He's very glad to see you, you know." She blushed, but he went on without a pause. "Then your grandfather must be told."

"Don't send Vasili. Sir George will be here before Vasili could ever get to Penloren. If I know him at all, he probably didn't sleep any more than we, and his horse is waiting for him. I'm sure he'll leave the instant he can see ten feet in front of him."

"You're sure?"

She nodded and whispered, "I'm positive," and he knew she meant of other things as well.

Again Vasili interrupted their privacy, this time bringing steaming cups of strong tea. He was neither surprised nor dismayed at the length of the list of errands Mikhail gave him and would have gulped down his tea to set out at once but once Mikhail and Alexandra insisted he stay.

As Alexandra began to explain not only the events of the past few hours but the weeks leading to them, she realized Mikhail, too, knew none of this. The last time she had seen him, he had ignored her as though she had been a mote of dust in the air. He had accused her in his own silent way of betraying him and yet now he demanded that the child of that betrayal carry his name. She was more confused than ever.

Had he forgiven her or had he realized somehow that he had been mistaken? What had changed him and when? He touched her hand and all the pain receded. She didn't care why or how he had come to this new feeling for her; it was there and he was there and nothing mattered.

"I'm sorry for Valentina," Vasili said quietly. "I do not know what could have been done to save her from this end. For Tamara and the colonel, I can only be glad they are dead. Their hatred took up too much room in this world. Now that they are gone, we must see that the empty space they have left behind is filled with love.''

Sir George and Roland arrived at Vinewood while their shadows still stretched long and thin behind them. Five other horses, two of them familiar as Trabert's grey and the leggy chestnut Alexandra had taken last night, dozed at the porch rail. Sir George leapt off his own mount then bounded into the house.

"Alexandra!" he roared.

"Please, Grandfather, don't yell."

He hardly recognized her. Standing in the doorway to the summer parlor, she wore one of his old, frayed bathrobes over a nightgown in equally shabby condition. Her hair, which he had never seen loose, hung past her waist in slightly damp waves, as though it had just been washed. She obviously had not slept at all, but in contrast to his own grumpiness under such circumstances, she appeared as content as a well-fed cat. He suspected why.

"I've told you not to call me that," he reminded her as she threw her arms around him. "Stop it! You're embarrassing me in front of your uncle."

"Then I shall embarrass him in front of you."

But Roland was not embarrassed in the least, only relieved.

"Come, I have coffee and croissants in the dining room," she said, taking them both by the hand. "I have much to tell you and very little time."

They had no choice but to obey and followed where she led.

"Penhale the caretaker saw lights and brought up breakfast," she explained when they were all seated. "George, I believe you haven't really met Mr. Hawthorne. Mischa, my grandfather, Sir George Tregarth."

Both nodded and shook hands. Introducing Mikhail to her uncle proved more difficult, but at last it was accomplished. She skirted the important issues by introducing him as Michael Hawthorne—the name still felt strange—whom she had known in Paris and Moscow as Baron Mikhail Pavlovitch Ogrinov.

"Nancy was right," Roland said as he poured fresh cream into his cup and stirred it thoughtfully. "Your son looks just like you, Mr. Hawthorne."

Alexandra caught her breath and dropped her spoon with a clatter.

"Yes, I think he does, too," Mikhail replied. "I hope he has inherited his mother's temper and not mine, however. I've never seen anyone who combines patience and stubbornness as sweetly as she does."

"All right, all right, enough of this sentimental rubbish," Sir George interjected. "We didn't come here to watch you two make calf-eyes at each other. We brought some unpleasant news."

"Mother's all right, isn't she?"

"Yes, yes, Constance is fine. A bit impatient to have you back and damned worried, but other than that— No, it's something quite different. Betsy Lytle went back to that old gypsy, Rayna I think her name is—"

"Rayda," Alexandra corrected.

"Anyway, Betsy went there last night and found the old witch beaten half to death. Betsy had enough sense in her empty head to get the constable and myself, and before Rayda died she told us Trabert had done it and was on his way to find you. She was just an old gypsy, but murder is murder, and now he's wanted by the law. Roland and I left as soon as we could, but I was very much afraid that monster would find you before we did. I thought that was his horse outside, but I see he hasn't been here to harm you."

"And that brings us right up to this side of the story," Alexandra sighed. "Trabert did come here. And he hasn't left yet."

Before the first sentence was out of her mouth, Vasili, worried by the sight of more horses outside, roared into the house with Constable Race on his heels. Though she had hoped to delay the ordeal of interrogations as long as possible, Alexandra welcomed being saved telling the horrible tale twice. And now that the time had come, she was eager only to get it over with.

The sea battered the rocks with water turned to liquid gold by the setting sun. A stiff breeze pulled too many curls loose from their pins until Alexandra gave up and removed the others, tossing them defiantly over the cliff as her hair tumbled free and whipped behind her. Touched by the dying sun, the blue lights of those thick tresses glimmered as green as her eyes.

This day at last was done. It had been a day of death and hatred and the unrivalled ugliness of evil, yet as it lingered, Alexandra felt a tug of sadness at her heart. Out of this hell had come her salvation, the man who stood beside her and stared out at the eternal sea.

They had left Penloren to find the privacy they had craved all day and on the cliffs where the grass grew soft and only gulls peered curiously at them and asked no questions, they savored the aloneness, not speaking, touching only where her hand clasped his.

Water and sky changed from gold to copper, then rubies sparkled on the edges of the waves. The evening star appeared above the horizon as bright as the lights from Penloren and seeming as near. The soft call of a nightjar beginning his hunt sighed the last breath of the vermilion orb sinking into the sea. Brilliance faded swiftly now that the sun lay behind the world, but the delicate beauty of the night stole in to fill the void. Stars spangled the deepening sky, and the moon, round and irridescent, rose like a fabulous pearl over the Cornish moorland. The gulls settled on the silver sea or roosted on the rocks, while overhead the nightjar sang its eerie song.

"You said you wanted to talk, but I haven't heard a word from you," Mikhail whispered, afraid to break the silence too harshly.

"There are so many things. I was trying to put all the questions in order."

"I thought I explained all about Lydia's confrontation and my letter to Manette and how I misunderstood what I saw that night at the Kremlin."

She shook her head and turned to face him for the first

time since walking to the cliffs. Seeing her like this, early moonlight on one side, the last glow of twilight on the other, he could not resist a kiss.

"Is that what you wanted to talk about?" he asked mischievously.

"Partly. I suppose what I meant was I need to know about Tristan. You have no idea what a quandary I've been in these past few weeks about so silly a subject as his name, and when I'd finally accustomed myself to a solution, you had to throw it all into confusion again."

"Wasn't that settled this morning? He's my son; I expect him to have my name. And don't try to trap me into being suspicious. You can't prove he's mine—though just looking at him ought to be a damned good hint—but it's only a man with doubts who needs proof. I don't need it. I can find it right here."

Again his mouth descended on hers, a gentle passion stirring his hunger for the taste of her. He had left his coat at the house, preferring to stroll in just his shirtsleeves. As he pulled her against him, he felt more than the warmth of a summer's evening. Her arms slid around him, her fingers found their favorite hold in the curls above his collar.

"I love you," he whispered, his lips moving against her neck. Kissing the pulse at her throat, he found the buttons at the back of her dress and began to unfasten them. When she struggled, he said, "Please, my love, I want you. If you wish to take on the innocence you have always had in my eyes, then I will wait, but tell me now, so I can take you home."

"Wait? For what? And what has my innocence got to do with it? I was trying to unbutton your shirt, silly."

He laughed and tightened his embrace.

"You really don't understand yet, do you? Your mother did, even your Aunt Nancy did. Why not you? No, it is my fault. I have hurt you so often that my sly hints will not do. I must spell it out clearly so you do not misunderstand."

He pushed her away, and as he did, one shoulder of her

549

dress slipped down provocatively, almost but not quite baring her breast. Not letting go her hands, he dropped to his knees on the cool grass.

"I love you, you witch. I probably have since that night in Rosalie's garden or at least since the night I rescued you from Bonaparte and got you drunk on vodka. I have loved you, but I have also hurt you, because I refused to admit even to myself how much I loved you. I was so afraid that you would not love me back, that you would be like Tamara and betray me and I could only believe what I saw to prove that. Yet each time, I knew it wasn't true, and I only hurt myself. I want to make amends for some of the hurt I have caused you. I want Tristan to carry my name but, Alexandra, I cannot give our son my name until I give it to you first. My dear, sweet, beautiful Alexandra, will you honor me by becoming my wife?"

She sank in front of him, let him lift her palm to his lips.

"That word, honor," she said. "Yesterday I swore I never wanted to hear it again as long as I lived. Now it is the most beautiful sound, next to *I love you*. Yes, Mischa, I will be your wife, but only under one condition. The next time you *think* you see me with another man, please, ask me before you imagine the worst."

He laughed with her, then she fell into his arms and his kiss devoured her. Their clothes became fetters they struggled to be free of, and when at last the soft ocean breeze swept across her naked flesh, Alexandra let out a long sigh of pure pleasure.

There was no haste in his lovemaking, despite the desire that had gone so long unsatisfied. With newfound tenderness, he touched and caressed her, not to arouse the fiery passion that demanded fulfillment, but to prolong the sweet intimacy of the moment. He cupped her breast in his hand, teased the nipple erect with his tongue. The taste of her milk filled him with wonder, and he paused to whisper, "You are so beautiful. If this night lasted a thousand years, I could not enjoy you enough before morning."

"Then let us not waste the hours we have," she replied and pulled him to her.

He was part of her, loving her as he had never loved her before. His hand, warm against her cool skin, slowly travelled down the ripple of her ribs, rising and falling with each breath, to the hollow of her waist. He found the curve of hip and thigh, the soft tangle of silk between her legs, the warm eagerness that cried out for him. Slowly, with infinite gentleness, he entered her and felt her close around him with a sigh. Then and only then, when he knew her body craved the same delights as his, did he relax his conscious control and give in to the tempest of his need.

His senses tingled with the extraordinary delight as he thrust into her, pulled away, then met her arching body again in a continuing ecstasy that served as its own source and its own end. It was as though he were once more an innocent boy taking his first pleasure with a woman. The act itself thrilled him, this joining of flesh with loving flesh that seemed almost an act of worship.

She cried out once, not when he drove so deep into her that she felt him touch the very core of her soul, but when he withdrew and she was left empty. Rising to him, she found that which he had taken from her, drew it to her, and gently impaled herself upon it to be filled once again. When slow and gentle rhythm gave way to the growing storm, she let it carry her along. It broke with a thunderclap whose echoes died gradually, leaving her to bask in sudden peace.

"I love you," Mikhail murmured. He kissed her nose, her ear.

"I love you, too." Words she had longed to say, had said so many times when he was not there to hear, brought tears to her eyes.

She gasped, then laughed at the absurdity.

"Well, how would it look if we had a child only six or seven months after? Yes, it must be soon," she insisted in perfect imitation of his jesting.

"If it must be, it must be. But surely no sooner than

Sunday. After all, I hardly think your uncle can obtain a special license before then.''

"Oh, can he do that?" Alexandra asked honestly. "Can we really be married that soon?"

"Probably. And just in time to have our son christened. Ought to drive the parish gossips wild."

He chuckled and rolled onto his back, carrying her with him. Bathed in bright moonlight, her hair tangled with bits of grass, she straddled him like a victorious barbarian princess, except that she blushed hotly. Without a word, he began to move inside her again, chasing her shyness with sensuality that drove all else from her mind. When it was spent and she lay panting on his chest, she, too, laughed.

"No, love, no more," she begged as she swung her leg over him and then curled up at his side. "You may have the strength for a thousand years, but not I."

It was enough then just to lie together, tired and happy, yet too chilled by the breeze to sleep. All was dark now save for the moon and stars; only a single light still burned at Penloren.

Alexandra rose first, ran her hands through her tousled mane, and said reluctantly, "We must go back. We both need sleep, and Tristan will be hungry soon, if he isn't already."

"Will you sneak into my room when the rest of the household is asleep, or shall I come to yours?" he joked as he sat up to pull on the trousers she tossed at him.

"It would be easier for me to come to yours since I know my way, but—oh, Mischa, what are you making me say? Can't you wait until Sunday?"

He was all seriousness when he answered, "No, I can't. If you ask me not to touch you again until the marriage vows are said, I will not touch you. Just say it, and I will not even ask again. But for these few nights, let me be with you. I love you, Xan, and I have only just realized how many times I have almost lost you forever. I am afraid to be parted from you for even a moment."

She bent to pick up his shirt, using the task to hide the

depth of her reaction to his confession, but when she turned to hand the garment to him, she could not stop her tears.

"You know where my room is. Please, don't ever, ever, ever leave me again." She kissed the tips of his fingers and gently wiped his cheek dry.

"As God is my witness, Xan, I won't."

Chapter 52

MIKHAIL KISSED his son and extinguished the last candle, plunging the room into darkness. Once in the wide bed, he needed no light to find his wife. Their bodies met in the center of the mattress, warmth drawing warmth until they met and fused.

"Well, Mrs. Michael Paul Hawthorne, how does it feel to be married?"

"Do you want the truth, or some romantic nonsense?"

"The truth, so long as it is romantic nonsense."

"I feel relieved. All my life I've been using someone else's name without any right to it. I still don't have my own, but at least having yours is legal." She accepted his kiss, but no more, and even pushed him gently away. "There's something else, too, that's been bothering me ever since that night at Vinewood. I know our wedding night is no time to be discussing it, but I can't bear it any more. I thought I'd eventually forget about it, that everything else would cover it up, but it's still there, Mischa, nagging at me."

"Don't drag this out like some frightened virgin. What is it?"

"That's unkind. Anway, I can't stand the doubt any more. I've looked for it in your eyes, listened for it in your voice, and even though I can't find it I know it's there."

"You're right. This is no time to talk about doubt and trust. I ought to spank you for not trusting me, but God knows I've given you reason enough in the past. Besides, every time I put my hand to that lovely bottom of yours I want to do much more pleasureable things. Now what was it that I did Wednesday night that you've kept for yourself until after we're safely wed?''

She swallowed and moistened her lips nervously, and after a deep breath let the words canter off her tongue.

"Valentina told you I had carried another man's child and you called me a lying slut."

"No, my love," he crooned, slipping his arms around her, "I called her the liar. Tasha told me about your miscarriage long before we ever left the mountains. I said nothing because I wanted to wait until you were ready to talk about it yourself. I thought you would eventually, and it was not something I was going to let come between us. I knew, and it didn't matter when you came to me with it. The same was true of my conversation with Andrei Tchernikov at Vera's. I knew you had heard me tell him I would marry you."

"It took you long enough to get around to it."

"I know. But I was drunk that night and too ashamed afterwards. I couldn't tell you it was just the bragging of a man who didn't know what he was talking about; I couldn't tell you it was the truth; I didn't know what the hell to say. So I waited for you to remind me of it and make me face it when I was sober. Stupid pride again."

"Yes, I know. I've had my share of it, too. You never guessed I was pregnant because you were looking for signs that I wasn't and I carefully provided them because I was afraid you'd be furious when you found out. I thought I'd tell you when you asked me to marry you, when it was safe and I didn't have to think you were marrying me only because of the child."

"I think you know I would never do that."

But the time for talk had come to an end. He found her mouth, kissed it softly, then as desire sprang to life, more hungrily, tasting the inner reaches so familiar and yet so delicious. This time she did not push him away but drew him closer.

"I am going to do something I have never done

555

before," he said. "I am going to make love to my wife. But before I start, since I do not want any interruptions, are there any last words, any final questions, before I make you mine forever?"

"Only one," she whispered.

With a frustrated groan, he rolled away.

"What is it now?"

Like a penitent child, she inched closer, until he could not resist and took her once more into his arms.

"A long, long time ago, you told me there were two men in this world you could not protect me from. One was Alexandr, and I saved myself from him, though to this day I don't know how. But who was the other?"

With a strange laugh he said, "I remember that morning in the garden very well. And I was right, you know. I couldn't save you from the danger that one other man would lead you into, dangers like that nightmare at Vinewood."

"But you *did* save me from Trabert. If you hadn't come in when you did, he would have killed me, or worse. I still don't know who the other man is."

"I could not protect you from the one man you would risk anything, everything for, the man who didn't deserve a tenth of the love you gave him in spite of the way he treated you. He put you in that house that night because he didn't have the courage to admit he loved you and wanted you. Instead, he made you come after him, and left you a victim for Trabert and Tamara and poor Valentina too.

"I couldn't save you from the man you fell in love with. I knew he would be more dangerous than anyone else."

"So it was you," she sighed.

A low growl curled from his throat.

"Yes, it was I."

Her helpless giggle drowned in a moan of pleasure.

FORBIDDEN LOVE

Karen Robards

PASSION, TENDERNESS AND WIT

Justin Brant, Earl of Weston, had prided himself on meticulously fulfilling his obligations as guardian to his dead brother's adopted daughter, though he regarded the rebellious child as a nuisance. On her part, Megan considered him a stern figure, cold and distant.

Now, at seventeen, Megan had blossomed into a breathtaking beauty. For Justin, Megan was forbidden fruit dangling temptingly within his grasp. But Megan knew that in spite of everything, she must give herself to the one man in the world whose bride she could never be.

LEISURE BOOKS

PRICE: $3.50 US/$3.95 CAN
0-8439-2024-6

STORMY SURRENDER

Robin Lee Hatcher

WAR AND LOVE

At sixteen, lovely Taylor Bellman finds her gentle and elegant world crumbling around her with the death of her father. Forced by her half brother to marry a man over forty years her senior in order to keep their beloved home, Spring Haven, in the Bellman family, Taylor's platonic marriage becomes a source of strength and contentment to both herself and her husband. But Civil War threatens her peace—and a gallant Yankee visitor awakens her sleeping heart to the thrill of illicit love.

Though their passion cannot be denied, Brent and Taylor know they must part. So begins a saga of war and tragedy, and of burning love that will never die, no matter what obstacles fate has placed between them.

LEISURE BOOKS　　　　　　　　**PRICE: $3.75/$4.25 CAN**
0-8439-2073-4